MISFIT ANGEL

THE MISFIT SERIES BOOK 2

STEPHANIE FOXE

STEEL FOX MEDIA LLC

The Foxey Betas

A big thank you to my ART (Advanced Reader Team). Their advice cleaned up the book and helped me to be more confident launching a new series.

David Ravita, Jen Plumstead, Larry Diaz Tushman, Laura Cadger Rogers, Stephanie Johnson, Tami Cowles, Thomas Ryan

To Sarah, thank you so much for your feedback on the story. I will always have something to learn and your edits are always so insightful.

And to Carol, thank you for a speedy and thorough proofread to catch all those pesky typos!

To my husband

Who helps me through my bad days
And celebrates my good days

I love you!

CONTENTS

ELOISE

*E*loise yawned as she tapped another piece of the puzzle into place. It was still dark outside but she was already awake. The older she got, the harder it was to sleep through the night. She supposed it was insomnia. Or too much coffee after dinner.

Her seventieth birthday was in less than a month. The number galled her, so she refused to think about it. Her body was aging faster than her mind, and it was annoying, to say the least.

There was a quiet creak and she turned around expecting to see Evangeline coming down the stairs, but the stairway stood empty. Knitting her brows together, she reached toward the curtain to peek outside. The back door crashed open at the same moment as a flaming bottle flew through the kitchen window. It shattered against a cabinet and burst into flame.

Eloise jumped up from her puzzle and ran for the antique buffet where she kept her pistol. Just before she reached it, thick arms wrapped around her from behind and lifted her off the ground. She kicked wildly, hoping to catch his knee or something more sensitive.

The man grunted and slammed her against the wall. He grabbed a handful of her hair and yanked her head back sharply. "Where is the demon spawn?"

She bared her teeth at the intruder. "I'm looking right at him," she said right before she spat in his eye.

He reared back in anger and disgust giving her enough room to kick him square in the balls. Without hesitating, she lunged for the drawer again and ripped it open. As her fingers closed around the pistol as he yanked her back by her arm.

She pointed the gun at him, but he shoved her arm up and the first shot went wild. Her ears rang from the deafening blast of the Colt 45 and she prayed to God she hadn't hit Evangeline. She had to have heard the fight. Eloise hoped she had run.

The man's fist connected with her face and she felt her knees give out as her vision exploded into stars. She was too old for this, but she wouldn't let them hurt her daughter. She kicked blindly and kept a firm grip on the gun. It was her only chance.

As her vision began to clear, he swung her around and her back hit the bookcase. Something cracked, most likely a rib, and breathing became painful. Books toppled down onto both their heads. She lunged forward and sank her teeth into his meaty forearm. He slammed her against the bookcase again and she cried out in pain.

When he slammed her against it a third time, the whole thing swayed forward. He jumped back to avoid getting crushed, half dragging her with him. She pulled in the opposite direction then yanked her arm free. Aiming the gun right at his chest, she pulled the trigger as the bookcase crashed down on top of her.

Pain like she'd never felt throbbed through her leg where the heavy bookcase had her pinned. The intruder lay dead in a pool of blood across from her. She'd barely been able to shoot him before he killed her. His face was still contorted with rage and malice, but his eyes were empty.

Smoke filled the home she had lived in for thirty years. Flames licked up the wallpaper, turning the delicate flowers black. The air was thick with the scent of gasoline.

Her daughter stumbled down the hallway, clutching her pillow. Her face was pale from weeks of illness, and now this.

"Just run," Eloise choked out, willing her daughter to get out before they found her. Another bottle crashed through the window, shattering and igniting the carpet.

"I won't leave you!" Evangeline cried, limping toward her. As she drew closer, the flames lapped at her legs, but they didn't hurt her. They couldn't, because she wasn't human. Her daughter knelt down by her and pushed futilely at the heavy bookcase she was trapped underneath.

These bastards had managed to kill her, but not Evangeline. That was all that mattered.

"Eva, baby, you have to run before they find you," she

said, forcing her fingers to release their tight grip on the gun. She wiped away the tears streaming through the ash and grime on Evangeline's face.

"I can't leave you!" Evangeline sobbed, banging her fists against the bookcase.

"You can't move it--"

The demon mark on Eloise's chest tingled and he appeared, looking as he always did, like an old man cloaked in shadows.

"Why are you still here?" the demon demanded, surging toward Evangeline. "Get out before it's too late!"

"No!" she snapped back, slashing her hand through his smoky form. "Help her!"

"You know I can't," he growled. "But you can if you just stop suppressing your magic!"

For a brief moment, Eloise wondered if the demon had arranged this just to force Evangeline to accept her demon side, but she dismissed the thought. She didn't think he would truly risk her being harmed.

The demon leaned in, whispering something in Evangeline's ear. The fire was drawing closer and Eloise could barely catch a breath. Evangeline couldn't be hurt by the fire and smoke, but she could be hurt by whomever was outside.

Evangeline's scream of anguish cut off her words. Her black hair lifted from her shoulders, floating around her head. With a scream, wings of fire burst from her back. She sat there panting, then looked up. Her eyes were black as night.

Eloise gasped as she took in the transformation. She'd known from the day she found the baby abandoned in the woods and the demon had appeared to her, what Evangeline really was. She'd also known that people would hate her, and she'd protected the child as long as she could.

Her daughter lifted her shaking hands, tears still streaming down her face, grabbed the bookcase and threw it across the room. She blinked, delirious from the lack of oxygen. Her daughter scooped her up carefully but she still had to bite her tongue to keep from crying out as pain shot through her legs and her side. She wouldn't have to hold it back long though, her vision blurred as her mind tried to protect itself by sliding into unconsciousness.

Evangeline walked to the back door and kicked it open, then flew into the night. Cool air stung Eloise's burned skin as they raced through the sky.

CHAPTER 1

AMBER

*T*hree days earlier...

Amber's hand tightened on the armrest as they hit another patch of turbulence. She ground her teeth together and pretended the plane was just bumping down a gravel road and that they weren't thirty thousand feet in the air. There was nothing to worry about. Nothing at all.

"Are you sure there's room? I could camp in the woods if I had to," her brother, Derek said, for the tenth time.

"Dude, there are two extra bedrooms even with four of us staying there. It's fine."

"And your pack won't mind? I won't be intruding on your new family, or whatever?"

She punched him in the arm, maybe too hard judging by

his flinch. "They're not my new family. Stop saying it like that. And they're alarmingly excited to meet you."

The pilot announced the plane was beginning its descent. She double-checked her seatbelt and leaned back in her seat.

Her visit had ended up with a big family fight, of course, but Derek had decided he wanted to open his own mechanic shop after all. Since doing it in the same town as their father was out of the question, he'd asked to come to Portland with her. That had caused another family fight when he'd told their parents, but she just didn't care anymore. Derek had been fed up with it as well and stormed out.

She needed a job, he wanted a fresh start, and it seemed like the perfect opportunity for both of them. When she'd told her pack their plans, Tommy had volunteered immediately to help out, eager to have a job again himself. He was always fretting about helping to pay the bills.

As the plane bounced onto the ground, the demon mark on her chest twinged painfully. She rubbed it. It had been aching a lot like that ever since the wolf had somehow banished Angel during the fourth trial to prove her worthiness as an alpha. She kept expecting the demon to show back up that day...and the next...but he never did.

She had no idea how the wolf had done it, but she was insanely glad Angel had been absent while she had visited her family. Though, the temporary peace was probably going to come at a high price.

Everyone stood and crammed into the aisles, but Amber just relaxed in her seat. She'd wait out the crowd and avoid the mad rush for the exit. She didn't have a connecting flight to make and ever since she'd been changed being shoved around by strangers made her irrationally angry. It was better for her sanity and everyone else's health if she just waited. The wolf huffed in agreement in her mind.

"Who did you say was picking us up?" Derek asked, turning his cellphone back on.

"Ceri, she's a witch in my pack."

"That's so weird," he said, shaking his head. "How does that work?"

She shrugged. "I don't know, it just happened. I'm not convinced anyone actually understands how magic works."

"No kidding, there's no explaining how my baby sister ended up an alpha werewolf." He snorted in amusement.

She glared at him. Maybe she *hadn't* missed having her brothers around. "I could always beat you up."

"You could not!" he objected as she finally moved out into the aisle and grabbed her backpack from the overhead bin.

All her luggage fit in a backpack. Derek had chosen to only bring a carry-on as well, having mailed the stuff he wanted to bring to the house. He'd said he didn't have much in the way of furniture and hadn't thought it valuable enough to bother bringing with him to Portland, especially since there's wasn't anywhere to put it.

"Just keep telling yourself that," she said with a smirk.

They finally got off the plane and a knot of tension unwound from her shoulders. The wolf had not been a fan of flying, and she wasn't exactly a nervous flyer, but she was a grumpy one. The combination hadn't been fun.

Her phone buzzed about ten times, finally receiving all the messages that had been sent while she'd had it turned off.

She skipped all the ones from her pack and found Ceri's name.

"Ceri is here already and waiting for us at the terminal," she said, shoving the phone back in her pocket and picking up her pace. It was weird since she hadn't had many close friends in her adult life, but she missed her pack.

They passed through baggage claim, then headed outside. It was chilly out. She tugged her jacket a little closer around her and adjusted the backpack on her shoulder. The wind shifted and she caught Ceri's scent.

"This way," she said, hurrying in the direction the scent led without waiting to see if Derek actually followed.

When she spotted Ceri, the wolf practically howled inside her. Before she realized what she was doing, she'd run over and wrapped her friend up in a tight hug, inhaling her scent deeply. Blonde curls covered her face and drowned out all the other smells. It was nice.

"Hey there, missed you too," Ceri said with a laugh, hugging her back just as tight.

"Felt wrong to be gone," she muttered, feeling a blush grow on her face.

"Yeah, it did. Gen has been grumpy as a hungry pixie since the day after you left."

Amber forced herself to let go and moved back. She jabbed her thumb over her shoulder at her brother as he jogged up behind her. "This is Derek."

"Hey, I'm Ceri," the witch said, stepping forward with a bright smile and wrapping him in a hug as well.

Derek looked surprised and patted her back awkwardly, getting a face full of curly, blonde hair. "Nice to meet you."

Ceri let go of him. "You too! I expected you to be a redhead like Amber though."

He grinned. "Our oldest brother is the only other carrot top in the family. Other than Mom."

Amber rolled her eyes. She hated being called carrot top. "My hair is auburn, not orange. I'm not a carrot."

Derek slung his arm around her shoulder. "Whatever you say, alpha."

"Oh, shut up," she said, shoving his arm off. "Let's get out of here. I don't like the way it smells."

CHAPTER 2

TOMMY

*T*ommy gnawed on the end of his pencil as he stared at the problem. He'd been good at math, but after over a year off, he was rusty. Deward had taken away his formula cheat sheet and insisted that he work from memory. He glanced at the troll, wondering if he could wrestle it away from him and deciding against it. Deward was taller, buffer, and had probably been wrestling since before he could walk.

It had been Ceri's idea to hire the troll as his GED tutor. Deward was insanely smart, but he wasn't really the best teacher. If Tommy didn't understand the first explanation, he'd just shake his head and mutter something about humans, then tell him to try it anyhow.

"Don't forget the power rule," Deward prompted. "It tells you how to differentiate—"

"Yeah, I remember," Tommy interrupted with a sigh. "It's just all running together in my brain. Maybe we should have started with algebra."

"A challenge will strengthen the mind faster," Deward said, adjusting his glasses.

That was apparently the troll's favorite saying. Tommy rubbed his eyes and tried to refocus. If he knew the rule, he should be able to do the math.

An enraged squeak broke his concentration and he looked up, realizing Woggy was no longer in his box. "When did he get out?"

Deward looked in the box as well and frowned. "I don't know, I didn't notice either."

Tommy jumped to his feet and looked around, his ears straining to tell where the noise had come from. There was another squeal, then a shriek of pain. He took off at a run, headed straight for a bush near the edge of the house. As he rounded the corner he saw a swarm of pixies throwing small pebbles.

Woggy was on the ground, hopping and waving a stick furiously. The wingless pixie managed to deflect a few of the pebbles but most hit their target.

"Ah, a territorial fight," Deward said, sounding unconcerned.

Tommy darted in and grabbed Woggy to the displeasure of the attacking pixies. "Well they can buzz off, this is Woggy's yard," he said, swatting at them to try and shoo them away.

The little monsters swarmed him. One of them bit his neck while three more attacked the hand that held Woggy. He yanked the one off his neck and threw it away. The pixie managed to get its bearings and fly back toward him. Their teeth might be small, but they were sharp. He shook his arm to get them off, belatedly realizing that was probably really jarring for Woggy.

Deward finally stepped in and plucked the pixies off, tossing them over his shoulder. He managed to throw them hard enough that they hit the ground. One struggled to its feet and stumbled around in a daze.

"Don't hurt them," Tommy said, watching them struggle back to their feet.

"If you take that disabled pixie away, they'll feel they've won. You either have to kill them, or cede the yard to their control," Deward said, crossing his arms.

He took a deep breath to keep from snapping at his tutor. "I'm not going to kill them, but I'm not giving up that easy either." A pebble thunked against his cheek and he scowled at the attacking pixies.

Woggy was trying to escape from his hands, ready to fight to the death for his territory. The pixie reminded him of Amber. Fearless and full of rage. Unlike Amber, though, Woggy wasn't strong enough to fight off his enemies.

Tommy could relate to that. When he and Ceri had arrived at the house while it was being attacked, she'd run inside. He had tried to help. Despite the wolf's instincts, he simply hadn't known what to do. Of all of them, he could shift the fastest, and had the most control. Maybe too much control. He wasn't sure he *could* fight, even if he had to.

Deward shrugged. "Suit yourself, however, I consider it a waste of time."

"Noted," Tommy said drily, heading back toward the table where they'd left all their books.

Deward followed and began picking up his things, tucking them neatly away in his backpack. "My father suggested it would be polite to invite you over for dinner tomorrow evening."

Tommy glanced at the troll, raising his brow. He wasn't sure if that was an invitation, or if Deward was just letting him know his father had suggested it. Either way, he had no interest in going. "We have pack dinner tomorrow, if that was an invitation."

"Of course it was," Deward said, frowning at him as he slung his backpack over his shoulder. "I'll let my father know and confirm a different time that will work for my parents."

"Great," Tommy said, already thinking up various excuses to get out of going. He had a feeling Deward would trap him eventually. Trolls were too smart to be fooled forever.

Deward nodded his head farewell and headed toward his car. It was pretty small for such a big troll, but Deward said it got excellent gas mileage which allowed him to save more of his tutoring income.

That reminded Tommy that he still needed to find a way to pay Gen back for his tutoring. Somehow. Without a job. Hopefully Amber's brother would want to hire him.

The pixies started gathering together, looking like they were about to swarm him again. He piled his books in his free arm and jogged inside before they had a chance to attack. He checked on Woggy briefly, and the pixie was worse off than he thought.

He pulled out his phone and called Ceri, guilt already curdling in his gut for not watching the pixie closely enough.

CHAPTER 3

GENEVIEVE

Genevieve pinched the bridge of her nose between her finger and thumb and thanked every deity that her boss couldn't see her face. She'd taken this job because she thought this law firm cared more about pro-bono cases. She didn't understand why her boss was fighting her so hard on this potential case.

A bitten werewolf had been attacked at a bar. When he'd defended himself, he'd put the other guy in the hospital. Because he was bitten, it was being called a 'failure to maintain control', which meant he could end up in the System even though he had a pack. She couldn't let that happen.

"Look, I'm not saying we can't take it on, but I think you misunderstand how the pro-bono cases work. If you think this is a worthy cause, then take the case. Do the work.

However, you have to keep up with all your billable hours as well."

"Is that even possible?" she asked.

"Of course it is, you'll just have to work weekends. That's what this job is, if you haven't figured that out yet. It's actually a good opportunity to prove yourself if you're interested in becoming a partner in the next few years," Susan said, typing in the background. That woman never sat still. She was always doing two things at once and expected the same of every other employee. Especially the lowly associates.

Genevieve paused for a moment to steel herself for taking on another challenge. "Alright, I'll do it."

Susan shouted something at someone in the background, though the words were muffled. "Great!" she said, returning to their conversation abruptly. "Send Jorge all the information you find. The client interview needs to be done by Sunday evening, and then we can get into the rest Monday morning. Go ahead and come in early, maybe around seven a.m., so you can catch me up before the rest of the partners arrive."

"Alright, I can do that." She wasn't actually sure she could, but she had to try. She didn't want to spend the rest of her life getting people out of parking tickets. She wanted to actually help people. Besides, if she couldn't do this basic grunt work she'd never make it as a lawyer.

When she gotten into college she'd chosen law because her dad had always called her his little lawyer. She argued her way out of every punishment and had enjoyed debate in high school. This was nothing like she pictured.

Susan ended the call without saying goodbye. Genevieve

tossed her phone down on the table and put her face in her hands thinking, once again, that this had been a huge mistake. Someone's well-being depended on her ability to do her job. She had no idea how surgeons functioned. Hell, she wasn't even sure how Amber walked around all day like everything was fine when the pack's safety depended on her.

The door opened and she looked up. Tommy walked in with his arms covered in tiny cuts. They were already healing, so they must have been way worse a few minutes ago.

"What happened to you?" she asked in alarm.

He muttered something even her enhanced hearing couldn't make out.

She got up and walked over, grabbing his arm and inspecting one of the bloody spots. It looked sort of like a bite. "Did Woggy bite you?"

"No, but it was a pixie," he said with a sigh, lifting his other hand to show her Woggy. He was badly beaten, his gray body mottled with purple bruises. The tip of the pixie's ear was torn. "A whole swarm of them. I think Woggy started the fight, and by the time I got there and got him out, he was already in bad shape."

The pixie rolled over in Tommy's hand, whimpering. He opened his big, watery eyes and gave them an utterly pathetic look.

She wasn't as enamored with Woggy as the others, but even she felt bad seeing him like this. "Did you call Ceri?"

"Yeah, she said to give him meat and that if he's breathing without trouble to wait on doing anything else until she gets back. They're almost here by the way," Tommy said, heading toward the kitchen.

Genevieve started packing up all the paperwork spread over the coffee table. She was a little embarrassed how excited she was to have Amber back but was trying to learn to accept the odd instincts that came with being a werewolf. She could take the cure, but...she felt braver when she was with the pack. If she left, she knew she'd just go back to avoiding her responsibilities and never challenging herself.

"What do you think her brother is going to be like?" Tommy asked from the kitchen as he cracked open a can of pre-cooked chicken. It was normally a treat they gave Woggy at dinner to keep him from trying to get into their food.

She zipped up her briefcase and snorted at his question. "Bossy, probably."

He grinned at that. "As long as he doesn't run around worrying about everyone constantly."

"Oh my god, that would be miserable," she agreed with a laugh.

Tommy paused. "Do you think she'll be mad about...you know," he asked, gesturing down the hall.

"She's going to rage about it and demand to know who did it, and then whine about it, for days possibly, but she's going to be secretly thrilled."

He looked unconvinced. "I'm telling her it was your idea."

"You picked--"

They both stopped, their heads cocking toward the front of the house as the sound of tires on gravel drifted toward them from the driveway.

"They're here!" she said, running for the door. Tommy followed and they tumbled out onto the porch.

Ceri parked and the door to the truck opened. A tall man

with dark brown hair, a thick beard, and a shirt that said It's Bigger Down South stepped out. She sucked up the drool threatening to escape her mouth as he hoisted a backpack onto his shoulders and smiled at her.

Amber hopped down from the truck and Genevieve forgot all about the newcomer. She ran forward, Amber meeting her halfway, and slammed into her alpha. Tommy got there a half second later and wrapped his long arms around both of them, turning it into a group hug.

"You're finally back!" Genevieve squealed, her words muffled by Tommy's forearm and Amber's shoulder.

Amber laughed and squeezed them a little tighter. "I'm glad to see I was missed. I was worried I'd get back and you'd all be gone."

"Never," Tommy objected.

They pulled back, but Amber grabbed her and sniffed her again, carefully. "Why do you smell like...I don't even know what it is." She paused, a low growl rumbling in her throat as her eyes flashed red. "Who marked you?"

Genevieve busted out laughing. "Don't worry, whatever you're thinking is wrong."

CHAPTER 4

AMBER

*T*his was so much worse than what she'd been thinking. This was very, very bad. She was never leaving the pack unsupervised again.

The mangy, one-eyed cat hissed at her again, arching its back to make its already massive form look bigger. The thing had to weigh at least forty pounds. It was possible it was mostly fluff though. It had long, ratty gray fur that probably needed to be shaved off. The animal was filthy.

Genevieve pet it soothingly. "It's okay Captain Jack, she's not as mean as she looks. Her face just does that naturally."

"What the hell is that?" she demanded after a few moments of stunned silence.

"It was Gen's idea," Tommy said hastily, crossing his arms and taking a step back.

Genevieve glared at him. "Tommy picked him out."

Amber turned to Ceri, who was feeding Woggy little pieces of chicken. "Why didn't you stop them? And I thought y'all were planning on getting a *dog*?"

"Well, we saw this old guy in the shelter, and he'd been there for over a year," Ceri said, her blue eyes getting watery, like she might start crying. "We couldn't just leave him."

Amber put her face in her hands and muttered threats she knew she wouldn't follow through on. This was all part of her cosmic punishment for the bad things she'd done in her life. That was the only explanation.

She dropped her hands and faced the cat again. It was licking its leg now and ignoring her. Tentatively, she patted its head. It looked up at her and hissed. "Great, we're friends now," she said, wiping her hand on her leg.

Genevieve rolled her eyes and picked the cat up. Its legs hung down to her hips. She nuzzled her head into its fluff, which explained the smell on her, and the cat began to purr like a motorboat. "Captain Jack is the best cat ever."

Derek clapped his hand on her shoulder. "At least it won't bark. Now, where's my room?"

"There are two free rooms upstairs, pick whichever you like," she said, gesturing toward the stairs.

"So inhospitable," Derek joked as he headed toward the stairs.

"I'll show you around," Ceri offered.

"That'd be great," he said, his face lighting up in a smile.

Amber grimaced. She should have just done it. Genevieve caught her eye, then looked pointedly at Ceri and Derek heading upstairs. Genevieve's smile grew, clearly amused by the obvious chemistry between the two.

Her stomach growled, distracting her from all that. "What's for dinner?" she asked, looking at Tommy hopefully.

"I ordered pizza," Genevieve said. "Tommy had tutoring with Deward today, so he didn't really have time."

"Sorry," Tommy said, looking chagrined.

"Pizza sounds great, nothing to be sorry about. How's tutoring going? Did you get your driver's license?" she asked, eager to catch up.

"Yeah," he said with a grin, finally straightening his shoulders. "Passed with flying colors."

Amber heard someone turn down the driveway and tilted her head toward the noise. "Pizza guy?"

"What? Oh, I hear it now," Genevieve said, hurrying toward the door. She grabbed her wallet from her purse and yanked the door open before the guy had a chance to knock. The smell of pizza filled the house.

"You aren't too mad about the cat, are you?" Tommy asked, tugging his beanie down nervously.

Amber shook her head and looked at the beast. "No, I'm not mad. He's probably the perfect mascot for us."

Tommy laughed. "You've got that right. He's definitely not your average cat."

"Is he getting along with Woggy?" she asked.

"Yeah, surprisingly. We actually took Woggy to the shelter with us. He climbed on Captain Jack's back and the cat just sniffed him, then laid down."

"Huh, I would not have guess that'd be the cat's reaction. Glad to hear it though."

Genevieve walked back into the living room with the pizza. "DINNER IS HERE!" she shouted in the general direction of upstairs.

"Be right down!" Ceri shouted back.

Amber smiled to herself, she was glad to be home. Even if the cat was currently stealing a piece of pizza straight out of the box with its filthy paws.

CHAPTER 5

CERI

The house had gone quiet, and Ceri should be sleeping, but between the odd dreams and the anxiety she'd had since the Trials…well, she wasn't. Instead, she'd been living on caffeine and naps. Sleeping during the day seemed to result in fewer dreams.

Covering a yawn with the back of her hand, she shuffled into the work room. She'd been investigating the wards on the house to keep herself from brooding over everything that had happened. It was fascinating how the house had moved them around during the attack. She'd never seen magic like it before. It was almost as if it had been left alone and gotten unruly, coming up with its own ideas about how to protect itself. The only thing she knew for sure so far was that gaining new inhabitants had strengthened it and made it happy.

She lit a bundle of sage and began walking the perimeter of the room. Waving the smoldering herb gently, she directed the smoke with her free hand as she cleansed it methodically. It was important to make sure the space was clear of negative energies and spirits before she opened her mind to the magic of the house.

There were spirits in this world, born of pure magic, that were both good and bad. This was another thing her grandmother had taught her, all the while cursing people that lived their lives with a black and white view of good and evil.

Ceri rolled her eyes at the memory. Her grandmother had been wise, powerful, and vicious. And just as disappointed in her daughter as her mother was in her. Her grandmother had had such high hopes for her. She was probably rolling in her grave watching her now.

Setting the still smoldering bundle of sage in a bowl on the floor in the center of the room, she sat down in front of it. The scent surrounded her and cleared her senses. She crossed her legs and rested her hands on her thighs.

Her senses reached out and sank into the walls, the floor, and wards that were a part of the house. It looked back at her and she felt the air around her shift slightly.

The house was excited she was acknowledging it, almost like a happy puppy. The floorboards under her creaked and trembled slightly. A barrage of images flashed through her mind, too fast to process. A glimpse of the kitchen. The back door. The porch. The attic. Then, in a blinding burst, the wards themselves came into focus.

Her breath caught in her throat. Woven into every board, and into the air itself, were golden threads of elven magic. They burned as bright as the sun. Whoever had created them had been pure of heart and had poured love and creativity into them. She mentally snorted. That ruled out Thallan, the house's owner.

She lifted her hand, eyes still closed, and tentatively touched a spot where she knew one of the threads laid. The magic was warm at first but quickly became too hot to touch. She yanked her hand away with a pained hiss, sucking on the burned finger.

The house groaned in alarm. The curtains fluttered behind her and the light fixture overhead began to sway. It was then that she realized that she could see everything around her. She could even see herself.

"Shhh, it's okay. You didn't mean to hurt me," she whispered, trying to soothe the agitated house.

It seemed to huff at her as it curled around her once again. Emotions that weren't her own bounced through her. Worry, shame, fear...and hope.

She smiled and did her best to send back contentment, curiosity, and forgiveness. The trembling of the room stopped and she was filled with warmth.

Another image appeared in her mind. It didn't change abruptly this time, instead, it slowly came into focus, showing her Derek standing in front of the kitchen counter. She nudged it and found she was able to move slightly to see better. He was stirring honey into a mug of tea.

She almost jumped when he picked it up and turned around, then laughed to herself. He couldn't see her. She pressed her hand into the floor by her foot to ground herself. Despite what she could see, she hadn't moved. The house was simply showing her what *it* could see.

Instead of walking upstairs to his room, Derek headed out of the kitchen and down the hall that led to her and Amber's rooms. She expected him to knock on his sister's door, but he passed it up, and stopped in front of hers.

That was surprising. Though...perhaps it shouldn't be. She thought he'd been flirting most of the day, but she never liked to assume that sort of thing. She was a very friendly person, and he was new to the house.

Derek lifted his hand, then hesitated and turned around, walking away. Then he stopped and shook his head and walked back to her door once again. He squared his shoulders and knocked lightly.

She grinned to herself. He was nervous. He seemed so confident in all their other interactions, it was endearing to see him fretting about bringing her a cup of tea. It also made it clear that he *was* wooing her. While flattering, her stomach twisted with misgivings.

This was Amber's brother, and someone that now lived with the pack. They could date, but if either of them broke it off, it could get very awkward. She wasn't one for casual relationships either. She knew she always fell in love first, and way too fast. She'd never understood how people held their hearts back.

With a sigh, she released her connection to the house and stood. Derek knocked again, a little quieter this time. She hurried toward the door, pausing to take a breath before she cracked it open.

"Derek?" she asked in fake surprise, not wanting him to know she'd been spying on him.

He lifted the steaming mug of tea. It smelled like lavender and chamomile. "You said you'd been having trouble sleeping," he said. His smile drooped. "Aw hell, I didn't wake you, did I?"

She shook her head and opened the door wider. "No, you didn't. I was researching something."

"Oh, okay, that's good." He extended the cup of tea toward her. "I've heard this tea stuff can help you sleep, and you mentioned you'd been having some insomnia lately. I thought this might help."

She accepted the cup with a smile. "Thank you, it smells wonderful. And I love honey in my tea."

"How'd you know there's honey?" he asked, confused.

"Oh, I can smell it," she said, swallowing nervously. She wasn't quite ready to let anyone know the house let her spy on them. That was a conversation to have with Amber first, anyhow. She blew gently on the tea, then took a sip. Her eyes fell shut. He'd put in just the right amount of honey. "That's perfect."

Derek cleared his throat and rubbed a hand across the back of his neck. "That's great," he said in a slightly strangled tone. "Glad you like it."

"Stop flirting in the hallway. It's gross!" Amber whisper-shouted through her closed door, sounding like they'd woken her up.

Derek turned bright red and took a step back. "Hope it helps you sleep."

Ceri grinned at him. "Thanks for thinking of me."

That got his smile back. He glanced at Amber's door and mimed zipping his lips shut, then winked at her, and walked away.

She stayed standing in her doorway for a moment, sipping the tea, and chastising herself for flirting back. The tea *was* really good though.

CHAPTER 6

AMBER

*A*mber hopped down from her truck and looked at the rundown warehouse in front of them. The windows were broken with old, dusty glass still clinging to the weathered frames. It was made of brick but looked like a stiff wind might blow it over. On the side of the dilapidated building was an overhead door that was so badly rusted there were holes in it. "Derek, are we about to get murdered by a man wearing a mask made of someone else's face and wielding a chainsaw?"

"Nah, I'm getting more undead-welder-with-a-grudge vibes from this place. So, a blowtorch maybe?" he suggested with a shrug of his shoulders.

She rolled her eyes. "Who are we supposed to be meeting here?"

The door the warehouse opened and she flinched slightly. Derek snorted in amusement and shook his head, walking over to meet the guy heading toward them.

The guy didn't look like a serial killer. In fact, he looked like an old hippie. He had on cut-off jean shorts that showed an awful lot of thigh for an old man. He'd topped that with a tie-dyed shirt and a vest made of some kind of weird, faux-leather looking material.

"Good to meet you in person, Mr. Suthersby," Derek said, greeting him with a handshake.

"You too, my friend, but call me Bernard. We're all brothers on this great, green ball of life," he said, dragging Derek into a brief hug. Her brother grimaced and patted his shoulder awkwardly, pulling away as soon as he could.

Amber hid a smile behind her hand. Derek was getting ambushed by a lot of hugs recently. Served him right for bringing her to this creepy place. When he'd said he had a potential shop already lined up, she'd imagined something nicer. Something *useable*. This place would take weeks of work just to clean up, much less to get it ready for customers. Her savings account was dwindling fast just trying to keep everyone fed. Genevieve had insisted on covering things while she was gone, but it frustrated her to not be able to provide for her pack, or at least contribute more.

"Is this your sister?" Bernard asked, turning his attention to Amber.

"I am," she said, walking forward and shaking his hand as well. Instead of letting go, he wrapped both his hands around her and looked deep into her eyes.

"You're a werewolf," he stated. It wasn't a question, she could tell he was absolutely sure of it.

She inhaled carefully, but her first impression was right, he was human. She glanced at Derek, but he shook his head. He hadn't told Bernard. "Yeah. Is that a problem?" she asked, already feeling herself stiffen. If he was going to reject them because of what she was, then she wanted to know right now. "I'm bitten, too."

He smiled gently and patted her cheek. "Thought so. Mother Earth has blessed you with her magic, what is there to have a problem with?"

She raised a brow. "Everybody else seems to come up with a list of concerns."

He waved his hand at her and shook his head. "Ignorance leads to anger, which leads to hate. They need to smoke a little weed and meditate. Can't force a person to choose happiness though."

Well, this guy was nuts, but at least he wasn't a bigoted asshole. She managed to extract her hand from his and nodded. "You sure can't."

"Now," he said, rubbing his hands together. "I'm sure you'd like a tour. I know she looks rough on the outside, but my inspector promised she's safe to enter."

Amber groaned internally. 'Safe to enter' was a very low bar. Derek happily followed Bernard to the front door though, no hint of concern on his features. Maybe Ceri was right and she did worry too much.

She began to follow them, but her phone rang. Glancing at the caller ID, she saw it was Shane, the werewolf contact who'd helped her through the alpha trials, and quickly answered it.

"Alpha Hale," she answered with a smirk.

Shane chuckled. "Like the way it sounds?"

"Yeah, actually, I do," she said, unable to keep a smile from forming on her face.

"You might like it a little less after your first council meeting."

She groaned internally. Jameson, Shane's alpha, had originally planned on getting her up to date before she left on her trip, but ended up postponing it, though he wouldn't say why. "Is it going to be that bad? I'm not going to have to fight a bear again, am I?"

"Nah, nothing that easy. You instead get to learn about all your new responsibilities. I'll be picking you up at six a.m., by the way."

"No one should ever have to be awake that early," she muttered. "I hate Donovan. Have I mentioned that recently?"

He cleared his throat uncomfortably. "About Donovan..."

"What?" she prompted when he didn't continue.

"He disappeared from the cell the council was holding him in, then turned up dead a couple of days ago. Well, his head turned up. The police haven't found the rest of him."

She froze, her heart hammering in her chest. "What? Who killed him?"

"They don't know. I think you should expect a visit from the police soon, though. Your issues with him were pretty well-known. Honestly, he's lucky he got off with decapitation. His punishment was going to be way worse."

"Shit," she said, beginning to pace. She had an air-tight

alibi, but Donovan's murder couldn't be good news. She wasn't exactly sad to see him go, but she had a bad feeling about this. Her wolf growled in agreement.

"Yeah, that's one word for it," Shane agreed.

"What about Peter, the werewolf that turned us? Any sign of him yet?" she asked.

"No, we never did find him," Shane said. "Look, I can't discuss this any further over the phone, but Jameson will tell you more tomorrow. Just be ready to go at six a.m. sharp."

"Alright."

"Talk to you soon," he said before ending the call.

She dropped her hand to her side and rubbed her hand against the demon mark. It was aching again, as if it was responding to her emotions. She was going to have to get the pack together this evening and let them know what had happened.

"Amber!" Derek shouted from the doorway of the warehouse. "Get in here and check it out. This place is awesome!"

She mentally shook off the worry and jogged toward her brother. "I'm coming, don't get your panties in a twist."

~

One hour, two hugs, and three large rats later they were heading out. Derek was thrilled with the warehouse. All she could see was the mess, but her brother was more of a visionary like Dylan had been. They saw the potential in broken things, and had the patience to try and fix them.

"Replacing the door will be the biggest expense," Derek

said, scrolling through a web page on his phone. "Other than tools, obviously."

"A month ago, I'd have been able to offer a little more help with all that," she said, her hands tightening on the steering wheel.

"Don't worry about it, you're going to be free labor until we start earning enough to cover all the expenses. That's gonna save me a ton of money," he said, waving her misgivings away.

"Well, now I feel taken advantage of," she said, grinning at him.

"Tommy said he wanted to help, too. I'll work out a way to get him a little cash."

"Just make sure he always has time to study. He's trying to get his GED soon."

"Did he not finish high school?" Derek asked, looking up from his phone in confusion.

She shook her head. "Ran away from home when he was sixteen and dropped out of school."

"Damn, you really did find yourself a weird little pack."

"It wasn't his fault," she said, frowning at him. She didn't like him calling her pack weird, even though it was. They might be an odd group, but they'd managed to accomplish a lot.

"I didn't mean that in a bad way," he said, nudging her shoulder.

They fell silent for a few minutes as they drove; Derek lost in his research, and Amber lost in her thoughts. The song on the radio ended and the DJ's started talking about the new spots that had popped up where magic didn't work. Apparently, they were blaming overuse of magic now. She rolled her eyes and changed the channel. There was always a new conspiracy theory about what had caused it, but the truth was no one knew.

Her phone buzzed and she glanced at the screen. It was a short text from Ceri. She'd figured out something weird but cool about the house that she wanted to show her later. That reminded Amber of last night.

She turned back to Derek and narrowed her eyes at him. "What exactly are your intentions with Ceri?"

He looked up slowly. "That was out of nowhere."

"Answer the question, buster. All I remember from high school is that you brought a new girl home every week," she said accusingly.

"Geez, I'd forgotten how protective you were," he muttered. "It's been six years, and I've grown as a person, thank you very much. I'm not planning our wedding or anything, but I like her. She's all bohemian and cool, not to mention really nice. I don't know, I just couldn't help but flirt, and maybe I do want to date her. Or something."

Amber sighed at him. "Or something? That's the best you've got?"

"I'm being honest here. Do you want me to lie to make you feel better?"

"No, just don't screw her over, alright? She's in my pack, and I won't ask her to leave if you hurt her and make things awkward."

Derek looked offended at that. "Why do you assume I'd be the one to screw it up?"

She rolled her eyes. "You've met Ceri, I don't think she's capable of hurting anyone. For any reason."

He crossed his arms, still looking annoyed. "I'm not planning on screwing things up. Don't go all mama bear on me over it."

She knew she was being slightly overprotective. They were both adults after all, but all her instincts were going haywire over it. Learning that Donovan was dead was only making it worse.

"If she breaks your heart, I'll...ground her or something," she said finally, winking at her brother.

He snorted. "Thanks, that'll really show her."

"Bros over hoes."

He busted out laughing. "Your jokes are so bad, they're *almost* funny."

She reached over and punched him in the arm. "I'm hilarious. You're just jealous I'm the funniest one in the family."

"Oh please. Everyone knows I'm the funny one. You're the grumpy one."

CHAPTER 7

TOMMY

ommy was bored. Amber and Derek were off looking at a place for their mechanic shop, Ceri was napping with Woggy, and Genevieve was working. He wasn't sleepy, but he definitely wasn't interested in studying anymore.

He rummaged through the refrigerator until he found stuff to make a sandwich and slapped a couple together. He scarfed down the first one standing there but took the second with him. The estate was huge and he hadn't explored any of it yet. When Amber had been preparing to take the Trials, they were all he could think about. Now, he was curious.

He left out the back door and wandered in the direction of the main house. There was no way he was going inside

Thallan's creepy, old mansion, but there was no harm in checking out the gardens around it.

The garden by their guest house was decently well-maintained, if a little overgrown, but the closer you got to the main house, the worse shape everything was in. It was like the place was cursed and slowly killing everything around it.

He headed toward the back of the mansion, chewing as he looked around. There were remnants of wooden archways and a crumbling stone path. A big willow tree drooped over a scummy pond that was only half full. The narrow stream that used to feed it was dry. Weeds grew up through the cracks now. This place was probably really pretty once. It smelled weird around here, too. It wasn't exactly *bad*, but it definitely wasn't good. He sniffed the air, trying to parse it and got some combination of wet dirt, cut grass, and old fish.

He wondered what had made Thallan hate it so much that he'd let the place rot. The only thing elves loved more than themselves was nature. Their gardens were usually a little wild, but this was just…in ruins.

Shoving the rest of the sandwich in his mouth, he ducked under the drooping branch of an old tree and rounded a curve in the pathway. He caught a glimpse of a pixie in the shrub next to him and walked a few paces forward to try and get a better look. He needed to figure out a way to run them off, or gain their trust, so they didn't hurt Woggy.

"I was promised you wouldn't come snooping around the house," a gruff voice said from right behind him.

He jumped, not having seen Thallan when he was walking up. The creepy elf was sitting on a stone bench that was half covered in vines. He should have smelled the elf, but the scent of cigarettes wasn't noticeable until after Thallan had spoken.

"I'm just looking around. I didn't go in your house," Tommy said, backing up a step.

Thallan exhaled smoke through his nose and turned his eyes back to the overgrown rose bush in front of him. "Don't come lurking through my gardens either. You and your pack get the guest house, and the lands. But not this. That was the deal."

"Got it. Sorry." Tommy turned to go back the way he'd come.

"Has Amber been acting odd in any way since she got back?" Thallan asked before he'd even taken a step.

He paused and looked over his shoulder. "No. Why?"

Thallan shrugged. "No reason."

Tommy waited for some kind of explanation, but the elf just took another drag of his cigarette and stared at nothing. He decided to leave before he got asked anything else.

The question had unsettled him though. Amber never had explained how she got Thallan to agree to letting them live there, or to be her sponsor. Now the old creep thought there was a chance she might start acting weird. He wasn't sure if that's because he'd cursed her, or if there was some other reason.

When he made it back to the pack house he saw Amber's truck was back in the driveway. He frowned thinking he should have been able to hear them arrive. Maybe the garden had some weird wards on it that had prevented it.

The back door opened as he approached it and Amber

visibly slumped in relief. "Are you okay? You just felt really... disturbed for a moment."

"Oh, yeah. I was just wandering around and Thallan startled me," Tommy said with a shrug. He didn't want to talk about it yet. He wanted to bring it up with Ceri first, and see if she knew anything. "Did the place Derek found work out?"

She groaned. "He seems to think so."

"Just because there are a few rats and cobwebs doesn't mean it isn't perfect," Derek shouted from inside the house.

She turned back to her brother and Tommy followed her inside. "I can help clean up," he offered.

"That'd be great!" Derek said. "I was actually going to talk to you about your pay. I can give you fifty bucks a week for part-time work until the place opens, then I'll see about a raise. Until then, I thought maybe we could work something else out. Maybe teaching you how to work on the trucks so you can help out as a mechanic eventually?"

Tommy hesitated, the gears in his head turning, then tugged his beanie down farther on his head. He had something else in mind, but he wanted to talk to Derek about it in private. "Sure, sounds good. I'll just be glad to have something to do. I can only study so much."

"Perfect," Derek said, rubbing his hands together. "Studying is overrated anyhow."

Amber rolled her eyes and punched him in the shoulder. "Don't even start."

Derek just punched her right back, starting an impromptu wrestling match. Tommy grinned. It was good to see someone giving his alpha crap. She looked more relaxed than she had since...well, since he'd met her.

CHAPTER 8

GENEVIEVE

The werewolf was younger than Genevieve had expected. He was a skinny, blond college kid, and he looked scared out of his mind.

"I was out for my twenty-first birthday with my human friends and this group of guys started picking on a girl. I was feeling cocky, because what can they do to me, you know? So, I stepped in. I didn't think I was going to hurt him that bad. He threw the first punch and I didn't lose control. I didn't. I just hit him back and he crumpled," Davie said, his hands shaking as he rubbed them over his watery eyes. "I'm screwed, aren't I?"

"You should never have been arrested," she said firmly, reaching across the table to squeeze his arm. Her wolf was furious, all her protective instincts were raging inside her. If she'd been in his situation she might have actually lost control and ripped the dude's arms off. "My firm has agreed to take on the case, free of charge. We're going to get these charges dismissed."

"Really?" he asked, not looking like he believed her at all. "My alpha said it was a lost cause."

"No offense to your alpha, but that's bullshit," she said, pausing to take a deep breath. "What pack are you with? I'll need to talk with them."

He sniffled and wiped his nose on the back of his sleeve. "The Lockhart Pack."

Her pen snapped in her hand, ink soaking into her fingers. She quickly dropped it on the table. This werewolf belonged to Donovan's pack. There was no way she could just stroll up and talk to Donovan. He might kill her, or refuse to help just to spite her.

"You okay?" he asked, confused.

"Yeah, just fine," she said, clearing her throat and curling her stained fingers into her palm. "I'll be back to see you tomorrow, okay? Keep thinking about the details, and anyone that can vouch for your character. Especially any humans."

"Okay."

She got up and rapped on the door to let the guard know she was done. The guard opened the door to let her out, but she paused in the doorway. "Keep your chin up, okay Davie? It's going to work out. I promise."

Davie nodded, the tense line of his shoulders loosening just a little. "I'll try to believe that."

"Thanks," she said with a nod to the guard as she slipped

out of the room. Her fingers tightened on the handle of her briefcase. Being in the jail made her skin crawl. She'd come so close to being in this place herself. It hadn't seemed real until she'd walked in here today, though.

She made it out of the building and to her car before before the tears of frustration welled up in her eyes. She wanted to strangle Donovan. He'd abandoned his pack member so easily. She couldn't fathom doing that. Even now, she could feel the pack bond stretching between her, Tommy, Ceri, and Amber. It thrummed in her gut, a warm reassurance. How could an alpha turn their back on that?

She rested her forehead against the steering wheel and took a deep breath. Maybe, she could have one of the other associates talk to Donovan and convince him to give Davie the support he needed.

The only issue was if she could do it in less than a week. She'd spent the entire morning prepping to go to the jail and most of the afternoon interviewing Davie.

She checked her phone and saw an invitation from Steven to dinner, which she quickly replied to with a rejection. The last thing she had time for was a date. Her mother had also texted her now, which meant a phone call was imminent if she didn't reply. She opened the message and saw that her parents wanted to have dinner and catch up. That meant they'd probably heard something about her getting bitten. She wondered who had ratted her out. It was probably her sister, the little snoop.

She didn't hate her parents or anything. It was the opposite actually. They were frustratingly perfect. They never pried and always supported her. Her dad used to take off work to come to all her softball games. He'd cheer when she struck out and tell her *better luck next time, princess.* She knew he'd probably been embarrassed though.

Dropping her phone in her lap, she groaned in annoyance. Her mother would probably love Amber, want to adopt Tommy, and think Ceri walked on water. Logically, she knew it was a dumb thing to be frustrated by, but all she'd ever done was let them down. She'd graduated college only to avoid using the degree they'd paid for as long as she could. She was in her mid-twenties now and hadn't had a serious boyfriend yet. Unless you counted Steven, but they didn't know about him, and she still wasn't sure she wanted that to be serious.

She needed, desperately, to be able to help Davie. She wanted to prove she could do something right, and do it well. That, and she couldn't bear the idea of letting an injustice like this happen.

Angry, she threw the car into reverse and backed out of her parking spot. It was time to hunt down an alpha. She should probably let Amber know what she was doing first. And call Steven and see if there was any etiquette she needed to follow since she was also a werewolf.

"It just has to keep getting more complicated," she muttered to herself.

CHAPTER 9

CERI

*C*eri parked her car a few blocks from the store and climbed out. The wind whipped around her legs, scattering leaves across the sidewalk. She pulled her cardigan a little closer around her. It was time to start wearing leggings under her dresses again.

She hadn't wanted to come into the city. Despite its size, the chance that she'd run into either a family member or someone from the Blackwood coven was high. Witches ran in small circles, and the things she needed to get today took her right into the midst of them.

She was going to have to look into getting another job soon. Amber had told her not to stress about it, but there was no way she'd just mooch off the pack forever. Even if all she could do was contribute to the grocery bill, she would. There were things she could do to make the wards on the house stronger if she had the right supplies. With a little time and money, she thought she could actually improve the wards on the entire property. They just needed a little TLC.

A little bell tinkled overhead as she walked in. Pausing just inside, she scanned the sections for hyssop elixir and powdered pennyroyal. A sign in the back corner of the store pointed out what she needed. She wound through the aisles, refusing to look at the little jars that held pixie parts and other magical creatures. It had always bothered her, but now that she had Woggy, it made her nauseous to even think about it.

As she neared the back of the store, the scents of sage and other cleansing herbs made her nose tickle. She grabbed a few sticks of sage since she had a feeling she'd be using a lot of it in the coming weeks, then continued toward the back.

She paused in front of the shelf that had it and picked up two brands, comparing the strength of the ingredients versus the price. Despite preferring to use the more concentrated version, she was probably going to have to settle for the cheaper one and hope the strength of her magic could make up the difference.

"Ceridwen," a deep voice said behind her. Her heart immediately kicked into overdrive as her gut twisted in worry. He shouldn't be here.

She turned slowly to face her father. He was only slightly taller than she was and almost as slender. He had thin strawberry blond hair and a baby face that made many people underestimate him. Her mother was their coven leader, but he was her second. They'd married for no other reason than to combine the magical potential of their families. It had paid off with powerful and talented children.

"Father," she said, meeting his eyes despite her unease. *Don't show fear. Don't show weakness. Don't ever turn your back on an enemy.*

"Your mother is surprised you haven't come back," he said, rubbing his hand along the stubble on his jaw.

"But you're not."

He shook his head. "You've never been willing to commit to the coven. It was only a matter of time before you found a reason to leave permanently."

There were many reasons she'd stayed for so long. Wanting her parent's approval, fear of striking out on her own, and knowing that if she joined another coven they'd consider her an enemy. This meeting wasn't a coincidence. Her father had come specifically to speak with her. Perhaps to threaten her.

"I don't want to hurt other living things just to gain more power," she said, repeating the beginning of an old argument.

He shook his head in exasperation. "You've made that very clear."

"Why are you here then, if not to talk me into returning to the coven?" she asked.

He lifted his head and spoke formally, "You weakened the coven when you left. Normally this would justify retaliation."

She stiffened, preparing for an attack. Her mind went to the pack, praying they were still alright. She hadn't even considered that her family might move against them after her mother kicked her out, but she should have.

"However," he continued, "your actions at the Alpha Trials, and on Halloween, severely weakened our enemy, the Blackwood Coven. Your mother has chosen, as a final act of mercy, to accept this as an offering that balances out your transgressions. You are persona non grata with the Gallagher Clan from this day forward. Under the rules of coven engagement, we will not act against you unless you first act against us."

She had no idea how he knew about Halloween, or if he just suspected it had been her. Perhaps it had been a simple matter of deduction. Not many witches could get past the Blackwood wards.

"The Hale pack will not threaten or harm the Gallagher clan unless you first move against us," she said, echoing his words as the formal declaration demanded.

Her father nodded, then turned and walked away. Her heart was racing and, now that he wasn't looking, her hands shook slightly. That was it. She had no family anymore. Her mother had kicked her out before, but she had always come back. That wasn't a choice this time.

Relief and sorrow warred inside her. Her parents were cruel, but she hadn't seen that as a child. She didn't want to see it now.

Shaking off the self-pity, she straightened her shoulders and steeled herself. Enough was enough. She'd made her choice and she didn't regret it. Amber was her alpha now, and she was a good person. Tommy was like a little brother already, and Genevieve could be the sister she always wished she'd had. Her actual siblings were…like her parents. They'd never gotten along.

She grabbed the last thing she needed from the shelves and walked to the register, paying as quickly as she could. She knew her parents hadn't done anything to the pack or her father wouldn't have said what he did. Still, she'd feel better once she was back there and could confirm it in person.

"Thanks, have a good day," the cashier said cheerfully.

"You too," she replied, though her smile in return was wooden.

She grabbed the bag the cashier handed her and hurried out the door, almost running into someone trying to enter. With a muttered 'sorry', she sidestepped around them. She wished she'd parked closer now. Parking down the street had obviously done nothing to help avoid running into someone she knew. It took all her self-control, and the knowledge that her father or someone else might be watching, to walk and not run.

Finally, her car came into view, but…an owl sat on the roof. Her blood ran cold. Owls were ill omens. They portended death, misfortune, and illness. This was the last thing she needed right now. Running into her father had been enough of a bad sign. She didn't want another.

Glaring at it, she walked up to her car and waved her hands at the unwelcome creature. "Shoo!"

The owl flapped its wings and hopped out of her reach but didn't fly away. It hooted at her softly.

"Go away," she hissed.

It hooted again and walked sideways, hopping down onto the side mirror. Its eerie, orange eyes fixed on her. She tried to shoo it away again and it nipped at her finger, drawing a little blood.

She hissed in pain and shook her finger. Seemingly pleased with itself, it took flight. Instead of going over her head, it almost collided with her. She ducked to avoid it, then turned to glare at the persistent bird. It was sitting under a tree looking quite smug.

She thought about throwing something at it when she saw what was growing next to its foot. It had barely sprouted out of the ground. If the owl hadn't been practically standing on it, she never would have seen the slight, purple glow.

Crouching down, she cautiously reached for the little mushroom near its foot. The owl hooted happily and shuffled to the side. She brushed the dirt away and, sure enough, there was the beginning of a Fairy Ring. It was a super rare mushroom that had all but died out due to over-harvesting. It was useful in all manner of spells, as well as meditation. There were rumors it could help a powerful enough witch catch glimpses of the future, or at least its possibilities.

She brushed the dirt a little farther away and saw that there wasn't just one. There was a circle of seven little, purple mushrooms. That was a lucky number, and meant that she could collect the whole bundle and use them to grow more.

She looked at the owl again, suspicious now. It cocked its head at her as though it were analyzing her right back. This wasn't a normal animal.

"Thank you," she whispered.

It hooted, then took off, flying over her head and into the

sky. She was going to have to do a little research, perhaps they weren't always ill omens.

Turning her attention back to the Fairy Ring, she quickly dug around it and pulled out a whole chunk of dirt. With nowhere else to put it, she opened her purse and set it carefully inside. It'd wash.

CHAPTER 10

AMBER

Amber sat next to Ceri on the porch swing sipping coffee. She was tired, and the demon mark was throbbing like a headache. That couldn't be a good sign.

Mentally, she prodded the wolf, asking what she'd done to the demon. Amber got back a strong impression of smugness, but nothing else. She sighed. She didn't like being caught between the wolf and Angel.

Ceri shifted around, yawning. The witch had been in a weird mood since she got back yesterday, and she hadn't been sleeping much since the Trials. It was starting to worry Amber, but she knew Ceri would just say she worried about everything.

"I saw an owl yesterday," Ceri said, her tone suggesting that meant something important, and possibly bad.

"Are you allergic to them or something?" she asked.

Ceri snorted in amusement. "No, well, figuratively I guess we all are. They're considered ill omens."

"Great," Amber muttered before chugging the rest of her coffee. "Just what I needed to hear right before this meeting."

"Well, that's the thing," Ceri said thoughtfully. "It led me to something really good. Those mushrooms I told you about yesterday evening –– which I planted in the garden by the way. Anyhow, my gut is telling me it wasn't an ill omen, that it's something else instead. I just have to figure out what, exactly."

"You're probably turning into some kind of animal whisperer," Amber suggested. "All the forest creatures are going to start flocking to you. Witches don't ever join packs. It was bound to do something weird to you."

Ceri laughed, then sat up straight, her eyes going wide. "Amber, you're a genius."

"What?" she asked, confused.

"An absolute genius," Ceri said, jumping to her feet and running inside, slamming the door shut behind her.

"Well, okay then." She'd have to corner Ceri later and get an explanation, but she'd take being called a genius for now. She glanced at her phone. Shane was two minutes late. The bastard.

Leaning her head back against the back of the swing she let her eyes slip shut. Maybe there was time for a short nap. Of course, that was when she heard a car turn down the driveway.

She peeked her eye open and saw it was the same suburban he'd driven to pick her up for the Trials. She stood and hurried back inside to dump her coffee mug in the sink, then walked back out to the porch.

Shane hadn't bothered to get out to greet her; he just flashed his headlights impatiently. He had some nerve.

She yanked the car door open and glared at him. "You're late."

"I know, get in," he said, motioning for her to hurry.

She hopped up into the passenger seat and buckled her seatbelt. "Is something wrong?"

"Not really, it was just a late night last night. Since Donovan was ousted from the council, and you haven't filled his spot yet, Jameson has been handling all his duties. Which means I've been dealing with a lot of petty crap as his beta," Shane said tiredly.

"Great," Amber said with a sigh.

"Don't worry, I won't let them throw you to the wolves. Jameson is going to let me assist you for a while. He knows you're clueless," Shane said with a smirk.

"Gee, thanks."

"Oh, come on, you know it's true."

"I'm not *completely* clueless, just slightly under-educated," she retorted. He was right though. She'd be lost without help. "Thanks for the help though. I'd prefer to not screw everything up my first week on the job."

He chuckled. "Maybe you can take me out for coffee to pay me back."

"I don't know if it's appropriate to date my coworkers," she said, looking out the window to hide the slight blush on her cheeks. She really needed to date more if this was how she reacted to a little light flirting. This was just embarrassing.

"Think of us more as allies," Shane said, nodding to himself. "No rules against allies dating."

Shane had a lot of things going for him. He was attractive, confident, and best of all, he was straightforward about what he wanted.

"Fine, let's do coffee in a few days. I need to make sure you earn it before I take you out," she said, crossing her arms.

"That won't be a problem."

It turned out that Jameson only lived twenty minutes away. The drive passed quickly and Amber had to fight down the nervous energy that was about to make her sweat through her shirt. She hated not knowing what to expect, and this was all brand new. The wolf was pacing in her mind too, which didn't help calm her down at all.

They turned down a street that led into a small subdivision.

"Do these homes all belong to pack members?" she asked, looking at the rows of houses. The lawns were neat, and no cars were parked in the street clogging up traffic. It looked like any other human subdivision.

"Pack and their families," Shane confirmed with a nod. "There's another community about a mile north of here that's bigger. I live out there since Alpha Jameson wanted a high-ranking pack member in the neighborhood to keep the peace, and protect the pack."

"How big is Jameson's pack?" she asked in surprise. She'd always thought of packs as small, with ten to twelve members. Maybe that's just how it was in the South.

"He has fifty registered members. It's a big pack, which is part of why he's the head of the council. Not many people could keep a pack this big together."

"That's a lot of people to keep track of," she said, shaking her head in disbelief. She couldn't fathom what it would be like to be connected so intimately to so many people. How did he not go crazy feeling them all the time? And the strength she got from the pack bond was already crazy. Being able to draw on fifty people would make you insanely powerful.

Shane pulled into a driveway in front of a two-story house. It wasn't the biggest, or grandest house on the block. There was nothing to make it stand out at all other than the cars in the driveway and parked along the street.

"Before we go in, just remember, you're their equal. You don't have to be submissive to them," Shane said in a whisper.

She nodded. "Got it."

They climbed out and headed toward the door. She could smell the other alphas now, and recognized their scents from the Trials. It was odd to have some of her senses enhanced so dramatically, but she was getting used to it. Slowly.

Jameson greeted them at the door, waving them inside. There was none of the formality of the Trials this time. He was barefoot in a pair of cargo shorts and a t-shirt.

"Alpha Lawrence is running late, but we're getting started without him," Jameson said as he let them through the house. "Need coffee?"

"I already had some, thanks though," Amber said as she looked around curiously. There wasn't anything unusual about the place. He had family pictures on the wall. The living room was a mix of new furniture and a bookshelf that looked like an old, family antique.

She could smell that dozens of weres had passed through, but it seemed like only his immediate family actually lived here. She was glad her pack could all live together, for now at least. It still made her skin crawl to think about being separated. Maybe that was something that lessened in time.

"We have these meetings bi-weekly unless something is going on," Jameson explained as they walked. "We get them done early so everyone can be to work on time."

"What do you do outside of being an alpha?" she asked, curious.

"My wife owns a hair salon, and I'm mostly in real estate. I own a strip center in Portland, and a couple of apartment complexes."

"You don't own Rosewood Lake Apartments, do you?" she asked, narrowing her eyes at him.

"No. Why?" he asked, pausing to turn and look at her.

She shrugged. "I got evicted for being bitten. Just making sure it wasn't you."

"Ah," he said, looking annoyed. "The laws make it harder on bitten weres than it needs to be. They tend to have less control at first, generally speaking. You certainly proved that wrong. Humans worry too much, and have to regulate damn near everything."

They walked out the back door and she was hit with the scent of other alphas, and a sense of something *other*. Of magic. She hadn't noticed at the Trials. Maybe the ritual changed her somehow, or maybe she could just sense more as the wolf settled into her mind.

She could feel her eyes shifting to red as she surveyed the other alphas. Currently present were a man and a woman she recognized from the Trials.

"This is Alpha Salazar," he said, pointing at the woman, who nodded in her direction.

She was Hispanic with short, black hair. She wore a pantsuit with a bright teal shirt underneath the jacket. To be honest, she kind of looked like your average real estate agent.

"And this is Alpha Bennett," Jameson said, finishing the introductions.

This guy looked like he worked with his hands. He was a textbook burly, mountain man with a plaid shirt, worn jeans, and a bushy black beard that stretched halfway down his chest. A knit cap hid his hair. He inclined his head slowly, his eyes never leaving hers.

They didn't seem particularly welcoming, but no one was trying to bite her head off. She'd call that a win.

"Nice to meet you," she said, nodding at them in return. It was difficult, but she pulled the wolf back, and willed her eyes to return to normal. There was no need to piss off anyone with some kind of inadvertent werewolf challenge the day she met them.

Jameson plopped down on the porch swing and gestured at the chair next to Salazar. "Grab a seat, this is going to take a while."

Shane chuckled as he moved to stand behind her. She noticed he didn't sit, and Jameson didn't ask him to. There were several places he could have sat, so it must have been intentional. She crossed her arms and leaned back in her seat, unsure of how she felt about that. All this posturing didn't come naturally to her. Born wolves did have that advantage over the bitten wolves like her.

Jameson leaned back and pushed the swing with his foot. "As you all already know, Alpha Donovan Lockhart is dead. However, about a half hour before you two arrived," he nodded at Salazar and Bennett, "I found out some more information. The police found his body." He paused, as though collecting himself to deliver bad news. "His heart was gone."

"Shit," Bennett said immediately, running his hand down his face. "How was it removed?"

"Obsidian blade. He was bound with silver. And he was definitely alive when it was cut out," Jameson said, shaking his head in disgust.

"Wait, someone cut out his heart?" Amber interjected, both horrified and confused.

"A sorcerer," Salazar said, speaking for the first time. "Witches sacrifice animals all the time; cut them up into little pieces to fuel their magic. Sacrificing a werewolf or human? That's sorcery. It's as dark as magic gets."

"We have to assume that every alpha in the area may be a target next," Jameson said.

"I hope the bastard tries to take me," Bennett grunted.

Salazar scoffed at his comment. "You've obviously never fought a sorcerer then."

The door opened and a reedy man with thick, black-framed glasses hurried over to join the group. "Sorry I'm late."

He must be Alpha Lawrence. Despite his nerdy appearance, his rolled-up sleeves revealed wiry muscles. His eyes flicked to her and he nodded briefly, returning his attention to Jameson.

"You say that every meeting," Jameson said, raising a brow.

Lawrence shrugged and smirked at the older man. "Maybe we should have them in the evenings instead."

Jameson shook his head in annoyance, then continued the meeting, "With Donovan dead, his pack is in turmoil. Over the past two days, there have been five challenge fights." He turned to look at Amber. "This will be a good situation for you to learn what this council does. We are not here to try to tell the other packs what to do, but we are here to make sure they don't get out of control in these sorts of situations."

She forced herself not to fidget as the eyes of every alpha landed on her. "Alright. What do I need to do?"

"Go meet the current alpha, and register the names and positions of all the pack members. With every challenge, record the name of the winner, loser, and any other changes in rank. Someone has to be the alpha for one cycle of the moon, or they can't go through the Trials. Anything that can be done to calm down the situation would be better for everyone involved. I've seen packs completely unravel after losing their alpha if there wasn't a clear successor. If that happens, we'll have dozens of omegas in the region that we'll either have to take into our packs, or risk starting this whole process over again," Jameson said with a sigh.

Amber felt a headache forming behind her eyes. "So,

babysit their pack while they fight over who becomes the new alpha?"

A smile tugged at the corner of Jameson's mouth. "Yes."

"They won't try to challenge her, will they?" Lawrence asked, pointing at her.

Jameson frowned. "We've never had that issue before."

"Never had a bitten wolf on the council before either," Lawrence said with a shrug.

"I beat their alpha, why would they bother trying to challenge me?" Amber asked, irritated at the implications. Shane had warned her not to let them treat her like she wasn't their equal. If this guy had a problem with her, she was going to settle it right now.

"You beat him in a test of control, not a fight. Some idiot might want to see if they can take your pack instead," Lawrence replied.

"If I'm going to be a part of this council, they'll all have to learn to respect me eventually," Amber said, relaxing slightly. It sounded more like genuine concern than him trying to put her down. She turned back to Jameson. "If I hide behind the council it'll make me look weak. I never wanted Donovan's place here, hell, I never wanted to be a werewolf, but I'm not going to shirk my duties out of fear. If this is what I need to do, then I'll do it."

"No one else wants to do it, that's for sure," Salazar said under her breath.

Bennett didn't comment, but he did look like he thought she'd fail.

"I agree," Jameson said with a nod. "Shane will be there to back you up. I don't foresee any problems coming up that you can't handle. Honestly, if you can't deal with them, you aren't fit to be on the council."

Bennet snorted at that and muttered something that sounded like 'natural selection'. She ignored him and did her best to take in all the information Jameson shared during the meeting.

It turned out babysitting Donovan's pack was only part of what she'd have to deal with now. Who knew being a were-wolf would come with so much paperwork?

CHAPTER 11

TOMMY

ommy scooped the cheesy omelet out onto a plate and inspected it. It wasn't burned, hadn't broken when he flipped it, and it had just the right amount of gooey cheese. It was perfect.

Derek was sitting at the table oblivious, but perked up when he set the omelet down in front of him. He looked at the omelet, then looked at Tommy. "Why do I feel like this is a bribe?"

"Because it is," Tommy said, crossing his arms.

Derek picked up his fork and took a big bite. His eyes widened as he chewed. Swallowing, he said, "Okay, it worked. What do you want?"

"Could you teach me how to fight?"

"Shouldn't you ask Amber for that kinda help?" Derek

asked, scratching the back of his head.

"Yeah, probably," Tommy said shoving his hands in his pockets. "But I don't want her to think I'm completely incompetent. I'd like to learn a few things first. Even Genevieve can hold her own. I've lost every fight I've been in."

Derek shrugged like that made perfect sense to him. A mischievous grin spread across his face. "Alright, I can show you how to punch and I'll show you a few wrestling moves that always used to work on Amber."

"That would be awesome," Tommy said with a huge smile.

"But you're not allowed to use your werewolf strength while I'm showing you things. I don't need my arm getting accidentally broken or anything stupid like that," Derek said, pointing his finger at him.

"No werewolf strength," Tommy said, lifting his hands in surrender.

Derek nodded, then scarfed down the rest of the omelet. "Dude, where did you learn to cook like this?"

"My mom I guess, but most of the time I just follow the recipes," Tommy said. He hadn't enjoyed cooking so much when he'd been a kid. Now, it was one of the few things that could relax him when he started feeling anxious. He didn't have to go hungry anymore. He had a place to call home, and a makeshift family.

"Do you know when Amber is supposed to be back?" Derek asked, glancing at his watch.

"No clue, but I'll hear her coming before they even reach the driveway," Tommy said, tapping his ear. "Shane's suburban makes a weird noise."

"Oh, that's right, you can hear super well. That's going to come in handy when I start teaching you how to work on cars," Derek said as he stood, walking the plate over to the sink and quickly washing it. "Let's do what we can today before Amber gets back. There's no telling when else we'll have time."

"Sounds great," Tommy said, practically bouncing with nervous energy. He needed this, but he couldn't say he wasn't still worried. Like he'd told Derek, he'd lost every fight he'd been in. Before he was bitten, he was scrawny and weak. He had muscles coming in now, but he didn't know what to do with them.

"Let's go out back," Derek said.

They headed out the back door and behind the house. It was shady and grassy with plenty of room to move around.

Derek nodded in approval, then turned to him. "Okay, throw a punch."

Tommy curled his hand into a fist and swung his arm as hard and fast as he could. The momentum of the punch drug him forward and he stumbled slightly as his feet twisted in the grass. When he looked up at Derek to see how he'd done, the man had one hand covering his face.

"Okay, so…that was…completely wrong in every way," he said, taking a deep breath before looking up. "Come here. Let's start with how to make a proper fist. Never, ever stick your thumb out like that. You're just asking for it to get broken."

Tommy sighed. He knew he sucked, but he'd hoped he wasn't *that* bad.

CHAPTER 12

CERI

*C*eri flipped through her old spellbook, filled with notes from her grandmother's lessons, until she found it. She hadn't remembered her grandmother had even talked about it until Amber had said "animal whisperer". Her old notes were there, written in glittery pink ink and uneven letters.

"A witch belongs in a coven, lassie. There should be at least three, but a coven of seven or thirteen will be stronger. The number of witches must always be a prime number, so the coven cannot be divided. Always an odd number for luck," her grandmother said as she dissected the remains of the pixie.

Ceri kept her eyes on her notes so she didn't have to see. "Can't a witch be alone?"

"Pah, she could, but then she'd be vulnerable. Limited. This family is meant for powerful magic, not tricks a human could do."

She kicked her legs, trying to think of another question. She only got the knowledge she asked for, that was the rule. Sometimes it was risky to ask, because the lessons were...unpleasant. But her grandmother said not to let fear rule her.

"Has a witch ever been part of a pack?" she asked tentatively.

Her grandmother stopped cutting and glared at her. "Why would ya want ta consort with a bunch of flea-ridden weres?"

She lifted her chin stubbornly. "Never said I did, I just wondered if it had ever happened. Werewolves can't even control their magic. I'd never want to be one of them."

Her grandmother didn't speak immediately. She weighed Ceri with her gaze, as though she could see a lie written on her face. "If ya let a pack suck ya in, you'll turn into a pathetic little shaman. You'll end up spending all your time outside talking ta birds like you're some kind of animal whisperer. Shamans think every little bug that crawls the earth has a spirit inside it. They use soft magic."

Saying someone had soft magic was the highest insult her grandmother could give.

Ceri snapped out of the memory. Shaman. Her grandmother was probably rolling in her grave right now.

She'd never heard anyone else talk about shamans. Human magic users were either witches or sorcerers. Good or bad. Though she knew how often those lines got blurred.

This was something she needed to figure out, then talk to Amber about. Sooner rather than later. She wasn't sure if anyone outside the pack should know. They'd thought it odd

Amber was claiming a witch as part of the pack, but everyone seemed to think it was in name only. It had surprised both of them to discover it wasn't.

She closed the book and grabbed her sage. It was time to figure this out. She walked the room as she usually did, but hesitated by the window. She'd always left the curtains shut, but this time...she needed something different.

She yanked the curtains open and lifted the window. The screen was awkward to pop out, but she got it and set it aside. Taking a deep breath to re-center herself, she moved the sage around the edges of the window. Nothing could come in that meant her, or her pack, harm.

Placing the sage in a bowl in front of her, she sat cross legged in the center of the room. She closed her eyes and instead of focusing on the house, she turned her attention inward. The pack bond was intertwined with her own, innate magic now. She turned her hands upward and recited a spell for clarity. The energy in her body moved, shifting to her head and her heart.

A noise at the window startled her, and her eyes snapped open. Big orange eyes stared back at her as the owl she'd seen the day before settled itself on her work table. She forced herself to examine it rather than just shoo it away out of fear.

It was large, at least two feet tall. The tawny feathers were striped with black and brown. Two tufts that looked like ears sat above the round face. The creature's vibrant orange eyes watched her patiently as she inspected it.

"Umm, hello," she said quietly.

It hooted, fluffing its feathers out and shifting closer to her.

As she looked into its eyes, she felt like she was being tugged forward, but her body wasn't moving. She exhaled, letting the magic flow through her without struggle. The orange eyes grew larger in her vision until it was all she could see...and she was falling.

The warm glow of the owl's eyes grew, and it didn't stop. The warmth became heat. It grew hotter and hotter until it felt like she might suffocate.

Darkness. Fire. Screams. Pain.

The visions rolled over her so fast she couldn't process them. There were only glimpses. They terrified her. Strange magic pounded against her mind. This creature didn't just use magic, it *was* magic.

Help me.

The desperate plea for help washed over her, bathing her in someone else's terror. Her heart pounded in her chest and she struggled against the magic holding her in the vision. As though sensing her distress, the owl blinked and everything stopped just as abruptly as it had begun.

Ceri's eyes snapped open. Her hands shook as she pushed her hair back from face. She was sweating and her hands were trembling. She had no idea how long it had been, but her body ached from sitting in one position for so long.

She looked up, relieved to see the owl was still there. "What are you?"

The owl hooted, then turned and flew out of the open window.

She couldn't bring herself to stand, or move at all. Whatever she'd just seen was bad. Someone was in danger, though she had no idea if it was happening in the past, present, or future. It had been vague and confusing, but she had felt the darkness.

Something was coming and it was powerful. She pressed a clammy hand to her cheek and closed her eyes. Whatever it was, it was evil.

CHAPTER 13

AMBER

*A*mber waved goodbye to Shane. They had to go see Donovan's old pack later that evening, but they both had things to do before that.

She headed inside, her brain hurting from all the information she'd absorbed this morning. For every answer she'd gotten, she'd ended up with five more questions. She had a list of things to ask Steven, Genevieve's boyfriend. He'd been peppering her with questions for his thesis lately as they'd agreed to when he'd helped her prepare for the Trials, so she didn't feel bad using him for research. It made her life easier and made him happy as a clam.

She walked inside and saw Tommy and Derek standing in the kitchen. Looking *guilty*. Tommy's hair was standing on end and the side of his neck and face was all red. Derek's shirt had a tear under the sleeve that she knew hadn't been there before.

"Why are you both so sweaty?" Amber asked, her nose twitching as she looked between the two miscreants.

"We were...cooking," Derek lied, gesturing at the stove.

Amber was about to retort that he hated cooking and he would never, ever do it under any circumstances when Derek winked at her. She sighed. He was asking her to drop it. It looked like they'd been wrestling, so she doubted it was some kind of bad secret. Derek would tell her if it was important. She hoped. "Whatever. Has anyone heard from Gen?"

"Nah, but I think she should be home–" Tommy stopped abruptly, his head tilting toward the door.

Amber heard it then too; the car turning down the driveway. That wasn't Genevieve or anyone else she recognized. "I'll see who it is."

She looked out the peephole and saw an unmarked police car parking in front of the porch. The detective she'd met after those mercenaries had attacked her stepped out.

"It's the police. Stay inside, I'll go talk to him," she said, barely suppressing a growl. She knew he was probably here about Donovan. Luckily, she had an airtight alibi for his murder, but that wouldn't necessarily stop her from being a suspect.

She walked outside, shutting the door firmly behind her, and waited for the detective on the steps. Tommy and Derek were whispering inside. Tommy was probably explaining what had happened. She hadn't actually told Derek about all that yet. She glossed over the Trials too, making the whole ordeal sound easy. He was probably going to have a ton of questions now.

Detective Sloan stopped in front of her. He had bags under his eyes and looked even skinnier than last time she'd seen him, like he hadn't been eating or sleeping. "Ms. Hale," he said in greeting.

"Detective," she said, nodding her head at him. "How can I help you?"

"I'm sure you've heard about Donovan Lockhart's murder."

"Yes," she acknowledged, seeing no reason to lie about it.

"I've already looked into your whereabouts around the time of the murder and you aren't a suspect. I just came to warn you," he said, running his hand through his light brown hair. "I spoke with a friend that works up near Seattle. There were two alphas killed the same way out there."

She frowned. Jameson hadn't mentioned that. Maybe he didn't know. "Like a serial killer?"

Sloan nodded. "That's my suspicion. It looks like they might be working their way south."

"Do you have any idea who's behind the killings?"

"No. So be careful, and let me know if you see or hear anything odd. We have reason to believe there may be more than one person involved in the killings. I know you weres like to handle things on your own, but this may not be something you can stop." He pulled his card out of his pocket and handed it to her. "Call me if you have even the slightest suspicion you're being targeted."

She took it with a nod. "Alright."

Sloan turned and headed back to his car. She waited until

he was leaving the driveway before going back inside. Derek was standing in the living room, arms crossed, jaw set with anger.

"Don't start," she said, shoving the card in her pocket.

"What the hell, Amber? Don't start? You nearly got killed, on more than one occasion!" he shouted at her, throwing his hands in the air.

Tommy backed up so fast he was almost running backward and disappeared into the kitchen with a guilty expression.

"There was no point worrying anyone!" she shouted back, her eyes flashing red.

"You don't just keep something like that from your family," he insisted, jabbing his finger at her. "And now there's a serial killer after you? Would you have told anyone about that if we weren't here listening in?"

"Of course, I would have," she ground out. "This puts the whole pack at risk. I'm not gonna call Mom and tell the whole family though, if that's what you're asking. She made it clear I still wasn't welcome."

"The rest of us care though! She doesn't speak for the whole family."

"Look, you know now. Just let it go. This was the worst possible thing that could have happened to me at the time, but I got through it, and we're all going to be fine," she said, her breaths coming hard as she fought against the sudden, overwhelming emotions. She wanted to shift and run away. The wolf wanted to make her brother submit.

Ceri appeared in the hallway. She hadn't even realized the witch was home.

"Is everything okay?" Ceri asked quietly as she approached.

The mark on Amber's chest throbbed. She doubled over in pain, unable to catch her breath as it seemed to make every muscle in her chest contract. *No, not now. She couldn't deal with this right now too.*

Captain Jack rose from his spot on the couch and hissed at her angrily before fleeing the room entirely.

"Amber?" Derek asked, worry clear in his voice. "Tommy, get back in here. Is she about to lose control?"

Pain turned to agony and the wolf howled in her head. She could feel it struggling against something, fighting back viciously.

"What are you doing?" she demanded between gasps.

The wolf howled. Amber screamed.

CHAPTER 14

AMBER

The room grew dark and her vision swam in front of her eyes. Claws pressed out of her fingertips, scoring deep lines in the floor. She gritted her teeth and refused to shift.

Tommy was close. He was shouting something at Derek. A cool presence drew close. Ceri. Hands touched her face and she realized someone was pushing her backwards. The room spun and she shoved them away. They needed to leave.

"No, run, please go," she gasped, clutching at the mark on her chest.

Her hands were ripped away and her shirt tugged down. Ceri would know what it meant. Then they'd all know. The whole pack. What had she done? She shouldn't have trusted the demon.

A roaring sound overtook the buzzing in her ears and her muscles twitched. The war in her head raged on but she could feel the tide shifting. The wolf was being forced back. The shields it had erected against the demon were cracking. Pain engulfed her entire body as they gave way.

Darkness rushed out of the mark, pushing Ceri and the others back forcefully. Angel had never been solid before. Instead of his usual, small form, a massive demon filled the room. His dark body blocked out every bit of light, except for the flames that burned behind his eyes. Horns curled from his head and smoke poured from his nostrils.

"How dare you attempt to block me from your mind." Angel's voice shook the entire house and pounded against her eardrums.

Amber forced herself upright, bracing herself against the arm of the couch. "I didn't do it––"

"Shut up!" Angel shouted, growing even larger. Her nickname for him felt so wrong now. He wasn't an angel. He wasn't innocuous. He wasn't *funny.*

"Amber, what the hell is going on?" Derek asked, trying to edge toward her.

"She made a deal with a demon," Ceri said, her face pale and angry. Her hand curled into a fist and light flickered from inside the closed hand.

"Don't even think about it, witch," the demon snarled. "You can't force me out. Not when she's invited me in."

The demon turned to her and surged in close. She forced herself to hold his gaze. This hadn't been her fault...well, it had been. She made the deal with Thallan to take on his debt. The wolf had just made the demon angry. She had gone quiet now, and Amber was a little worried the demon had done something to her in retaliation.

"Leave them out of this," she said, pushing up to her feet. "What do you want?"

"I'm calling in your debt. Now."

The words made her heart sink into her stomach. She wasn't ready for this moment to come, but she had no choice. "What do I need to do?"

"Amber, don't--"

Ceri clamped her hand over Derek's mouth. "She has to fulfill her end of the bargain, or her soul is forfeit. She'll die."

The demon looked deep into Amber's eyes. "There is a girl outside of Timber, Oregon, lost somewhere in the woods. Find her, and her guardian, and protect them. If she dies, I'm holding you responsible."

"Where is she, exactly?"

"She's lost, that's why you need to find her. I'll give you three hours."

"It'll take us an hour just to get there," she objected.

"Then you better drive fast," the demon said, before disappearing with a pop.

Amber stood there, staring at the space he'd left behind. A thousand thoughts were racing through her mind. She could still feel his presence too. He wasn't really gone, just invisible.

"Why the hell did you make a deal with a demon?" Ceri demanded, startling her. She'd never seen the witch this mad before.

She looked up, forcing herself to meet Ceri's eyes. "I took

the demon mark from Thallan in exchange for him being my sponsor for the Trials and a place to stay."

Ceri shook her head, pressing her lips tightly together. "You *idiot*."

"I was out of options," Amber said angrily. "You can stand there and judge my choice all you want, but we'd be in the System and you'd be homeless if I hadn't done something."

Ceri's pale face went red. "That doesn't make this right."

"I'm going to go deal with this. Stay here. Someone find Genevieve and make sure she gets back to the house as soon as she can. No one leaves until I say so," Amber said, ignoring her last comment.

"You can't just order everyone--"

"I can," Amber snapped, drawing on the pack bond roughly. The power she rarely used burned behind her eyes. "And I will."

"I'm going with you," Tommy said, stepping out from behind Ceri.

"What?" she asked in surprise.

"You need to find this girl, and fast. I tend to notice things before you, and we can cover more ground if we both go and split up."

"This is dangerous," Amber objected.

"Everything we've done since we were bitten has been dangerous. I don't care. Losing our alpha to a demon because she couldn't find someone fast enough is more dangerous than whatever might be in those woods," Tommy insisted.

She wanted to turn him down and make him stay, but he was right. She needed to be practical. If she died, the pack may not be safe. "Fine, let's go."

Amber turned and headed toward the door. She didn't have time to argue, or to overthink any of this. She hadn't even had time to take her jacket off when she got home before everything went to crap.

Tommy followed her outside. She could feel his anticipation, worry, and frustration through the pack bond. It was Ceri's anger that beat against her mind like a drum though. She wished, yet again, that she could block how much of her pack's emotions she felt.

Halfway to the truck, the door opened behind them and Ceri jogged out. She had her bag slung over her shoulder and had to hold it down as she ran.

"I'm coming too," she said, jaw set stubbornly. "I don't like this, but I like what would happen if you failed even less. Derek is staying behind to wait for Genevieve."

Amber nodded, and climbed in the truck. The day had started off bad enough, but now it had completely spun out of control.

CHAPTER 15

TOMMY

*T*ommy sat between Amber and Ceri and kept his eyes forward. Amber was driving like a crazy person, passing every person she got behind on the narrow, two-lane road. Ceri was *stewing* in anger.

He got why Ceri was freaked out, but the anger really surprised him. It's not like Amber had summoned a demon for fun. She hadn't even been the one to do it. Thallan had. Amber had been protecting them when she took the demon mark.

Amber had driven straight here without directions. He looked around the cab of the truck again, but didn't see any hint of the demon. Something told him it was still here, though.

His nose twitched as the scent of smoke washed through the truck through the open windows. "Do you smell that?"

Amber nodded, then pointed off to the left. "There's smoke over there. Looks like a house fire, it's all black."

They turned down a short, gravel road which seemed to lead straight toward the house. The smell grew worse and he noticed a strong smell of gasoline as well.

Amber slammed on the brakes and turned down a dirt driveway. She drove just far enough that the truck wouldn't be visible from the road, and parked.

"Is this it?" Tommy asked.

"No," she said, opening her door and hopping out. "This is just as close as it's safe to get in the truck. The demon thinks there's still a threat at the house. And he doesn't want us drawing attention to ourselves."

Tommy nodded. He was conflicted about this whole thing. He'd never heard of a demon demanding protection for someone before. Then again, the only thing he knew about demon marks were from tv shows. In those, it was always about murder and chaos. There was something odd going on here. The demon had scared the hell out of them all and hurt Amber, but it had seemed almost...fearful.

"We're a half mile away. We're going to go that way, quietly," Amber said, pointing north, deeper into the woods.

The trio walked quietly, each of them watching the woods intently for any sign of movement. All of Tommy's senses were on high alert. He could hear people in the distance, but he couldn't make out any of the conversations yet.

The smell of smoke grew stronger as they drew closer to

the house. He focused on trying to catch the scent of a person underneath it all, but no one had come this way recently.

Soon, the charred skeleton of a house was visible through the dense forest. All that was left of the house was a crumbling shell of still smoldering beams. He could hear faint voices now, and put his hand on Amber's shoulder, then tapped his ear to let her know.

Amber nodded and motioned for them to slow down. They crept in a wide circle around the house until they could see the people that were talking.

There were two men. The one Tommy had heard first turned out to be on the phone. He had long, blond hair tied back in a ponytail and wore some kind of linen suit. He looked like he belonged on a yacht or something, not standing in ash. The way he moved was graceful, unnaturally so. His skin almost glowed with health, and that was when Tommy realized what he was. He was half-angel.

They weren't common, but every single one of them was beautiful and talented. They were always models, actors, or singers. Everything they did seemed effortless, and they were even more beautiful than the elves.

The other guy was no angel, that was for sure. He wore dark jeans and a long sleeve shirt. The sleeves were pushed up, exposing strange tattoos and old scars. His hair was buzzed short making his face look harsh. He walked a short distance away from the half-angel and crouched down in front of the house.

Tommy tensed when he drew a knife from a sheath in the back of his pants. The man curled his hand into a tight fist, then drew the blade over the back of his forearm, leaving a fairly deep cut. Blood dripped into the ash and dirt as he began to chant.

Ceri grabbed Amber's arm and motioned for them to move back. They retreated a decent distance back into the trees where they could talk.

"If you want to find this girl, you have to do it now," Ceri whispered urgently. "That's a method for tracking someone. It's an insane method, but extremely effective. It will also hurt her."

"How long do we have?" Amber asked.

"Fifteen, twenty minutes tops," Ceri said, glancing back at the house. "I might be able to buy you more time, but you have to hurry. Does the demon have any idea where she is?"

Amber glanced to her left, then shook her head. "No."

"Find her, and get her to me as fast as you can. I can protect her, but I need her blood," Ceri said, grimacing slightly.

"We have to split up," Tommy said, already pulling his shirt over his head. He knew he could cover more ground in wolf form.

"Be careful," Amber said, her eyes flashing red like it was an order.

"I will be," Tommy said before turning around to shuck off his pants. Nudity still made him intensely uncomfortable, but they didn't have time to worry about that right now.

The shift came easier every time he did it. The wolf grew in his mind as he dropped to four feet, his paws forming before he hit the ground. He shook out his fur and panted for a moment, processing the changes. The acrid scent of the smoke made his nose burn.

He turned around and saw that Ceri was already headed back toward the house. Amber nodded at him, also in wolf form now, and took off at a run. He went in the opposite direction, skirting around the side of the house, heading into the densest section of the forest.

He ran until he could smell something other than burnt, then paused to take a deep breath. He sniffed the ground, getting a nose full of pine needles, but nothing that smelled like a person. This might be harder than he thought.

CHAPTER 16

CERI

*C*eri's blood was boiling with rage. Amber had been an idiot. This demon had led them into extreme danger because that was what demons did. She hated that Tommy had come. If she'd known there was going to be a sorcerer here, she would have made him stay at the house.

Blood magic was one of those things you rarely saw used. There were so many other ways to enhance your magic. Sacrificing your own lifeblood to power a spell damaged you. It twisted something inside of you and left a dark mark on your soul.

The owl was perched on a branch above her. She didn't have to look up to know it was there. This was what it had been trying to warn her about. In some ways, she had been right. It was an ill omen, but if it hadn't warned her she would have been even more unprepared.

Ceri crouched behind a tree and lifted the strap of her purse over her head. She had what she needed to slow the sorcerer down. Stopping him was borderline impossible. The raw power needed to do that was beyond her without a coven. Luckily, he was alone, or she wouldn't be able to do a thing.

She lifted out her spellbook first, then her little tin of mugwort. The plant was helpful in protection against a psychic attack, which was, at its heart, what the sorcerer was casting. It attacked the natural mental protections of the target. The spell could leave physical wounds as well, depending on the strength of the caster.

Finding a decent branch nearby, she grabbed it and drew a circle of protection around herself. She added a triangle with a second horizontal line that cut through the bottom third of it. Invoking the element of air to give her strength and embrace its energy.

Most witches viewed these rituals as weak and unreliable. Her grandmother had hated them. Without a coven, and without a living sacrifice such as a pixie or other animal, it was all she had.

She crossed her legs and dug her fingers into the earth to ground herself, literally and figuratively. The magic inside her would have to be enough to slow this sorcerer down.

"Spiritus defendat," she chanted softly. Magic welled up within her. Instead of sinking into the ground, it lifted up from the top of her head. A breeze picked up around her.

Her eyes slipped shut and her other senses came into

focus. The sorcerer's magic was hot and dark to the west. It crept through the forest like a hunter after its prey. Though it passed her by, she felt its attention turn toward her briefly, inspecting the competing magic. The sorcerer would know she was here, but he would not attack her until he'd accomplished his task.

The owl flew down and stood at the top point of the symbol she'd drawn. It twisted its head, picking at its feathers until one came loose then dropped the feather, which floated down onto the symbol. She felt a surge of energy and clarity.

In her mind, she saw her magic flare up, cutting through the darkness that pressed around her. The sorcerer's spell shuddered. Her hair lifted off her shoulder as the breeze tickling her skin grew stronger. It was tinged with magic, both hers and the spirits. The owl was aiding her. The strength of help that was freely given could never be matched by a sacrifice ripped from the animal's body.

The darkness around her shifted as the wind pushed against it. She continued chanting to give herself something to focus on. The wind lifted the words from her lips and carried them like daggers through the forest. Her magic cut through the sorcerer's spell. It groaned and shuddered.

She could feel the sorcerer's attention turn to her briefly. He didn't falter in the pursuit of his target, but she could feel his anger growing in the darkness like a storm.

The pack bond shifted inside her and she felt a *push*. Instead of drawing strength from her, it was being poured into her. Amber was helping, the only way she could. A smile spread across Ceri's face. This was the strength of the pack, of being a shaman.

The wind howled like a hurricane, whipping her hair up into a frenzy. The trees around her strained against the onslaught. A branch cracked and snapped off the trunk, flying through the air like a missile. Her magic pushed against the sorcerer's spell, slowing its progress and stripping away its power.

Lifting her face to the sky, Ceri poured every ounce of her strength into the battle. She would not falter. She would not show fear. She was strong enough.

CHAPTER 17

AMBER

*I*t was an odd sensation to be sending the strength of the pack to one of the pack members instead of drawing it into herself. The wind buffeted Amber as she jogged through the forest. There was magic in the air, both Ceri's and something that smelled like blood and fire.

The demon drifted beside her, glaring at the forest around them. He hadn't spoken. Just watched. Every few minutes he'd float away until she felt a strange tug in her chest, then he'd reappear. It seemed like he was tethered to her.

A sound behind her, muffled by the wind, made her pause. The scent of metal and gunpowder had her dropping to her stomach. Splinters exploded from the tree trunk in front of her as a bullet impacted it. Her ears ached from the loud crack of the gunfire.

Not wanting to be a stationary target, she darted to the side, running as low as possible. Her first thought was that she had to get to Tommy, her second was that they were all screwed. Two more shots cracked through the air, one hitting a tree, the other striking the dirt right in front of her.

She zig-zagged as best she could, but she had to get to the shooter fast. If those were regular bullets, she could afford to get hit. It would hurt but she could deal with that. If they were silver...she didn't want to have to draw on the pack's strength. Ceri needed it.

"He's moving that way," the demon said, pointing in the same direction she was running. "There are two, I think."

She changed directions to try to get behind him. Her heart was racing in her chest and the wolf was finally fully awake.

There was another shot. The pain didn't register until she stumbled. Her shoulder burned and blood seeped into her fur. Growling in anger, she pushed herself to go faster. She didn't know anything about the girl lost in this forest, but she couldn't imagine a good reason for her to be hunted like an animal.

She ran recklessly, no longer worried about being shot. The wound hurt, but it wasn't silver. It would heal. Over the rush of the wind, she heard the man's footsteps. Smelled his cologne. His fear. He was right to be afraid.

The wolf pushed her even faster, thrilled to be chasing prey. The wolf's instincts overrode her fear and worry. There were two of them. She was closing in on the first, but the other was coming up behind her.

The demon surged ahead of her and she heard a scream. She pushed herself to go faster and a man hit the dirt in front of her, scrambling on hands and knees trying to get away. The demon loomed over him, larger than he'd been even in the house. He backed right into a tree and was left with nowhere to run.

She lunged for him as he lifted the gun, aiming it with shaking hands at the demon. Her teeth closed around his forearm and the bone snapped in her powerful jaws. She shook viciously and the gun fell to the ground. The man's head hit the tree with a crack and he fell limp.

She wasn't sure if he was dead, and she didn't have time to worry about it. Three fast shots rang through the air, but the other man was shooting at the demon as well. They didn't realize he couldn't touch them.

"Charlie!" the other attacker shouted behind them in alarm.

Amber turned and ran toward him. He swung his gun toward her as she leapt. The bullet hit her in the gut and knocked her to the ground. She scrambled to her feet, but her legs were like jello. She couldn't breathe.

"Who the hell sent a damn werewolf out here?" the man shouted as he fumbled to reload his gun.

Her body was already healing, but it was slower than she'd expected. She drew on the pack bond for one moment, just to give herself strength, then charged the man.

He locked the slide in place a half-second before she collided with him. It wasn't a clean takedown, she'd missed his throat. The pain had been greater than she'd expected. He scrambled for a place to grab her as they hit the ground. His fist connected with the bullet wound and she yelped, tearing at him with her paws. One of his hands wrapped around her throat, holding her at a distance.

She yanked her head away, then snapped at his arm. Her teeth tore into his skin and he screamed in pain. It made him slow, and her jaw closed around his neck. One bite was all it took. His throat collapsed under the pressure. The scream abruptly cut off.

Excitement pulsed through the pack bond from Tommy as she stumbled away from the body. She could barely process it as she looked at the carnage at her feet. Bile rose in the back of her throat and she vomited as she backed away. She'd had to kill him. She hadn't had a choice…but it was awful. There was so much blood.

The excitement from Tommy changed to fear and her head snapped up. He had found them.

CHAPTER 18

TOMMY

*H*e took a winding path through the woods, trying to cover as much ground as possible. They had two hours left. He was pretty sure bloodhounds got to smell something that the person they were tracking owned before they were sent out to find them. It would have been really helpful to have *something*. Instead, he was just wandering aimlessly hoping to get lucky.

At the back of his mind, the wolf seemed unconcerned. It was patient. Tommy huffed in annoyance and picked up his pace. He was afraid to run in case he missed something, but he wasn't making enough progress.

His ears twitched as he took in the sounds of the forest. It was surprisingly noisy now that he could hear for miles in every direction. Wind ruffled his fur lightly and he reveled in the cool breeze. In this form, he'd found it was easy to feel overheated.

The wind grew steadily stronger, making him pause. He looked around and saw the trees waving wildly. The steady breeze shifted, buffeting from different directions. A particularly strong gust hit him in the side and he stumbled from the force of it.

Magic tickled his nose. He lifted his face toward the sky as the wind howled through the trees. It smelled like magic, and Ceri. He hoped this meant she was winning.

The pack bond began to grow inside him like it did whenever Amber pulled on it. Ceri must be fighting the sorcerer, or Amber was in danger. He shifted anxiously on his feet, but there was nothing he could do to help except find the girl. He hoped Ceri could slow the sorcerer down. And that she could stay hidden. He knew she could probably fight way better than he could, but he still didn't like her being alone out there.

He took off again, moving at a steady trot this time. A faint scent whipped past him and the wolf woke up inside of him, going from patient to excited. He changed direction, following where his instincts led him despite the scent fading. It wasn't exactly human, but it wasn't an animal. It reminded him of the strange, sulfur smell he'd noticed around the house. And the smell in the truck when the demon had been there.

He followed the trail with his nose to the ground. The wind shifted, swirling around him like a tornado, and for a split second, he almost lost the trail. A branch snapped off a tree overhead and he dropped to the forest floor, ducking underneath it just in time.

Taking off at a run, he stopped hesitating. The girl had to be somewhere in this direction. The wind was blowing so hard now that he had to lean his head down just to run.

He heard her before he saw her. She was crying and shouting curse words at the wind. He slowed his pace, creeping up slowly toward the sounds. At first, he wasn't sure where he was, then he saw a glimpse of pale blonde hair through the underbrush. She was crouched behind a tree.

The smell of blood and burnt flesh hit him and he froze. Then he realized there was someone with her. They weren't moving.

He ran toward the two of them, his heart racing with excitement. Her head snapped toward him when he got close and she jumped up, her eyes going wide with fear. Slowing down to a walk, he stepped toward her trying to look friendly.

She grabbed a fallen branch off the ground and ran at him, holding it like a bat. Her long blonde hair swept behind her like a veil and he was momentarily mesmerized. Until she swung the branch at his head.

He dodged the attack and skittered backward. Maybe he hadn't fully thought this plan through. He'd been so focused on finding her that he hadn't thought about how she'd react to a wolf showing up.

"Get back!" she shouted again, swinging the branch at him. The harsh wind kicked her blonde hair into her face as she tried to fend him off. She was wearing pajamas and didn't even have on shoes.

He ducked underneath it and yipped, trying to look more like a puppy than a wolf. She swung the branch again viciously. Well, that didn't work.

Backing off, he ran behind a tree. She didn't follow, staying in front of her tree holding the branch like a shield.

He shifted, feeling very vulnerable standing naked in the woods. "I, uh, come in peace," he said, sticking his arms out from behind the tree. The wind was blowing so hard now he had to shout.

"Wait, you're a werewolf?" the girl asked, lowering her weapon. She didn't drop it though.

He peeked his head out from behind the tree, keeping himself carefully hidden. "Yeah, we were told you were lost and sent to find you."

Her blue eyes narrowed as she brushed her hair out of her eyes. She pressed her lips into a thin line. "Who sent you?"

"Well…just someone that was….concerned," he deflected. The demon hadn't told them if she knew who he was, and she looked pretty suspicious. He wasn't sure admitting it was a demon was the best move.

"It was Kadrithan, wasn't it?" she demanded, anger leaking into her tone.

"If Kadrithan is a demon, then…yes?"

She snorted in derision. "How in the hell did a scrawny teenager like you get a demon mark?"

"Oh, I don't have the mark. My alpha does, but I wanted to help."

"Great, an idiot has come to rescue me," she muttered, dropping the branch and walking back to her hiding spot.

She paused and looked back over her shoulder. "I don't suppose you have pants anywhere close, do you?"

"Not really close, no," he said. A noise caught his attention. He wasn't sure if it was a branch hitting a tree or a footstep.

She sighed and rolled her eyes. "Well, I can't carry her, so you're going--"

"Be quiet," he said urgently, interrupting her. The wind had shifted and he'd smelled something out of place. Another person.

She opened her mouth -- probably to tell him not to talk to her like that -- when a gunshot cracked through the air. Her eyes went wide as she hit the ground.

Tommy ran for them, shifting as he went. He didn't know what to do. He could smell her blood. He should have just taken them and run, but he'd been standing around like an idiot chatting.

His paws dug into the dirt as he sprinted toward them. As soon as he was close enough, he launched himself toward them, landing right behind her facing the direction the shot had come from. He couldn't see anyone. The wind was blowing too hard for him to hear or smell them properly. Were they moving?

He backed up until his hind foot bumped into the girl. She groaned and scooted away. He sighed in relief. She was alive, for now.

Amber had to have felt his panic. He thought he could feel her headed his way, but it was hard to focus on the pack bond right now.

A man stepped out from the trees a few yards away. He

had a shotgun held up to his shoulder and pointed straight at them. Tommy growled and took another step back, standing over the girl to protect her. He was tempted to charge the man, but he could hear two other people closing in from either side. They were surrounded.

CHAPTER 19

EVANGELINE

Another gunshot blasted through the air, making her ears ring. Evangeline curled over her mother as the werewolf leaped over her. The first shot had only grazed her arm, but it still stung like a bitch.

She could barely hear anything over the panicked beating of her heart. Blood from the werewolf's wound dripped down onto her, staining her pajamas. The second shot had hit him. He'd thrown himself in the path of the gunfire to protect her, which was insane, and further confirmed she was being rescued by idiots.

The wind was blowing so hard her hair was practically standing on end. It whipped up dirt and leaves around them like a tornado.

Her mother was deathly still beneath her. She was breathing, but it was labored. Evangeline cursed herself for not trying harder to get her to a hospital. She'd never forgive herself if her mother died out here in the woods. It was her fault she was hurt in the first place. This was all her fault. She tightened her grip on her mother's arms and tried to convince herself to just end all this. But...she didn't want to die. Even if she did deserve it.

She looked back over her shoulder, weighing her options. During the day, her demonic side slept. She couldn't use the fire magic at all. Instead, her other side awoke. It wouldn't be much help here though, it wasn't the type of magic you could use in a fight, especially with the talismans hanging around the men's necks. She was as helpless as a human.

Scooting forward, she dug through the leaves until her fingers hit a rock. The werewolf howled as two men circled around them. Another shot rang out and the wolf flinched from the impact but didn't flee. He pressed down closer against her as he howled again, hopefully calling the rest of his pack. Werewolves weren't her favorite –– they tended to be arrogant blowhards –– but she'd welcome a whole pack of them right about now.

A ruddy wolf appeared out of nowhere, ripping out the throat of one of the men. Evangeline flinched as blood sprayed from his neck, soaking into the leaves. It didn't seem like any of this could be real. She'd always known what she was, but she'd been able to ignore it all her life. She'd never seen someone die.

The black wolf ran toward the ruddy wolf and they attacked the second man together. Evangeline frantically pulled at the rock buried in the dirt. A twig snapped in front of her and she looked up, straight into the eyes of a third attacker.

He lifted his gun toward her. It felt like everything was moving in slow motion as she ripped the rock free. He peered down the sight of the rifle. She threw the rock, a scream erupting from her throat. The rock hit his gun, knocking it off just enough that the shot went wide.

A red blur flew toward him, hitting him so hard his neck snapped to the side. The gun flew form his hands and the werewolf's jaws clamped around his throat. She squeezed her eyes shut, not wanting to see what happened next.

Something nudged her shoulder. She peeked behind her to see the gray werewolf looking at her expectantly. He nodded, as if to say *yes, it's safe now.*

Hesitantly, she sat up and looked around. The bodies were still there, laying in growing pools of blood. Bile rose in the back of her throat and she forced herself to look away.

The ruddy wolf shifted into a woman as she approached. Her wavy red hair fell down over her shoulders but did nothing to hide the fact that she was buck ass naked. Or the blood dripping from her chin and slipping down her neck in little rivulets.

Evangeline's eyes were immediately drawn to the black demon mark on the woman's chest. It twitched as her uncle appeared behind the woman. It wouldn't be visible to everyone but she could see those sorts of things.

"If you want your mother to live, go with them," Kadrithan said, still scowling at her from their last argument.

She didn't want to go with these people, but, once again,

her uncle had outmaneuvered her. It was easy when he had all the information and she had none of it.

"We have to go, can you walk?" the woman asked.

"Yeah, but my mother can't."

"I'll carry her," the woman said, brushing past her and kneeling at her mother's side.

"Be careful!" she warned, hovering over them.

The woman glared at her. "Obviously."

With more tenderness than she'd expected, the woman eased her arms under her mother's knees and shoulder. She lifted her like she weighed two pounds. It was effortless. Damn werewolves and their superhuman strength.

"You could be stronger too if you would just give someone a mark," her uncle whispered in her ear as though he could read her mind.

She pressed her lips together in annoyance and ignored him. She jumped when she felt fur brush her hand. The other wolf, the guy, was standing next to her looking around warily. His ears were perked up, twitching this way and that.

He huffed softly and the woman nodded. "I know, let's go." The woman turned to Evangeline for a moment. "We're going to go as fast as you can. If we get in trouble, Tommy is going to shift and carry you on his back."

Evangeline nodded and started walking. Her feet ached and she was so thirsty it felt like her throat was cracking, but none of that mattered. They had to get her mother to safety.

CHAPTER 20

CERI

*T*he strain of channeling so much magic was beginning to wear on Ceri. She pressed her fingers deeper into the dirt but she couldn't feel them anymore. They'd gone numb. Sweat dripped down her forehead as she struggled to breathe past the burning in her lungs.

Wind swirled around her in a funnel that grew narrower and narrower. Darkness pressed in from all sides invisible to the naked eye. She could see it though, even with her eyes shut.

"You can't win this battle." The sorcerer's voice drifted past her. The wind tickled her neck as though it was his breath.

She ground her teeth together. He was getting closer to the girl, but he hadn't found her yet. She was slowing him down more than she had thought possible. He could taunt all he wanted, it was merely a sign of his frustration.

"Neither can you," she whispered back.

Amber and Tommy had to be close to finding her. She'd felt something through the pack bond. A tug. It had almost made her falter, but it had been brief, and she'd held onto the spell through it. If Amber could get to the girl first, Ceri could protect her.

The owl squawked and her eyes flew open in alarm. The large bird fell back, wrapped in ropes of darkness that threatened to crush its wings. She lifted one hand and a gust of air rushed past her, hitting the bird and the dark magic and loosening the bonds just enough for the owl to struggle free. It lifted into the air, circling overhead.

"Just go!" she shouted, fear sinking into her. The darkness was closer than she realized. The sorcerer's magic was closing in around her and she was about to lose this fight. He was too powerful.

The weight of the magic slammed into her. She fell back, pinned against the ground, unable to move. It felt like her teeth were going to crack as her jaw clenched tight. Breathing became harder with every breath as her lungs tired.

Something wet touched her face. After a moment, she realized it was a tongue. The weight of the magic lessened, but she felt fur pressing against her neck and arms. Another lick, then warmth enveloped her. The darkness vanished.

With a gasp, her eyes flew open. Genevieve was looking down at her in wolf form, whining softly.

"How the hell did you get here?" she croaked.

The wolf rolled her eyes and scooted back far enough that she could sit up. Blood dripped from Ceri's nose and she coughed, tasting it on the back of her tongue as well.

Genevieve was looking around them warily. She stood abruptly, her ears perking up as she looked to the west. A moment later, Amber burst out of the trees, naked, and carrying an old woman. Ceri wasn't sure the woman was alive. She was badly beaten, and had severe burns on the lower half of her body.

Behind Amber was Tommy, in wolf form, and a blonde girl that looked around his age. Her bare feet were torn up and her pajamas were filthy from the run through the woods. Tommy quickly grabbed his and Amber's clothes, carrying them in his mouth.

"Run," Amber said urgently.

Her legs wobbled underneath her as she turned to flee, but Tommy was right there, supporting her. She wound her fingers into his fur and let him drag her forward as she attempted to keep up. The blonde girl kept her eyes glued to the woman Amber was holding.

"You're jostling her too much," the girl hissed, trying to grab Amber's arm.

"She's unconscious, she can't feel it," Amber snapped. "Stop complaining and run."

As Ceri grabbed her bag, she could still feel the sorcerer's spell pressing down on them. He would find the girl any second now. They needed to go faster. She was exhausted, but she had to save what strength she had left to protect the girl once the spell found its mark. She would have one chance to fight him off then.

The forest thinned slightly and Amber's truck came into view. Genevieve had parked behind the truck and left her clothes in a pile by her driver's side door, which was hanging open. She'd been in a hurry.

Amber ran to the passenger side of the truck and the girl yanked the door open. She laid the woman down on the bench seat.

"Has that sorcerer done whatever to the girl yet?" Amber asked as she grabbed the clothes Tommy had dropped next to her. "Tommy, go with Gen, there's no room," she shouted over her shoulder.

Genevieve, who was hopping on one foot trying to get redressed, shouted back, "When is someone going to explain what the hell is going on?"

"When we're back, just take Tommy and drive home as fast as you can," Amber said, running toward the driver side of her truck.

The girl was already sitting in the truck with the old woman's head in her lap. Ceri jumped in the passenger door and crouched on the floor. She dumped half the contents of her bag out between her legs, scrambling to find something that would help the old woman until she could properly heal her, or get her to a hospital.

Amber started the truck and threw it into reverse. The truck whipped around, slinging Ceri into the dashboard. Amber gunned it toward the main road, gravel flying from under her tires.

The girl glared at someone Ceri couldn't see and flicked them off. "This is all your fault anyhow!"

Amber rolled her eyes. "Do you know who is after you?"

"No, I don't know, and I don't care," the girl snapped. "I--" Her eyes rolled back in her head and a red glow thrummed around her body. Her muscles rippled under her skin as she began to shake.

Ceri grabbed the bundle of herbs she'd been putting together and shoved it in the girl's mouth, holding her jaw shut.

"What the hell is that?" Amber demanded.

"The sorcerer," Ceri said, pushing up onto her knees so she could get a hand around the back of the girl's neck. This was going to be tricky, but lucky for her, psychic attacks were one of her family's specialties.

"Custodiat cor tuum. Custodiat animam. Custodiat cor tuum." Ceri's fingers dug into the girl's neck as she repeated the chant. There was magic inside her, and it was helping Ceri fight back. It was hot and uncontrolled. Whatever this girl was, she was completely untrained.

The sorcerer's spell worked by using the blood in its victim's body to force them to return to the sorcerer, by any means. If the spell couldn't be stopped before it reached its target, the only option was to change the victim's blood. Ceri abhorred what she had to do, but the only way to fight the sorcerer's blood magic, was with more of the same.

The darkness lashed at the truck. There was no time left. Ceri looked up at Amber as fear curled in her gut. If she didn't do something to stop this, Amber would die. Just like that. All because she was doing the only thing she could to protect her pack. Ceri couldn't let that happen.

Never hesitate.

Fuck you, grandmother, she thought as she squeezed her

eyes shut and grabbed the blessed knife from the pocket in her bag and drug the tip along the back of her arm. There was only one other scar there from years ago. It had almost faded completely. It would have a twin now. Two times Ceri hadn't been able to find a way to avoid using black magic. Two failures.

Sorcery was dark magic, but she wasn't strong enough to fight back with only white magic. As the blood seeped from her palm, she swore to herself to find a way to do so in the future without having to resort to this. The pack bond curled around her but she wanted to shove it away. This was going to leave its mark on her and the pack.

The blood seeped out of the wound, writhing on her skin instead of dripping. She began chanting again, calling on her own magic, and whatever she could drag from the pack bond. Flipping the knife around, she sliced through the sleeve of the girl's pajamas, opening a small wound at the same time. The girl didn't even flinch, too lost in the haze of the sorcerer's spell.

Her blood stretched toward the wound and sank into it. Ceri's gritted her teeth as she forced herself into the girl's body and mind.

"Ceri, what the hell are you doing?" Amber asked as she skidded around a turn.

"Saving this girl's life so you don't die," she replied quietly. The dark magic pulsed around her as her magic blazed to life. It was always warm and comforting, but this... this was different. This was like standing on the surface of the sun. It didn't hurt her, it raged inside of her with an addictive thrill. This was the rush of heroin and crackling energy of cocaine. Sorcerers weren't just power hungry. They were addicts. She was going to regret this.

The spell she was using wasn't straightforward. It was an off the cuff combination of a white magic spell of psychic protection with the power of a blood sacrifice. Her family had always been inventors and creators. They twisted magic in new ways. Ceri had always excelled at this. She was the only one of her parent's children to truly match her grandmother's talents. Some days she hated it.

She pushed the old guilt away and plucked at the threads of magic weaving around her and the girl. Ceri cocooned her in blood, magic, and the pack bond. It wouldn't make her pack, but it would let Ceri use the strength of the pack and her own magic to protect her from the sorcerer's attack.

Amber swerved sharply, her breath coming in pants. "How much longer?"

"Shut up, I need to focus," Ceri said sharply, forcing her mind back to the task at hand. It was uncomfortable, but it wouldn't truly harm Amber. The still angry part of her mind considered this Amber's penance for taking the demon's mark in the first place. This was affecting the whole pack, not just her.

Something in the girl shifted, as though it was coming awake. The hot tendrils of magic inspected Ceri. They poked and prodded, searching for a threat, but when they found none, retreated. Ceri's hands shook as the nature of the magic finally became apparent.

Ceri's protective spell slid into place, locking around herself and the girl. They were tied together until she released the spell. Ceri opened her eyes and pressed herself back against the dash, horrified. If Amber's life hadn't been at stake she would have ripped the spell away and thrown the girl out of the car.

"What's wrong? Is it over?" Amber asked, still breathless.

"She's...a demon, but..." There was something else, but it didn't make sense. Ceri looked up at her alpha. "She's part angel as well."

"That's impossible," Amber said, eyes going wide.

CHAPTER 21

AMBER

*A*mber thought she might be sick. She could still taste the blood that had coated her tongue. It was drying on her skin and it made her want to bathe in acid. She wasn't sure she'd ever feel clean again.

They'd tried to kill that girl in cold blood. They'd deserved to die, but for some reason that didn't take away the guilt she felt. She'd seen the fear in their eyes when she'd killed them.

Angel appeared behind her just as she was about to take off her shirt. "We need to talk."

Angry that he couldn't leave her alone for ten damn minutes, she ripped her shirt off over her head anyhow, not caring what he saw. She'd been wandering around the forest naked. It didn't matter at this point and she needed a shower. Now.

"Then you can talk while I shower," she said, throwing her clothes straight in the trash.

"If her guardian dies, Evangeline will become completely unmanageable," Angel said testily, following her into the shower and hovering above the soap dish. He kept his head turned slightly away as if he cared about her modesty. She knew better. He didn't care about anything except himself.

"She's not going to die. Ceri said she can heal her, without a hospital, just like you wanted," she replied before dunking her head under the hot water. It stung, but she reveled in it. Needed it. She groped blindly for the shampoo, then poured a large amount into her hand.

"She needs to be monitored closely. We can't risk any complications," Angel insisted.

Amber leaned her head out of the flow of water and slathered the shampoo into her hair, scrubbing furiously. "Ceri is not going to let the woman die. Stop harping on it."

The demon snorted and mumbled something she couldn't understand, then said, "You have no idea what's at stake here."

"Are you going to explain it?" Amber asked, peeking one eye at him.

The demon sneered at her. "No."

She rolled her eyes and began rinsing out the shampoo. The water swirling around her feet was pink from all the blood. The need to vomit roiled up in her gut and she squeezed her eyes shut again, breathing through her nose.

Her enhanced senses weren't helping right now. She could smell it like it was fresh, and she hated it.

"Who is this girl anyhow?" she asked as she lathered up the rag.

"You don't need to --"

"Just answer the damn question. I already know she's part demon, and part angel, so that cat's out of the bag."

He grew in size, filling up one corner of the shower. His burning eyes fixed on her face. "You don't get to demand anything. Not after that stunt you pulled. You're lucky I've left you alive. I'll tell you what to do, and you will obey. That's the bargain."

Turning away she began scrubbing at the blood again. She wished she could scrub away the demon mark. Or punch Angel in the face.

He vanished, finally, and she slumped against the wall of the shower. Tears burned at the back of her eyes but she didn't deserve to cry. This was all happening because she thought it was the only choice she had. It *had* been her choice.

Everyone was waiting for her to come out and explain herself and fix everything. She didn't want to. She wanted to curl up in bed and hide but she couldn't. That was never an option for her.

Straightening back up, she finished scrubbing off all the blood and sweat, then climbed out of the shower. She could break down when this was all over, but until then, she had to put her pack first.

CHAPTER 22

GENEVIEVE

Genevieve sat on the couch with Captain Jack and watched the argument unfolding in front of her. She'd been furious they'd gone off on some half-cocked rescue mission without her, but now that she knew why…well, she was still furious.

Derek was yelling at Amber, for the third time, that it was total crap she'd let him come out here to start a business without telling him about the whole demon mark thing.

"I would have still come but I can't believe you'd keep something like that from me!" he said, slamming his fist onto the coffee table for emphasis.

"I was trying to figure out what it meant!" Amber shouted back.

Ceri finally stood. "Both of you, just shut up."

Genevieve raised a brow at her tone. Little Miss Sunshine was angry too. That meant things were probably about to get ugly. She glanced at Tommy. He was hiding in the kitchen with Woggy trying to ignore the whole argument.

"Amber, is there anything *else* you haven't told the pack?" Ceri asked, crossing her arms.

Their alpha's face reddened to match her hair. "No," she ground out.

"Alright. Then enough with the whole conversation. The two of you can argue about it later. We have a severely injured woman and an unconscious, half-demon, half-angel teenaged girl to worry about. Along with a sorcerer who has apparently already killed one alpha werewolf." Ceri, looking exhausted, sat down on the couch next to her and crossed her arms.

"Do the police know about the attack today?" Genevieve asked, speaking for the first time since they'd gotten home. She hadn't been able to get a word in edgewise once Amber and Derek had started arguing.

Amber rubbed her hand over her face. "The police weren't there when we arrived, so I doubt it."

"Is there any reason we can't report it to the police? Or that you didn't call the police when you got there?" she asked, raising a brow.

Amber shook her head. "We didn't have much time to find the girl. Now, I have to protect her and the older woman."

"Protect them until what?" Genevieve asked.

Amber looked at her, brows furrowed. "What do you mean?"

"Protect them is super vague. There's no end to it. How long do you have to protect them?"

Amber turned to her right, facing no one. "Well?"

Everyone looked at the blank space uncomfortably. Only Amber could see or hear the demon most of the time. And right now, she didn't like what it was saying.

"I think you're lying," Amber said, crossing her arms.

"I want to talk to this demon," Genevieve said, frustrated at being left on the outside of all this. Everyone else had been here when the demon had appeared. She was the only one that hadn't seen it. The others all seemed to be afraid of it, but she knew a little something about demons. Theoretically.

They had a reputation for murder and mayhem, but when you looked at actual events of a demon appearing, the facts showed something different. Sometimes bad things happened, but sometimes they didn't.

Amber flinched, her hand flying to her chest. The air next to her twisted and a shadow grew, enveloping that corner of the room.

Horns extended from the creature's head. Its face was a cross between a bull and a dragon. Smoke curled from its nostrils and mouth, which was curled into a menacing, fiery grin. His dark form seemed to suck all the light from the room. "Speak then, mortal."

Everyone else took a step back, but Genevieve rolled her eyes. If it was trying to intimidate her, then it needed something from them. Badly. That was something she'd learned from Donovan. They still hadn't found out why the dead alpha had needed Amber's power, but he had desperately wanted it for some reason.

"How can Amber fulfill the bargain she made with you and have your mark removed?" Genevieve asked, walking slowly toward the creature until she was standing beside Amber. It seemed that the demon was taking something from her in order to appear like this. She couldn't feel anything odd in the pack bond but that was probably because Amber wasn't pulling on it.

The demon shrank until he was more or less her same height and began to float around her. She let him, choosing instead to inspect her nails. She wasn't concerned about him being at her back.

"As I told her, I need her to protect the girl," the demon said.

"And as I said, that's too vague. You have to be more specific, and it has to be possible for her to succeed, therefore, there has to be a way to measure that success. What is she protecting the girl from? And for how long?" Genevieve asked, placing a hand on Amber's shoulder. Immediately, the pack bond grew in her chest. She let it draw strength from her and give it to her alpha. Of course, Amber-the-stubborn had been holding back doing so.

The demon sneered at her. "You don't get to negotiate for her. Amber has to do it herself."

"I can negotiate for her if she asks me to," Genevieve said, gently squeezing Amber's shoulder to prompt her.

"I want her to," Amber said, glaring at the demon. "You haven't exactly been straight with me."

The demon changed shape. His smoky form was

dressed in a suit, but his head remained the same. "You are very bossy. I guess I shouldn't expect any less from a lawyer."

Genevieve snorted. He had no idea. "What do you want?"

"Someone is trying to kill Evangeline," the demon said, striking a relaxed pose. "I will consider the obligation of the mark fulfilled if Amber can find out who, stop them, and ensure Evangeline's safety until that is done."

"Do you already know who is trying to kill Evangeline?" she asked, narrowing her eyes at the demon.

A smirk lifted the corner of his mouth. "No, not for sure."

"Who do you suspect is behind it?"

"The angels."

Genevieve pinched the bridge of her nose and held back a sigh, with effort. "Sarcasm isn't helpful."

"Who said I was being sarcastic?"

She looked up at him, suspicious. "Why the hell would *angels* try to kill someone?"

"There was a half angel at the house when we got there. He was working with the sorcerer," Ceri said, speaking up for the first time since the demon had appeared. "And the girl is half angel."

The demon turned his attention to Ceri. "Who told you that?"

"No one had to, I sensed it when I was protecting her from the sorcerer's spell. She's half angel, and half demon," Ceri said, walking toward them. "Which shouldn't be possible, but I know it's true. Is that why you're protecting her?"

The demon snorted and turned back to Genevieve. "You know as much about who is trying to kill Evangeline as I do.

My offer remains the same, and is more than fair. Take it, or leave it."

"We'll accept it on one condition," Genevieve said, stepping up to the demon to make sure he understood she was serious. "You help in any and every way you can, and share any new information you discover about who is trying to kill Evangeline with us."

The demon stared at her, and she got the sense he would have set her on fire if he could have. Lucky for her, he couldn't.

"It's a deal." He moved in closer, his red eyes flickering with dark amusement. "You looked good as a demon, by the way."

He must have been here on Halloween, watching them. She leaned away from him. "Stop being creepy."

The demon vanished and it felt like a weight had been lifted from the room. Amber groaned, bracing her hand against the wall so she could stay upright. "I hate that," she muttered, rubbing the spot on her chest where the demon mark must be.

Genevieve walked toward her and stood over her alpha, hands on hips. "I can't believe you didn't tell us you made a deal with a demon. But what really makes me mad, is that you didn't even try to negotiate with him. You were just going to let him walk all over you!"

Amber squinted at her. "I didn't know it was negotiable!"

"Everything is negotiable," she said, crossing her arms. "Also, my parents and my sister are coming over for dinner tomorrow evening to meet all of you. I don't want them to have even the *slightest* clue that something weird is going on," she said, glaring at each of her pack mates in turn, finishing with her alpha. "My sister is nosy. She's going to ask intrusive questions if she thinks anything might be amiss."

Amber looked worried. "This isn't really a good time, can they come some other week?"

"No," Genevieve said, crossing her arms. "That will worry them."

CHAPTER 23

CERI

*D*emon. The word repeated over and over in Ceri's mind. She should have noticed sooner. Magic that dark should have been apparent, but she hadn't sensed it at all.

She smoothed her hair back with angry strokes and bound it into a loose bun on top of her head. A few curls spilled out, tickling the back of her neck. For a split second, she was tempted to shave it all off. She took a steadying breath, then grabbed her supplies.

The girl's guardian, a woman named Eloise Berger, was injured, but not enough that required a hospital, luckily. She'd treated her share of smoke inhalation –– witches tended to get into all sorts of trouble as kids, and telling their parents they were hurt meant getting grounded –– and it had been simple to fix once they were somewhere safe.

She'd sedated the woman simply so she didn't have to deal with her, but now they needed to wake her up. Ceri wanted a couple of minutes alone with her before she called Amber in. She needed to know if the girl was a danger.

Coming out of the sedation, she'd be loopy, and more likely to be honest. Ceri made sure her bedroom door was shut then knelt by the cot they'd made from a few blankets they'd found in a closet. She pressed her hands tightly together and spoke the words for silence and privacy. The sounds from outside her room became muted and she felt the spell press around her. Until she broke it, the pack wouldn't be able to eavesdrop on her. They'd only hear muffled sounds.

She unstoppered the bottle of Perk Up and waved it under Eloise's nose. The woman's eyes flew open and she jerked with a gasp.

"Shhh, calm down," Ceri said, pressing her back against the blankets to keep her from hurting her ribs any worse. "You're safe. The girl is safe."

Eloise's eyes were wide with confusion as she looked around the room. "What happened?" Her voice was hoarse and thready.

"You were attacked by someone. Your house burned down, but somehow you and your…daughter ended up in the woods. My alpha has a demon mark. He sent us to find you and the girl, and protect you."

Eloise instantly relaxed. Her eyes fluttered shut and she covered her face with her hands. "Oh, thank goodness."

Ceri sat back, completely surprised by her reaction. Normally saying demon wasn't cause for an 'oh thank goodness'.

"You, uh, know this demon?" she asked.

"Of course," Eloise said, dropping her hands. "He's Evangeline's uncle." She said it so casually. She had no idea what this demon really was, or how dangerous he could be.

"Has Evangeline ever hurt anyone?"

Eloise's eyes narrowed and she pressed her lips into a thin line. "No, and she wouldn't. She is harmless."

"How can you be sure?"

"Because I know her. I raised her from a baby. I taught her how to walk and how to read. She used to rescue insects that got into the house and carry them out to the garden. Wouldn't let me squash them. She's a good girl."

The door opened and Amber walked in. Ceri subtly canceled the muffling spell and nodded toward her alpha.

"Eloise, this is Amber. She is the one that rescued you," Ceri said as Amber sat down on the bed on the other side of Eloise.

"The demon mentioned you. He said a red-headed woman would help me," Eloise said with a smile. "Where is Evangeline? Is she okay?"

"Yeah, she's upstairs. I'll bring her to see you in a few minutes," Amber said, returning the woman's smile tensely. "Do you have any idea who attacked you?"

"They were humans, at least the one that got in the house." Eloise's hands shook slightly in her lap. "I knew they'd come one day, but I didn't think it'd be so soon."

"You knew they'd come one day?" Amber asked, her brows drawing together in confusion.

"Not them specifically, but someone. I've been so careful to make sure no one found out what Evangeline is. I never let her go out at night, she never had friends. Kadrithan told me that there have been others like her, and they'd all been killed. None of them made it past infancy, but they hid Evangeline better. They'd learned from their mistakes."

Ceri sat back in shock. How many had there been? Were they conducting some kind of experiment?

"Kadrithan...is that the demon's name?"

Eloise nodded. "It's not his real name I suspect. Not the one you'd use to summon him, but it's the name he gave me."

"How long have you been raising Evangeline?" Amber asked.

"Since she was a baby."

"Did the demon give her to you?"

Eloise nodded. "He's been with us since I found the girl. She was laying in the woods outside my house still covered in afterbirth. I have no idea how she got there, but he asked me to care for her."

"You have a demon mark, what deal did you make with him?" Amber asked, crossing her arms.

Eloise blushed, the color stark on her otherwise pale face. "Money. He gave me money in exchange for caring for her. My husband had died and I was about to lose the house." She looked up, meeting both their gazes. "I loved her right away though, treated her like my own child. I didn't care about the money, but I needed it. I needed it to care for her and to pay the bills."

Ceri sighed, brushing her hair back again. The wind had tangled it hopelessly and it was a huge mess now. She couldn't blame the woman for taking the money, and she obviously did care for Evangeline. It was just…the girl was a demon. At least half a demon.

She considered herself open-minded and non-judgmental, but demons and sorcerers were the exceptions. The things sorcerers did were evil and wrong. She'd always believed that demons not only committed evil acts, but were evil. Inherently.

"And that's all the demon wanted? For you to care for Evangeline?" Ceri asked finally.

Eloise nodded. "Care for her and keep her safe. And, of course, keep the secret. I've had to be strict with her because of that, and she hasn't been able to make many friends. I always regretted that, but there was no way around it."

"Why not? Were you worried she'd tell someone?" Amber asked.

"Not exactly. When it's daytime, Evangeline looks like a normal, pretty girl. When the sun sets though, she…changes. Physically. If anyone were to see here at night it would be obvious she was a demon."

"Does she act differently?" Ceri asked, glancing out the window to see the sun was already low in the sky.

"Not in the way you might think," Eloise said, shaking her head. "When she was a little girl, there was no change. But, as she got older, she started to understand it made her different. She hates it, so she gets all moody and irritable." Eloise paused then, hesitating.

"What is it?" Ceri prompted. They needed all the information they could get.

"She's been sick lately. Kadrithan knows why, but won't tell me, and neither will she. Every day it seems she gets weaker, and now sometimes, the-- she'll pass out or throw up. I just want to help her, but she won't tell me what's wrong." Eloise wrung her hands together, clearly upset.

"We'll keep an eye on her while y'all are staying here too, okay?" Amber said, trying to reassure the woman.

Ceri, however, had no interest in doing that. Eloise was acting like these were just normal teenage issues. The girl was a *demon*. Whatever was happening to her could have serious repercussions for her, and everyone around her.

"Can I see her?" Eloise asked.

"Yeah, she's been wanting to see you to. I'll go get her," Amber said, glancing at Ceri to make sure that was okay.

Ceri nodded and rose to her feet. "Just a quick visit. I need to sedate you again, Eloise, to help you heal. Your body can recover faster when you aren't moving or exerting yourself."

Amber knelt by Eloise to offer her more reassurances, but Ceri was done for now. She needed a break. Derek was standing in the hall when she walked out. He looked as angry as she felt.

"You okay?" he asked as she approached.

"I'm fine, what do you need?"

He glanced at the closed door and shook his head as if he disapproved. "Is this demon girl going to be safe to have here?"

Ceri thought about his question before answering. She

felt even more confused now than she had before they'd talked to Eloise. "Yes and no," she said honestly. "She's not going to hurt us, as far as I can tell, but whoever is after her might try to, if they find out she's here."

Derek took a deep breath and nodded. "I have to go to the mechanic shop. *Call me* if something happens."

"I will," she said with a tight smile. She probably wouldn't until it was over, but if it made him feel better to hear it, she'd reassure him. Humans weren't completely defenseless, but with a sorcerer threatening them, he'd be safer far, far away from the fighting.

He lifted his hand and squeezed her shoulder, but didn't pull away. "Thanks for looking out for my sister. Lord knows she doesn't think things through sometimes." He dropped his hand and took a step back. "I'll see y'all this evening for dinner. Try not to summon any more demons while I'm gone."

She snorted. "We'll do our best, but no promises."

"Oh, and you might want to check on Tommy. Apparently, he got shot while he was out there, but didn't tell anyone."

Her heart plummeted. "Thanks for telling me. Dammit, I can't believe he didn't say anything."

"He's a teenage boy trying to look tough, what do you expect? I think he's okay." He flashed her a charming grin that, for a second, lifted her spirits. Then, he was walking away and she was left with nothing but anger for Amber and the situation she'd drug them into.

CHAPTER 24

TOMMY

*T*ommy was halfway through his third sandwich when Ceri stomped into the kitchen. She looked even angrier than she had when she'd found out about the demon mark. "What's wrong?"

"You didn't tell me you were shot," Ceri said as she grabbed his arm and spun him around, looking for injuries.

"Because I'm fine. They healed," he protested.

"Do you know for sure that every bullet was pushed out and not just healed over?"

"Well, I don't know, but I feel fine," he said, batting her hands away.

"Where were you shot? Show me," she said, finally letting go and putting her hands on her hips. Her hair was even frizzier than normal and her fingers were white she was digging her fingers into her waist so hard. He didn't *want* to get checked over right now, but decided she needed it.

"Fine," he said with a sigh. "Left leg and my side, right here." He lifted his shirt and she began carefully palpating the area.

"Are you okay? I know it healed, but being shot had to hurt," she asked quietly.

He hesitated before answering. "It doesn't seem real. I don't know, I'm not freaking out, but maybe I should be. I'm more worried about Amber. What she did was brutal, and she's had this *look* on her face ever since."

Ceri snorted. "Amber will be fine."

He didn't like the tone in her voice, but he wasn't sure what to say. "Why are you so mad at her?"

She paused and looked up at him. "She put the whole pack in danger."

"There wouldn't be a pack if she hadn't made that deal."

Ceri straightened and crossed her arms, looking away. "We could have found a different sponsor. She shouldn't have done that without telling us."

Tommy shook his head. "It's easy to say that looking back, but we barely knew each other when she did that. And I don't think we could have found a different sponsor. Just, I don't know, give her a break. Derek is all over her about leaving him out of the loop, and now you are too. She actually listens to you. She needs you."

Ceri glanced toward Amber's room where Evangeline was laying, still sedated. "Easier said than done."

He shook his head, still confused. "What are you *actually* mad about?"

Her eyes snapped to his and she gnawed on the inside of her cheek. "I'm worried we're going to fail."

Tommy looked at his feet. He hadn't let himself think about that yet. Failure just wasn't an option. "We can't, so we won't."

"Since when are you so optimistic?" Ceri asked with a short, humorless laugh.

"Since some wise old lady told me it was just a choice, or something silly like that," he said with a grin. "She also told me to believe in myself, and my pack."

Ceri pressed her lips together, failing to completely hide her smile. "You're not supposed to use my advice against me."

Genevieve strolled into the kitchen. "Did you eat all the bread again?"

Tommy grabbed the bag and tossed it at her. "Nope."

"He's right, by the way, you're the only one Amber really listens to," Genevieve said as she fished a piece of bread out.

"She listens to --"

Genevieve cut her off with an unimpressed look. "And then does what she wants. *You* can change her mind when you need to. You are the alpha whisperer."

Ceri laughed, finally relaxing a little. "What a grand title."

The tension bled from the room and Tommy took a deep breath. Just being with pack like this had a way of calming him. It was a sense of safety he hadn't felt since his mother died. He'd do anything to keep them safe, and to keep the pack together. Even help a demon.

He just had to find a way to get stronger. He'd frozen in the forest, and he couldn't afford to do that again. Amber couldn't fight every fight for them. She needed them just as much as they needed her.

CHAPTER 25

EVANGELINE

*E*vangeline grasped onto consciousness and forced her heavy eyes to open. She was inside. An old-fashioned light fixture cast yellow light on the white ceiling. She rolled her head to the side and saw the woman with red hair who had found her in the forest. The woman was sitting in a chair, watching her.

"Are you feeling okay?" the woman asked. Her eyes were freaky, like all alpha werewolves. They were tinted with red from the magic that flowed through her.

She forced herself to sit up, though the movement made her arm ache. "I'm thirsty."

The woman leaned down and grabbed a bottle of water, then carried it to her. Evangeline took it and drank from it, swallowing as quickly as she could. Her throat felt like sandpaper, but the water soothed it.

"My name is Amber, by the way," the woman said. "And as Tommy told you, the demon I owe a favor to sent me to find you and protect you."

She nodded and swung her legs over the edge of the bed. "Yeah, I got all that."

Amber crossed her arms. "Any clue who attacked your house? Did you see anyone?"

Evangeline fiddled with the bottle cap and shrugged. She didn't want to rehash all of this with some stranger, especially one stupid enough to take a demon mark. Anyone working for her uncle didn't have her best interests at heart. "Where's my mother? I want to see her."

Amber looked annoyed for a moment, then took a deep breath and headed toward the door. "Come on, she's in the bedroom across the hall."

She scrambled to her feet, ignoring the wooziness that hit her as soon as she stood, and followed Amber. As they passed through the hall, she caught a glimpse of three other people watching them expectantly. The witch, and the two other werewolves who'd been in the forest earlier.

Her mother was laying on a cot on the floor. Her eyes popped open as soon as they walked in. "Oh, Eva," she said, lifting her arms for a hug.

Evangeline ran toward her and buried her face in her mother's neck. Distantly, she heard Amber saying she'd give them a minute, then the door shut again and they were alone. She knew the werewolves would still be able to hear them, but at least they weren't staring at her.

"Are you okay?" she whispered.

Her mother smoothed her hand down her back. "I've felt better, but that witch is healing me. I'm going to be just fine."

She sat back and wiped a tear from her cheek angrily. She hated crying in front of people. "Are we going to have to stay here?"

"Yes," her uncle answered, startling her.

She turned and glared at him, not realizing he was in the room. "I wasn't asking you."

"You will stay here and stay hidden as well as you can, or you will be killed. As I keep reminding you, all I'm trying to do is keep you alive," he sneered.

"I believed that when I was five, but I know better now," Evangeline hissed, glancing toward the door suspiciously. She didn't really want anyone listening in on this conversation.

"Don't worry, they can't hear us," the demon said.

"If you wanted to keep me alive then you would have warned us those people were coming to kill us, but you weren't even there!" she said, all the pent-up anger from the last twelve hours spilling out.

He ground his teeth together and glared at her. "If I'd known they were coming, I would have gotten both of you out days before. Someone found out you exist, and when I find out how, I will punish whoever screwed up appropriately. However, until then, you have to stay here, and stay safe."

Evangeline wanted nothing more than to just run and disappear, but she could never escape her uncle. He'd dug his claws into her mother long ago with a demon mark she could never be rid of as long as she lived. He knew she loved her mother, and so she was trapped.

"How are you feeling today? You used magic to get the two of you to safety," he asked, floating over to the bed.

She felt sicker than ever and weak. Her bones ached and she knew it would only grow worse when the sun set. "I feel fine."

"You can keep lying to yourself, and to me, but eventually it will break you," he sneered.

"Kadrithan, leave her alone. She'll come to the decision in her own time. I told you I wouldn't tolerate you trying to scare her into it," Eloise objected.

"She should be scared. If she doesn't do what she needs to, she will die." He stepped over her mother and got in her face. "If you die, then Eloise has failed. I'll take her soul."

She jumped to her feet. "You can't do that!"

"I can and I will! Come to your senses and stop putting off the inevitable."

She curled her hand into a fist and yanked the bedroom door open. Amber, who had been waiting just down the hall jumped, clearly startled. "I'd like to go back to sleep."

"Okay, we have a room for you upstairs," Amber said, pointing toward the stairs.

Evangeline nodded, then turned back to her mother for a moment. "Love you, and see you in the morning."

Her mother smiled, but it didn't have the usual joy behind it. "Love you too, sweetie."

CHAPTER 26

AMBER

"How's your arm? Ceri said you'd probably need to change the bandage when you woke up," Amber asked as they walked upstairs.

The girl looked angry, and Amber had felt a slight tug on her demon mark while she was alone in that room with Eloise. She wondered what the demon had said to her, if anything. Or if he'd just been lurking and eavesdropping.

Evangeline pulled her sleeve up and shrugged. "It's only bled through a little bit."

"Here," Amber said, making a quick detour to the upstairs bathroom. Ceri had left a first aid kit on the sink with a big band-aid set on top. She picked it up and showed Evangeline. "You don't need the full bandage anymore."

Evangeline didn't respond, just pushed the sleeve of her

hoodie up and started unwinding the bandage. She hissed in pain as she started to peel the gauze away from the wound. It had bled a little and then dried, which made it stick.

"I can keep that from sticking if you want," Amber said, reaching for the bandage.

"Don't touch me," Evangeline snapped, flinching away from her outstretched hand. "I can do it myself."

Amber lifted her hands in surrender. "Fine. You should change the band-aid every morning and evening." She picked up a little tub of ointment Ceri had added to the kit. "And smear a small amount of this on it. Ceri said it should help it heal within a few days."

It wasn't hard to believe this girl was a demon. She was rude, ungrateful, and looked like she wanted to punch anyone that came near her. The angel part seemed to have only affected her appearance.

"Great," Evangeline said, grabbing the tub opening it. She dabbed the ointment on while standing as far away from Amber as physically possible in the small bathroom.

The band-aid made it onto her arm but it was crooked and only partially covered the wound. Evangeline tossed the trash, most of it making it in the actual trashcan, the rest falling on the floor. Angered by its apparent uncooperativeness, she bent down and picked up the pieces, throwing them in one at a time.

Amber crossed her arms and waited. When Evangeline was finally done, she tried to leave the bathroom. She grabbed the girl's uninjured arm. "We need to talk."

"Why? You're supposed to keep me alive, not get to know

me," Evangeline said, flipping her long hair over her shoulder.

Amber's eye twitched. She wondered if shaving the girl's head would count as 'harming her'. "Did you see any of the people that attacked you?"

"Only the one my mom killed, but he was already dead," she said, turning her head away. But she couldn't hide the slight tremble of her lips.

"Have you seen any other half angels around recently? At school? Following you?" Amber asked.

Evangeline shook her head. "People like that don't come to Timber. It's in the middle of nowhere. They would have stuck out."

"Has anything weird happened around you recently?"

"Yeah," Evangeline said, shrugging her shoulders. "But everybody already knows about that."

"Well *I* don't. What was it?"

"A no-magic spot showed up right outside our school," she said, crossing her arm and looking uncomfortable. "There was a rumor going around that it must be demon related."

"Is it?" Amber asked bluntly. That earned her another glare, but at least Evangeline didn't look like she was about to cry anymore.

"No. At least not anything *I* did. I don't know what Kadrithan gets up to in his spare time."

Amber's phone buzzed with a message. She pulled it out and saw Shane's message letting her know he'd be there in ten minutes. "Shit."

She'd completely forgotten he was going to pick her up

this evening to go visit Donovan's old pack. The timing couldn't be worse.

"What?" Evangeline asked, eyeing her suspiciously.

"I need you to stay in your room and stay *quiet*. There's another werewolf from the council stopping by." She shoved Evangeline out of the bathroom and pointed toward the spare bedroom she'd be staying in.

"That I can do," Evangeline muttered. She hurried into the room, slamming the door shut behind her.

Amber put her hands over her face and cursed Angel, demons, and teenagers. She was never, ever having kids.

She left the first aid kit where it was so Evangeline could find it later and hurried downstairs. The pack was in the kitchen and...they were laughing. She stopped in the living room and just watched for a moment, completely confused. Less than an hour ago they'd been at each other's throats. Well, they'd been mad at her. Not each other.

"Hey, Shane is on his way here. I completely forgot he was coming by this evening to pick me up. We have to go to Lockhart's old pack to check in on things and see if they have a new alpha yet," she said, feeling strangely left out for the first time.

Genevieve immediately perked up. "I need to go with you."

"Why?" Amber asked, frowning.

"I wanted to talk to you about it earlier today, but..." she waved her hand around to indicate the chaos that had taken over the afternoon. In some ways, it felt like it had been days since the demon had appeared in the living room and called in his debt. "Anyhow, I have a new client. He's a bitten wolf, and about a week ago he was charged with loss of control. He was attacked in a bar, and when he defended himself, he hurt the other guy pretty badly. Without his alpha to vouch for him, they won't even consider letting him out on bail."

"It may be a while before the pack accepts a new alpha," Amber warned. She hated the injustice, but she had no idea if they'd be able to help this bitten wolf anytime soon.

"That's okay, I just need to talk to *someone*," Genevieve said. She grabbed a slice of bread from the bag she was holding, then retied it and tossed it at Tommy. He caught it easily thanks to his werewolf reflexes.

"Alright, when Shane gets here I'll make sure it's not against some kind of rule, but it'd be good to have more backup there." She dragged her hands through her hair. "I think it's best if no one knows we have guests."

"I definitely agree," Ceri said with a gentle smile that took Amber off guard. The witch had been pissed last time she saw her. "I'll make sure he can't smell anything out of place. How long do I have?"

Amber glanced at her phone. "Maybe ten minutes, but I wasn't going to let him inside."

Tommy started cleaning up the kitchen and Genevieve ran up to her room to grab something.

Ceri walked over and put her hand on Amber's arm. "After you get back, we need to talk about that whole animal whisperer thing."

"Okay," Amber said, her eyebrows drawing together. "Is everything okay?"

"Yes. There's just a lot to explain, and we need to start

figuring out how to track down whoever is trying to hurt Evangeline."

"As soon as we get back, I'm all yours."

Ceri smiled and squeezed her elbow lightly. "Be safe."

~

*A*mber finished tying off her braid when Angel appeared at her shoulder. Her phone vibrated on the counter and she saw Shane's message on the screen letting her know he was in the driveway.

"You don't have time for these sorts of distractions," he said, blocking her view of the mirror. He had reverted to his little red devil form, but his humor still hadn't returned.

"If I don't take care of this, Shane and the council will be suspicious," she said, grabbing her jacket and hurrying toward the front door. "Just stay out of it and let me get it over with."

She hurried for the front door, shouting for Genevieve over her shoulder. Angel followed her as well, much to her chagrin.

Amber plastered a smile on her face before yanking the door open. Shane froze, his fist still in the air, ready to knock.

He lowered his hand. "Everything okay?"

"Yeah, sorry, running a little late. Also, Genevieve is coming with us," she said, slightly breathless from scrambling to get ready. "She's representing one of members of the Lockhart pack. She needs to talk to whoever the alpha might be right now and see if they can help the werewolf. I'm bringing her along if that isn't against some kind of weird werewolf code of conduct I don't know about."

He raised a brow, but didn't object. "Fine with me. She'll need to be careful not to challenge anyone and stay by you."

Amber nodded. "That shouldn't be a problem."

"I didn't realize she was a lawyer."

"No one ever does," Genevieve said, popping up behind Amber. "Are we going to leave, or just stand in the doorway all evening?"

Amber threw a glare over her shoulder. Genevieve winked at her.

Shane just laughed and swept his hand to the side. "Ladies first."

She headed toward the suburban, walking a little fast so she could get shotgun and make Genevieve sit in the back. It was uncomfortable leaving Evangeline with the pack, but she knew Ceri could take care of her and protect the rest of them if needed.

Angel settled on the dashboard as they climbed in the suburban. He glared at Shane and Amber found herself glad she was the only one that could see him, even if it did make her feel a little crazy sometimes.

The drive was uneventful. Shane spent most of it asking Genevieve how she'd ended up a lawyer, and all about the bitten wolf that had been arrested. Amber had trouble focusing on the conversation. Angel kept making snide comments she couldn't respond to.

That wasn't what really bothered her though. Her heart was beating faster than normal and her palms were sweaty. She felt a strange disconnect from everything around her. It didn't seem possible that earlier today she had killed four people. It had been in self defense, but the memories of the violence made her skin crawl. And now she was just going on an errand for the council like nothing had happened. Maybe she was going crazy.

The wolf felt nothing but fierce pride over the kills. She rubbed the hem of her jacket between her fingers to ground herself. She had to calm down before they saw the other pack or she'd end up setting someone off. Or letting someone get to her.

Genevieve's hand landed on her shoulder and squeezed. Some of the tension bled out of her as the pack bond wrapped around her. She forced herself to turn her attention back to the conversation. In just a couple of hours this would be over, and she could go take care of what really mattered. Her pack.

CHAPTER 27

AMBER

*A*mber grew tense as they pulled into the driveway of Donovan Lockhart's house. It belonged to the pack now according to his will and would house whoever managed to claim the title of alpha. It was a nice house, though a little gaudy for Amber's taste. It was a mix of five different architectural styles, all mashed together in an attempt to make it look expensive.

Cars and trucks were parked in the driveway, with the overflow spilling into the side yard. Even from inside Shane's suburban, she could hear shouting and growling in the distance.

"They must be in the middle of a challenge," Shane said as he parked next to the car farthest from the house.

"After all these years you'd think they'd move to some kind of election-based system instead of literally fighting for the position," Genevieve muttered from the backseat.

Shane shook his head. "The wolf in us would never respect something like that. We could never follow someone weak."

Amber would never admit it out loud, but a small part of her craved the chance to fight off a challenger and prove her worth to her pack. Being a werewolf didn't change who you were, exactly, but it did give you new instincts. She wasn't alone in her head anymore.

"Wolves are savages. You should know that, Amber," Angel purred, twisting around her shoulders.

She glared at the demon as they climbed out of the suburban, but couldn't respond. He seemed pleased to have gotten a reaction.

They headed toward the sounds of fighting. The wolf peered out of her eyes and took it all in. There was a sense of excitement in the air. She could smell it.

"Stay calm, and don't make eye contact for too long," Shane cautioned, for a third time, as they walked toward the crowd gathered in the backyard. "The pack has no clear leadership right now and everyone is keyed up from the fighting."

"Shane, you worry more than Amber, and that is really alarming," Genevieve said, patting him on the shoulder.

Amber snorted in amusement, but tried to hide it behind a cough.

Shane gave them both a dirty look. "See if I try to keep you from getting in a fight ever again."

"You know you will," Amber said with a grin that didn't feel entirely forced. "You want to hand off these crappy duties too bad to let me get hurt or killed."

He sighed dramatically. "That and you are still supposed to buy me dinner."

Genevieve made a gagging noise. "Please don't flirt in front of me. I *just* ate."

Amber was about to make a smart remark back when she saw the fight. She stopped in her tracks and just stared.

To say it was violent would be an understatement. The two wolves were huge. One was dark gray, and the other a muddy mix of red and brown. Their lips were curled back revealing long, sharp teeth streaked with blood. Their fur was matted with dirt and grass that had been torn up by their sharp claws.

The wolves collided with a furious snarl. The gray one bit into the thick muscle of the other wolf's shoulder. The brown wolf yelped and twisted, clawing at the gray wolf's gut. The snarls were almost drowned out by the jeers of the crowd as they shouted insults and encouragement.

Amber couldn't tell who they wanted to win, or if they even cared. It seemed like they were caught up in the thrill of it. The whole thing made her sick, but the wolf was merely curious. It looked at the two fighting as potential challengers. They were slightly bigger than she was, but they fought recklessly, depending on their size and strength to dominate the other.

The wolves broke apart and circled each other slowly. Genevieve pressed against Amber's side. She was just as tense as Amber felt.

"You can't tell me this isn't barbaric," Angel whispered. "But people fear *demons*."

She wished her wolf could banish Angel again, even if it was just for a few days. He needed to shut up. This was awful enough without his commentary.

The gray wolf lunged, jaws open, but this time the brown wolf didn't meet his charge. He skittered backward, then ducked underneath the attack. His jaws clamped around the gray wolf's neck and he dragged him to the ground, managing to twist at the last moment so that he ended up on top.

"That's a common move," Shane said, whispering directly into Amber's ear. Despite the current situation, she felt a shiver go down her spine as his breath tickled the skin of her neck. She glanced back and caught his gaze. He was standing very close. Close enough to touch.

"The gray wolf seems like the better fighter, but not by much," Amber replied quietly.

Shane nodded. "He's a little older. Jameson expects him to end up as the alpha. He was one of Donovan's gammas, but he was dominant enough to be a beta at least."

Amber looked around at the crowd. There must have been thirty people here. She recognized a couple from the night they'd been changed, but they weren't paying any attention to her. They were completely focused on the fight.

The former beta whose ass she'd kicked when he'd showed up at her apartment to gloat over her eviction was watching as well, though he had a sullen expression on his face. He must have tried to take the position early on and lost.

A sudden cheer from the crowd brought her attention back to the fight. The gray wolf had the brown wolf's ear in his mouth. He jerked his head viciously and ripped the ear off, taking a hunk of fur with it. Bile rose in Amber's throat, but she forced it down and didn't look away.

He attacked again immediately, forcing the brown wolf onto his back with his jaws clamped firmly around his neck. The other wolf struggled for a moment, but it was clear he couldn't breathe.

"He'll forfeit now, don't worry," Shane said, touching her back briefly. True to his word, a moment later the brown wolf shifted back to human form. He lay still underneath the gray wolf who tilted his head back and howled in victory. She had hated Donovan, but she hated this more. There had to be a better way. A less violent way.

The gray wolf shifted into human form and glared down at his defeated opponent. His body was streaked with sweat and the wounds from the fight were even more obvious on his bare skin. "Do you submit?" His voice carried over the crowd, silencing every conversation as the pack waited for the response.

The other man kept his eyes on the ground, but his body was shaking with anger, or embarrassment. She wasn't sure which. "Yes."

The pack erupted into howls, celebrating their newest alpha. A few of the men and women watching didn't join in though. Amber looked at each of them in turn. The wolf thought they were potential challengers, and she agreed. At the very least they didn't like their new alpha.

"You look disgusted, but I can sense your strongest

emotions. You wish that was you," Angel, morphing into a vicious looking wolf with a pointed tail and horns.

She took a deep breath and sent all the hate she could muster at the demon. If he could sense her emotions, then she hoped he suffered.

He wagged his tail at her. "You can do better than that. I know you have a lot of anger and hate in that savage, wolfy heart."

Shane tapped Amber on the arm and motioned for her to follow him. She turned her back on Angel and tried to put him from her mind. Engaging with him never turned out in her favor.

The winner was exiting the circle and accepted a pair of loose shorts handed to him by another pack member. He paused to pull them on, then continued to a table where he grabbed a pitcher of water and downed it. The water spilled over his jaw and chest, washing away some of the blood.

"Congratulations, Kevin," Shane said, raising his voice loud enough to be heard at a distance.

The man lowered the pitcher and nodded toward Shane, though he didn't look excited to see him. "I didn't expect the council to show up so soon."

"We waited a few days to show up, but you know how the government gets. They want their paperwork," Shane said with an easy grin, completely ignoring the tension in the other werewolf. "Alpha Hale is with me. She took Donovan's position on the council."

Kevin turned his dark eyes to her and she felt her skin crawl. "I know who she is." He seemed to bite back something he wanted to add on to that statement.

Amber took her cue from Shane and simply stared at him impassively. The wolf rose up in her mind, hackles raised and red bloomed along the edges of her vision. She would tolerate a certain amount of attitude, but she wasn't going to cower in front of him.

"We need to record the names and rank of every pack member. Are you going to help, or do you want your beta to do it?" Shane asked. "Assuming you have someone in mind for the position."

Kevin pointed at the man who'd handed him the shorts. "He'll do it."

Shane nodded and headed toward the guy, but Amber walked over to Kevin. Genevieve followed her.

"What do you want?" he asked, looking her over. It wasn't sexual though, it was fear, which surprised her for a moment. She had defeated his alpha in the Trials though, something no one thought possible.

"Genevieve is representing one of your pack members that has been arrested. She has some questions, and needs your help. Are you willing to talk to her?" Amber asked, holding his gaze. Shane had said no prolonged eye contact, but she wasn't going to act scared. Kevin could look away first if he didn't want another fight on his hands.

"Sure, but she needs to make it quick." Kevin opened up an ice chest and grabbed a beer, cracking it open and chugging half of it immediately.

Amber turned to Genevieve for a moment. "I'm going to go help Shane, and make sure the other guy is alright. If you need help, just let me know."

Genevieve patted her arm. "I'll be fine."

Amber nodded and caught up to Shane, cursing Donovan in her head for being stupid enough to get murdered.

CHAPTER 28

GENEVIEVE

Genevieve locked gazes with the interim alpha. He hated her. And the feeling was mutual.

"Davie is a little shit and I'm not bailing him out of trouble," Kevin growled, his eyes flashing red like that could make her cower. This asshole wasn't more dominant than she was. He had won that fight but he was nothing special. He'd be knocked out of his position by tomorrow, if not sooner.

"You are worthless," Genevieve said quietly, leaning in slightly and baring her teeth at him.

He sneered at her. "Unless you intend to challenge me, you better keep that pretty little mouth shut. Insult me again and it might start a fight you can't win."

She rolled her eyes and grabbed her briefcase. This

conversation was going nowhere. Absolutely nowhere. This pack was in shambles, and every single member was going to suffer until someone managed to come out on top.

Genevieve stood and glared down at him. "I won't have to challenge you, you'll be ousted by the end of the day."

He growled and made a move like he was going to lunge at her, but Shane appeared out of nowhere and slammed him back down in his chair.

"Let it go, Kevin," Shane warned. "You try to challenge her, you'll have to go through me."

The werewolf sneered at them, but didn't make another move. Genevieve turned and walked away, heading back toward the car. Amber was off to the side talking to the werewolf that had lost the fight. She looked back over her shoulder to make sure Genevieve was alright. She nodded at her alpha and kept going.

This entire pack were idiots. All of them. She tightened her grip on her briefcase and thanked every deity she could think of that Amber had been there the night they were attacked. If it had been someone else...she may have ended up in the System. Or worse, in this pack.

Halfway through the impromptu parking lot she noticed a man with light brown hair underneath a well-worn ball cap leaning against the side of his car. She couldn't quite pin down his age. He wasn't young, but she didn't think he was middle-aged yet either. He was dressed casually in jeans and a white t-shirt. He had a bag of donut holes in one hand but wasn't eating them.

She paused when she felt his eyes on her. It felt like he was waiting for her to show up. He wasn't checking her out and he didn't look nervous. His expression was more... expectant. She changed directions and headed straight for him.

He waited until she was about a foot away to lift the bag in her direction. "Hungry?"

"Always," she said, extending her hand for a treat.

He picked out three donut holes and placed them in her hand before grabbing one for himself. She wasted no time scarfing down two of them, eyes slipping shut as she enjoyed the melt-in-your-mouth glaze and the soft dough.

"Who are you and why are you handing out donut holes?" she asked, holding her hand in front of her mouth as she continued chewing.

"My name is Paul Greer, and I have a proposition for you."

She narrowed her eyes at him. "Alright, Paul Greer, let's hear it."

"This pack has gone to shit," he said without preamble. "And it's going to stay that way until the idiots get done fighting amongst themselves. I intend to claim it; however, I've been waiting for the right moment. No matter how good of a fighter I am, I can't defend three challenges a day for very long."

She nodded. "Yeah, that'd be pretty insane."

"I've heard a lot about your alpha, and I was there for the Trials, watching." He opened the bag again and ate another donut hole, chewing it thoughtfully. "It's weird seeing a bitten wolf pull something like that off, but I think I like it. Werewolves have been getting complacent in recent years. Getting humanized, and acting like they don't have to prove themselves if they were born that way." He shook his head in disapproval.

"What are you planning on doing about that?" She wasn't sure if she should be creeped out by his little speech or not. He didn't give off crazy person vibes, but there was something...wild about him.

"Not much," he admitted with a shrug. "But I'll run this pack differently, and I think I'll get along well with your alpha. If I win my challenge, I want her as my sponsor."

Genevieve's jaw dropped, but she quickly clamped it shut. A sponsor would need a certain amount of money, and she wasn't sure Amber could come up with it. "Oookay, why aren't you talking to her about this?"

His mouth quirked up into a smile. "It's tradition to contact the alpha's beta first, which I assume you are. It's meant to be an introduction. Tell her what you think of me." He pulled a slip of paper out of his pocket. "This is my contact information. I'll be challenging whatever knuckle-head is the alpha in a few days, on the night of the Full Moon. Then, I'll come call on Alpha Hale. If you have any questions for me between now and then, let me know."

This was completely unexpected, but the wheels in her head were already turning. She wasn't even sure if she *was* Amber's beta. The pack had never talked about pack ranks since there were so few of them. They just worked together and didn't overthink it.

She wanted to ask Paul to swear to help out Davie before she passed along his info to Amber but decided against it. This guy seemed like he was fairly honest and blunt. She didn't want to try to manipulate him. He couldn't do anything for Davie right now, so she would wait until he become the alpha to present the case to him. There were a few details she needed to figure out anyhow, since it was starting to look like Davie wasn't being entirely honest with her. She had wanted to get him out on bail but that just wasn't an option anymore. The Full Moon was in three days. Davie could wait until then.

She put the paper in her briefcase and nodded. "Alright, I'll be in touch."

"Have a good day," he said, tipping his head toward her. He pushed off the car and strolled back toward the area where the pack had congregated.

She watched him go as she stuffed the last donut hole in her mouth. They were really good.

CHAPTER 29

CERI

Ceri handed Derek a mug of tea. "You look like you could use something to relax. A friend recommended this to me recently, and it was very effective."

He smiled for the first time in twenty-four hours as he accepted her offering. "Your friend sounds smart."

Leaning back against the counter she picked up her own mug of tea and took a sip. The lavender and honey tasted like heaven and she felt her muscles slowly un-tensing.

The house was quiet. Eloise was still sleeping off the sedative, and Evangeline had no interest in talking to or seeing anyone from the pack. It was almost blissful. Ceri knew she was an introvert, but sometimes she forgot just how draining other people could be. The magical battle had drained her too, and was still draining her. She needed to talk to Amber about that as soon as she got back.

"Am I being too hard on Amber?" Derek asked, startling her out of her thoughts.

Ceri blew on her tea, taking a moment to think. "I think we both are. Maybe. She knows she should have told us sooner. I'm done being mad at her, it doesn't help anything."

Derek nodded in agreement. "I can't really blame her for keeping it to herself, I guess. She was real messed up after Dylan died. We weren't there for her. I think that kind of thing could make a person forget they can actually turn to family for help."

"She's mentioned that her mom blamed her for what happened, but she doesn't talk about it much."

He sighed and shook his head. "Yeah, mom definitely blamed her. It was stupid, but Amber just always took care of Dylan. Kept him out of trouble. He was the risk-taker. It caught us all off guard that they'd both tried to join a pack. It's something I would have expected her to talk him out of, but I guess she wanted it too." He cleared his throat. "But enough about all that. How'd you end up in the pack?"

Ceri laughed. "That's not any less depressing. My family kicked me out because I won't join the coven properly."

"Why not?" Derek asked. His blue eyes watched her over the brim of his mug with genuine interest. It made something warm curl up in her gut to see. All her dating prospects had always been other witches, and they only saw her family name, and her reputation as a tree-hugging disappointment.

"The magic witches use is based on a trade. You have to sacrifice something. A plant is a small sacrifice. It's alive, but its life force doesn't hold the same...oomph that something sentient does. A pixie, like Woggy, is a common ingredient." She looked down into the amber liquid of the tea, her fingers tightening on her mug. "No one talks about it, but they'll do bigger animals too. Cats, dogs, horses. It's all about power."

"The elves don't have to do that to work their magic, why do y'all?" he asked, looking a little disturbed.

"They tap into something else. Some theorize there's a type of spirit realm, or that magic is in the air we breathe but that not every race can access it," she said with a shrug. "Hard to say, really. These spots where magic doesn't work might give us some insight though."

A loud squeak caught her attention and she looked down to find that Woggy had escaped from his box yet again. "Are you hungry?" she asked, signing along as she spoke just like Tommy had taught her.

The pixie squeaked and signed back with a very emphatic yes.

"Is that sign language?" Derek asked.

Ceri nodded. "Tommy suggested it. It's completely brilliant, and I'm mad I didn't think of it first."

"And he really understands it?"

"Yep. Woggy is learning more every day too." She grabbed a can of tuna from the pantry, opened it, and sat it on the floor. Woggy dived into the meat immediately, eating with gusto. And making a mess. "We're working on teaching him to clean up after himself too, but he hasn't been very interested in that lesson."

Derek snorted. "Of course not."

The front door opened and Genevieve walked inside

yawning. She grimaced. "We have got to get Woggy something other than tuna. The whole house reeks all the time now."

"Better than just smelling like cat," Amber said, appearing behind her and glaring down the hall. Captain Jack appeared, his tail swishing behind him. He made a beeline for the tuna, but Woggy turned and hissed at him, hugging the can of fish close to his chest.

"Captain Jack does not stink," Genevieve said, picking up the giant cat. "He's very cleanly."

Amber rolled her eyes and muttered something about putting him outside to catch rats. Ceri hid a smile behind her tea. It was refreshing to see them arguing about something normal.

But, there were still things to discuss before the night was over. She caught Amber's gaze and nodded toward the porch.

Derek seemed to understand that they needed to talk. "Gen, did that alpha end up agreeing to help you get that bitten wolf out on bail?"

Genevieve groaned and launched into a long explanation. Ceri took the distraction and headed toward the porch with Amber. It was cool outside, borderline cold, now that the sun was down.

"This has been the longest day in history," Amber said, plopping down on the porch swing. She held it still so Ceri could sit, then pushed off the ground with her toe, rocking them gently.

"Yeah, it has been," Ceri agreed. She was tired down to her bones. They sat quietly on the porch swing and enjoyed the breeze for a moment before continuing. "What you said the other morning reminded me of a conversation with my grandmother. She was a nasty piece of work, but I learned a lot from her. Have you ever heard of a shaman?"

Amber shook her head. "Is that some kind of witch?"

"Technically, yes." She pulled her foot up onto the porch swing and hugged her knee to her chest. "When a witch joins a pack, it can change her magic. That owl I was complaining about the other day wasn't just an owl. It was a spirit. I don't know what it wants, but it helped me when I was fighting that sorcerer. Without it, and the pack bond, I would have been completely outmatched."

Amber ran her hands through her hair and pulled her feet up on the swing as well. "What does that mean for you? It doesn't sound bad, but you didn't exactly sign up for having your magic changed."

Ceri rested her chin on her knee and stared out at the night sky. "I don't know what it means, but it definitely isn't bad. I've always hated how weak white magic is. This…was different. It was more powerful."

"More powerful is better, right?"

"Mostly, but more power generally requires a greater sacrifice. At least for a witch. I shouldn't be able to just tap into the source like an elf." She rubbed her temples, wishing she had answers for herself and Amber. "The second time this owl visited me, right before the demon called in his favor, I had a vision of fire, pain, and darkness. Then the demon showed up and we rescued Evangeline. I don't know if I was being warned she was in danger, or being warned that *we* were because of the demon." The vision had been gnawing at her ever since the demon had appeared.

"In some ways, I guess we both are. Whoever is hunting Evangeline is a threat to us now. Too bad this shaman stuff doesn't come with a guidebook," Amber said with a snort.

"No kidding. That'd make our lives so much easier," she agreed with a laugh. "Speaking of no guidebook, I might have done something kind of risky."

"Risky?" Amber asked, sitting up straight.

"To stop the sorcerer, I had to kind of...create a shield for Evangeline," she said, twisting her fingers in the hem of her sweater.

"Ceri, just spit it out," Amber said, frustration evident in her voice. Her whole body was tense, like she was ready to fight someone.

Ceri sighed and dropped her head back to her knees. "My magic is shielding her. We're kind of tied together until I undo the...well, it's basically a psychic shield. But it's the only thing keeping the sorcerer's spell from killing her."

Amber put her hand over her mouth, her fingers digging into her cheeks slightly, then dropped her hand. "Can it hurt you?"

"It's not likely."

"Why doesn't that sound very reassuring?" Amber asked, making it sound like an accusation.

She wanted to say *because it shouldn't*, but Amber had enough to worry about. "We have to find this sorcerer and stop him. But I'm more worried about the demon than I am the sorcerer. Does he know anything about who is hunting her?"

"Not much. I think we may know more than Evangeline or the demon at this point. The blond guy was a half angel, and he has a sorcerer working with him. Maybe we can start asking around. Would a sorcerer leave any signs if he showed up in town?" Amber asked.

"They tend to fly under the radar. It's technically illegal, after all. But…they might buy supplies wherever they end up," she said, her mind racing. The black market for magical supplies was alive and well in Portland. There were a dozen people the sorcerer could contact, but it was somewhere to start. "I know a few people that my family used to buy from when we needed something not on the record. We can start by talking to one of them."

Amber nodded immediately. "How soon can we talk to them? Is it like a night time only thing?"

Ceri laughed. "They're not vampires, well, not all of them. There's someone we can definitely talk to tomorrow before Gen's parents come over for dinner."

"Ugh, don't remind me. They couldn't be coming at a worse time," Amber groaned, putting her head in her hands.

"When it rains it pours," Ceri agreed. Part of her was glad though. She wanted to cling to every bit of normalcy as tightly as possible. A gentle hoot caught her attention and she saw the owl, her near constant companion, sitting in a tree near the porch. She twisted her fingers tighter in her sweater and tried to ignore the sense of doom she hadn't been able to shake since the vision.

Amber shifted on the swing, starting up the rocking again. She cleared her throat, like she was gearing up to say something, but only ended up chewing her nails.

"What is it?" Ceri asked, nudging her gently.

"I'm sorry I wasn't honest with you," Amber said quietly.

Ceri turned her head to rest her cheek on her knees instead and reached her hand out, entwining her fingers with Amber's. "I know. And it's okay. No one is perfect, not even a woman who's only been an alpha for just over a month and who had no idea she was about to be dumped into a dangerous, magical world."

Amber glared at her, but there was no heat behind it. "Are you mocking me while I'm trying to apologize?"

"Only a little," Ceri said with a grin.

Amber shook her head, but she was smiling now. "Everyone in my pack is a jerk. That is my karmic punishment."

Ceri laughed, and it felt good. She felt lighter than she had in days. "Oh, that reminds me...our house is kind of sentient."

"What?" Amber asked in alarm.

She grinned and launched into an explanation. Freaking Amber out with magic was the best form of therapy.

CHAPTER 30

GENEVIEVE

"You promised you could get me out!" Davie said, his voice cracking. "Come on, I can't stay in here."

"Listen to me," Genevieve said, leaning forward. She was about as frustrated as he was, but all this panicking didn't help anything. "I am going to help you, but until an alpha is chosen, there's nothing we can do. Do you know Paul Greer?"

Davie wiped his nose on the back of his sleeve and nodded. "Yeah, why?"

"He's going to try to take the position on the night of the full moon, and I think he would help," she said, sitting back in her chair.

He snorted and shook his head. "No way. He's just some quiet loner, he's not gonna be able to win a challenge."

She pinched the bridge of her nose between her thumb and forefinger. "Well, you better hope he wins, because if Kevin keeps it, he won't vouch for you and we'll have to try a different strategy. What I need you to do for me now is *stay out of trouble*. I can't believe you got into a fight in here."

Davie looked chagrined. "They told me bitten wolves might as well be puppies."

"So what? They're just trying to get a rise out of you. If you can't show some semblance of control while you're waiting for your hearing, there's no way the judge is going to let you out on bail no matter what your alpha says." She was starting to think Davie *did* have a problem with control. He definitely had an attitude problem. Someone like him should never have been bitten, but from what she knew of Donovan's pack, he hadn't exactly chosen the most upstanding citizens to bring into the fold.

"I'll try, okay? Just please get me out of here as soon as you can," he begged again, giving her puppy dog eyes.

"That's my job," Genevieve said as she rose from her chair. She had so much paperwork to do today for other cases. This visit had been a last minute decision after she'd gotten a phone call from Davie where he'd been sobbing about a fight he'd gotten into.

She rapped on the door for the guard to let her out. He opened the door and she hurried down the hallway. She wasn't sure if it was a good sign or not, but she was getting used to coming here.

Halfway back to her car, her phone rang. She saw

Steven's number and almost ignored the call but a twinge of guilt stopped her.

"Hey," she said, tucking the phone between her cheek and shoulder while she unlocked her car.

"Finally," Steven said, irritation clear in his tone.

"I'm sorry, it's been a really weird couple of days." She climbed into the car, tossing her briefcase in the passenger seat.

"You could at least text me back. It takes two seconds."

"I know, I know. I said I was sorry." She backed up quickly and checked the time. She was going to be at least thirty minutes late getting to the office, and she'd missed the morning meeting completely.

"Can you come over tonight? It's been a week since we've had dinner."

"I can't, my parents are coming over for dinner to meet the pack." She mentally groaned. It was the last thing she wanted to deal with right now, but she'd put them off even longer than Steven. When he didn't reply, she checked her phone to make sure the call hadn't dropped. It still showed connected, but he was completely silent. "Steven?"

"You know we dated for a year and you barely even mentioned your parents, much less let me meet them."

"We weren't...it just didn't seem like the right time," she said, cringing as the words came out of her mouth.

"Genevieve, why can't you just be honest? You were never serious about our relationship, and still aren't," he said in clipped tones.

She sighed and ground her teeth together. Normally, this was the part where she just agreed, and they broke up for a few weeks before they got back together. "Then just come tonight."

As soon as the words left her mouth, she wanted to drive her car into a telephone pole. It wasn't that she didn't want to be with Steven, it's just that the idea of forever made her skin crawl. She didn't want everyone to think they were madly in love and then be disappointed if they broke up. So, she'd just...not told anyone. It was easier that way. For her at least. It obviously wasn't easier for Steven.

"Are you serious?"

"Yes," she said hesitantly. She couldn't tell if he was still mad, or excited.

"Are you going to introduce me as your boyfriend or try to pretend I'm just part of the pack?"

"As my boyfriend," she said, exasperated at him now. "Look, I'm not good at this stuff. You know that. Just take the invitation and stop making me repeat it."

He sighed. "Fine, but we're going to hold hands, and sometime in the next month, we're going to have a dinner with just us and your parents. No hiding behind the pack."

"Fine. Look, I'm almost to work, I really need to go."

"I'll be at the house at four this evening, unless they'll be over earlier?" he asked.

"No, they're coming around five."

"Okay, see you then. Have a good day at work, bye," he said, sounding a little more chipper.

"You too. Bye," she said, hanging up the phone. As soon as she tapped end, her heart dropped into her stomach. "Ah, hell."

She'd completely forgotten about Evangeline. She still

hadn't told Steven about her, and he would know something weird was going on. With a sigh, she picked up her phone again, and texted Amber.

She was so busy now that she was working all the time, she felt like she'd abandoned the pack. Ceri, Amber, and Tommy had run off to rescue Evangeline without her and she hadn't gotten there in time to help. She left before everyone was awake, and barely made dinner most nights.

Taking on this case felt like a mistake but if she hadn't, then Davie would just rot in prison. She wished she was smarter and had a way to help him *now*. Paul Greer might be able to help but the full moon was still two days away. She also had no guarantee he'd want to help Davie either, especially as a new alpha.

Her fingers twitched on the steering wheel as the sudden urge to shift and run flowed through her. The wolf was restless and tired of being restrained. The more frustrated she got, the harder it was to stay in control. None of the others struggled with it as much as she did.

After the Trials, she'd thought she could just turn her life around and *do something*, but it was silly to assume she'd be able to succeed just like that. Maybe it had been silly to try at all.

She parked the car on the far end of the parking lot in the only space left and shook her head at herself. She couldn't even manage to get to work on time.

CHAPTER 31

CERI

*C*eri had a headache, and this downtown traffic wasn't helping. "Oh my god, learn to use your accelerator," she muttered as she changed lanes to pass a slow driver.

Amber looked askance at her. "I never suspected you'd have road rage."

"I don't have road rage!" she objected, glaring at the road. "Normally. I might be a little hungry and tired."

Amber smirked and propped her foot up on the dash. "Who are we going to see today?"

"My cousin. And, just be warned, she's awful. She actually managed to get kicked out of the coven for using too much black magic. Well, for getting caught using it by the wrong people." She twirled a curl around her finger. That had been a huge mess. Her mother had done a lot of damage control, but it had been yet another step on her coven's downward spiral into oblivion. Her grandmother had probably been rolling in her grave.

"Is it common for so many covens to use black magic whenever they can get away with it?" Amber asked. "I didn't know that many witches back in Texas, or here for that matter, but I thought it just wasn't done anymore."

"It's probably fifty-fifty," she said with a shrug. "Newer covens are more likely to be completely legal, but the older covens gained their power through spells that no one could consider white magic. They aren't about to give that up just because the laws have changed, and no one is going to rat them out."

Her cousin worked at a beauty shop owned by some elves that sold elf-spelled cosmetics in the front, and more interesting things in the basement, if you had the money. It was in a nice part of town; the kind of place you felt comfortable letting your kids run around alone. And, to be fair, it was safe for them. You only got into trouble if you pissed someone off, and then it wouldn't matter where you were.

The shop had a big parking lot filled with new, shiny cars. Ceri parked near the door, but didn't get out immediately.

"What?"

She sighed and yanked down the visor to use the mirror. "You can never tell anyone about this, but if I walk in there without looking perfect, we're just going to spend the whole time with her insulting my hair."

Amber raised a brow. "What's wrong with your hair?"

"Nothing," she said as she pulled a small tub of Friz-B-

Smooth out of the center console. She scooped the smallest amount possible out and rubbed it on her hands. "But she's a pompous turd-face. If we didn't need information, I wouldn't bother, but I'd rather spend as little time in there as possible."

Magic tingled on her palms. She waited for it to feel warm, then vigorously brushed her fingers through her hair. The curls detangled easily, then popped back into shape perfectly smooth and shiny. Her blonde hair practically sparkled in the sunlight.

"Will you hate me if I say that's actually kind of awesome?" Amber asked, leaning over and sniffing slightly. "You smell like fruit."

Ceri arranged the curls in the mirror and examined the final results. It *was* awesome. "I love the stuff, but it's expensive so I save it for special occasions. I don't need to look perfect all the time, and besides, any spellwork will make it fall out right away. This kind of elf magic is delicate." She nodded into the mirror and steeled herself for a miserable conversation. "Alright. Let's do this."

They hopped out of her car and headed inside. The first thing that hit her was the impossibly fresh scent of the store. It was spotless, as always. The shop was to the right and the salon area was to the left.

A tall, willowy elf with pastel pink hair was shampooing a customer's hair. Her hands danced through the air as she guided the water -- spelled to the perfect temperature of course -- over the woman's scalp. Elves used an elemental type magic and could manipulate the base elements, like water, fairly easily. The stronger and older they were, the larger quantity of the element they could manipulate. Even an elvish child could do what she was doing though.

"Welcome to Glow Up," a cheery saleswoman said, appearing from behind one of the shelves. Her ears weren't as pointy as an elf's usually were, so she probably had some human in her heritage. "How can we help you today?"

"Hi, I needed to see Siobhan," Ceri said, forcing herself to keep her hands where they were and not fidget with her hair. "I heard she has something in stock for discerning witches."

The saleswoman's smile stiffened slightly. "Of course! Come right this way."

Amber stuck close to her as they followed the woman through the shelves filled with glittering potions and spells that promised beauty, happiness, and confidence. It all worked, but it was also all very expensive. Witch's potions could do many of the same things, but anyone who could afford it used elf products instead. They were just classier. And tasted better if they were the sort you had to drink.

"If you can wait right here I'll see if she's free," the saleswoman said, gesturing toward a plush, red velvet couch. "Can I get your names?"

"You can tell her that her favorite cousin is here," Ceri replied with a smile. She didn't want anyone here having their names, it was bad enough they'd had to stop by.

"Alrighty, be right back!" The woman hurried through the 'Employee Only' door a few feet away, letting it swing shut behind her.

"Why do I feel so...refreshed?" Amber asked, sniffing slightly. "The air smells odd."

"They spell a little more oxygen into the air to give you an energy boost every time you visit the shop. It's all part of the experience."

Amber wandered toward the shelves and picked up a little vial that promised to change your eye color. She coughed when she saw the price tag on the bottom and quickly set it back down. Shaking her head, she walked back over to Ceri, putting her hands in her pockets.

"That cost more than I made in a month as a nurse," she said with a shudder.

Ceri laughed. "It takes them almost two weeks to make, and it's permanent, unlike most cosmetic spells. This is why elves have money coming out of their long, pointy ears."

The door the saleswoman had disappeared through reopened and she peeked her head out. "Siobhan will see you now."

They followed her into the back room. It looked completely normal. Concrete floors, stacks of boxes, and a small table for the staff to eat lunch at. The door that led to the basement was easy to miss. It was tucked behind some industrial shelving in the corner of the room.

"Go ahead," the saleswoman said, pointing at the door. "You can leave out the back when you're done, please."

Ceri nodded and took a brief second to compose herself before pulling the door open. Soft, flickering light shone at the bottom of the stairs. It was warm and inviting, but she knew that was all an illusion. Siobhan was as mean as their grandmother, but not quite as talented, which had made her bitter. It was an unfortunate combination.

The stairwell led them down into a cozy room. The light came from a fireplace, but the room wasn't hot like it should have been with a huge fire in one corner. Siobhan stood over a large cauldron stirring what smelled like chicken noodle soup. Knowing her, it could be anything.

Her long, red hair cascaded down her back in perfect, effortless waves. She turned to them with a welcoming smile that made her baby blue eyes sparkle. Nothing about her was real anymore. She'd darkened the red of her hair, lightened her eyes, erased all her freckles, and doubled the size of her boobs.

"Ceridwen! It's been too long," she exclaimed, hurrying over for a hug. Ceri endured the brief hug, patting her once on the back, before untangling herself from Siobhan's grasp. The witch's eyes turned to Amber, examining her intently. "Who is this with you? You've never brought company here before."

"This is my friend, Amber," Ceri said.

"Hmm, the rumors said she was your alpha," Siobhan said, cocking her head to the side. She walked toward Amber and held out her hand, which Amber shook firmly, never dropping her cousin's gaze. "You're definitely a werewolf, and surprisingly an alpha. I guess the rumors are true."

"That's not why we're here." She didn't want to spend forever down here discussing her personal life with the town gossip.

Siobhan turned back to Ceri and rolled her eyes. "Are you here to finally get that hair under control? The Frizz-B-Gone can only do so much, sweetie."

"Oh, come on, Siobhan. You can do better than that. Where are the insults about me getting kicked out of the house?" Ceri asked with a grin.

"That's too easy of a target, besides, your hair always bothered you more whether you admit it or not. Why else would you try to fix it just to see me?" She sashayed back to her cauldron, her tight pants accentuating her curves.

"I thought Ceri was exaggerating, but you really are a bitch," Amber said, crossing her arms.

Siobhan looked back over her shoulder with a smirk. "It's a family trait."

"Speaking of family traits, have you been selling supplies to any sorcerers lately?" Ceri asked.

Siobhan stopped stirring and turned around, raising a brow. "Not since Grandmother died, may her soul burn in hell." She narrowed her eyes at the two of them. "Why?"

"If you do, be a good cousin and let me know, please," Ceri said with a smile.

"Why should I? You aren't even in the coven anymore," she said, cocking her hip out to the side.

"You still want the spell, don't you?"

A muscle in Siobhan's jaw jumped as she ground her teeth together. The pleasant facade dropped from her features and she glared at Ceri. "She did not give it to you."

Ceri grinned, taking sick satisfaction at finally putting her cousin on the defensive. "I was her favorite. That's why you always hated me."

Siobhan's hands curled into fists. "I want it now."

"Grandmother would come out of her grave and strike me down if I just *gave* it to you," Ceri said, shaking her head. "You can have it for information. The name and the location of the sorcerer that just showed up in the area. I *know* you've heard something."

Siobhan's fingers twitched like she was considering throwing an attack. She straightened her shoulders instead and turned back to her cauldron instead. "I'll be in touch."

"Always a pleasure seeing you," Ceri said with a smile while nudging Amber toward the stairs. Siobhan didn't bother with a reply, she just glared at them while they headed back up to the storefront.

Ceri's hands were shaking by the time they made it outside. They hurried through the parking lot and climbed back into the car.

"What the hell was that about?" Amber demanded as soon as both doors were shut.

She sighed and rubbed her hands over her face. "My grandmother left me a spell that isn't in the family spellbook. It's something she created, one of dozens of powerful spells actually. The family thought she died without sharing them with anyone, but she gave them to me. All of them."

Amber sat back in shock. "Why you?"

She picked at the seam of her dress. "When I was around seventeen, I made a conscious choice not to follow in my family's footsteps. Before that, I was my grandmother's favorite. And her experiment, most likely. I got all the attention, all the lessons, and it made the rest of my family jealous. But, anyhow, I have the spells, and there's one that Siobhan has always wanted."

"What does it do?"

"It binds a demon to your control for one night," Ceri said quietly. "It's supposed to be a way to get what you want from a demon without having to pay the price."

"Shit," Amber said, sitting back in her seat.

"It doesn't..." Ceri hesitated, shaking her head. "It doesn't work. My grandmother died trying to use it, but, uh, no one knows that."

"Did they think she just fell over dead?"

"No, I made it look like an attack by another coven," Ceri whispered, her hands shaking. She'd never told anyone this before. That one little lie had launched a war between their covens. The Blackwood coven had been trying to ruin them before that, so they'd been the perfect cover. "I hated my grandmother, but watching that demon kill her was terrifying. And I blamed myself for a while even though it was my grandmother's own fault. What she did was insanely stupid, but she thought she was invincible."

"Seeing that demon show up in our house must have been a shock then," Amber said, staring out the passenger window with a guilty expression.

"It was, and I still don't trust him, but he'll abide by the bargain," Ceri said with a shrug. "When my grandmother tried to bind the demon, it pissed it off. This is a different situation."

Amber laughed humorlessly. "Pissing them off is definitely not a good idea."

"Yeah," Ceri said with a weak smile.

"Well, let's get that stuff Tommy wanted for dinner," Amber said, visibly shaking off her thoughts.

Ceri nodded and put the car in drive. They'd keep searching for the sorcerer, but Siobhan's contacts were their best bet for finding him before he found them.

CHAPTER 32

TOMMY

*T*ommy signed *no* emphatically, then crossed his arms. Woggy's bottom lip trembled and he signed *outside* again before throwing himself down on the floor and squealing.

"What the hell is that noise?" Derek shouted from the living room.

"Woggy," Tommy shouted back. He headed toward the kitchen with a sigh. He was going to have to bribe the pixie with chicken again to get him to calm down. Woggy hated being cooped up inside, but if he let him out, he was going to get attacked by the other pixies that had moved into the yard.

"Did you pinch him or something?" Derek asked walking up next to him at the end of the hallway where Woggy was having his temper tantrum.

"No, I just won't let him outside," Tommy said tiredly, tugging his beanie down on his head.

"Because of those other pixies?"

"Yeah."

Captain Jack peeked around the corner, watching the scene disdainfully with his one good eye. He prowled toward Woggy, sniffed him, then planted his paw on the pixie's head. Woggy's squeals were cut off and he flailed, trying to get free.

"No, bad kitty," Tommy said firmly, pushing his paw off of Woggy's head.

The cat swished his tail and gave him a dirty look.

"I think Captain Jack had the right idea. You're encouraging Woggy if you keep giving him treats when he acts like this." Derek took another bite of the bread he was holding. "Why don't you just get the other pixies out of the yard?"

"I'm not sure how to do that without hurting them."

"Then Woggy is just going to be stuck inside," Derek said pragmatically. "You want to get a little training in while Amber and Ceri are out?"

Tommy nodded. He'd been feeling especially useless lately. Amber had asked him to stick around the house while they were out so Evangeline and Eloise weren't left alone, but it felt more like she was just worried about taking him somewhere potentially dangerous.

He sighed. At least everyone liked his cooking. Maybe he'd just be a werewolf chef. Make food, not war.

"Yeah, let's go ahead and train. I just need to go check on Eloise real quick," he said, pushing himself back up to his feet.

He hurried upstairs and knocked on the door to the room

right next to his. Eloise spent all day with Evangeline in their room resting. She was recovering, but still too sick to do much more than sleep all day, and Evangeline refused to leave her side.

The door opened, but Evangeline didn't open it wide enough for him to come in. "What?"

"Do you need anything? I'm about to go outside for a little while." Every single interaction with Evangeline had gone the same. She glared at him. He felt awkward. Then she slammed the door in his face.

"You brought up a gallon of water and two plates of food an hour ago. We're fine," she said sarcastically.

"Great--" The door shut in his face right on cue. He pressed his lips together and turned on his heel, hurrying back downstairs.

"She seems friendly," Derek commented, nodding his head toward her room.

"She's grumpier than Amber," Tommy muttered as he pulled on his shoes.

Derek shuddered in mock horror. "That's terrifying."

～

*H*e tried to punch quickly, but not too hard. Derek slapped it out of the way and he stumbled forward a half step. Derek's leg hit the back of his knees and swept his legs out from under him. He hit the ground hard and all the air rushed from his lungs.

"You alright?" Derek asked, staring down at him with concern.

Tommy let his head fall back against the grass. "I think I'm getting worse. How is that even possible?"

Derek scratched his jaw. "I'm probably not teaching you right. And you're too worried about hurting me. It might be time to talk to Amber."

He groaned. "I'm not ready for that kind of embarrassment." A car turned down the driveway and he scrambled to his feet. "That's them."

They both hurried back inside and Tommy met them at the door. Ceri walked in, her arms full of bags.

"How much did you get?" he asked as he took in the huge haul of groceries.

Amber walked in behind her carrying just as much and kicked the door shut. "Way too much probably, but Genevieve texted us with a bunch more stuff she wanted."

Tommy scratched the back of his head. "Well, I guess we'll have lots of leftovers."

He followed them into the kitchen and began unloading the bags, trying to organize by item.

"Do you know when Gen is supposed to be back?" Amber asked as she dumped a bag of pears into the fruit drawer in the refrigerator.

He shook his head. "She just said before dinner, which based on her usual schedule, means after we've all eaten."

"Something tells me she's going to be here two hours early this time," Ceri said with a snort. "I'm starting to worry her family is awful and judgmental."

"Did you find anything out about the sorcerer?" Tommy asked. Neither of them looked particularly upset, so they probably hadn't found anything useful.

Amber waffled her hand. "Ceri asked her cousin to let us know if she hears anything. If that doesn't pan out in the next couple of days I might go back to Eloise's house and see if I can find something. For now though, Evangeline is safe, so that's all that matters. No one knows where she is. We can take our time figuring this out."

Tommy had a feeling Evangeline wouldn't be so patient, but he kept that thought to himself. "Are they joining us for dinner?"

"Not sure. I asked Eloise earlier and she said she'd love to if she was awake, but Evangeline didn't look enthused about it," Amber said with a shrug.

There was a knock on the door and Amber frowned, then recognition dawned on her face. "Why is Steven here?"

"No clue," Ceri said.

Amber hurried over to the front door. "Hey, Gen isn't here, but you can come in while you wait for her."

Steven sighed deeply. "She didn't tell you, did she?"

Tommy had to clamp his hand over his mouth to suppress his laughter. Ceri caught his eye and turned away, her shoulders shaking slightly. Steven was a nice guy, but he and Genevieve were a mess as a couple.

Steven followed Amber into the kitchen and she wrapped her arms around his shoulders. "Steven is meeting Genevieve's parents tonight!"

He was blushing furiously and looked like he might be sick. His skin definitely wasn't that shade of pale green normally.

"That's awesome!" Ceri exclaimed.

"She was supposed to be here by now though. She said

she'd be home by four," he said, adjusting his shirt, which had come untucked.

Tommy laughed. "She's always late, don't worry about it," he paused, cocking his head to the side. "She's actually coming down the road right now."

Steven's nervousness immediately fell away and he pulled out a notepad. "How far away is the entrance exactly? Have you noticed your hearing getting better the longer you've been a werewolf?"

Amber backed away with a smirk and gave him a thumbs up for distracting Steven. He glared at her and whispered, *"Traitor."*

"What was that?" Steven asked, looking up and adjusting his glasses.

"Nothing," Tommy said quickly. "And no, not really. It's just easier to sift through all the noise now. It was just chaos for a while."

Steven nodded and scribbled down his answer. Tommy sighed and pulled out a cutting board. So much for getting to relax while he cooked.

CHAPTER 33

GENEVIEVE

Genevieve tucked her hair behind her ears and tried to smooth a wrinkle out of her shirt.

Steven grabbed her by the shoulders and turned her away from the mirror. "You look beautiful, quit fussing. Is your family really so bad?"

She sighed and dropped her head to his shoulder. "No, they're just...freaking perfect all the time. And I'm not. I'm a mess."

"Were they really hard on you growing up?" He wrapped his arms around her and she let herself enjoy the comfort, even though she knew she was overreacting.

"No, I mean actually perfect. They're super supportive and want me to follow my dreams and be happy. But I keep screwing everything up. I barely got a job with the degree they paid for, and I don't stay in touch even though they invite me to everything. I'm such an asshole."

"That sounds like it'd be nice. Why are you freaking out?" he asked, pushing her back slightly so he could look at her face.

She glared at him. "Will you just let me be irrationally freaked out without trying to fix it?"

He looked completely baffled by that request. Steven was logic personified. He was a fixer of problems and a scientist at heart. Emotions were not his strong suit.

"Gen, how did you want these place settings again?" Amber shouted from downstairs.

"Ugh, I should go help her," she said, pulling away from Steven and hurrying toward the stairs. He followed, and she knew he was shaking his head at her, but he hadn't had to grow up with her parents.

Amber was in the dining room examining the table. It was already filled with food and each place setting was neatly arranged. They'd busted out the good china they'd found in one of the cabinets for the occasion.

"It's perfect," she said as she hurried over to straighten one of the spoons.

"Uh huh," Amber said, raising a brow at her.

The doorbell rang and her heart stopped for a split second before jumping into overdrive. She started to scramble for the door, but Amber grabbed her, forcing her to be still.

"Calm. Down." Her alpha's eyes flashed red like it was an order, and, despite herself, her muscles un-bunched slightly.

She took a deep breath and nodded. "I'm calm."

"That's a lie, but at least you're trying," Amber said, shoving her toward the door. "If they're mean, I'll kick them out."

"They're not…" she sighed. "You'll see."

Bracing herself, she walked toward the door. Each step made her heart stutter. It had been over six months since she'd seen them. She'd been dodging dinner invites and coffee dates with increasingly weak excuses, but she hadn't wanted to update them on her lack of a life. At least now she had a job to talk about.

She opened the door and was immediately tackled and wrapped up in a hug so tight she could hardly breathe. Blonde hair tickled the bottom of her nose and she realized her sister was here.

"Susannah? What are you doing here?" she exclaimed, hugging her younger sister back. "I thought you were still in Washington."

Her sister stepped back, beaming at her. "I flew down to see you after mom told me you were a werewolf now! That is *wicked* cool."

"Are you gonna let us in, kiddo?" her dad asked, holding up a pie dish.

"Oh, yeah, sorry," she said, opening the door wider and stepping back. Her dad and sister filed in, looking around the entry way curiously. "Where's mom?"

"She's grabbing something from the car, she'll be right in," her dad said. "Now, where can I put this?"

Amber walked into the living room just then with Tommy trailing nervously behind her. "Hi, Mr. Bisset, my name is Amber, I'm Genevieve's alpha."

They started the introductions, and Tommy took the pie dish from her dad. Genevieve watched it all in a slight daze. Seeing her family here with her pack was like two alternate realities colliding.

"I see your hair is still pink," her mother said from right behind her, startling her.

"Yeah, the law firm didn't..." She stopped when she saw her mother. She was wearing a wig. No. That wasn't a wig. She'd dyed her hair pink. And she was wearing a shirt that said *Bitten = Born* in...glitter. "What. Are. You. Wearing."

Her mother beamed at her and struck a pose. "I made it myself."

"Why is your hair pink?" Genevieve could feel herself becoming slightly hysterical. Her voice cracked as she attempted to keep from shouting.

"I retired from my job! My last day was Thursday, so I went to the salon, and got my hair dyed. I just thought it'd be fun, it always looked so cute on you," her mother said, her smile faltering slightly at Genevieve's expression.

She put her hand over her mouth, completely taken aback, then burst out laughing. There was nothing else she could do. She pulled her mother with a big hug. "You are so ridiculous."

Her mother laughed, clearly relieved, and hugged her back. "I'm too old to be not-ridiculous."

She should have known her mother was going to show up and do something like this. That was how she showed her love. She threw herself behind you one thousand percent. That made it all the more awful when you failed, but she'd never known how to tell her that.

Pulling away from the hug she turned toward the pack who were watching with varying degrees of shock and amusement. "Mom, this my pack."

"You must be Amber," her mother said, walking straight toward Genevieve's alpha.

"I am," Amber confirmed with a smile.

"Thank you for saving my daughter." Her mother wrapped Amber up in a big hug then stepped back, keeping both hands on her arms. "Not many people could have done what you did. Or would have even stepped in that night to help a stranger."

Amber looked intensely uncomfortable with the thanks, which made Genevieve relax even further. At least she wasn't the only one overwhelmed by it all.

Steven shuffled forward, looking at her expectantly, but before she could introduce him her father approached him and crossed his arms.

"You're dating my daughter," he stated without preamble, staring Steven down.

"Uh, yes, yes, he is," Genevieve said, hurrying over and linking her arm with his. "Dad, this is Steven, Steven, this is my Dad, Levi Bissett."

Her dad shook Steven's hand firmly. "My daughter can take care of herself, but you should know that she has me for backup. And I'm not scared to go to jail."

Steven swallowed, his face paling. "I would never hurt--"

"Ooookay, let's not do this," she said, pushing her dad away. "No threats, just get to know him."

Her dad's face split into a grin. "Oh, come on, I totally had him going. It's my right as a father to terrorize your suitors."

Steven relaxed slightly, but she could still hear his heart beating so fast she thought it legitimately might explode.

Her mother whacked her father on the arm. "Be nice or we won't get invited back for dinner."

Ceri appeared at the top of the stairs with Eloise, thankfully interrupting the conversation. Evangeline was on the woman's other side and they gently helped her walk down. She had a hoodie on with the hood pulled so far forward you could hardly see her face. Talk about anti-social.

"This is Eloise and Evangeline," Amber explained to her parents. "They're staying with us for a while. Eloise was in a...car crash."

Amber could keep a secret, but she was a crappy liar. It seemed like those were the same thing, but Genevieve had learned they were two very different skills. Her sister raised her brow, but neither she nor her parents called Amber out on it. Genevieve sighed in relief. Maybe her parents had gotten better about being too nosy.

The whole group filed into the dining room and sat down. Susannah grabbed the chair right next to her while her parents took the two seats across the table. Steven managed to get the seat on her other side, leaving her completely boxed in as the center of attention.

Amber smirked at her from the head of the table, clearly able to read all her emotions. Genevieve cursed the pack bond and its lack of privacy.

"I kind of thought you might look different, but you don't," Susannah said, inspecting her closely. "What does your wolf look like?"

"It's black. I'm not as big as some werewolves, but I'm fast," she said.

"Can you shift for us later?" Susannah asked, her eyes going wide with excitement.

"That would be awesome to see," her mother agreed. "I don't think I've ever seen a werewolf shift in person before."

"Uh, sure," she said hesitantly. "Well, I'll show you my wolf. I'm not stripping down naked in front of you."

Steven wrapped his arm around her shoulders. "She is a very beautiful wolf."

Her mother practically melted at that, looking at the two of them with so much hope in her eyes. Genevieve forced a smile onto her face. Tommy really needed to get the rest of the food out here soon so she could distract herself.

CHAPTER 34

AMBER

*A*mber grabbed the mashed potatoes and handed them to Mr. Bissett, or Levi as he had insisted they call him.

"These are excellent, Tommy," Levi said, scooping a third serving onto his plate. "Genevieve never ate this good at our house growing up. She was forced to survive off sandwiches and frozen dinners."

"Oh, stop it," Genevieve's mother said, smacking his arm. "She got overcooked meatloaf every Sunday too."

Tommy blushed under all the praise, but he was happier than she'd seen him all week. Amber had been worried this visit would be awkward, and it was a little with Evangeline sitting at the end of the table looking miserable, but it was also nice. The problem was, she hated it.

Amber had started questioning whether or not she was a good person about two minutes after she watched her brother die, but now she knew it for sure. Genevieve's family was basically perfect. Maybe a little too enthusiastic to the point where they might smother you if you let them, but they loved her. She'd never been so jealous in her life.

Derek caught her eye and she knew he could tell what she was thinking. Clearing her throat, she put down her fork and excused herself to the kitchen. She'd find something to bring back to cover her absence, but she needed a minute alone or her feelings were going to flood the pack bond and freak everyone out.

She'd learned to control that on her trip back to visit her family right about the time her mother had ordered her to leave as soon as she'd walked through the front door.

Derek released her from the tight hug and she shifted on her feet, waiting for the rest of the family to react. They never got a chance.

"Get out," her mother said, her voice cracking. An angry red flush was crawling up her neck and her jaw was clenched so tight Amber wondered how her teeth hadn't cracked.

"Miranda, that's enough," her father said gruffly, striding into the room.

Her mother glared at him, then turned and walked away, disappearing into the hallway. Amber watched her go and wondered how fast she could get back to the airport. She clamped down on the pack bond so tight she could barely feel the others at all.

"I know what you're thinking," her father said, walking up and

grounding her with a hand on her shoulder. "But you ain't leaving yet."

"Why the hell shouldn't I?"

"Because I said so. Your mother is just shocked, that's all. She'll come around by tomorrow."

She hadn't come around. Her mother had stayed as far away as she could the whole week until the day she was leaving; when she'd found out Derek was planning on going back to Portland with her.

Amber yanked open the freezer and pulled out the ice cream. It needed to thaw a little before they ate it with the pie the Bissett's had brought.

She heard the chairs in the dining room pushing back, and something about starting a bonfire. The air shifted behind her and she heard, and smelled, Derek walking up behind her. She was starting to get used to the enhanced senses, but being able to *smell* someone coming was probably always going to be strange.

"You okay?"

"I'm great," she said turning around with a smile plastered on her face. "I take it everyone is headed outside to start a bonfire or something?"

"Yeah, nothing like a fall night outside under the stars," he said, still looking at her with concern. "We used to do that all the time when we were kids."

"Dylan always tried to set the grass on fire," she said, looking down at her feet.

"And you always stomped it out before it could spread." Derek sighed and shoved his hands in his pockets. He was silent for a moment, but finally looked up at her with a determined expression. "Mom is just...she's being an asshole."

Amber's eyebrows shot up in surprise. Everyone always danced around the issue, talked about how she was grieving. "What?"

"She's being an asshole. Dad lost a kid too, and we all lost a brother. You lost your other half. I mean, you two were never apart when you were kids," he said, shaking his head. "She has no right to blame you for what happened, and we've all let her get away with it for too long because we didn't know how to handle it either."

She gnawed on the inside of her cheek to keep from crying. She hated crying, and she certainly didn't want to cry at the dinner party for Genevieve's parents. "I just can't stop wishing she'd forgive me."

Derek dragged his hand over his mouth. "I'm sorry. Me too."

The others could probably hear them even though they were outside, but no one was coming inside to bother them. An unspoken rule had developed that they just didn't comment on things they overheard. Privacy had become difficult with their enhanced senses, so they tried to just pretend it still existed.

She took a deep breath and opened a cabinet, pulling out some paper plates. "Let's take the pie out there so we can enjoy it by the fire."

Derek nodded and came to help her, letting the conversation drop. Sometimes, certain things just couldn't be fixed, and she didn't want to wallow in it. Her mother had stolen enough of her happiness. She had a new family now, and her brother was here. They were going to build something together that she was excited about. She wouldn't let the past keep her from enjoying what she had now. Dylan wouldn't have wanted that.

They headed outside, their arms full of plates, forks, and desserts. Genevieve's mom had an arm around Tommy and her dad was helping Ceri start the fire.

Amber smiled. "Ceri, can't you just do that with magic?"

"No, no," Levi said, waving his hand at Amber. "We're going to do this the hard way. It's more satisfying."

Ceri shrugged and kept helping him place little twigs in a tee-pee formation. Amber set her pile of things down and went to join them.

CHAPTER 35

AMBER

*A*mber pulled on her softest flannel pajama pants and her favorite worn shirt. She'd eaten too much pie and was ready to face plant in her bed. The pack was still wired but the noise wouldn't keep her up tonight. It was comforting.

She pulled her covers back and slid in between the freshly washed sheets. They were a little cold, but she ran hot these days. With a happy sigh, she tugged the comforter up to her chin and squished the pillow up so that it cradled her head perfectly. Her eyes slipped shut and she felt her entire body relax into the soft mattress.

Genevieve's shout echoed down the hallway. "Amber, we have a problem!"

A spike of panic shot through the pack bond and she

jolted upright, all remnants of sleepiness vanishing immediately. She jumped out of bed and ran out of her room. Her fluffy socks slipped on the hardwood floor as she rounded the corner and she had to grab the wall to keep from falling.

The pack was gathered in the living room, their eyes glued to the television. The first thing she saw was Evangeline's picture. Bold red text cut across the bottom of the picture, "DEMON THREAT?". Her heart dropped into her stomach and the demon mark on her chest flared to life.

Genevieve turned up the volume and the reporter's voice filled the room.

"The areas where magic does not work have been growing. Early this morning, one of those spots was discovered in downtown Portland. Before today, something like this hadn't been seen outside of rural areas. Mr. Hudson, a representative with ATD, an organization devoted to stamping out black magic, is here with us today claiming he has information on what is causing these spots to pop up," the reporter turned in her chair and the camera shifted, another face popping up on the television.

Amber recognized him immediately. He'd been there when they rescued Evangeline, but it wasn't the sorcerer, it was the half-angel. This wasn't good. The demon materialized next to her, drifting toward the television.

"Thank you for having me, Ms. Laramie," Mr. Hudson said with a brilliant smile.

The reporter blushed slightly before responding. "Mr. Hudson, you're claiming that demons are behind the destruction of magic in these areas?"

"I am, however the threat is even more insidious than

that," he said, his flirtatious grin turning serious. He looked directly into the camera, every word intent and clear. "The demons have always been a threat against humanity and the supernatural races. We used to be protected from them because even a summoned demon that has escaped will be banished back to their realm when the sun rises. However, they have found a way to walk among us by creating hybrid demonic abominations through mating with humans, witches, and other supernatural races. These creatures are now using their infernal powers to consume magic, which is part of the very fabric of our world."

"These are very serious accusations. Do you have any proof?" the reporter asked.

It was absolute crap, but everyone was going to believe it. Evangeline was kind of moody, but she wasn't doing anything nefarious. She couldn't use magic at all as far as Amber could tell, much less eat it. Amber had to wonder if Angel would do something like that though. She glanced at him. He looked angry, offended even, but he didn't look guilty.

"I do. However, I must warn your viewers that what they are about to see is disturbing," Mr. Hudson said, shaking his head slightly.

A "Viewer Discretion is Advised" warning flashed on the screen before a video started playing. A house was engulfed in flames. A figure burst up into the air, and appeared to be holding someone. Through the smoke you could make out horns and fiery wings, but their face was obscured.

The video ended abruptly and switched back to the reporter, who looked truly alarmed, and Mr. Hudson.

"This was a recent attack by the demon. It has been masquerading as a human teenager named Evangeline Deschamps from a small town less than an hour from Portland, called Timber. As you know, another town recently had an area appear where magic no longer works. We believe this demon fled to Portland, and this morning, another spot appeared. The pattern is clear."

"Where is this demon hiding in Portland? There haven't been any sightings of a fiery winged creature flying over the city," the reporter said, chuckling nervously.

Mr. Hudson's frown deepened. "My organization believes she is being harbored by a werewolf pack. We're not sure which pack, but we *will* find them."

A picture of Amber in wolf form appeared next to Evangeline.

"Shit," Amber said.

Genevieve looked at her with wide eyes. "That is an understatement."

CHAPTER 36

EVANGELINE

*E*vangeline stopped at the bottom of the stairs. Her face was on the tv screen. The witch looked back at her with a worried expression that made her want to shrink back into the woodwork.

"Have they found us?" Her question seemed to startle the rest of the pack, who apparently hadn't noticed her walking down the stairs. That wasn't a good sign. She tugged the hood of her jacket down a little farther to make sure they couldn't see her hair. She wouldn't have even come downstairs after sunset but she'd heard them freaking out and had to know what was going on.

"No," Amber, the alpha, said. She tried to say it like it was a fact, but Evangeline could hear the *not yet* that she hadn't spoken aloud. They had her freaking picture on the news.

"But they're going to," she said angrily. The least these people could do was be honest with her. Kadrithan never was -- he wouldn't even tell her his *real* name -- but she'd expected better from the pack for some reason.

"Until we track down the sorcerer and this pretentious blond dude you'll have to stay in the house, but that's doable," Amber insisted. Tommy nodded along eagerly, but he always did that when his alpha spoke.

The witch, at least, didn't look convinced. Evangeline got the impression Ceri hated her, but she'd saved her mother's life. So, she didn't hate her enough to hurt her. Maybe just enough to not worry about her *feelings*.

"They have a picture of you, too," she said, pointing at the television. "They're going to look here eventually." She was half expecting someone to knock on the door right then.

"Can they identify you by a picture of your wolf?" Amber's brother asked, casting a suspicious glance at her. She wasn't surprised a human would be wary. They tended to be warier of anyone supernatural that might be a threat.

"I...don't know," Amber said with a frown. "I doubt it. It's not like it's on file somewhere."

Genevieve shook her head. "Everyone saw you at the Trials though. Like, every werewolf in a hundred square miles."

"Freaking out isn't going to help anything," Ceri said, finally stepping into the conversation. "They can't prove it was Amber based off a fuzzy picture."

She felt the air shift at her back and looked over her shoulder. Her uncle was there, watching the drama, as usual.

"I won't let them take you," he said, watching the news play on impassively. He didn't speak out loud, just in her mind. It was something he didn't do often because she tended to ignore him when he did it.

This time she didn't. "You couldn't stop them when they attacked the house. Why would next time be any different?" she replied silently.

Amber glanced at them, her eyes lingering on Kadrithan before her brother drew her attention again. Other than Eloise, she was the only one that could see him when he showed up like this.

"They revealed their hand and lost their greatest strength. The element of surprise. Now, if you would just accept your heritage and ––"

"SHUT UP," she shouted mentally, as loud as she could. "I won't do it."

He shook his head. "You will, and dragging it out is just a waste of time."

And that was why she normally just ignored him. It was like talking to a brick wall. Only that brick wall thought it knew everything.

The pack could debate whatever useless plans it wanted, but it was all pointless. She turned away and walked back up the stairs as quietly as she could. No one tried to stop her. Her uncle just drifted down the stairs, probably to go bother Amber again. She should probably just keep walking right out of the house and disappear forever.

She shoved her hands into the pocket of her hoodie and curled them into fists. Her mother wasn't going to be healed enough to leave anytime soon, but even if she was, as long as she was with her, her mother would be in danger.

At some point she was going to have to really leave. Maybe the pack could fix all this in another couple of days, but if they couldn't...She had to protect her mother. She wouldn't let them hurt her again.

CHAPTER 37

AMBER

*A*mber stood in front of the pack and tried not to look as nervous as she felt. Her mind was whirring through all the possible catastrophes that might be headed their way. No one knew Evangeline was with them yet, but it was only a matter of time.

Everyone would be looking for her now, and Zachariah knew a werewolf pack and a witch had rescued her. It wouldn't take them long to connect the dots once they started asking around. Word had traveled fast about her odd little pack.

Angel was floating around her brother, but he wasn't being silly, he was just watching them. The demon's sense of humor hadn't returned along with him. Instead, he was everything she had expected a demon to be. Demanding. Mean. Dangerous.

Clearing her throat, she decided to just get this over with. "When I took the mark from Thallan, I didn't think I would have to pay the debt anytime soon. He'd had it for years. I was just...fed up that day. I'd been fired and evicted, and we were running out of options." She paused, dragging her hands roughly through her hair. "Anyhow, it was a decision I made without y'all, so, if you want out, I'll find a way for you to join a different pack. And, of course, I can try to cure you."

Genevieve immediately stood and put her hands on her hips. "I'm not going anywhere. You risked all of this for us, the least we can do is support you now that you have to deal with the fallout."

Tommy nodded along. "I'm not leaving. We're in this together."

There was a long silence, and Ceri stayed still, staring at her hands. Amber's heart dropped into her stomach. She could barely breathe at the idea of losing one of her pack, and Ceri was special. She understood Amber better than Tommy and Genevieve did. Amber curled her hand into a fist as she waited for Ceri to say what they all knew she was thinking.

Genevieve looked back at her and broke the silence. "If you're going to bitch out, then just say it and leave."

Amber's eyes grew wide. "Gen, don't say that. She's allowed to leave if she --"

"I can speak for myself," Ceri interrupted. She rose from the couch and glared at Genevieve. "I'm not sure what we're doing is right."

"So, you don't want to help this girl?" Genevieve demanded, looking sincerely offended.

"She's a demon," Ceri said, exasperated.

"She's also an angel. And from what I've seen, she's just your average teenage girl who's done nothing wrong, but people are trying to kill her because she's different. You lose your shit if someone tries to kill a pixie, but you'll let them kill her?"

Ceri stiffened. "I'm not saying she should die, but--"

"I don't want to hear the *but*," Genevieve snapped. "She either deserves to die, or she doesn't. There is no caveat."

"Evangeline is scared," Tommy interjected, finally speaking up. "She's terrified that someone else is going to get hurt because of her. How could we turn our back on her even if there wasn't a demon mark involved?"

"I want to help Evangeline, I just don't want to help *him*," Ceri said angrily. Her face was flushed with anger. "This demon is using Evangeline somehow, and we're letting him. Helping him even. We have no idea what the consequences might be."

Amber looked at the demon. He looked back, his expression neutral. Nothing Ceri said seemed to have bothered him. She had the same concern as Ceri, she just hadn't wanted to think about it too hard.

"Well I'm not willing to let Evangeline die just to keep a demon from possibly carrying out a nefarious plan," Genevieve said, crossing her arms.

Ceri pinched the bridge of her nose and sighed. "I'm not either. I just hate this."

"So do I," Amber admitted, shoving her hands in her pockets. "I'm sorry."

Ceri dropped her arms and pushed back her shoulders. "I've waffled enough. After everything you've done for us, there's no way I'd ever leave. We're in this together, whether it's good or bad. We'll get through this, and then we'll be free from the demon."

Angel drifted behind Ceri, invisible to her and grinned darkly. "You'll never be free of me, Amber. Not if I get my way."

She ground her teeth together and ignored the taunt. "You can always change your mind, any of you."

Genevieve marched over and wrapped Amber in a hug. "Shut up."

She let the warmth of the pack bond soothe her for a moment.

~

*A*mber was bone tired. Tommy had passed out on the couch after their conversation. Ceri and Gen were outside on the porch talking about something just quietly enough that she couldn't hear. She grabbed a blanket and laid it carefully over Tommy. He didn't stir.

Sleeping like this, he looked so young. He *was* young. And she'd drug him even deeper into a dangerous world. She dragged a hand down her face as she walked down the hall. Maybe tonight she'd be able to just sleep.

Evangeline was upstairs. She could still hear her heartbeat, so she hadn't run off. Yet. Eloise was up there with her, sedated once again so she could finish healing. Amber pushed her bedroom door open and caught a whiff of cat.

Her eyes adjusted to the dark room and she saw a fluffy lump on her pillow. She ground her teeth together in irritation. The last thing she needed was a mangy cat sneaking into her room. She must have forgotten to shut her door in her haste to get out to the living room to see what was going on.

She walked over and picked him up, dumping him unceremoniously on the floor. "Shoo," she said, waving her hands at him before climbing in bed.

"Mrow," he said irritably.

"I don't care, get out," she said, pointing at the door. His tail swished unhappily as he climbed down from the bed.

Her sheets were still cool, but they didn't have that same super fresh feel and the cat had squished all the fluff out of her pillow. She smacked it a few times to get it back to normal and laid down with an angry huff.

Captain Jack hopped back up on the bed, walked over her legs, and curled up against her knee. Sighing, she scooted farther down in the bed then flipped her pillow over to the clean side and curled up under the covers. Her movements disrupted his position. She felt him circle a few more times before curling up against her back.

Despite herself, the warmth and steady, slow beat of his heart made all the tension bleed out of her shoulders. He was still annoying, but he could stay for the night. As long as he left her alone. Her eyes slipped shut and she fell asleep.

CHAPTER 38

CERI

The snow was feather soft and freshly fallen. She curled her toes into it, expecting to feel icy cold seeping into her skin, but there was nothing. Neither heat nor cold. Her entire body felt...neutral.

The sparkling powder stretched out in every direction as far as she could see. The wind had blown it into drifts like sand dunes, but there was nothing to break up the endless white. No trees. No people. No life.

She took a deep breath and felt her lungs and chest move, yet, when she looked down, she was nothing more than a formless shadow. It was a surreal mix of real and not real. She lifted her ghostly hand and moved her fingers one by one. The shadow shifted, showing glimpses of the hand she knew was there, but couldn't quite see.

Content she wouldn't float away, she started walking. She didn't have a particular destination in mind but felt the urge to move. This was a time to let her intuition guide her, rather than her logical mind. She had no idea why the spirit had brought her here.

As she walked, she realized she was headed uphill. She paused and looked behind her. It looked like that way led up as well. Shaking off the dizziness that caused, she turned back around and continued. There was no point in trying to make sense of it.

The powdery snow firmed beneath her feet as she walked, then gave way to rock. Wind tugged at her hair and whipped her skirt around her legs. She blinked and found herself at the top of a mountain on a narrow ledge. Despite knowing this was only a vision, her heart caught in her throat as she looked down from the dizzying height.

She picked up her pace, hugging close to the cliff face. The wind blew harder and harder. Her footing slipped and she dug her fingers into the rock, but the wind only grew stronger. A sudden gust lifted her from her feet and tossed her into the air.

A scream caught in her throat as she grasped uselessly at the air. Another current of wind caught her and she was flung upward toward the top of the mountain. Tears stung at her eyes from the force of the wind. She forced herself not to look down again.

The wind shifted and she was thrown forward, landing in a pile of snow that went up her nose and blinded her for a moment. She pushed up to her hands and knees and shook her head to clear it, coughing slightly.

"Oh, sorry about that," a melodic voice said, drifting past her like a breeze. "You're heavier than I expected."

Ceri looked around but didn't see anyone. "Where are you?"

"I'm right here," the voice replied as a breeze danced through her hair.

She lifted her hand and trailed her fingers through the wind. It felt almost solid. "Are you...air? Or wind?"

"I am not all of it, only my part," it replied.

"Are you a spirit?"

It swirled around her as though it were thinking. "That's a good word for it in your language."

"Have you been visiting me through the owl?" she asked as she finally pushed to her feet, brushing the snow from her ethereal body.

"Yes," it replied, sounding pleased she recognized it. "I saw you through the veil like a beacon and felt you calling to me. You need guidance."

"Something bad is coming, isn't it?" she asked.

A shimmery creature with a body like a ribbon formed in front of her. Its body drooped forlornly. "Something very bad."

"Is it the sorcerer?"

The spirit shook its head. "He is only the beginning."

"Can I stop it?" she asked, the sense of doom growing in her chest.

The spirit drifted closer. "I don't know. No one can tell the future. I can only warn you."

"What is the sorcerer trying to do?" She turned in a circle, trying to keep the spirit in sight. It floated around her, it's body undulating like an eel.

"It's not about him, he's just the beginning. A tool," the spirit said again.

"Who is he working for?"

The spirit charged at her and she fell back, sinking into the snow. It covered her chest and her legs, then her face.

She was falling again. Through darkness and absolute silence. Then, there was fire. The flames roared, reaching out across the inky blackness, but it was met with bright, searing light. The two collided with a deafening crash.

She jerked with a gasp and found herself back in her work room, breathing like she'd just run a race. Her head was spinning and for a moment, it was hard to tell which way was up. She wiggled her feet to ground herself and forcibly slowed her breathing, letting out a slow exhale.

As the room came back into focus, she saw Derek was sitting in front of her. He looked worried. He reached out like he wanted to touch her, but kept his hand hovering in the air. "Ceri, can you hear me?"

She blinked a few times and unclenched her fingers. "Yes. Sorry. How long have you been sitting there?"

He still looked skeptical that she was alright. "About ten minutes. I was about to call Amber."

She looked up at the clock. Only an hour had passed since she entered the vision. It had felt like longer. "It's okay, I mean, you can tell her, but I'm okay."

"What were you doing?"

She uncurled her legs and grimaced at the pins and needles feeling in her foot. Next time, she needed to just lay down. There was no way she could explain what she'd just seen. It hadn't made any sense. "It was a vision. I know it sounds crazy, even for a witch, but being a part of this pack has changed my magic a little. I have a stronger connection to the spirit world, and one of them sent me a vision."

"A vision of what?" he asked, brows furrowed tightly together. He and Amber had similar eyes, but his were piercing. The way they contrasted with his dark brown hair made it hard to tear her eyes away from his face.

"I'm not sure. It was another warning, but either the spirits don't know, or can't tell me, exactly what is coming." She rubbed her fingers over her temples. Her head ached slightly, but that was to be expected with the amount of magic she was using lately. Maintaining the shield that protected Evangeline was a constant drain.

He extended his hand and helped her to her feet. "Do you think someone's going to try to hurt the pack?"

"Yes and no. I'm not sure it's about us, in particular, just that we're going to be caught up in it. My instincts are telling me Evangeline is involved, but I'm not sure how," she said with a shrug. "I'll talk to Amber about it whenever she gets back. There's not much we can do until we find this sorcerer."

"He's working for Zachariah, that guy from the news, right? Maybe you can track him down and find the sorcerer that way," he suggested.

The vision of fire and light colliding flashed through her mind again at the mention of Zachariah. She frowned and rubbed her temples again, trying to ease the headache. "Maybe. We'll have to be careful though. Zachariah wants

Evangeline dead, too. The sorcerer must have convinced him that she was to blame for the magic disappearing."

"Are you okay?" Derek asked, his fingers brushing over her shoulder. She melted into the touch and he dug his thumb into a knot. "You've been really tense."

"I'm just not sleeping well," she said, rolling her head forward to give him better access. If he came and gave her a back rub, she'd probably sleep like a baby. He dug his thumb in a little deeper and she almost let out a groan, which sent her thoughts racing in an entirely different direction. She felt her cheeks heating and pulled away, smiling at him awkwardly. "Thanks, that helped a lot."

"Anytime." He was still standing close. She could smell his cologne and the shampoo he used. They locked eyes and her heart skipped a couple of beats. "Maybe you can take a break, and we could go get dinner tomorrow evening," Derek said, holding her gaze. "And I mean a date, just to be clear."

She swallowed and stared back dumbly for a moment. They'd been flirting, but for some reason she hadn't expected him to ask her out so soon.

He ran his fingers through his hair and started to look nervous. "That looks like a no."

"I don't...think it's a good time," Ceri said quietly. She wanted to say yes, but she had to put the pack first. If things went bad with Derek, it could hurt Amber. The pack couldn't afford any more conflict right now, not with a literal demon in their midst.

Derek shoved his hands in his pockets and nodded. "I can take no for an answer," he said carefully. "I'd still like to be friends, especially since we live together, so don't take it as me pushing you if I'm still friendly."

Ceri smiled at him. "Of course not, we can certainly be friends."

He turned to leave, then paused, clearing his throat. "If you change your mind though, just say the word. I won't wait on you or anything pathetic like that, but if the timing changes..." he shrugged. "Just say something."

She nodded and he left. It had been a perfectly polite exchange but she felt sick to her stomach. This was the right choice, she knew it was. Dating in your friend group was tricky, and dating your alpha's brother was just asking for a disaster. Especially in the middle of all this chaos.

It had been the right choice. She curled her hand back into a fist and willed it to be true.

CHAPTER 39

TOMMY

*T*ommy tried to focus on the problem in front of him, but Deward was staring at him intently, and it was unsettling.

"Is there something on my face?" he asked finally.

The troll frowned. "No."

"Then what ––"

"Why are you hiding bruises? They're fresh, and you winced when you picked up the books," he said, suspicion and concern clear on his face. "If you are being hurt by your pack, my family would be willing to assist you. Just because you can heal quickly does not mean abuse is justified."

"Oh, it's nothing like that," Tommy said, finally understanding. "I'm trying to learn how to fight. Apparently, the bite doesn't automatically impart that knowledge."

The troll continued to frown. "Who is teaching you? Your alpha?"

Tommy shook his head. "Nah, I don't want to embarrass myself in front of her yet. Her brother Derek is trying to help me, but I can't use my werewolf strength on him because he's human, and I suck, so I keep screwing up."

"You should not be fighting humans. You will never learn how to fight if you are constantly holding back. You will only learn how to hesitate, and therefore fail. That builds bad habits that are hard to break." Deward's frown deepened, as if he was unhappier with the idea of bad training than abuse.

Tommy snorted. "Well, I don't exactly have any other options."

Deward picked up his phone and started typing a message. Tommy turned back to the problem, assuming the conversation must be done. He'd learned the troll was generally very abrupt, not bothering with small talk. Their culture tended to be blunt like that. Trolls got straight to the point and didn't tolerate bullshit.

"I have received permission to bring you to our training grounds this afternoon," Deward said, startling him.

"Wait...what?" Tommy stared at Deward with his mouth hanging open.

"I told my father of your predicament, and he has invited you to train with us," Deward repeated, slower this time.

He cleared his throat nervously and eyed Deward's biceps. The fabric of his button-down shirt was straining against the bulging muscles. "Umm, how much?"

Deward waved his hand at him. "Free. Trolls do not charge for training, ever. It is as important to us as air or water, and always freely given. Only a dishonorable coward would try to demand payment for such knowledge."

Tommy pursed his lips, considering. On one hand, he might get crushed if he went. On the other...Derek was trying, but Tommy wasn't improving with his help. It was starting to feel pointless. He knew what he wanted to say: no. But he also knew what Amber would say if she was given an opportunity like this.

Curling his hand into a fist to suppress his nerves, he nodded. "Okay, I'll do it."

A rare smile crossed Deward's face, revealing teeth sharper than humans, and making his tusks look even bigger. "I look forward to testing your courage."

All Tommy could think was, *what the hell have I gotten myself into?*

~

*D*eward pulled his shirt off over his head and folded it neatly, laying it on the bench. Tommy stared at the rippling muscles and felt...small. He had filled out quite a lot since being bitten, but all that meant was that he was now lean with muscle, instead of just lean.

"So, is shirtless a requirement?" he asked.

Deward nodded. "It will likely be ripped if you don't remove it anyhow."

The last thing Tommy wanted was to ruin the clothes Amber had bought for him. Reluctantly, he removed it, folding like Deward had, and setting it on the bench. He crossed his arms over his chest and stood there, practically shivering with nerves.

"This way." Deward led him out into a large, circular room. The walls of the building were concrete, but the roof was wooden. It arched up, creating a vaulted ceiling that made the place feel even bigger than it already was.

It had a dirt floor with two traditional style boxing rings and three matted areas to their left. Heavy weights and what looked like a troll-sized jungle gym took up the right side of the training area.

"This place is huge. Did your parents build it?" Tommy asked, looking around in awe.

"The tribe built it. We use it as a community center on the weekends, and for training during the week," Deward said, rolling his head around in a circle to loosen up. The muscles in his back flexed with every movement. "We should start with a light sparring session to see how you move."

Tommy scratched the back of his head and shrugged. "I'm not even very good at punching yet, but I guess I can try."

"Just fight, and we will go from there." Deward waved away his concerns. The dirt floor was cool under Tommy's feet as he followed Deward to the closest mat. "No hits to the groin and no eye gouges. I will start light, then match the power of your punches, so you get to decide how hard you are hit."

"Uh, great," Tommy said, cringing internally. Deward was assuming he'd be able to land a punch, which so far in his training was only a fifty-fifty shot.

Deward shifted into a fighting stance. His right foot moved back and he brought his hands up in front of his face.

The muscles in his shoulders bunched up as he began to move a little, advancing on Tommy, who quickly brought his hands up as well.

He had no idea what he was doing, but it seemed like Deward wanted him to attack first. Swallowing down his nervousness, he threw a punch. The troll didn't bother moving, but his fist still didn't hit anything but air.

"You need to hit *me*, not the air in front of me," Deward said with a hint of confusion in his voice. "I promise you cannot hurt me if that is your concern."

Tommy grimaced. "I just…missed."

Deward took a step forward. "Try again."

He sighed and adjusted his feet. This was going to be just as humiliating as he'd feared.

CHAPTER 40

GENEVIEVE

Genevieve was sprawled on Steven's futon with an empty box of pizza to her left and a watered-down iced coffee on the floor to her right. She'd spent the past two hours looking at case files and making notes. Her brain was fried and all the caffeine in the world couldn't resuscitate it right now.

She sighed, rolling over onto her side and pulling out Greer's card. It had been two days since she'd spoken to him and she still didn't know much about him. Or how to deal with his request. Or if she was even Amber's beta.

Steven closed his textbook and leaned back in his chair with a groan. "I should have just been an accountant."

"Don't be ridiculous," Genevieve scoffed. "You'd have hated it."

He sighed, dragging his hands down his face. "Yeah. I would have."

"Hey, in all that research we did about sponsors, did you find anything on how the sponsor decides if they're willing to vouch for a potential alpha?" she asked, tapping Greer's card against the palm of her hand.

Steven shrugged. "Probably, why?"

She hadn't talked to Amber about it yet, and she really needed to, but it felt like her responsibility to figure this out first. "Well, this werewolf, from the old Lockhart pack, approached me when I was there trying to get help for my case. He wants Amber to sponsor him."

"Why?" Steven asked, looking somewhat alarmed.

"I don't know. I think he might want to shake things up a little. It seemed like he was impressed by her performance at the Trials. He said he wanted to run things differently once he became alpha." He'd also said werewolves had become a little too humanized, which she wasn't sure she agreed with, but she kept that little tidbit to herself.

"That is an interesting perspective." Steven got up and started digging through a box of his whole notepads. He wrote everything he learned down in them, then stacked them, organized by date, in various boxes around his room. She'd tried to talk him into putting it all in his computer, but he had insisted handwritten notes helped him think.

He pulled out a notebook and flipped through it before stopping on one page. "Here it is. Actually, I still have the book. Keating's *Politics of the Wolf*." He leaned over and grabbed a thick book out of the stack next to his desk.

Genevieve grabbed it and flipped to the table of contents.

It looked like it had five chapters on alphas, with one that focused entirely on an alpha's rise to power. "This is perfect."

"I made a few notes on how the sponsor chooses an alpha just in case Amber had needed to try to convince someone. Most of it appears to be centered around future alliances, favors, and sometimes even a payment. Though that 'paying your sponsor' is a new thing. It's looked down on."

"This guy wouldn't want to do that. The alliance though...he'd probably be interested in something like that."

"You'd have to be careful not to be taken advantage of when negotiating a deal," Steven said, flipping to the next page in his notebook. "He'll probably press for whatever he can get. It's a natural part of the process. A sort of dominance game."

"Would I negotiate, or would Amber?" she asked.

"You would start the negotiations, with your alpha's permission, but Amber would have to have the final discussion with him. That's the most important conversation where last-minute concessions or demands are made." He lowered his notebook. "You need to know what he wants, and why he wants Amber as his sponsor."

"I know. We can't negotiate with him until I know what he's hoping to get." She leaned back on the futon again. It was time to get creative.

CHAPTER 41

TOMMY

"You're still holding back," Deward said with a grunt, flexing as he paced in front of him. "Where is the wolf? The hunter inside of you?"

Tommy ground his teeth together, tempted to shift and show him exactly where the wolf was. They'd been at this for over an hour. He'd finally figured out how to hit Deward, but his attempts at sparring were still pathetic.

"Maybe bitten wolves *are* weaker," Deward taunted, dropping his hands like Tommy wasn't even the slightest threat.

Anger rose in his chest, pushing power into his limbs. He charged the troll, slamming right into him. Deward dropped his hips, stepped, and pivoted. He flipped Tommy over his hip in a blinding fast move and let him fall to the mats.

"Anger is better than apathy, but you must focus it!"

Tommy groaned from his place on the ground, but Deward wasn't having it this time. The troll grabbed his arm and yanked him back up to his feet, giving him a slight shove backward to create space.

"We're going to do this again, and you're going to fight me. No more training, no more sparring. You either fight, or I will beat you until you can no longer lift a hand to defend yourself," Deward said, his eyes flashing with irritation.

"Wait, wha--" His question was cut off with a sharp jab that snapped his head backward and blurred his vision. Tears stung at his eyes from the impact on his nose. He bobbed under the next punch, just barely avoiding catching another blow with his face.

The pace of the fight had changed. They were no longer student and teacher. They were opponents. Tommy felt it in every fiber of his being. The drive to fight. To win.

The wolf peered out of his eyes and the instincts of a predator took over. There was nothing to fear. His body would heal. The nervous energy he'd been stuck under for so long began to lift.

He struck back with two fast strikes to stop the barrage Deward had been throwing. He threw all his power behind a third punch. It only grazed Deward's ribs, but he had been close.

The troll was stronger, taller, and heavier, and that wasn't going to change anytime soon. But Tommy wasn't by any means slow. His speed was the only thing that saved him from the surprise uppercut. He threw himself backward, tripping over his own feet, but avoiding the knockout blow.

Deward's foot slammed into his solar plexus, driving all

the air from his lungs and picking him up off his feet. He hit the ground at least a yard away and immediately tried to roll back to his feet, but two-hundred fifty pounds of troll landed on top of him before he could move. Deward's first punch hit his jaw, the second his nose.

Feral rage rose up inside of him. He was tired of being beaten. Tired of losing. He'd frozen when those men were shooting at him and Evangeline. He didn't ever want to freeze again.

He swung his fists wildly while bucking his hips in an attempt to throw the troll off. It wasn't even close to the technique Deward had shown him earlier, but he wasn't just going to lay there and take it. He reached up blindly. His fingers caught on a tusk. He grabbed it and wrenched Deward's head to the side as hard as he could.

The troll roared in outrage, hitting Tommy even harder as he attempted to pry Tommy's hand off his tusk. Tommy's pulled even harder. Deward's weight shifted slightly and he bucked his hips again. The troll was thrown just far enough to the side that he was able to get the leverage to shove him completely away.

He immediately lunged at Deward, tackling him and driving him back down to the mat. He rained punches down on the troll's head. Deward shielded his face with one arm and drilled two hard punches into Tommy's unprotected side. The first one hurt, the second cracked a rib.

Breathing suddenly became extremely difficult. He tried to keep punching, but he could barely move his left arm through the fog of pain. Deward threw another punch, his fist narrowing in on the injury mercilessly. Tommy crumpled and Deward flipped him over with ease.

It only took on more punch and then everything went dark.

～

*T*ommy came to what felt like hours later. Deward's father was crouched over him with a look of concern.

"You should not have injured him," the older troll said and he snapped his fingers in front of Tommy's face. "Can you hear me?"

His mouth didn't want to work and it felt like he was outside of his body watching all this happening from above. "Whaaa..."

"He needed to be pushed, father. He was still holding back," Deward protested, only looking slightly remorseful.

"Am fiiiiine," Tommy said, waving away their concern. He wasn't sure he was fine, actually, but he wasn't dying. His ribs felt weird. It hurt, but there was magic rushing through the bones and muscles healing them. "Healin' jus' fine."

"Is his alpha here yet?" Deward's father asked. He was taller, bigger, and nerdier than Deward. Black, thick-framed glasses were perched on his nose and gave him a scholarly look...if you ignored the bulging muscles and the long tusks.

"Almost, she'll be here in about five minutes," Deward replied.

Tommy's eyes went wide and he suddenly felt much more awake. "What? Alpha?"

"Deward called your alpha as soon as you were injured. She'd be able to sense it, of course, so it was proper to call and reassure her that you were safe. Allowing her to believe you were under attack by an enemy would be irresponsible and callous to her responsibility to protect you." Deward's father narrowed his eyes at Tommy, then at Deward. "She should have been informed before the sparring even took place."

"Ah, well," Tommy said, trying to push up to a sitting position. "I didn't want to worry her."

"Foolish and immature," the old troll said, shaking his head. He extended his hand and, very gently, helped Tommy to his feet. "You will apologize when she arrives."

Tommy swallowed, feeling embarrassed. "Yes, sir."

"Wait for her, I will get refreshments for our guest," Deward's father said before turning and walking away, leaving them alone.

Deward shifted on his feet, looking properly chastised. "Are you okay?"

Tommy grinned at him. "I feel awesome."

Deward looked up, his green face a picture of shock. "What?"

"I lost, but...not because I gave up. I've never done that before. I've never stuck it out," Tommy said, rubbing the back of his head awkwardly.

"Well, you're not dead." Amber's voice cut through the training center. He looked back in surprise, he hadn't felt her coming. She didn't look particularly mad, just curious. She'd kicked off her shoes by the door and was strolling toward them, her hands in the pockets of her jeans.

"I must apologize for the liberty I took in fighting one of your pack without speaking to you first and obtaining your permission," Deward said with a short bow of his head.

Amber raised a brow, glancing at Tommy before responding. "Uh, that's fine. Assuming this idiot agreed to receive a beating?"

"Yeah, I did," Tommy said quickly.

Amber shrugged. "You and Derek have been beating on each other all week. This seems like it'll be more effective. It's no big deal."

Tommy's mouth fell open in shock. "You knew about that?"

She laughed. "Of course I did. You think I don't know when my own brother is hiding something from me? That and the bruises you both had, and pretending nothing was going on every time I got home even though you were both panting? It was either that or a torrid love affair and we both know Derek has the hots for Ceri."

Tommy crossed his arms, feeling even more idiotic for thinking he was hiding it from her. "Well, I guess we were kind of obvious."

She patted him on the arm, then turned back to Deward. "Do you want to keep training him?"

Deward looked between them, then nodded. "If Tommy is amenable."

Tommy nodded quickly. "Yeah, this is great."

Amber shrugged. "Then feel free to keep knocking each other out."

Deward's father returned at that moment carrying a tray

of sodas with a glass of ice in front of each one. There were also two beers on the tray.

"Alpha Amber Hale, welcome to our home," he said with a polite smile.

Amber returned it. "Thank you for welcoming me and Tommy here."

Deward pulled Tommy aside while they continued to exchange small talk and apologies. "Did you mean what you said? That this was helpful?"

He nodded. "It was. I need to know how to fight." Evangeline had brought a new kind of danger to their pack. It felt like he was running out of time, and if he didn't learn fast, he might end up dead. Or someone he cared about would.

This also gave him an idea for how to help Woggy. He'd have to talk to Ceri and make sure it was okay, but he was pretty confident she'd be on board.

"Can you start coming here for tutoring? We can do that first, then train. Most evenings my friends come over to train as well. It would do you good to fight different people so you can see the different strengths and weaknesses we have."

"I'll be over here as often as you'll have me," Tommy said.

Deward slapped his hand on his shoulder. "Then I'll see you tomorrow evening."

CHAPTER 42

AMBER

*A*mber walked back inside to a disaster. A loud shriek split the air and a grey blur streaked past her, headed toward living room. An angry, yowling mass of fluff followed close behind as Captain Jack pursued the pixie. His hair was mussed and streaked in…grape jelly?

"What the hell…"

"Dammit Woggy, get back here!" Ceri shouted, stumbling after them as the caboose in the crazy train. She lunged for the cat, but at that moment Woggy took a sharp turn and the cat darted after him. Ceri tripped over the hem of her dress and was sent sprawling onto the floor.

Amber couldn't help but laugh. "Graceful."

"Quit laughing at me and help!" Ceri demanded as she untangled her legs.

Tommy hurried around to the other side of the couch and grabbed Woggy just as he shimmied out from under it. Purring loudly, and completely failing in his attempt to look innocent, Captain Jack curled through Tommy's legs. His one eye was locked on the tasty treat Woggy still had clutched in his hands.

Evangeline was peeking over the balcony upstairs to see what was going on, but she disappeared as soon as she noticed Amber looking at her.

Amber walked over and gave Ceri a hand up, which she took with a sigh. "I see you're having a good day."

Ceri just glared at her. When she saw Tommy though, her eyes went wide. "Tommy, what the hell happened to you?"

He grinned, making his bruised eye close completely. "Trolls."

"He fired Derek as his trainer and is now letting Deward beat him up," Amber said cheerfully.

"That actually makes sense. Do you want a poultice to help it heal quicker?"

Tommy shook his head. "It should be fine by dinner. I've noticed bruises heal within a few hours."

"I'm going to go take a shower," Amber said. She'd spent the day at the warehouse cleaning -- until she'd gotten the call from the troll -- and she was filthy. Derek had shown up about an hour after she'd gotten there, and he'd been in a rotten mood, but wouldn't say why.

She and Ceri had both agreed they shouldn't go around asking questions the day after a picture of her had been on the news, even if it was just her in wolf form. But she needed something to keep herself occupied, so murdering spiders it was.

"Same. I'm covered in Deward's sweat." Tommy sniffed his arm, then grimaced. "Sweaty trolls don't smell great."

"I'm going to clean up the *giant mess* these two knuckleheads made." Ceri grabbed Captain Jack and lifted him with both hands. He meowed mournfully. "No complaining. You're getting a bath."

Amber snorted and headed toward her room before Ceri could rope her into helping bathe the vicious beast.

As she dropped her things on the dresser next to her bedroom door, the faint scent of cigarettes drifted toward her. Frowning, she looked for the source and noticed a single, folded sheet of paper sat on the dresser where she'd just dumped her keys. She grabbed it, Thallan's scent filling her nose.

Come see me, alone.

Alarm bells went off in her head and she crumpled the paper in her hand. He must have seen the news like everyone else. He'd know why she was involved.

Only Ceri was still in the living room when she walked back through. She could hear Tommy upstairs in the shower. Eloise and Evangeline were talking quietly.

"What's wrong?" Ceri asked.

Amber handed her the note, worst case scenarios running through her head. Would he try to hurt Evangeline? Or kick them out? They'd be screwed if he told them to leave. "I'm going to go see him and get it over with."

"Maybe I should come with you."

Amber shook her head. "I don't want to piss him off. This could already be dicey."

Ceri looked hesitant.

"If he tries to murder me, you'll feel it through the pack bond. I'll be fine."

"Fine. But you're coming straight back here and explaining what's going on."

"I'll be back as soon as I can," Amber agreed with a nod.

She left out the back door and jogged across the lawn. The wind had picked up since they got home. It smelled like rain.

Thallan's house looked ominous in the moonlight. It would be a full moon in a few days, but the heavy clouds were blocking most of the light tonight. She hopped up onto the porch and let herself in through the front door.

Her footsteps echoed through the empty house. It really was like a tomb in here. It even smelled like death. Like something rotten. She wrinkled her nose and hurried to the study she knew Thallan was hiding out in.

The door was open and warm light spilled into the hallway.

Thallan stepped into the doorway, a disturbing excitement on his face. She'd never seen him look so alive, but the tension in his body worried her. "I told you it wasn't your friend."

"What's your point?" she asked.

He turned away and vanished into the office. Rolling her eyes, she followed. He was pacing the length of the room puffing on his cigarette like he needed the smoke to live.

"You wanted to talk?" she prompted, feeling a strong urge to leave. He looked completely manic.

His head snapped up and he pointed the glowing end of the cigarette at her. "The demon has called in its mark."

She nodded impatiently. "Yes."

He took one last drag on the cigarette then flicked it into the hardwood floor, grinding it out with his foot, not caring about the scorch mark it left on the wood floor. "Is it here?"

"No, not that I can see." Her hand went to her mark automatically. The sensation she'd come to associate with Angel's presence was gone, for now.

"Then we have to talk, quickly. We won't have many chances to execute my plan," Thallan said, a dark grin spreading across his face.

"What are you talking about?"

"I'm going to kill it."

Amber's gut twisted. Angel was a threat to her. She shouldn't care, but she did. The idea of just murdering him made her skin crawl. "What? Why?"

"Because he killed my wife!" Thallan shouted, spittle flying from his lips. He advanced on her, forcing her to move backward until she hit the bookshelf. "He's a liar and a murderer, and I swore I would have my revenge!"

"He killed your wife? Is that why you have the mark?"

Thallan turned away, disgust clear on his face. "I made a deal with the devil. Traded my soul. All I wanted was for him to heal her. For two months, I thought he had done it, and that my sacrifice was worth it." He lifted his face toward her. "Then she was killed in a car accident. I know he did it. That monster manipulated me and stole the only thing that mattered. He killed her!"

Amber swallowed and pushed herself off the bookshelf. She wasn't sure if she should believe Thallan or not. Why would the demon kill his wife? But if he had, would he betray her too?

"What's your plan?" she asked. If he was going to do this, she at least needed to know what he was thinking.

Thallan straightened slightly and walked over to his desk. He opened a drawer and pulled out a long, flat box. Lifting a thin, silver chain from around his neck, he pulled a key out of his shirt which he used to open the box.

He picked up a thin, white blade. It glowed as though it were filled with light, casting a strange pallor over his skin. He rotated it slowly and it pushed back the shadows of the room.

"This," he said, his eyes fixed on the shimmering metal, "can kill a demon."

"What the hell is it?" Amber whispered.

"That doesn't matter. All I need is an opportunity. The demon must be visible to the physical realm, not just the apparition you sometimes see. It will be at its most vulnerable then." He tightened his grip on the knife. "That will be my moment to strike."

"I can't do this," Amber said, shaking her head.

Thallan's lips peeled back from his teeth and he advanced on her, reminding her of the two wolves she'd seen fighting for alpha. He looked feral. "You don't get to say no."

"Your wife died in a car wreck. Why do you think it was his fault?"

"It's the only explanation!" Thallan shouted at her, spittle flying from his lips. "She was my light, and that bastard killed her! I know he did, even if no one believes me."

He was insane. She'd always suspected it, but she hadn't realized how bad it was. His insanity was infecting everything around him. The house, the grounds...they were rotting from the inside out because of the hate he held inside him.

"I can't just summon him," Amber said, trying to deflect.

"The witch knows how. She used to dabble in black magic." Thallan sneered at her. "Find a way. Before you fulfill the bargain."

She ground her teeth together. There was no way she was going along with this plan, except as a last resort if Angel tried to kill her. She still had a hard time imagining he would despite how much of an asshole he'd been lately.

"I have to talk to my pack."

Thallan snorted. "Talk to the witch. She'll know how to get the demon at his most vulnerable. If nothing else, he wants to protect this girl you have stashed away in my guest house."

"You're not hurting her," Amber said, immediately angry.

"That's up to you," he said with a mock bow.

Amber turned and left, her mind racing. She wouldn't let him hurt Evangeline, but he could be unpredictable. If he thought she wasn't going to help him, he might try to do something on his own.

There was so much to do. And so many ways it could all go wrong. She stopped in the middle of the grounds and kicked off her shoes, then stripped her shirt off over her head. She couldn't think right now.

The shift rolled over her like a wave and she dropped to four feet. Normally, she tried to maintain control while she was shifted. This time, she just let go.

The wolf shook out its fur and trotted toward the woods.

CHAPTER 43

CERI

*C*eri had waited over an hour for Amber to return, and had started getting a little nervous that something was wrong. But the pack bond stayed calm, so she forced herself to sit and wait instead of marching over to Thallan's house to demand to see her alpha.

She sighed and started the porch swing rocking again. It was getting too cold to sit outside but she didn't much feel like sleeping either.

A pair of bright red eyes appeared in the darkness right in front of the porch and she tensed up. "Amber?"

The wolf stepped into the light, holding her clothes in her mouth. She nodded her head.

"Where have you been? You were supposed to come talk to me."

Amber sighed and looked away guiltily then trotted up onto the porch where she shifted. Ceri looked away while she pulled on her clothes, waiting to glare at Amber until she sat down on the porch swing next to her.

"Well?"

"Sorry," she said, crossing her arms. "I needed a minute to clear my head."

"That bad?"

Amber nervously picked at the hem of her shirt. "Thallan wants me to kill the demon," she whispered, glancing around like the demon might pop out at any moment.

Ceri was quiet. She just stared down at her hands. A thousand thoughts raced through her mind in an instant. None of them good.

"You can't seriously think I should go along with his plan."

Ceri knew she expected her to be her sounding board. The voice of reason.

"I mean...it would free you," Ceri said hesitantly, barely able to meet her eyes.

"And what would it mean for Evangeline? He's protecting her." Amber crossed her arms.

"That's what he's told you he's doing, but it could be a lie. He's a *demon* for heaven's sake. They *lie*," Ceri said, exasperated.

"There's something else going on. I just don't know what yet."

"Honestly, my biggest issue with it is just that it's risky. If we can get through this and free you from the mark, that's better than trying to kill...you know who." She drained the last of her tea, grimacing as she swallowed down the dregs at the bottom.

"Do you think Evangeline is evil?" Amber asked, turning to look at her.

Ceri gnawed on the inside of her cheek as she rolled the question around in her mind. She'd been avoiding this question, so of course Amber had to bring it up. "She's not really a demon."

Amber gave her an unimpressed look, raising one of her eyebrows.

"She's not," Ceri insisted. "The angel side of her changes things."

"Before the whole incident with Angel, he really seemed just like any other person. Maybe a little bit of an asshole, but so are most humans."

"And when you crossed him he threatened your life and put everyone in danger." Ceri sighed, rubbing her temples. The headache was back. "I'm not saying you should do it, but I wouldn't exactly cry. Do you think Thallan will try without you?"

"Probably. I want to keep an eye on him. He's not exactly...stable."

"That's an understatement."

Amber glanced at her. "What was that favor you did for him before? The one you thought you could trade for the whole sponsor thing."

"Ah..." she grimaced at the memory. "I tracked his daughter down for him. She disappeared after he went all crazy after his wife died. He didn't know where she was or if she was okay, and she refused to speak with him."

"I really can't picture him as a father."

Ceri snorted. "She said he was a good one, before his wife died. Grief makes people do awful things sometimes."

Amber's face fell. "Yeah, it does."

Ceri reached across the bench and grabbed her hand. "I'm sorry."

She wished she could fix all of this. Maybe killing the demon was the only way. It scared her how deep he had his claws in Amber already. Amber always wanted to see the best in people, and sometimes, it just wasn't there.

CHAPTER 44

EVANGELINE

*E*vangeline grabbed the shower handle, turning on the water just in time to drown out the sound of her throwing up her dinner. The room spun as her stomach heaved. Her skin was clammy all over. It had been all day and she had thrown up every time she'd eaten.

She yanked some toilet paper off the roll and wiped her mouth, then sat back, leaning her head against the wall. Her skin ached, especially where the boils had started popping up. She thought she'd have more time, but using her demon side's magic the other night seemed to have accelerated the illness.

She lifted her hoodie a little and saw that the boils had grown even larger. The skin around them was red and inflamed.

There was a soft knock at the bathroom door and she froze. "I'm busy."

"I heard you throwing up. Again," Tommy said quietly, just audible over the noise of the shower. "Are you okay?"

"I'm fine," she said, glaring at the door and cursing werewolf hearing. She'd hoped the shower would drown it out. It had always hidden it from Eloise.

"Even if I couldn't hear your heartbeat stuttering all over the place, it'd be obvious you were lying."

"I'm fine is code for go away," she snapped, pushing up to her feet. Her vision blurred from the sudden movement and she had to pause to catch her breath. She tried to take a step forward, but her legs buckled.

Instead of hitting the tile floor, she landed in Tommy's arms. She hadn't even heard the door open, but somehow, he was in the bathroom. He lifted her like she weighed nothing then set her down gently, with her back propped up against the wall.

"Are you sick? You smell like...I don't know what. It's really weird though," he said as he smoothed the hair back from her face.

Her eyes popped open and she pushed his hand away but it was too late. Her hood slipped back and she felt him freeze, his eyes locked on her head. She knew what he was seeing. Black hair, and her least favorite part...

"Are those horns?"

"You cannot tell anyone," she said angrily, pulling her hood back over them. They'd gotten bigger over the years and she hated it.

"Did they just grow or something? Your hair was definitely blonde before too." He sat back, watching her curiously. She felt like a zoo animal.

She stared at the floor so she didn't have to see his expression. "They grow when the sun sets. My demon side comes out. I don't like to talk about it."

He shrugged and stood up, grabbing one of the disposable cups they kept by the sink. "You should drink some water."

"I'm not thirsty."

"You've thrown up three times today. You're bound to be dehydrated. I know you want to be left alone, but don't be dumb." Tommy thrust the little cup of water toward her. She wanted to knock it out of his hand and run away, but he was right. She needed whatever she could manage to keep down.

"Fine," she said, taking the cup and draining it quickly. It still made her stomach churn but she didn't vomit right away.

"This isn't the flu, is it?" Tommy asked, crossing his arms.

She looked down at her hands. "No."

"Does Eloise know what's going on?"

Her head snapped up and she glared at him. "Do not tell her."

"Why are you hiding it from her?"

"Because she already has enough to worry about and I don't want to make it worse. There's nothing she can do anyhow."

"We could take you to a doctor."

Evangeline snorted at that. "Hey doc, this half demon recently accused of eating all our magic is sick. Can you help? Yeah, that's going to go over real well."

"What about Ceri? She knows how to help with most things."

She wrapped her arms a little tighter around her herself. "I don't want her help. There's nothing anyone can do about it anyhow. It's...genetic." That wasn't exactly a lie. Maybe not the whole truth, but the curse was woven into her genes in a manner of speaking. Her biological mother had passed it on to her just like every other demon.

"Are you dying or something?" he asked, his brows knitting together in concern.

"No," she said, rolling her eyes. "I'm just sick. I'll be fine."

Unless she never did what she had to in order to make the sickness go away. Some days she thought it might be better if she didn't. Kadrithan acted like everything depended on her staying alive, but she didn't want that responsibility. Certainly not for the demons. Anything they wanted from her couldn't be good, and he wouldn't explain it.

Tommy shifted on his feet as the silence became awkward. She wanted to just leave, but she didn't have the energy to get off the floor right now.

"I'm going to ask Ceri if she has anything for nausea," he said finally.

"I don't want--"

He cut her off with a glare. "I'm going to, and then you can stop throwing up all the delicious food I make."

"Why are you such a mother hen?" she muttered, twirling the cup in her hands.

"Why are you so determined to keep feeling like crap?"

"I'm not, I just don't want everyone fussing over me." She

tossed the cup into the trash and pushed herself off the floor. Slowly.

"If you just told Ceri you needed something, she'd give it to you, and then no one would worry. You're seriously over-thinking all of this," he said, catching her arm as her legs wobbled again and pulling her upright.

The front door opened and Genevieve walked in. "Please tell me you saved me some dinner this time, Tommy," she shouted as she dumped her stuff on the couch.

Evangeline jerked away and slipped out of the bathroom. She knew he meant well, but she just wanted to be left alone. She'd disappear if she could. Sometimes she thought she *should*. She was evil after all. Or at least half evil.

She shut the bedroom door behind her and shuffled over to the bed. Her mother was already asleep as she slid under the covers and curled up behind her. At least while she was sleeping she didn't have to think.

CHAPTER 45

AMBER

*A*mber parked in front of Jameson's house and frowned. She wasn't late, but the others were already here. The wolf perked up in her mind as a feeling of dread settled in her gut. She'd been slightly worried about this meeting, but maybe she should have been *really* worried about it.

She hurried to the front door and let herself in. Jameson said he knew everyone by the sound of their vehicle, so driving up was as good as knocking. The house was quiet except for the sound of voices coming from the gathered werewolves.

Shane was waiting outside. He looked up, and she stopped in her tracks. He was furious. Wordlessly, he opened the door to the room and motioned for her to enter ahead of him.

Part of her was tempted to run, but the stubborn, alpha side of her refused to do that. She was going to deal with this.

Everyone was silent as she stepped into the room. Salazar was watching her curiously, but Bennett's expression was one of disgust, and hate. She didn't bother going to the one empty seat at the table. Instead, she just looked to Jameson.

"Do you have Evangeline Deschamps?" he asked without preamble. She could at least appreciate that he didn't beat around the bush and draw this out.

"She's not responsible for the magic disappearing," Amber replied, crossing her arms and holding his gaze.

"I'll take that as a yes," Jameson replied, rising from his seat. "We have a rule. We don't report other alphas to the police, no matter what the infraction is. If it's serious, we simply take care of it ourselves. If you believe this girl is innocent, then I will give you the benefit of the doubt."

"You can't be serious——"

Jameson cut off Bennett with a glare. "I lead the council. It is my decision, and without definite proof, I'm willing to acknowledge the girl may be innocent." He turned back to Amber. "You have a week to prove this demon-child isn't responsible."

"Or what?" Amber ground out.

"Or the council will come get her ourselves, and you will be punished as I see fit."

One week. Amber curled her hand into a fist and nodded. She was lucky she got that much based on the way Bennett was looking at her. "Can I trust that no one will come looking for trouble during that week?"

Jameson nodded. "You have my word."

Amber nodded. "Then I guess we'll talk again in a week."

"You're relieved of your council duties until this is resolved, and you won't be needed for this meeting," Jameson said, turning away in a clear dismissal.

"Just a word of warning. When I rescued Evangeline, there was a sorcerer there. He was trying to kill her. He's probably the same one that killed Lockhart," Amber said.

Jameson looked back at her. "I'll look into it."

She nodded, then turned around and walked out of the room. Shane shut the door behind her and followed her. They were silent as they left the house and walked back out to her truck.

Pausing by the driver side door, she crossed her arms. "Spit it out."

"What the hell are you thinking?" he demanded, just as angry as she expected. "You're a brand-new alpha whose reputation is already shit, and now you're harboring a demon? That's not just irresponsible, that's insane."

"You have no clue what you're talking about," she snapped, her eyes flashing red. "All of you idiots saw a man on the news making crazy claims, and you what? Just believed him? That asshole burned down an old woman's house, then sent men with guns into the woods to hunt down a seventeen-year-old girl. If she is part demon, no one knows what that means. You can't execute her without giving her a chance."

"You don't have the right to risk the safety of an entire

city just because you feel bad for her," Shane snapped back. She could see the struggle not to flinch back under her gaze, and any other time, she'd feel bad for using the dominance that came with being an alpha like this.

"I'm not going to sacrifice my conscience because some people are afraid of anyone that is different," she ground out. "I'm going to find out what the hell is actually going on, and kill the sorcerer that's behind all this. I don't miss Donovan one tiny bit, but a sorcerer killed him and cut out his heart. Something everyone conveniently forgot today. Jameson might be next, but sure, let's worry about the girl that hides in her room all day because she's terrified someone is going to find her and hurt her mother again."

Shane finally looked away. "If, in a week, you discover this girl is responsible, what will you do?"

Amber knew he could hear a lie just like she could. If she said she'd just hand the girl over that wouldn't be the truth. She couldn't. Not without dying. But if the council was going to come after her pack she might not have a choice.

Thallan thought he could kill the demon, but something about that plan made her skin crawl. If it came down to it though...she couldn't let Angel take her soul for failing to fulfill her end of the bargain.

"I don't know," she said finally.

He shook his head in frustration. "Sometimes I wish you'd just lie and tell me what I want to hear."

She shrugged and climbed into her truck. She didn't have time to sit here and baby Shane.

"Wait, I'm coming with you," he said, heading around toward the passenger door.

"What? Why?"

He hopped up in the truck. "You're going to go try to figure out what's going on, right?"

"Yes."

"Then I'm going to help." He pressed his lips into a thin line. "So you don't get yourself killed."

She sighed and cranked up the truck. "Do you know anyone that might know where to find a sorcerer?"

"Actually, I do."

She backed out of her spot and headed out of the subdivision. "If you try to screw me over, or hurt Evangeline, I will rip you apart. Just so we're clear."

He looked at her from the corner of his eye. "I never doubted that for a second."

CHAPTER 46

AMBER

"*H*is name is Bram? Seriously?" Amber asked, raising her brow.

"He's older than the other guy. And he's very sensitive about those sorts of jokes, so just…don't bring it up." Shane pointed at the light ahead. "Turn here."

She did as instructed, nervously checking the rearview mirror to make sure they weren't being followed. It was completely paranoid, but she was starting to feel justified in her paranoia. The council had connected the dots after seeing the news report, there was no reason someone else couldn't have as well.

"How old is this vampire, exactly?"

"I have no idea. Old enough to be a little crazy," Shane said with a shrug.

"How do you know him?" she asked, glancing at him curiously.

"I was an omega briefly when my original pack fell apart. I ended up in a less than savory crowd. We used to get things for him." Shane's shoulders tightened at whatever memories that question had brought up.

"Ah," she said, letting the conversation drop. He was already pissed enough at her without her pressing him on an obviously sensitive topic.

"It's that gate."

A chain link fence topped with barbed wire protected an old, brick building. It was unmarked, and every window had been boarded up. A man in a hoodie with his face and hands covered lounged near the gate, watching them. She turned into the short driveway and stopped, rolling down her window.

The man strolled over, tugging down the bandana that covered his face a little. He was pale, his eyes were a light almost golden color, but the teeth were what really gave it away. When he grinned, his sharp incisors were impossible to hide.

Vampires could go out in the sun with the right spell to protect them, but they'd still get a nasty sunburn in about an hour if they didn't keep their skin covered.

"Shane Weston, it's been a few years," the guard said, resting his forearms on the window ledge and leaning farther into the truck than Amber was comfortable with.

"Yet, you're still out here doing the grunt work," Shane said, returning the smile. All the tension was gone from his posture now. Even his heartbeat was slower. She had no idea how he did that, but she needed to learn that trick.

The vampire, of course, had no heartbeat which was creepy as hell now that she was used to hearing them.

"Ah, you know how it is. I like to party, and Bram doesn't like it when I party."

"Is that what you call those ragers? Parties?" Shane asked, raising a brow.

"Psh," the vampire said, waving a hand at Shane. "Semantics. Anyhow, you didn't come by just to see me. What do you need today?"

"I need to talk to Bram."

The vampire glanced at Amber. "Her too?"

"Yes," Amber said, answering for herself.

The vampire shook his head with a laugh. "Your funeral." He pushed off the truck and walked over to the gate, unlocking with a key he kept in his pocket.

"What does he mean 'your funeral'?" Amber asked, looking at Shane suspiciously.

"He's just goading me. Mostly. Bram can be weird about new people. He's slightly obsessed with...blood," Shane said, grimacing.

"Aren't all vampires?" The gate slid open and she drove through, parking in the only open spot.

"Not like this. You can tell him no when he asks for...well, you'll see..." he trailed off with a guilty expression, "but he will definitely be more cooperative if you say yes."

"You could have told me that before you brought me here," she said, a little angry that he hadn't warned her before they were driving through the gate.

"I had a lot on my mind," Shane said sarcastically.

They climbed out of the truck and she followed him toward the front door, where another guard sat. This one wasn't a vampire though. She was a werewolf.

The woman rose as they approached and opened the door. "I'd say it's good to see you again, Shane, but since you're just here for business..." She shrugged and gave Amber a curious look.

"Sorry, Bella, I'll try to make one of the game nights sometime. Being Jameson's beta doesn't leave me with a whole lot of free time."

"Excuses, excuses," Bella said, waving them inside. "Have fuuuun."

Amber stepped into the dimly lit building and almost gagged as the scent hit her. Blood, both old and fresh, was all she could smell. Her hand shook as she covered her mouth and nose, trying to breathe shallowly.

Her ears buzzed with the pop of gunfire and Tommy's frantic howls. She tasted blood in her mouth. Felt it dripping from her muzzle. Red tinted her vision as she lunged at the last attacker.

"Are you okay?" Shane asked, pressing his hand against her back.

His touch shocked her out of the flashback and she forced herself to focus on the concrete under her feet and the light scent of his cologne.

"I'm fine," she said sharply. She wasn't. She needed to get out of here, but running away wasn't going to make those memories go away. "Let's just go."

Shane kept his hand on her back, something she would

have objected to at any other time. Right now, it was the only thing keeping her from bolting.

The hallway led into the open lower floor of the building. It had been some kind of manufacturing business in the past, but all the machinery had been taken out and replaced with clutter. Couches were placed haphazardly around the room. Most looked like they'd been reclaimed from dumpsters. A few people were sleeping on them, curled up without a blanket or pillow.

There was a huge flat screen tv hung from one of the walls. A troll rugby game, that was playing silently on it, was the only source of light down here.

She expected Shane to lead her toward the rickety stairs that led up to the second level, but he took her down instead.

"In the basement? Really? That's borderline cliche," she muttered as they descended into the narrow stairwell.

"It's easier to block the light down here."

"Is he that worried about a sunburn?"

"Bram refuses to use the protective spells," Shane said, his voice suggesting this was an old argument he'd had many times.

There was a chuckle ahead of them and the door at the bottom of the stairs opened, revealing a tall, thin vampire -- there was no doubt in her mind that he was a vampire, even without the teeth visible -- wearing a pair of black leather pants and...nothing else.

"I'm a vampire. Why would I want to prance around in the sun like some sparkly elf?" He waved them down, his ropey muscles flexing under skin so pale it was almost white.

"No one is suggesting you go sunbathing, Bram, but

knowing that you won't burst into flames at the first lick of sunlight is a nice reassurance for most vampires."

Bram pulled Shane into a hug at the bottom of the stairs. Amber kept her distance. It was obvious Shane liked the weird, old vampire. He seemed eccentric, but not too dangerous.

"Come in, then you can introduce me to your friend," Bram said as he waved them inside.

Amber walked in and looked around. The place was covered in paintings. They were all the same color, a kind of sepia-toned red. Bram seemed to have an obsession with portraits. All of the faces stared out at her. Some angry, some happy, some terrified. She walked over to one still sitting on an easel and leaned in for a better look. That's when she realized…it wasn't paint that he used. It was blood.

"Beautiful, aren't they?" he whispered from right behind her.

She jumped and whirled around, coming face to face with the artist himself. "You paint them with blood?"

"Yes, their own blood. Art is a kind of magic all its own. The sacrifice makes it even more special," Bram said with a grin. His eyes were so light that his iris blended into the rest of his eye at the edges.

Shane cleared his throat. "This is Amber. She's ––"

"The bitten werewolf who became an alpha. I know." Bram finally turned away. He walked over to a long workbench piled with supplies and picked up an apron. It used to be white, but was now streaked with red. "I am curious what she might need from me though."

"What do you know about demons?" Shane asked.

Bram looked thoughtful, and slightly surprised at the question. "Not terribly friendly, similarly afflicted to not walk the earth while the sun is up, and rather long-lived. They've also been recently accused of destroying magic, though I doubt that." He grabbed a packet off the workbench that Amber immediately recognized. It was a blood draw kit.

The vampire walked toward her, watching her expression carefully. "I think I know what you're concerned about, and I'm happy to answer your questions, and keep the knowledge that you were here to myself, if..."

"If I give you some blood," Amber finished for him.

He smiled. "I simply want to do your portrait."

She ground her teeth together, but nodded. It was creepy, but it's not like it would kill her. He directed her to sit down in an armchair next to a table, then sat across from her and opened the kit. She laid her arm on the table and tried to focus on slowing her heart rate, but this whole process made her feel slightly ill.

He pulled out the needle and adjusted the angle of her arm.

"I'd rather do it myself, actually." She snatched the needle from his hand and clenched her hand into a fist to make the vein on the inside of her arm pop, then slid it in smoothly.

He watched her, swaying slightly as the blood began to pump into the tube. His eyes were locked onto her arm as though he were hypnotized. "This is even better, you doing it yourself."

"Do you realize how creepy you sound, or do you just not care?" She switched to the second vial. Only three more to go.

"Oh, I just don't care." His lips curled up into a smile and he dragged his eyes away from her arm to look at her. "You don't strike me as a drug addict. How did you learn to do this?"

"I'm a nurse. Or was. I got fired after I was bitten."

"Ah, yes. Those are some silly laws. I'm surprised they haven't been overturned yet."

She switched to the third vial and Bram grabbed the first two, carrying them over to the long, paint-splattered bench near the wall. He dumped the contents into a small bowl, using a thin piece of plastic to carefully scrape out every last drop.

Amber glanced back at Shane, who had on a neutral expression. How many times had he watched Bram do this? Had he let Bram do it to him?

Bram hummed happily as she disconnected the final vial. There was a band-aid sitting on top of the other supplies. She grabbed it and opened it with her teeth, then quickly slipped out the needle and tried to put on the band-aid, but it went crooked.

Shane startled her when he grabbed it. "You looked like you could use a little help." His hands were steady as he pressed the band-aid on.

"Thanks."

Bram collected the other vials and dropped them in the pocket of his apron. He looked more like a butcher than a painter splattered with all that blood.

"What do you know about Zachariah Hudson?" Amber asked, sitting on the edge of the armchair. She felt restless and wanted out of this room.

The vampire adjusted his canvas and began painting. "Well, he's a half-angel that works for the angels as far as anyone can tell. Their organization is perfectly above board in all their dealings, which I find terribly suspicious. No one is that perfect."

"Have any new sorcerers showed up in town recently?"

He switched brushes, dipping it in water this time before adding the blood. "Hmm, I'd say so. Lockhart having his heart cut out was a dead giveaway," he said, smirking at his own pun.

"Do you know where the sorcerer is?" Shane asked, pacing the edge of the room.

"I find it interesting that you ask about demons first, then an angel, then a sorcerer. It's as if you think they're all connected," Bram mused, ignoring Shane's question.

Amber resisted the urge to roll her eyes. "Maybe they are. Have you ever talked to a demon?"

"Yes, a few times. We used to summon them for fun." Bram switched paintbrushes again and leaned in close to the canvas. "They're very interesting. Determined to get you to agree to a favor, of course, but not nearly so menacing as most people would have you believe."

Summoning demons for fun...who the hell was this guy? Amber dragged her hands through her hair and shook her head in disbelief. "Have you ever heard of someone that was only half demon?"

"I've heard rumors, but I've never met anyone that was that sort of hybrid. It kind of makes you wonder though, doesn't it? There are so many half angels running around, but no half demons," he mused.

"This sorcerer, do you know his name?" Amber asked.

"Interesting you'd assume it was a man," Bram said, his eyes flicking to her for a moment.

"I saw him in the woods. I know he's a man."

"Ah, of course, my mistake. I believe he goes by Caligo. Sometimes they leave their real names behind in order to seem more mysterious, or simply to maintain their anonymity."

Amber narrowed her eyes at him. It felt like he meant something else. She didn't think there were two sorcerers. Donovan had been killed right before this guy had showed up. It had to be him.

"Have you sold anything to him?" Shane asked.

Bram shook his head. "No, not directly at least. It's possible some of my regular clients worked as a middle man." The vampire looked at Amber again. "Siobhan, for example. She also recently started asking around about a sorcerer. I believe she's your witch's cousin, right?"

Amber nodded. This guy seemed to know everyone. "I saw her yesterday."

"It was a smart choice to speak with her. She might be able to find him faster. A lot of paranormals owe her favors these days." He switched brushes again, a disturbing smile forming on his face.

"You never did answer my question about where the sorcerer is. Do you know?" Shane pressed. He looked as impatient as she felt.

"It makes you uncomfortable, doesn't it?" Bram asked with a broad grin. "You look like you'd rather rip off my head than stay in this room for another minute."

Amber curled her hand into a fist. "The thought has crossed my mind."

Bram threw his head back and laughed. "Shane, you can't handle this one, but I like her."

Amber glanced at Shane, who looked slightly embarrassed. He crossed his arms and sighed. "Can you answer our questions, or not?"

"Still so impatient," Bram grumbled. "And of course I can, however, I doubt you'll like my answers."

"Why is that?" Amber asked, trying to encourage the crazy old bat to get to the point.

"Because it won't help you." He dabbed the paint brush into the little cup of blood and added a final flourish to his macabre painting, then spun it around.

Amber stared at her likeness, painted in her own blood, and felt sick. Her eyes were striking, probably more so than in real life. Her face was tight with repressed anger and he'd made her hair look like flames wrapping around her head. She looked dangerous.

"What do you think?" he asked eagerly.

"It's the most awful thing I've ever seen," she said bluntly.

"You have got to be kidding me," Shane mumbled, dragging his hand down his face.

She glared at him. If Bram hadn't wanted her honest opinion, he shouldn't have asked. He didn't seem offended though, if anything, the answer had delighted him.

"It is awful to see yourself through the eyes of another, isn't it?" he purred, gazing at his own painting with adoration. "I'm sure that if you could paint me, my portrait would be just as horrifying to me."

"Somehow I doubt that," Amber said tiredly. "Look, if you don't want to give me the answers we came here for, then just say so. But I'm not staying any longer and playing these weird games with you if you can't tell us anything."

Bram looked up at her and grinned, revealing twisted yellow teeth. "Of course, of course. I've had my fun." He hopped up from his stool and grabbed a slip of paper. "I don't know where the sorcerer is staying, but I can tell you exactly where Zachariah Hudson is, and that he purchased a large amount of very odd ingredients from me recently. He wanted it off the record, but he failed to pay the full amount, so I consider any expectation of confidentiality void."

"What did he buy?" Amber asked as she accepted the note from Bram.

"It's all in the note, but I found the items particularly interesting. They are all things that could be used in spells, but they are not common ingredients. They're also normally bought by a witch. Interesting coincidence, don't you think?"

"Yeah, I do," Amber said, staring at the list. She looked up, that stupid painting catching her eye for a moment before she forced herself to look at Bram instead. "Thanks for your help."

He nodded. "You're welcome. Would you like to keep the painting?"

"Hell no."

He grinned. "Perhaps you should come back some time, when you hate yourself less. You might find that it has changed."

CHAPTER 47

CERI

*C*eri parked next to Shane's suburban and hopped out of her car. Amber had texted her a half hour ago and nearly given her a heart attack.

> *The council knows I have Evangeline. We're in deep shit if I can't prove she's innocent in a week.*

> *Going to a no magic spot with Shane. Need to see it for myself.*

Announcing that the council knew they were harboring a demon in their house required a *phone call*. That was not a text-and-then-not-respond-to-any-replies kind of situation.

She jogged into the woods, following the path worn by

investigators and probably tourists that wanted to see the freaky place where magic didn't work.

There was police tape around the area, but there weren't any guards. I guess they figured no one would want to come here. Being near it made her skin crawl. There was something off about the air. A strange smell that made her want to turn and run away. Every instinct she had was warning her against getting any closer.

Amber and Shane were waiting for her right next to the affected zone. Her alpha looked particularly grumpy, which she'd expected. She'd never seen Shane look so irritable though. He'd always been sunny and happy, even before the Trials.

"Took you long enough," Amber said as she approached.

"I can't believe you didn't call me. And what is he doing here?" She jabbed her thumb at Shane, then felt bad. "No offense, it'd be good to see you under different circumstances."

"None taken," he said, nodding in greeting. "And I volunteered to help since Amber is stubborn and won't just hand the girl over."

So, the council didn't know everything. That was probably for the best.

"We met with this old vampire named Bram, and he said he sold a bunch of stuff to Zachariah Hudson, that half angel we saw." Amber handed her a list scribbled down on a piece of paper. "He bought it all before the attack on Evangeline's house."

She read the list quickly, her brows knitting together as she thought about the supplies. They had to be for multiple spells because she couldn't think of anything that would require all this. Some of the ingredients would even work against each other. Then the name of the vampire registered and she looked up sharply, glaring at Shane. "You took her to see *Bram?*"

He lifted his hands and took a step back. "She was safe, Bram trusts me."

"You have got to be kidding me. That guy is insane. He *uses* people."

"He was a little weird but he didn't seem that bad--"

"You don't know his reputation," Ceri snapped before turning her glare back to Shane. "Are you actually trying to help or are you just here to keep an eye on her for the council?"

"I think Amber is being an idiot, but I'm trying to help."

Well, that sounded honest at least. "Fine. Let's get this over with."

It was impossible to miss the spot. She'd seen the pictures on the news, but nothing could prepare you for the wrongness of it. She braced herself and ducked under the police tape. It was a perfect circle about ten feet across where all the light and life seemed to have been stripped away.

Amber leaned in toward it and Shane grabbed her arm, yanking her back a step. "Don't step inside it!"

Amber batted his hand away. "I'm not an idiot. I'm just trying to smell it."

Ceri rolled her eyes. They were like children. "Sniff it from farther away. We can't risk you tripping into it. They're not sure what it would do to a werewolf."

She crouched down and opened her bag. Dozens of

witches, elves, and other magic users had done tests to try to find out how these spots were made, and if they could be fixed. None of them had come up with anything, but she had something they didn't.

Her owl flew down from the tree and landed on the ground next to her, startling both the werewolves.

"Where the hell did that thing come from?" Shane asked, eyeing it warily. "I didn't hear it."

"Guess you should pay better attention," Ceri said, smirking at him. It was fun to see him a little freaked out, and she didn't want to explain the owl anyhow.

Amber simply looked at it curiously. She knew what it was now, though she'd never seen it up close.

Her bag was a mess. She'd dumped everything in it in a hurry so that she could meet them here. After digging around for a moment, she brought out the sage and a little vial of holy water. She knew she had some lavender in there too but--

Her hand hit something warm and wiggly and she shrieked, almost falling backward as she jerked her hand out of the bag. Woggy was flung through the air, shrieking as well.

"Oh shi--"

Shane grabbed the back of Amber's shirt as she reached over the no magic spot, catching Woggy before he could fall into it. Shane yanked them both back and Amber toppled onto her butt, holding the pixie close to her chest.

"Well, that was close," Amber said drily.

Ceri put her head in her hands and tried to get herself

under control. She was *not* going to cry. "That's it. Woggy is grounded."

Shane laughed. "Is that pixie some kind of a pet or something? I thought witches just used them for parts."

Ceri lifted her head and glared at him. "They're sentient. He's not a pet, he's part of the pack."

"Oh...okay." Shane glanced at Amber as if expecting her to tell him that was just a joke, but Amber was busy making sure Woggy was alright. The pixie seemed rather excited actually and was signing something at her about *outside* and *happy*.

Taking a deep breath to shake off the trauma of nearly dumping Woggy into a no magic spot, she found the lavender and set it next to the sage. This was a chance to see if demons were actually involved in the creation of these spots, something that had been bothering her since it had come on the news.

She didn't trust Zachariah. The way he'd acted at the house that day, and on the news, set off warning bells in her head. But just because he couldn't be trusted didn't mean he was entirely wrong. Evangeline didn't seem to be the culprit, but that didn't mean Amber's demon wasn't doing something shady on the side.

Shane crouched down near the edge and sniffed it carefully. "It's weird that magic doesn't work inside it since it smells like magic."

"It smells like death and decay to me," Ceri said as she lit the sage stick. She pushed up to her knees and waved it gently around the edge of the no magic spot. The smoke curled around it, and drifted upward, but couldn't seem to pass over the edge. She frowned and blew gently, trying to coax it into the circle. It simply spread even further in either direction, none of it able to drift forward.

"Is there some kind of barrier?" Amber asked. Woggy was struggling in her hands, so she set him on her shoulder. He liked to climb in everyone's hair and hide in it, which he promptly did, disappearing into Amber's.

Shane grabbed a stick and tossed it into the circle. It passed through unimpeded and landed on the ground. Nothing seemed to happen to it. "Not a physical one."

"Whatever spell created this was evil. The sage won't touch it." Ceri set the bundle of sage next to her, letting it smolder. Having it nearby was calming. It afforded her a little protection against any evil spirits that might be lingering nearby.

The owl shuffled closer, climbing onto her knee. She pet it tentatively. It had never let her touch it before, and she wasn't sure why now was different. It seemed content just to sit on her knee for now though.

She grabbed the holy water and whispered a quick incantation -- infusing the water with her magic to give it a little more oomph -- then squirted some into the circle. The droplets hit the ground and...did nothing.

She frowned. "If this had been created by demons, the holy water should have done *something.*"

"Could it be a natural phenomenon?" Amber asked.

Ceri shook her head. "No, there's something very wrong about it. It feels the opposite of natural."

The owl turned its head to face her and she met its deep,

orange eyes. All the sounds around her faded away, including Shane and Amber.

The ground shook. Red eyes glowed in the darkness, surrounded by magic. A voice chanted, growing louder and louder, but she couldn't make out the words. Only the feel of them. They were wrong. Cursed. Hollow.

The owl blinked and she snapped out of the vision.

"Ceri?" Amber prompted again, looking a little concerned.

"Sorry, what?" she asked, rubbing the back of her hand over her eyes.

"I think I hear someone coming down the road, we should go."

Ceri nodded and began gathering up her things. The owl hopped off her knee, then launched into the air, disappearing into the trees. Shane watched it go suspiciously.

"I think that whatever answers we're looking for, we won't find here," she said as she pushed up to her feet. "I don't know what the council wants as proof, but I don't think any demon did this."

Shane shoved his hands in his pockets. "Jameson will stand by his word if you can prove it, but I don't think he knows what he wants to see either. The biggest issue is just disproving Hudson publicly. If it gets out that the council was protecting you, it won't matter what the truth is. It'll be a shit show."

"We'll figure something out." Amber untangled Woggy from her hair. He'd fallen asleep and simply rolled over in her hand. She walked him over to Ceri who took him and set him back in her bag. "I have to take Shane home. I'll see you back at the house."

Ceri nodded and hurried back toward her car. The more they learned about all this, the more it bothered her. Something wasn't adding up. They were missing something important.

She followed Amber's truck back to the main road. As they turned onto the highway, a sleek black sedan turned down the gravel road. She thought she saw a glimpse of blond hair through the tinted windows, but she couldn't be sure.

CHAPTER 48

GENEVIEVE

Genevieve's favorite part of her job was research. Digging into a client's past and finding every skeleton was important for a defense lawyer. She had to know her client's weaknesses better than the prosecution. If she got blindsided by evidence or something they'd done in the past, the client was screwed.

Finding out everything she could about Paul Greer was probably an abuse of power. After all, she had access to information most people didn't. She didn't feel the slightest bit guilty though.

"Here's your waffles," the waitress said cheerfully as she slid the plate in front of her.

"Thanks," Genevieve said with a smile.

The waitress set Paul's food in front of him –– steak with

a side of mashed potatoes –– then hurried away to the next table.

He picked up his fork and knife and raised an eyebrow at her. "Aren't waffles normally a breakfast food?"

"They're delicious, therefore they're breakfast, lunch, and dinner food." She grabbed the blueberry syrup and poured a liberal amount on top of the perfectly golden waffles. This was going to hit the spot. "Thanks for meeting with me on such short notice."

"It was no problem. I was surprised to receive your message, actually. Many new alphas aren't interested in taking on the responsibility of sponsoring someone, especially for a pack that has caused them trouble." He cut into his steak and blood leaked out. In the past that would have grossed her out, but now it just looked good. The wolf was jealous he had steak and she didn't, but she pushed the urges down.

"It is a lot of responsibility, which is why I'm interested in negotiating a few things before I approach Amber. I guarantee she'd turn you down without hesitation if we can't work out something that will help her before I bring it up." She watched his reaction closely. He did look a little surprised. Perhaps he hadn't expected her to be so prepared.

He finished chewing his bite, then set his fork down and clasped his hands together in front of him. "Alright, that seems fair enough. What do you want?"

She smiled, expecting the question. "I think we should start with what you want. Seeking out Amber is an odd choice. Most potential alphas would go to someone like Jameson first."

"You haven't been a werewolf long, so you haven't seen the way things have changed in the past decade," he said, his eyes going distant. "Some of the packs are becoming more like gangs than a werewolf pack. We're meant to be family, not mercenaries for hire. The alphas also try to suppress the instincts of their pack members so much that they end up acting out like rebellious teenagers."

"There has been a rise in gang violence associated with werewolf packs," she agreed with a nod. "Especially in cities."

"Born or bitten doesn't matter to me. If anything, the bitten wolves help the packs. Their issues with control remind us that we aren't human. We aren't tame. There is a balance between control and accepting the wolf that lives up here." He tapped a long finger against his head. "Lockhart never got that. He never accepted how much the wolf drove him, and he became mean. And selfish. He wouldn't allow challenges within the pack and simply chose his favorites for various positions. No one respected his beta or gammas as a result."

"They were definitely assholes," Genevieve muttered, sopping up some more syrup with an already soggy piece of waffle. "How does Amber fit into all this?"

Paul smiled at that. "She didn't give a fuck about what people thought. She demanded their respect, and found a way to not only enter the Trials, but survive them. I have changes to make in this pack, and allying myself with someone like Amber sends a message not only to my pack but everyone else as well."

"It doesn't also have to do with the fact that Jameson refused to sponsor you once before?"

Paul sat back, a smile forming on his face. "You looked into my past in more detail than I expected."

"I might be recently bitten, but I wasn't born yesterday. You might want to send a message, but I knew that couldn't be it." She took a drink of water and waited for him to explain. She already knew the gossip, but hearing from him why he'd been turned down was important.

"My original pack fell apart. I was the beta, and I expected that I'd be able to take control and move on. I expected it to be simple, but I made a mistake." He sighed and tapped his thumb on the table, an almost nervous gesture. "I didn't gain the pack's respect. A few of them broke the rules, went out on a full moon and got drunk, and someone got killed. It was my fault. I'd seen the signs and thought simply forbidding it was enough. I'd barely been alpha for a day but thought my word was law. It was naive."

"What should you have done?" she asked curiously. Amber never really told them what to do, but with such a small pack, they hadn't had any issues with idiotic pack members.

"Watched them. One of them showed disrespect when I gave the orders, but I didn't want to be too hard on them since their alpha had just died. I should have challenged him and forced his submission, for his own good. He was wild with grief. His wolf wanted a fight and I could have given it to him." He rubbed his hand along his jaw with a sigh. "Instead, he is spending life in jail. That is my fault."

"Well, we all make mistakes. Sounds like you've learned from yours," she said, setting her fork to the side. It was time to get down to business. "So, Amber is a bit of a last resort for you. All the risk is on her if she does this for you. What can you offer to my pack?"

He leaned in and rested his arms on the table. "I think the first thing we should discuss is an alliance. However, I would also like to offer to cover the sponsor's fee. From what I understand, Amber doesn't necessarily have the funds for it."

Genevieve nodded. "That sounds like an excellent start."

She smiled as they got down to the nitty-gritty. This was something she was good at. Hopefully, Amber wouldn't be pissed about it, but this could be really good for the pack. Right now, no one really respected them. It would only cause problems in the future if that wasn't remedied. Even if Amber asked Ceri to be her beta instead, she wanted to do this for her.

CHAPTER 49

AMBER

*A*mber rubbed the demon mark. Angel had been mysteriously absent today. Normally, he followed her around trying to ruin her mood. The absence made her suspicious, but perhaps he was spending his time harassing Evangeline instead. She'd seen him talking to her the night that half angel had come on the news.

"Is the mark hurting?" Derek asked, sipping on a beer. He'd been at the warehouse all day, and she felt bad about not helping, but everything had gone downhill fast after that council meeting.

"Yeah, I just haven't seen the demon in a while. Makes me antsy," she admitted with a shrug.

Eloise grunted as she sat down on the couch. They'd decided to include her and Evangeline in tonight's conversation. They needed to know about the most recent issue, and Amber was hoping they might be able to remember something helpful from the night of the attack.

Ceri handed Eloise a small vial to help with the pain of her healing ribs, then turned to her and Derek. "You ready?"

"Yeah, let's get this over with." She headed into the living room and plopped down in the armchair she'd dragged into the room just for this.

This needed to be a pack meeting, not just her standing in front of them telling them what to do, and she thought sitting might help with that. Genevieve and Ceri sat on either side of her, while Tommy took the last seat on the couch next to Evangeline.

With a sigh, she leaned forward, bracing her elbows on her knees. "This morning when I arrived at the council meeting, they demanded that I hand Evangeline over to the police."

Eloise visibly tensed, her hand going to her daughter's arm. "You can't--"

"I know," Amber said, waving her concerns away. "I wouldn't do that, and I can't anyhow with the deal I've made with the demon, Kadrithan. Fortunately, they're willing to give me a week to prove that Evangeline isn't the one destroying magic."

"Only a week?" Tommy asked, his face pinched in concern.

She nodded. "Ceri's cousin is looking for the sorcerer, and I talked to someone else today who gave me some interesting insight into that guy on the news, Zachariah Hudson. I have an address for him, and I think I should go see him tomorrow."

Ceri and Genevieve turned on her in sync, each of them in varying states of shock.

"You can't be serious," Ceri choked out.

"I'm not going to say I have Evangeline, but I want to try to figure out what he's after, really. He's working with the sorcerer, so he has to have a different reason for wanting her dead."

"That is the worst idea you've ever had. Hands down," Genevieve said, shaking her head. "If you go try to talk to this guy he's going to show up here with the police, and they're going to find Evangeline."

"We can't just sit here and wait for something to fall in our laps." Amber crossed her arms and sat back in her chair, exasperated.

"What if you just send me away somewhere?" Evangeline suggested. "If I leave, then everyone will be safe."

As if summoned by the utterance, Angel appeared. "She's not going anywhere until I figure out how she was found in the first place. I won't risk sending her into greater danger."

Amber met Evangeline's gaze. The girl looked as furious as she felt. They didn't have much in common but they both hated Kadrithan's constant interfering.

"If you're going to barge into our pack meetings, you should show yourself," Genevieve said, glaring around the room.

The demon obliged, pulling strength from the demon mark to appear to them all. He'd taken on his red devil form again, only bigger this time, and sneered at Genevieve. "Better?"

"It'd be better if you disappeared forever, but yeah, I prefer getting to hear both sides of the conversation," she snapped.

"And you wonder why I don't hang around for chats," Angel muttered as he arranged himself on the arm of the couch.

"Maybe you just need to find the sorcerer, then call the police," Derek suggested. "No matter what else is going on, he is breaking the law. You don't necessarily have to do this all on your own."

Amber stared at her knees. He wasn't wrong, it'd just be tricky. "We still have to find him."

"Siobhan should be getting back to me soon. She can talk to people we can't. She'll find him." Ceri seemed confident, and Amber hoped she was right.

"I hate waiting around," Amber said, dragging her hands down her face and taking a deep breath. "Okay, we wait to hear from Siobhan, but if she hasn't found him in two days, I'm going to have to do *something*."

No one seemed particularly enthused with the plan, but it was all they had. Amber felt completely out of her depth. She wasn't a detective or a bodyguard. She probably shouldn't be an alpha either at this rate.

CHAPTER 50

CERI

*C*eri sat across from Woggy, who was watching her hands intently. She was trying to expand his vocabulary now that he'd adapted to using sign language every day. He always enjoyed the lessons, but that was probably because of the treats he got.

She began signing *chicken* when pain shot through her head. It was so intense her vision blurred and for a moment, she thought she might vomit.

"Evangeline..." she gasped out as she collapsed to the floor. Her magic flared out from inside her, trying to defend her against the sudden attack. Gritting her teeth, she forced herself to shout, "EVANGELINE!"

Footsteps sounded on the stairs and through the tears of

pain she caught a glimpse of the girl kneeling over her. She looked frantic. "What's wrong?"

"Call...Amber...attack," she managed to force out. Each word was a struggle. Her muscles began to seize as magic flowed through her. She shut her eyes and pulled desperately on the pack bond. It came alive and poured into her, giving her just enough power to let her breathe again.

She'd known this was coming, but she'd hoped she had more time. That maybe they'd find the sorcerer first.

Her fingernails scraped against the wood floor and she felt the house come alive around her. It groaned, panicking at the rage and pain it felt in her.

Please help me, she begged.

All around her, the wards burst to life. The house's magic unfurled and lights danced behind her vision as she opened her mind to it.

The painful sensations racking her body faded away as her mind linked with the house. The sorcerer's attack was all around them, pounding on the windows, curling through the rafters, and seeping under the door.

The house roared, sounding like a dragon in her mind, and light burst from it, driving the darkness back. Her view shifted and she saw Evangeline shaking her limp body. It was odd to see her own face staring blankly at the ceiling.

"What do I do?" Evangeline begged as tears slipped down her face.

She drifted toward her, trying to be comforting, but the girl shrieked as she mentally touched her, whirling around like someone had touched her. "Who's there?"

The air shifted to Ceri's left and she saw the demon

appear. He looked straight at her as though he could see her even though Evangeline couldn't.

"What's happening?" he demanded.

"I don't know! She said something about an attack, then just stopped moving! She said to call Amber, but I don't have a phone!"

"Use hers," the demon said, keeping a suspicious eye on Ceri's ethereal form.

"It's in the pocket of my cardigan," she said, finding her voice suddenly.

"Check the pocket of her cardigan," the demon passed on, drifting toward her body.

Evangeline dug through her pockets and found her phone. She never kept it locked with a password, so the girl was able to unlock it and find Amber's number with shaking fingers.

"Hello? Amber? Something is wrong...I don't know... Amber? AMBER?" She dropped the phone and put her face in her hands.

"What's happening?" the demon demanded.

"I don't know," Evangeline sobbed. "I think something is attacking them. We're screwed."

Ceri's heart fell out of her chest. The sorcerer wasn't just attacking her, he was attacking her pack too. The house felt her fear and wrapped around her, pulling her out of the living room.

Her view changed and she saw everything around the house as though she was sitting on the roof. The house was an island in a sea of darkness. The black magic churned around it like they were in the midst of a hurricane.

Ceridwen Gallagher, a voice said, sliding around her like a snake. *I told you I'd find you.*

The flap of wings startled her and she looked up. Her owl was flying toward her but a gust of hot air knocked it aside, sending it careening toward the ground.

"No!" she cried, reaching out with her magic to protect it. The sorcerer's magic whipped upward and wrapped around her ankle, yanking her from her feet. Cold seeped into her leg as it dragged her toward the edge of the roof.

The spell had grown in power tenfold. She could feel the sorcerer's evil intent in the very air. The house groaned beneath her as it strained against the relentless attack.

Inch by inch the spell dragged her to the edge. She looked over her shoulder and saw the darkness waiting for her. Its maw stretched wide open, sharp teeth and a swirling, fiery throat that eagerly lifted toward her.

How many people did you have to kill to steal this power? Ceri demanded as she held onto the roof with aching fingers.

A chuckle floated past her. *Are you jealous?*

No, I pity you.

A vicious jerk ripped her hands free and for a moment she was falling. Her view shifted once again as the house dragged her inside to protect her. Her body was shaking now, teeth chattering as her head rocked from side to side.

"It won't work!" Evangeline shouted at the demon, hands curled into tight fists.

"Try it regardless! Or would you rather die crying in the corner?" He sneered at her. "Don't be *pathetic*."

A window shattered, glass spraying over the carpet. Ceri rushed toward it, chanting a spell of protection, but without her physical body, she was struggling to use her magic. If the spirit had been able to make it to her, she might had had a chance.

"Evangeline," Eloise said from the top of the stairs. "Look at me."

The girl turned toward her mother, eyes red with unshed tears. "I can't do this."

"Remember that lullaby I used to sing to you? The one about the castle. Sing that for me, just shut your eyes, and sing." With a pained grunt, Eloise lowered herself down to the floor and leaned against the banister, a gentle smile on her face.

Evangeline nodded tremulously and, keeping her back to the demon, began to sing. "Ah! Mon beau château…"

Her voice lifted all around them, twisting through the air as if it were pure light. Ceri had never seen anything like it, then again, she'd never watched an angel sing from the spirit realm. This was powerful magic, though not the type most people would understand. It wasn't a simple spell. It was life…power…and beauty. It was everything the sorcerer's spell wasn't.

Evangeline's magic, which was tied to the protective spell Ceri had cast, surged through their shaky bond. Her white blonde hair lifted from her shoulder and her pale skin glowed with a light that pulsed inside of her.

The lyrics didn't matter, they were nothing more than a focus for the magic inside of Evangeline. With renewed determination, Ceri took hold of the strength Evangeline was giving her, and opened the front door.

I'm going to kill you! the sorcerer howled, the darkness whipping into a frenzy.

Not today.

She lifted her hands and light poured forth.

CHAPTER 51

AMBER

*A*mber smashed another spider with the end of the broom. "We will, we will, smush you," she sang along with the radio, changing the lyrics to suit her current activities.

The warehouse was starting to look less like a haunted house and more like a place someone might actually want to leave their truck to have it fixed. They'd already cleared out all the trash in the main area where they'd work. She was tackling the office today.

There was a crash and she poked her head out. Tommy was sprawled out in front of a stack of now broken wooden pallets and Derek was cackling. "Told you that was too many."

"I almost had it!" Tommy hopped up to his feet and brushed the dust off his shirt.

She rolled her eyes but smiled at their antics. Her brother and Tommy got along great. He had a knack for bringing out Tommy's adventurous side that she appreciated. Between her brother and Deward, Tommy was really coming out of his shell.

Crouching down, she swept the dirt into the dustpan then headed outside to dump it. Derek had forgotten only one thing. A trash can. So, they had to get creative until he had time to go to the store and grab one.

She tossed the dirt and turned to head back inside when her phone rang. Tucking the dustpan under her arm, she pulled out her phone.

"Hey Ceri, what's--"

"Something is wrong."

Her fingers tightened on the phone as every sense jumped into high alert. That wasn't Ceri. "Evangeline? What's wrong?"

The wind shifted and the smell of something wrong blew past her. It smelled like fire and death. She stepped back outside and saw something moving in the trees. There was more than one of them, whatever they were, and they were big.

"I don't know," Evangeline said sounding frantic.

Amber felt Ceri pull on the pack bond and desperately sent her every ounce of strength she could. At the same time, a monster burst out of the trees. It wasn't like anything she'd ever seen. It was as if the earth itself had spit the thing out. Thick arms made of dirt and debris from the forest dragged along the ground as it lumbered toward her on thick, tree trunk-like legs. The thing had no eyes, but its wide, gaping mouth roared as it charged toward her.

She dropped the phone and shouted over her shoulder as she ran toward it. "Run!"

She didn't hesitate to shift. Her clothes tore and fell away as her body changed. The wolf came alive inside her, ready to fight. The creature was faster than she expected and it caught her midair with a swing of its massive fist.

Disoriented from the blow, she hit the ground and slid. With an enraged howl, she leaped back to her feet and raced after the thing. It was headed for the warehouse. Derek stood right in its path, a look of shock on his face. She wanted to scream for him to move, but she couldn't.

The creature lifted its fist, swinging it at her brother. Derek was shoved to the side and Tommy caught the blow with his side, stopping the creature's momentum completely. His teeth were bared, and a wild look was in his eye as he shoved the arm away, then shifted and lunged at its face.

Amber jumped on its back as it roared its displeasure. It reared up, trying to grab her. She dug her claws into the dirt that made up its body and bit into the back of its neck. Her mouth filled with soil and rocks and the sickly taste of magic. She spat it out and struck again, biting and tearing.

The ground shook as it stomped around, swinging its arms wildly. With one particularly vicious shake of its head, it threw her off. She hit the ground on her feet this time but was frozen in place for a moment.

Emerging from the trees were two more.

CHAPTER 52

TOMMY

*T*ommy saw the other two charge out of the forest and he wanted to run. There was no way they could defeat all three. They hadn't even managed to hurt the first one. There had to be something they could do to slow it down, but it wasn't made of flesh and bone. It was dirt and rock and magic.

A gunshot rang out and he dropped to the ground in a panic before he realized it was Derek. He racked his shotgun and fired again, hitting the first monster in the face and knocking it back. It seemed to stun the monster more than their attacks had.

He darted in and bit a chunk out of its ankle before hurrying back out of the reach of the thing's huge arms. It was slower than they were since it was big, but it was still faster than he'd expected. Faster than something that huge should be.

Amber charged toward the two new monsters, trying to get their attention. They roared and began following her, almost stumbling into each other in their haste to attack her. She wasn't going to be able to keep them running in circles forever though. They had to kill these things.

Derek shot the first one again, this time in the chest, and that's when Tommy saw it. There was something glowing inside it. If they couldn't damage the creature's themselves, maybe they could destroy whatever was powering them.

He yipped at Derek to get his attention so he didn't get shot, then ran toward the first creature. As soon as he got close enough, he bunched his legs up underneath himself and jumped. The force of his impact knocked the creature back slightly. He tore into its chest, ripping away chunks of dirt until he saw it.

Stars exploded behind his eyes and he felt himself flying through the air. He wasn't sure what hit him, he hadn't seen it coming. All the air rushed out of his lungs as he hit the ground, but he rolled immediately and forced himself back up to his feet.

"Stay down!" Derek shouted, reloading his shotgun as he ran. Sliding to a stop not far from Tommy, he swung the gun up to his shoulder and fired another shot. This one hit the glowing, red spot in the monster's chest.

It stumbled back, its arms flailing in panic, then it exploded. Dirt and debris flew in every direction and Tommy's ears rang painfully. He couldn't hear anything around him anymore, just his own panicked breathing.

Derek had been thrown onto his back, but he pushed himself upright and climbed back onto his feet. "Holy shit that worked. Amber! There's something in their chests!"

Tommy howled in victory, adrenaline rushing through him as he regained hope they could stop these things.

He and Derek worked like a well-oiled machine as they attacked one of the two chasing after Amber. She kept their attention, attacking as needed to make sure they kept following her.

Tommy darted in, his ears still ringing from the sounds of gunfire. He launched himself onto the back of the closest one and bit down hard on the back of its neck. It leaned back, trying to grab him as expected. Running into range, Derek swung his shotgun up to his shoulder and shot it in the chest twice, drilling a hole into the dirt.

Tommy leapt away and Derek fired again. The shot hit the thing in its chest and it exploded, tossing him a little farther than he'd expected with the resulting shockwave. The last creature turned, roaring its displeasure, and ran for Derek.

Derek, using common sense, took off at a run toward the warehouse. Amber leapt on the thing's back, but it immediately grabbed her and tossed her aside. A pulse of magic glowed within the creature, growing brighter and brighter as it ran.

As Derek ran into the warehouse, it launched itself after him in a leap that left craters behind in the soft dirt. It hit the front of the warehouse, its massive head catching on the top of the already broken roll-up door.

With one final, bright pulse, it exploded. A fireball

erupted from the center of it, engulfing the front of the warehouse in flames.

Amber raced toward it, jumping through the fire without any concern for herself. Tommy followed close behind, his heart beating a million miles a minute. As he skidded through the smoke inside the building he saw Derek running for the fire extinguisher. He had survived.

~

*T*ommy couldn't stop shaking even though it had been an hour, but he knew it was just the after effects of all the adrenaline that had been pumping through his body. That made it a little better, knowing that he wasn't just trembling in fear. The monsters were gone and they had all survived.

"It's a perversion of a golem." Ceri's face was drawn and pale. Dark circles stood out in stark relief under her eyes. She'd come as soon as she'd heard about the attack and filled them in on what had happened to her. "They're usually peaceful. Whatever magic was used to create them was twisted and filled with malice."

"The sorcerer did this, right?" He wrapped his arms a little tighter around his chest. He'd started keeping a pair of shorts in Amber's truck but apparently, he needed an entire spare outfit.

She stared at the pile of rubble, her eyes unfocused. "It could be. There's just something that bothers me about it. This sorcerer is all about psychic attacks. The whole time I was under attack at the house, he was taunting me, but he never mentioned this."

The sound of an unfamiliar voice startled Tommy. He looked over his shoulder and saw a black sedan had driven up. The detective that had come by their house after the attack there was talking to Amber in the driveway. He didn't look happy. Then again, neither did she.

"I think the same sorcerer that killed Donovan did this," Amber said, hands on her hips. She was still streaked with mud. None of them had had a chance to clean up.

Ceri nodded her head toward them tiredly. "Let's go help her out."

He nodded and trailed after her. The blackened front of the warehouse loomed in front of them. So much damage had been done. The fire hadn't spread far, but it hadn't needed to.

Derek hauled a pile of charred debris out of the warehouse. His eyes flashed with anger as he tossed it onto the growing pile. He'd been mostly silent since the attack. This place meant everything to him. Having it damaged like this had to be infuriating.

They'd almost lost everything. He couldn't imagine something happening to Ceri. He curled his hand into a fist and cursed the demon and the sorcerer.

CHAPTER 53

GENEVIEVE

*I*t had happened again. Her pack had been fighting for their lives while she was miles away, unable to get to them in time to help. She'd just hurried back to the house to find Ceri having convulsions on the living room floor. Then she'd had to stay behind to protect that demon girl while Ceri had gone to see Amber and the others.

Genevieve bit another hunk of chicken off the sticky drumstick in her hand and glared at the wall as if it were to blame.

"Did you eat that entire chicken?"

Amber's voice startled her out of her angry thoughts. She looked down at what used to be a rotisserie chicken and sighed.

"Apparently I did. Guess I'll order pizza for dinner." She

tossed the bone onto the now ravaged carcass and threw the whole mess away. "Is Ceri feeling better?"

Amber shrugged. "Yeah, she's just...angry. Everybody is on edge. Evangeline is scared out of her mind."

"Tommy said he thinks she's going to try to bolt." Genevieve walked over to the fridge and pulled out two beers. If any conversation required alcohol, it was going to be this one. With all the chaos going on, it was even more important to get the stuff with Greer nailed down. And it made her feel like she was actually contributing instead of just goofing off while her friends nearly got murdered.

"She probably will. He's keeping an eye on her. As is the house," Amber said, looking around like it might hear her.

It probably could. It probably watched them all the time. She was glad it decided it liked them because living in some kind of sentient house that had it out for you was her worst nightmare.

"It's kind of cool it can do all that. Makes me wonder who put all that magic into it." She looked up at the ceiling curiously. The house was older, but it wasn't anything too special design-wise. She took a sip of her beer, then decided to get the awkwardness over with.

"So..." she paused and tried to remember how she'd wanted to phrase this. "When we were visiting the Lockhart Pack, or whatever the hell it's called now, one of them approached me. They want you to sponsor them if they can take the pack on the next full moon."

"Seriously?" Amber looked about as surprised as she'd felt that day. "Why? Not that I have the money anyhow."

"Well, I had dinner with him yesterday and asked him that very question," she said nervously.

"You're taking this request seriously?" Amber laughed and took a long drink of her beer.

Genevieve's fingers tightened on the icy cold bottle she was holding. "Yeah, I am. It's actually a really good opportunity for the pack, especially since you are on the council. We're a little bit of a target right now. I mean, honestly, we're lucky no one has come to challenge you yet."

That sobered her up a bit. "Is that common?"

She nodded. "Smaller packs don't tend to last long."

"I still don't see how I could sponsor this guy, and there's no guarantee he'd help us after we did regardless."

"According to the deal I've begun negotiating with him there..." Genevieve began, pulling her notes out of her pocket.

"You started negotiating without even talking to--"

"Slow your roll," Genevieve said, holding up her hand. "So, traditionally, a potential alpha approaches the beta of the alpha they want to sponsor them. He, uh, assumed that was me."

"Oh."

"And nothing is set in stone, these have all been preliminary negotiations. It's all part of the game, basically. I told him it wasn't even worth bringing up to you if I couldn't show you that it would help the pack in some way. And I was right," she said, giving Amber a look.

Amber snorted. "Ok, fine. I'm cynical and suspicious. What can he give us?"

"First, he will cover the sponsor fee, and we will return

the funds to him if he passes the Trials. Second, a basic alliance. He won't act against us, and we won't act against him. Third, he will, personally, come to your aid any time you call to fulfill a single favor." She smirked at her alpha. "I took a little inspiration from the demon for that one."

"Lawyers, demons, same thing really," Amber said with a smirk.

"Hey! I'm trying to help here and now you're insulting me?"

Amber threw her head back and laughed. "Sorry, it was too easy."

Clearing her throat, she folded the paper back up and shoved it in her pocket. "Anyhow, that's what I have for now. You have to do the final negotiating if you agree to meet with him. And...you should also choose who is your actual beta. Though, since I started the negotiations it's probably best if I just finish it with you."

She crossed her arms and stared at Amber, waiting for some kind of response.

"This is a trap, isn't it?"

"It's not a trap. You just have to tell me who your beta is." Genevieve shrugged like it didn't matter.

"I don't know. I've never thought about it." Amber looked like she wanted to bolt. "This is worse than trying to pick your maid of honor for your wedding. Maybe I should make y'all fight for it."

Genevieve glared at her. "I'm not fighting for anything. Just pick."

Amber shook her head, her lips pressed firmly together. "Nope, not going to happen. You can deal with this little sponsor issue, then we'll just go back to normal. Nobody needs a rank."

She then fled to the living room while shouting for Ceri.

"This conversation is so not done," she muttered as she dialed the nearest pizza place, knowing full well that Amber could still hear her.

CHAPTER 54

AMBER

*R*ain pattered against the window in a soothing rhythm. Amber yawned as she stared absently at the gray fog outside. Maybe she could get to bed early for once.

The mark moved under her skin and she felt the demon now known as The Asshole behind her. "I see you're hard at work staring out a window now."

She rolled her eyes and turned to face him. "When are you going to stop being a dick? You were almost pleasant when you first showed up, but now you're acting like an angry sixteen-year-old girl who lost the title of Prom Queen to her little sister."

He sneered at her. "I had every right to kill you for what

you did when you banished me. I'm surprised you would complain about my *tone*."

"I didn't ask the wolf to do that or help her do it. She just did it on her own! So quit fucking blaming me for it!" Amber shouted at the demon, fed up with the attitude and constant digs. Red bled into her vision as she glared at him. The urge to shift and rip something apart crawled under her skin. "If you had told me a young girl was going to be killed for being half demon, I would have helped without the damn mark. We saved her. She's here, safe and sound, and she's going to stay that way. Quit being a damn drama queen about it!"

"You have no idea how important she is!" Angel shouted back. Flames shot from his mouth and he doubled in size, as he always did when he got pissy.

"So tell me, you stubborn asshole!"

He solidified for a split second and knocked a pile of books off the table, sending them scattering across the floor. His chest heaved as he panted from the exertion of affecting the material world. He shrank as he turned away and crossed his arms. "She's my niece, as you know."

Amber sat down in her armchair but didn't reply. This had been a long time coming, and she didn't want to interrupt. She pressed the palms of her hand into her eyes until she saw stars. She *was* sorry the wolf had banished him. He had completely overreacted though, and it was hard to trust him now.

Angel floated toward the fireplace and settled in front of it, a smoky chair appearing behind him. He grew legs and sat down, crossing them at the ankle as he stretched out. He looked mostly human in this form. His face wasn't fully formed, just shifting shadows. She caught a glimpse of a strong jaw, eyes that burned red, and aquiline nose. She wondered if this was close to what he really looked like, or if it was just another illusion.

He sighed before finally speaking. "My sister, the idiot that she was, fell in love with an angel. It was a real Romeo and Juliet situation. And everyone knows how that ended."

He fell silent again and Amber looked down at her hands. She knew the pain of losing a sibling. It was something most people didn't get.

"Angels hate us. Well, everyone hates us. We're monsters. Tricksters that are after your soul." He snorted and shook his head. "Nobody knows or cares about the truth."

"Are you saying you aren't after people's souls?" Amber asked, skeptical. It was indisputable that a deal with a demon came at the price of a demon mark. If you failed to fulfill your end of the bargain, you died. What happened to your soul was debatable, but she doubted it was good.

"It's complicated," he said, waving away her question. "Evangeline was never supposed to be born. She's an embarrassment for the angels. There have been others like her in the past, but none of them ever made it past infancy."

She looked up sharply. "The angels killed them?"

He nodded slowly. "Killed them and their parents. That threat is enough to deter most romances, but not all of them. Some people are too stupid to be helped."

"Why do the angels hate you so much?"

Angel stood and ignored her question for a second time. "I have things I need to do. Get some sleep."

"Why can't you just be honest with me?" she asked quietly.

She wanted him to give her a reason not to kill him. The thought of it still made her sick to her stomach, but she didn't know if that was because he was manipulating her, or if it was because her instincts about him were right.

He paused, glancing back over his shoulder. "It's for your own good."

CHAPTER 55

TOMMY

ommy had been paying attention, and he knew what she was going to do. It's what he would have done in her situation, what he almost did. If Amber hadn't come back early that day he'd be wandering in the woods somewhere as an omega.

He stood outside her window and waited quietly. Evangeline was zipping up the backpack she'd taken from his room earlier that day. He had no clue why she thought she could get away with it, but she seemed more stubborn than smart. She was too angry to think anything through clearly.

The window slid open and the screen flew out, follow by the backpack, then her foot. He crossed his arms and waited for her to hop down. She straightened her jacket, pulling her hoodie farther down over her face, and picked up the backpack.

"Nice backpack," he said in a normal tone.

She jumped with a strangled yelp and whipped around to face him. "What the hell are you doing out here?"

"Convincing you to not run away and getting back my backpack. Not gonna lie, it was a little crappy of you to steal it after I took a bullet for you."

Her eyes flashed with anger and she didn't look the least bit remorseful. "Just buy a new one. I'm not staying, and neither is your backpack."

"No, you need to stay here and stop being an idiot."

"I'll be better off alone, and everyone will be safer with me gone. Get your fake mom to buy you a new backpack," she said with a sneer.

"You're going overboard with the whole tragic, teenager thing," he said, shoving his hands in his pocket.

"Excuse me?"

He shrugged. "You're a demon, and you don't have any control over that. But the whole woe-is-me act is getting old."

"Woe is me? Seriously? I have people actively hunting me because one of my dead parents was a demon, and you're mocking me? You have no idea what it's like––"

"We're a brand new pack that everyone already distrusted simply because we were bitten and not born. I know exactly what it's like to be an outcast. And now, I have a monster in my head that likes the taste of blood, and every time I get angry, I think I might lose control." His voice rose with every word until he was practically shouting. "You've been a total ass to every single person around you since we rescued you. We're all having a shitty week. Do you think anyone wanted to deal with this? "

"So just let me leave!"

"If you leave and get hurt, not only will it devastate Eloise, but it will *kill* Amber."

Evangeline yanked the backpack off her shoulder and threw it on the ground. "What am I supposed to do then? Just sit in my bedroom and hope for the best?"

"Yes. Stay optimistic, help your mother heal, and learn how to control whatever magic you have. And maybe try admitting that you're sick."

She looked at him, expression furious with her lips pressed into a thin line. "It's not that easy."

"I never said it was easy, but running away isn't going to help anything. It's just going to get someone hurt and break your mother's heart. Did you even think about how she'd feel when she woke up in the morning and you were gone?" She had no idea how lucky she was to still have her mother. He'd never left his mother's side when she was sick. He'd stayed as her hair fell out and her skin grew pale. He'd stayed when his dad escaped into the bottle. He'd stayed until she took her last breath. There was no way he'd let Evangeline run away from this when she still had a chance to be with her mother.

"You don't understand what Kadrithan wants from me," Evangeline said quietly.

Tommy sighed. "Then tell me."

She looked away and shook her head. "Can I at least sit outside for a while? I'm going stir crazy in there."

He wanted to shake the truth out of her, but if he pressed

now, he knew she'd just clam up. She was stubborn like that. "Fine, but I'm staying with you."

She turned on her heel and walked toward the porch without responding. He followed, shoving his hands in his pockets and wishing he was a mind reader instead of a shifter.

CHAPTER 56

GENEVIEVE

*G*enevieve's palms were sweating, but she was managing to keep her face straight at least. Having to sit here silently while Amber negotiated this part was killing her. Maybe she should have taped her mouth shut before they started, just to remove the temptation.

Amber didn't look nervous at all. If anything, she looked bored. "Honestly, if I came here just to quibble over the details of an alliance, I will consider this time wasted."

She had to actually bite her tongue after that comment. Cool and untouchable was good, apathetic was not. They had talked about this beforehand, but Amber was already striking out on her own and *improvising*.

Greer snorted and shook his head. "You're too impatient. The details are what matters in this agreement, unless you want to end up having to take over my pack in the event of my death?"

"Then let's make this clear and simple." Amber grabbed a fresh sheet of paper and numbered it one through three. "First, I don't act against your pack, and you don't act against mine. Second, if I have any knowledge of someone that intends to harm you or your pack, I tell you. You do the same. Third, in the event of my death, you agree to sponsor my chosen successor if they successfully claim the position, and vice versa."

Amber pushed the paper toward him and leaned back, crossing her arms. Paul reread each of the points, tapping his finger against his cheek thoughtfully. This was exactly what she and Amber had talked about earlier. The alliance would help them, without requiring them to exert much time or energy. It was the perfect balance for a small, isolated pack like theirs.

This all depended on Paul now. She couldn't quite read him despite the research she'd done. He kept a cool, thoughtful expression on his face, making him look almost bored at some points in the conversation. The only time she'd gotten him to break was the other day when she'd brought up his last try at being an alpha.

His eyes flicked up to hers, then he turned his attention to Amber once again. He extended his hand toward her. "I accept."

Amber shook his hand firmly, sealing the deal once and for all. Werewolf agreements were always sealed with a handshake. If you couldn't be trusted to uphold your word, then you were worthless in the werewolf community.

"Is that it?" Amber asked.

Genevieve nodded. "Now Paul just has to win his challenge, and pass the Trials, of course."

"I'm not concerned with either," he said, rising from his seat.

"Glad we worked this out. You aren't half bad, Paul," Amber said with a smile.

He chuckled as they all headed out to the parking lot. "You're just as determined as I expected."

As they exited, Genevieve paused in front of the door. "Thank you for reaching out, and for meeting with us today."

Paul looked at her, a genuine smile turning up the corners of his mouth. "It was a pleasure."

"See you around," she replied with a self-satisfied smile.

"Absolutely."

She turned and headed toward the truck, jogging to catch up to Amber. Maybe she wasn't really Amber's beta, but for today she had been, and she hadn't let her down. The pack was better off than it was the day before and it was because she'd figured out what needed to be done and had helped her alpha. She could get used to this.

CHAPTER 57

AMBER

*H*igh on the thrill of actually accomplishing something as an alpha, Amber wrapped Genevieve up in a big hug. "We did it!"

Genevieve stiffened with surprise for a moment, then returned the hug with gusto and actually lifted Amber off her feet, swinging her around in a circle. "You owned that negotiation! Even though you deviated from our plan of attack which you *specifically* agreed not to do." Genevieve lost her grip and Amber almost tripped over her own feet trying to save herself from falling.

"I'm the alpha! I'm supposed to negotiate!" she objected. "I get no respect around here. Bunch of unruly werewolves."

Tommy walked in at that moment and stopped, looking at them suspiciously. "Why do you two look so happy?"

"Something has gone right for a change," Amber said, heading toward the kitchen. She was pretty sure Tommy had been stress baking again, so there should be more pie. As suspected, a fresh one was on the stove, still cooling. "Oh, did you make apple this time?"

"Yeah, but what happened?"

Ceri walked into the kitchen carrying Captain Jack who was straining to reach Woggy on top of her head. The pixie had ahold of her hair like reins and was taunting the cat by staying just out of reach.

Amber waved a hand at Genevieve. "You explain."

Genevieve happily launched into an explanation of not only the meeting they'd just had with Paul Greer, but also everything that had led up to it. Amber dug out a piece of pie and listened contentedly. She'd been worried about Tommy after the fight at the warehouse the day before, but with all them together right now, the pack bond was practically purring with contentment. Her pack still felt safe together.

Derek had borrowed her truck and met Bernard for coffee this afternoon to discuss the damage to the warehouse. She took a big bite of pie to distract herself from thinking about that anymore. She was furious that someone targeting her had damaged something so important to her brother. He'd taken a huge risk coming out here with her to start a business, and so far, it wasn't exactly paying off.

The road that went past their house wasn't very busy, but a few cars still drove by every hour. She had learned to tune out the noise unless one slowed, or turned down their driveway. She frowned as a vehicle that definitely was not her truck slowed and drove into their driveway.

"Who is that?" As soon as she spoke, she realized there was more than one car. There were at least three.

Tommy frowned. "I have no idea. It's not Deward."

She set her pie down and walked to the living room, peeking out the window. Her heart dropped into her stomach. "The police are here."

Ceri dropped Captain Jack and ran upstairs. "Give me two minutes before they come in!"

Amber turned back to the others and tried to remember how to breathe. They had to be here for Evangeline. "You two should leave. Go out the back. Can you carry Eloise?"

"I'm not going anywhere. And they aren't coming in this house without a warrant," Genevieve said stubbornly.

There was a bark from outside and Amber cursed, looking outside the window again. They'd brought a K9 unit. There's no way they could sneak Eloise and Evangeline out the back now, the dogs would notice immediately. Ceri had better be working some serious magic up there.

The demon mark twitched under her skin and Angel appeared. Because, of course, this needed to become even more complicated.

"Why are the police here?" the demon demanded.

She glared at him. "If I knew that, we would have been gone before they showed up."

"Are you talking to the demon again?" Tommy asked, staring hard at the air next to her.

"Yes." She let the curtain fall back as Detective Sloan stepped out of the first car. She was starting to get sick of this guy showing up. It was never good news.

"That is so creepy," Tommy muttered.

"What do I do?" Amber asked, looking at Genevieve.

"Answer the door like normal. If he asks to come in, ask for a warrant. Be polite."

Amber nodded and took a deep breath to steady her nerves. She really should have asked Shane how he slowed his heart rate like that. This would have been a great moment to look perfectly calm.

There was a brisk knock at the door. "Police, open up!"

"You cannot let them in! Evangeline is just upstairs. Why haven't you gotten her out?" Angel demanded as she walked toward the front door.

"Shut up and trust me."

She opened the door wide, but stood in the center of the doorway and crossed her arms, looking Detective Sloan in the eye. Behind him, six other officers were waiting, one of them heading toward the side of the house with his police dog.

"I would ask if there's been another alpha death, but something tells me you didn't bring all these people with you just to update me on the case," Amber said drily. Her heart was pounding in her chest.

"An anonymous tip was called in, naming you and your pack as harboring Evangeline Bissett. I have a warrant to search the house." He lifted an official looking piece of paper to emphasize his point. "Please step aside, I don't want this to get ugly." The detective looked run down. His suit was wrinkled and the lines around his eyes had deepened since the last time she'd seen him; when he'd been warning her about Donovan's murder.

"You can let him in now," Ceri whispered from the

bottom of the stairs, just loud enough for her enhanced hearing to pick up.

"It's not going to get ugly, but I would like to see that warrant," Amber said, stepping back and inviting him inside. She had to trust Ceri right now. There was no time for arguing or worrying. The police were coming in whether she wanted them to or not.

"If they find her, you are dead," the demon threatened, furious at her compliance.

She ignored him and waved the detective inside. "We have nothing to hide."

Angel practically growled at that remark. He circled the detective as he walked in, trying to read the warrant over his shoulder.

"I'd like to see the warrant," Genevieve said, holding out her hand. She and the detective stepped to the side, and he handed over the piece of paper.

Ceri grabbed Amber's arm and dragged her back a few steps. "The house is helping."

"What?"

"Shh, just...act normal. The house won't let the police find them," Ceri whispered quickly before walking away and joining Genevieve and the detective.

Amber stood off to the side watching two officers head upstairs, with Angel following close behind, her heart pounding in her chest. How the hell was she supposed to act normal in the midst of possibly breaking her deal with a demon?

She heard her bedroom door open and had to dig her nails into her palm to keep from running over and demanding they get out. She'd always hated people going into her private spaces, but that feeling was amplified by the wolf's instincts. Everything inside her was screaming that there were intruders in her home. Her den. The wolf snarled impatiently as she stared down the hallway.

"What the hell is that?" One of the officers demanded, sounding alarmed.

"Oh crap, Woggy." Ceri jogged toward her room. "Do not hurt that pixie!"

"No, the...is that a cat?" he sounded even more appalled.

Captain Jack hissed loudly before being shushed by Ceri.

No one upstairs was shouting yet, so that must mean they hadn't found Evangeline or Eloise. She focused intently on her hearing and realized she couldn't even hear their heartbeats anymore. What the hell had Ceri, or the house, done with them?

Amber was distracted by the sound of her truck pulling into the driveway. She wanted to pull out her phone and warn Derek, but she thought it would look suspicious. Frustrated, she headed toward the front door so she could at least meet him outside so he didn't panic.

He parked haphazardly in the middle of the driveway and jumped out of the truck. She jogged toward him and managed to intercept him before he made it to the porch.

"What the hell is going on?" He was practically shouting. So much for not panicking.

"They have a warrant because someone claims we have that demon girl they were talking about on the news in our house. It's total bullshit, but I had to let them in," she said, trying to sound as exasperated as possible.

A muscle in Derek's jaw jumped as he ground his teeth tightly together, but he stopped freaking out. "Who is trying to pin this on you?"

She shrugged. "No clue, though I could probably make a couple of guesses. One of the council members has been kind of pissy since I made it through the Trials."

Detective Sloan walked out of the front door and headed over to them. He held out his hand to Derek. "Detective Sloan, I don't believe we've met."

"Derek Hale," her brother said shortly as he shook the man's hand.

"I need to talk to your sister alone for a moment," Sloan said, putting his hands in his pockets.

Amber almost agreed but decided that with Derek's current level of anger, it might be better if he stayed. "My brother can hear anything you might have to say, if it's all the same to you."

Derek looked surprised at that.

Sloan shrugged. "Alright." He sighed again and scratched his bristly jaw. "I didn't want to run this warrant. The tip that got called in was clearly from someone that had it out for you, in my opinion, but it wasn't my decision to make."

"Who was it?"

He shook his head regretfully. "I can't tell you that. Just keep an eye out, alright? I shouldn't be warning you about this at all, but my investigation into Lockhart's death is turning up some weird inconsistencies with the other murders. I don't think they're connected, but I can't prove it. Yet."

"There's a second sorcerer?" she asked in surprise.

"I think so."

"Are they working together?" Derek asked.

The detective shrugged. "I don't know. Sorcerers are generally loners, but they could be working together for a time. It's impossible to tell right now. Just watch your back, alright?"

She nodded. "Thanks for the warning. You keep going out of your way for me, and I appreciate that."

He smiled ruefully. "My sister was bitten, like you. I wish she'd managed to find an alpha."

"Is she an omega?"

"No, she killed herself before they could put her in the System." He nodded and walked off, his shoulders hunched with exhaustion.

Amber watched him go, her arms wrapped tightly around her. "We should get back inside."

"How--"

"Later," she said sharply.

They walked silently back toward the house. In her peripheral vision, she saw a curl of smoke drifted up from Thallan's porch. She almost hadn't seen him watching from the shadows.

She frowned. Maybe she was wrong about who had called in the tip. The alpha council and Selena Blackwood weren't the only people with reasons to hate her. Thallan wanted to punish the demon and didn't care who got hurt in the meantime.

CHAPTER 58

CERI

Ceri almost walked into a wall. The house was showing her everything all at once, laid over her own vision, and it was extremely disorienting.

Hiding Evangeline and Eloise had been fairly simple, but it definitely wasn't easy. The house's wards had come alive as soon as the police had pulled into the driveway. It sensed their intent and had reacted to protect them. With only a little coaxing, the room Eloise and Evangeline were in had simply...disappeared. They were still here, but they also weren't. She wasn't sure where the house had put them and was trying not to think too hard about it.

The police had been here for almost an hour already. Most of the nerves had faded into frustration and boredom.

She was also tiring from the effort of maintaining a connection to the house, but she couldn't risk letting it go.

Amber had planted herself in the middle of the living room and was simply glaring at everyone touching all her things. Genevieve was following Detective Sloan around prying for further information. She glanced over at Tommy. He was holding up surprisingly well but had hidden in the kitchen with Woggy and Captain Jack. That was probably for the best.

One of the officers walked down the stairs, then waved Sloan over. "They're not here. We've searched the place up and down. Carter even cast a finding spell and she came up empty-handed."

Ceri could barely contain her sigh of relief. Now, if they could all just leave she could finally release the magic.

The front door popped open and Detective Sloan looked back at it, brows furrowed.

"Oh, sorry, it does that," Ceri said with a slightly hysterical laugh as she hurried over to close it. "So windy out here."

"Windy. Right," Sloan said skeptically.

The house pouted a little and she tried to send reassuring thoughts. It had only been trying to help, but that was only going to cause more questions.

She surreptitiously patted the wall behind her back like she was soothing a nervous dog. Sometimes the house felt a little like a dog. Eager to please, extremely social, and boisterous. The more she connected to it, the more alive it became as well.

"Alright, make sure you put everything back where you

found it, and let's get back to the station. We all have a lot of paperwork to do tonight," Sloan said loudly.

The officers started heading outside one by one until only Sloan was left. Thankfully, they hadn't torn the place apart completely. They had been thorough, but under Sloan's watchful eye, each of them was considerate about the way they conducted the search.

Sloan paused in the doorway and nodded in Amber's direction. "I hope I don't see you again anytime soon."

Amber snorted. "Likewise. Have a good day."

He walked out and the door slammed shut behind him. And locked. Ceri cringed, but Sloan didn't turn around. He seemed as eager to leave as they were to have him go.

"What the hell was that?" Genevieve whispered.

"The house is...eager for them to be gone," Ceri said quietly. "Amber, can I let Eloise and Evangeline out yet?"

"Wait for them to be off the property," Amber said, listening intently to the cars drive away with her head cocked to the side.

It was a painfully long minute as they all waited with bated breath for the last car to drive away. As soon as Amber nodded, Ceri darted upstairs and pressed her hands against the blank wall where their room used to be. It was simply gone as if it had never been built. The magic was similar to The Market, the way it compressed space without the slightest consideration for the laws of physics.

"Where is their room?" Amber asked in alarm.

"One second," Ceri said, panting with exertion as she coaxed the house to release them. It was a little nervous, and required some reassurances, but finally it groaned and everything snapped back into place.

She stumbled back and finally dropped the connection to the house. Her vision cleared and she blinked rapidly, feeling disoriented all over again.

The door to the bedroom flew open and Evangeline burst out of the room panting, her hair wild. "Never do that again."

Ceri rushed over. "Where were you? Are you hurt?"

"We were...flat. It's like it just...squished us. But it didn't hurt it just...mush..." Evangeline could barely speak, she just kept bringing her palms together like she was crushing something between them and shaking her head.

"This house is weird," Genevieve muttered, looking around suspiciously.

Ceri glared at her. "It saved all our asses today, be nice. Tell her she did a good job."

"Are you serious?"

"Yes."

Genevieve sighed but looked around with a softer expression. "Thank you."

Ceri felt the house perk up. The picture frames in the hall all jiggled happily, which made Gen's face go pale.

"She's happy," Ceri said gently. "She likes it when we talk to her."

Genevieve gave her a fearful look and nodded, then hurried back downstairs.

"Do you want some pie?" Tommy asked tentatively.

Evangeline gave him a hateful look. "Don't even talk about food to me. I think I'm going to barf."

Ceri laughed and glanced downstairs, realizing Amber had disappeared. She was arguing quietly with someone only she could see. Fear twisted in her gut even though the danger had passed. This had been close. Too close.

CHAPTER 59

CERI

*C*eri hadn't slept in almost twenty-four hours. Her body still ached and every sound and shadow made her twitchy. She couldn't relax until this sorcerer was gone.

Which was why she was standing on the sidewalk outside of a nightclub at one a.m. Her cousin, Siobhan, was holding court in there, and had summoned her here with promises of information. This wasn't the type of place she wanted to bring Amber, or any of the rest of the pack.

She'd gotten the message when everyone was asleep, and had used a spell to leave without anyone noticing. Derek might have seen her leave, but he hadn't said anything if he had. The thought of Derek made her head hurt even worse. She just needed to find out what Siobhan knew, then she could head back to the house and tell the pack. The note on her nightstand let them know where she was just in case something went wrong. But that was unlikely.

She sighed and headed toward the back door of the club. Her hair was a frizzy, curly mess, and she was wearing leggings under an old, beige cardigan, but tonight she did not care. Siobhan could mock her all she wanted as long as she told her where the sorcerer was so she could end this nightmare.

The back door was the employee entrance, but it wasn't locked, as usual. One of the shot girls looked up curiously, but didn't ask any questions. People were always coming and going back here, and she didn't look like someone trying to sneak into the club.

Bass thumped overhead, a never-ending beat since the club never closed. Vampires had lobbied hard for that win years ago. After all, two a.m. was just the middle of the day for them. They owned most of the nicer clubs now and found both their living and their daily meal in them.

She pushed the door that led from the break room into the club open and the music grew louder. The neon, flashing lights hurt her eyes as she looked around, trying to remember where the VIP section was. She'd always come here already drunk when she was younger, so some of her memories on the layout were a little fuzzy.

An argument just loud enough to carry over the DJ caught her attention and she saw a group of three, well-dressed young women getting turned away by a bouncer. Behind him was a short staircase roped off from the rest of the place. It led up to the VIP section that had the best view of the peasants that couldn't afford to gain access to it.

Wading into the crowd was like getting sucked back in time. She brushed off the memories and walked faster, using her elbows as needed to get people out of her way. No one was paying attention to anything other than their drink or potential one-night stand. Or their next meal.

As she brushed past the girls that had gotten rejected by the bouncer, she heard one of them giggling about her outfit. The bouncer also raised an eyebrow when he saw her approaching, but that she expected.

She stood on her tiptoes and shouted into the bouncer's ear. "Siobhan sent for me."

He nodded and lifted the velvet rope, allowing her to pass.

"Are you serious? You're letting *her* in?" the giggler from before complained.

The bouncer ignored her and placed the rope back in its place. They were lucky they couldn't get in. Maybe one day they'd realize that, but until then, a little disappointment on a Friday night wouldn't kill them. Unlike what was up here.

This place was owned by Bram –– another reason she was pissed Shane had taken Amber to see him –– but he didn't bother running it. He left that to his lackeys and just raked in the money. Siobhan was a staple here, and in most of the vampire's bedrooms. She didn't care about that though; her cousin could sleep with whoever she wanted. It was the drugs she sold to naive college students that made her mad.

She reached the top step and paused to look around. Everything was cast in shadow up here. Even the music wasn't quite as loud, though it was still enough to keep anyone from overhearing your conversation.

In the far corner she spotted her cousin sitting in the lap of a vampire. Siobhan noticed her at about the same time and whispered something in her conquest's ear, then stood. The vampire left and Siobhan sat back down on the loveseat alone. Ready to get this over with, Ceri marched over to her, trying to ignore the ever-increasing headache.

Siobhan draped her arm over the back of the loveseat and watched her approach, looking elegant as always. She had on some sparkly black number that was just long enough to qualify as a dress. Barely. "Dear cousin, I thought you'd never get here."

"You're lucky I came at all at this hour," Ceri muttered, inspecting the other two chairs for signs of bodily fluids before picking the one closest and sitting down.

"Don't be silly, I know you're desperate." Siobhan shifted her weight and swung her legs off the couch.

She wanted to punch her in the face. Maybe she could beat the information out of her. "Get to the point, Siobhan."

"I think I like watching you squirm." Siobhan grinned, something manic glinting in her eyes. "I can't believe you got in here wearing that atrocious cardigan. I mean, honestly. You could have thrown on a dress."

"Yes, I'm sure it's truly shocking. You'll live," she said shortly, rubbing her fingers against her temple. She was surprised her cousin hadn't gone after her hair first. Siobhan knew that was a sore spot. She'd said as much the last time they saw each other.

"I think I should get my payment first," her cousin said

abruptly, leaning back and crossing her arms.

Ceri raised her brow. "No way in hell. Tell me where he is and then I'll give you the..." she hesitated, just for a moment, a gut feeling of worry cutting through the mental fog. "I'll give you the spell my mother made."

Siobhan sighed, pushing out her bottom lip in a pout. "Fine, but only because you're too much of a goody two-shoes to screw me over."

She forced herself to keep a blank expression on her face, but her heart started pounding in her chest. This wasn't her cousin. Not only did she know that Ceri would screw her over given even half a chance, goody two shoes or not, Siobhan knew the spell she wanted was made by their grand-mother. That's not a slip of the tongue she would have ignored.

"Well? Where is he?" Ceri asked, quickly pulling magic into the palm of her hand. She'd have to fight her way out of here somehow. If she could manage a diversion, she might have a chance of succeeding.

The woman who was not her cousin looked at her care-fully, her smile growing wider. The pretense fell away and she changed her posture, crossing her legs and sitting up straight. "You know I'm not going to tell you that."

"Who are you?"

"Someone you shouldn't have screwed over," the impostor said with a vicious grin.

The attack didn't come from across from her, it came from behind. A quick prick against the back of her neck before a defensive spell could leave her fingertips. Every-thing went black.

CHAPTER 60

GENEVIEVE

*G*enevieve pulled up a fifth news report but it didn't have any new information. What she really needed was the actual police report. There was no way she could get her hands on it though. She didn't know any of the officers well enough to get a favor like that.

Detective Sloan had told Amber he didn't think the same sorcerer had killed Donovan that had killed the others. That begged the question of whether the sorcerer they'd been fighting had killed Donovan, or the others. Or both. Sloan could be wrong after all.

She yawned, covering her mouth with the back of her hand, and wondered how her life had come to this. Awake early on her day off investigating a murder. The house was quiet. Tommy, Amber, and Derek were asleep. Ceri must have gone somewhere early this morning, because she was already gone when Genevieve woke up. Sometimes she disappeared into the woods on a walk when she couldn't sleep, something about *communing with nature*.

A door upstairs opened and someone started down the stairs. She glanced over her shoulder when they stopped.

Evangeline stood at the bottom of the stairs and looked around uncomfortably. She tugged down the hood of her jacket. "Have you seen Ceri?"

"Not recently, why?"

"She comes every morning to give my mom her pain meds and she hasn't shown up. Mom woke up and she's really hurting now."

Genevieve frowned. That wasn't like Ceri. She was a total mother hen as soon as someone got hurt.

"Maybe she's in her room," Genevieve said. She suspected that Ceri occasionally soundproofed her room with magic. There were times where her heartbeat would vanish abruptly or a conversation would end mid-sentence. It was subtle, but she paid attention.

Knowing how sleep-deprived Ceri had been recently, she very well could have fallen asleep with the spell up, or be in one of her weird visions and lost track of time.

She set her laptop aside and uncurled from the couch. Evangeline followed her to Ceri's room. She knocked twice and waited. There was no response.

Frowning, she pressed her ear to Ceri's door. The witch wasn't in there but she could hear Woggy snoring.

"Is she there or not? My mom needs another dose of that

pain medication she makes," Evangeline repeated impatiently.

"I heard you the first time, give me a minute." She pushed the door open and looked around, sniffing the air. It smelled so much like Ceri in here it was hard to tell how long she'd been gone. Nothing seemed out of place, just the normal clutter. Except for the note on the bed.

"What's going on?" Tommy asked, appearing in the doorway behind her.

Genevieve ignored him and grabbed the note. It had been written quickly and was almost illegible.

Going to Redrum, a nightclub in town. Siobhan called. Will be back by three a.m.

Her hands shook as she reread the note again, hoping she'd misunderstood. But she hadn't. Ceri was supposed to be home five hours ago.

"Gen, what's wrong?" Tommy demanded, shoving past Evangeline into the room.

She thrust the note at him then ran to Amber's room, banging her fist on the door. "AMBER!"

The door flew open a second later and Amber stood in the doorway, wild-eyed, wearing her pajamas. "What's wrong?"

"Ceri isn't here, and she left a note saying she was going to go see someone, her cousin I think, last night, but she'd be home by three a.m. She isn't here. She's gone." She stood there panting with her hands shaking. This couldn't be happening. She didn't want to believe it but every instinct she had was screaming at her that something was wrong.

Amber's face went hard and she ran back into her room, quickly changing clothes. "Where did she go to meet Siobhan? I don't feel her through the pack bond. Like nothing. I didn't notice until you said something."

"Someplace called Redrum, I don't know. She said it was a nightclub?"

"We'll go there first." Amber ran out of her room and shouted for Derek.

Genevieve's head was spinning as she ran to the front door and pulled on her tennis shoes. She was wearing shorts and a tank top but there was no time to change. If the sorcerer had taken Ceri she may not even be alive. The fact that Amber couldn't feel her through the pack bond made her want to vomit. She couldn't be gone. She just couldn't.

Tommy was standing in the middle of the living room with his hands balled into fists. She realized he was about to lose control and ran over, wrapping him in a tight hug to ground him.

"We're going to find her. I promise," she said, squeezing him even tighter.

"You can't know that. She could already be--"

"Shut up. She's always saying to be optimistic. So do that for her, okay?"

Tommy nodded, and his breathing slowed a little. "Okay."

Evangeline was hovering awkwardly behind him looking both terrified and angry. She couldn't blame her.

Derek barreled down the stairs holding a shotgun. Another pistol was tucked in the waistband of his pants and his other hand held a massive tire iron. "I'm going with you and I'm not going to argue about it. You'll need help, and if you say a human won't be able to help, I'll deck you."

"What about Eloise and Evangeline?" Genevieve asked as she stepped away from Tommy.

Amber dragged her hands through her hair. "Tommy, I need you to stay."

"You can't be serious!" He looked angrier than she'd ever seen him before, but Amber was right to choose him. He was the best one to stay here. Evangeline trusted him more than the rest of them.

"We cannot leave her alone. If this is a trap, they may come here, too. I need you. Please," Amber pleaded, desperation clear in her eyes.

Tommy still looked unhappy but nodded reluctantly. "Fine, I'll stay."

"Thank you." Amber jogged over to the front door and grabbed her keys, then headed outside at a run.

Genevieve and Derek ran after her, but pausing at the front door, Genevieve looked back at Tommy. "Call Deward. If you think he can be trusted. I don't like you being here alone."

He nodded. "I will."

Genevieve pulled the front door shut and ran after Amber and Derek. As soon as they piled into the truck, she pulled out her phone and texted two people. Amber would probably kill her for this, but this was their chance to prove to the council what was happening.

Shane replied right away.

CHAPTER 61

CERI

*C*eri woke up choking. She rolled to the side only to be stopped by arm restraints. Pushing up as far as she could, she vomited over her shoulder. It hit the floor with a wet splatter. Her chest heaved as she tried to catch her breath.

They'd dosed her with something at the nightclub to knock her out, which explained the vomiting. Her magic was trying to purge the poison from her body to protect her.

Wherever she was, it was dark. She couldn't see anything, not even her hand where it was tied to the cold, stone slab she was laying on. Closing her eyes to block out the oppressive darkness, she wiggled her toes just to make sure they were there, then did a mental check on the state of her injuries.

Everything still ached and she somehow felt even more tired than before, but whoever had taken her hadn't hurt her more. Yet. Lying there, alone in a cold, dark room, the fear began to creep in. Her imagination filled in all the ways they could hurt her. All the things a sorcerer might do before taking her heart and killing her. Pain and blood powered their black magic spells and it was easier if they could use someone else's.

Frustrated tears rolled down her cheeks. She should have seen this coming, but she'd walked right into the trap. She'd gone to see Siobhan without her pack, like an idiot. Though, part of her was thankful Amber hadn't come. She probably couldn't have stopped them either. Maybe it was better if only *she* died.

She had to get out of here. There were spells she could use, though they were harder tied up and weakened like she was. Giving up just wasn't an option. This was not how she was going to die.

Gritting her teeth, she pulled magic into her hands. Unlocking whatever held her wrists was step one. If she could get her hands free, she could find her way out.

"Conminuo," she whispered, pushing her magic into the shackle. It grew warm, struggling to hold its shape under the pressure of the spell. Using a spell like this without a ritual or any spell ingredients was extremely difficult. It would take time and patience.

She repeated the spell and pushed harder the second time, regaining a little of her energy. Whatever they'd dosed her with was continuing to wear off. She pushed, and rested, over and over. Finally, the hinge creaked slightly.

Hope bloomed in her chest. She almost had it, and they didn't know she was awake. Perhaps the drug had worn off faster than expected. She began pooling the magic in her palms once again, focusing hard on drawing enough to finish the job.

"Conmi--"

Agonizing pain exploded over her arm and chest. She screamed, jerking away from the green fire spreading over her body. It illuminated the room with a sickly color, revealing a figure standing in the corner.

Ceri thrashed under the attack, trying to get away, and unable to focus her magic to stop whatever was happening to her while in so much pain. The figure threw their head back and laughed, then the fire vanished, disappearing without a trace.

"You were so close. I could practically see the hope on your sniveling little face," the voice from the darkness hissed. "That makes failure all the more painful, doesn't it? Being so close you can practically taste it, then having it all ripped away."

Ceri ground her teeth together and glared in the direction the voice had come from. "Who the hell are you?"

"I already told you. Someone you shouldn't have screwed over." A light flicked on overhead, casting light throughout the room. Selena stood before her, clutching a wooden wand. Her long, beautiful black hair had been shaved off. Her delicate features were sallow, as though she hadn't been getting enough food or sun. Gone was the glittery black dress she'd worn in the club. It was replaced by dirty jeans and a threadbare shirt that hung off her frame. "You have no idea what you did to me, do you?"

Selena prowled closer, holding the wand in her hand. Ceri's eyes followed it fearfully. The witch stopped a few feet away, green eyes boring into her.

"I thought at first that you were doing it for your coven. That you thought it was a way to reclaim the prominence your coven had once had, but then..." Selena laughed hysterically, but there was no humor on her face. "Then I realized it was all over a stupid, fucking pixie. You ruined my life over a pest."

"You got me fired and tried to kill––"

"SHUT UP!" Selena pointed the wand at her again and the green flames spread over her stomach, eating through the fabric of her shirt.

Ceri held back the scream by sheer force of will. Her teeth dug into her inner cheek and her mouth filled with blood as the pain coursed through her. As abruptly as it started, it stopped, and she was left panting.

"I was showing you your place in the world! You had overstepped, and you should have known better. You don't cross the Blackwood coven." Selena took three quick steps toward her and grabbed a handful of her hair, wrenching her head up harshly. She leaned in close, her face flushed with anger and hate burning in her eyes. "Did you think I wouldn't come after you for what you did?"

Ceri spat in her face. The resulting slap rocked her head back against the stone slab and stars exploded across her vision. She tasted blood.

"I am going to watch you scream while Caligo cuts out

your heart and I won't feel anything but glee," Selena sneered, wiping her hand off on her dress. "Or maybe we'll make you watch Amber die first. She's a pathetic excuse for an alpha, but you're the real embarrassment here. I didn't think even *you* were pathetic enough to join a werewolf pack. You've sunk so low."

Blinking to try and clear her vision, she tried to make sense of what Selena had said. "You're working for him?"

"No, I just sold you. I'll get a bonus if your pack comes for you and then I can buy my way back into my coven. Money covers a multitude of sins," Selena said with a particularly nasty grin. "And as a free perk, I get to make you suffer."

"Where is my cousin?"

Selena dug the wand into her cheek and pushed her head in the opposite direction. The sight that met her eyes made her want to scream, or cry. She had no love for Siobhan, but this was too awful to wish on anyone.

The long auburn hair she'd loved so much had been hacked off. Her eyes were gone and her mouth was locked in a silent scream. She was dead now, but she hadn't been when her eyes were taken. She'd been alive when they'd cut out her heart. When they had ripped her magic from her body.

"It's horrible, isn't it?" Selena whispered directly into her ear.

Ceri jerked away from her, looking at the woman in horror. "You're sick."

"And you're going to die." Selena lifted the wand again and Ceri braced for the pain, wishing she was already dead.

CHAPTER 62

AMBER

*A*mber grabbed the bouncer by his jacket and jerked him forward so hard he lost his footing. "You either let me in, or I'm going to rip your arms and beat you to death with them you piece of shit––"

Genevieve got in between them and shoved her back, and kept a hand on both of them to hold them apart. "My pack-mate disappeared from here early this morning, around one a.m. We need to talk to someone, or look at video surveillance."

He shoved Genevieve's hand away angrily and sneered at her. "We don't have video surveillance. And you're sure as hell not walking in there now. You can leave or I'm calling the police and pressing assault charges."

Amber growled and her vision bled red. She was two

seconds away from shifting right there and forcing her way inside.

"Amber, enough!" Angel shouted. He swooped in front of her, blocking her view of the bouncer and Genevieve. "Ceri is counting on you, if you lose your shit in public, she will die."

"They can help us!"

Angel rolled his eyes. "You don't need him. All you need are your senses. Find her scent. Her car is parked right over there, so you know she made it here. Stop and think."

She jerked around, seeing Ceri's car for the first time and felt like an idiot. Dragging her hand down her face, she forced herself to breathe.

"The sorcerer most likely took her to lure you into a trap," Angel said, drifting around her. "While I wouldn't normally recommend walking into a trap, I think this one is unavoidable. This is a chance to kill him."

"Shut up and let me think," she said angrily as she walked over to Ceri's car. Pausing next to the driver's side door, she shut her eyes and inhaled deeply. The wolf, already at the front of her mind, sifted through the scents until it found the one that was distinctly Ceri. Citrus, lavender, and magic.

She followed it across the street, though it was faint beneath the smells of exhaust and other people. Instead of leading to the front door, it led around back. Derek hurried after her, while Genevieve followed a little slower, still apologizing to the bouncer.

Ceri's scent led in through an employee's only door, but it also led back out. Not back to her car though, it led into the alley, then...vanished.

"It ends here," she said, dropping to one knee and inhaling deeply to draw in as many scents as she could.

"If someone took her here, perhaps you can get their scent."

"Dozens of people have been through here. I'm not a bloodhound, I don't know what to follow." Amber pushed back up to her feet angrily. This couldn't be a dead end. There had to be a way to find Ceri.

"Can you use the pack bond somehow?" Genevieve asked.

"I can't feel her at all," Amber said, pacing nervously.

"Perhaps you should try again," Angel suggested, swooping in front of her to force her to pay attention. "You don't know as much about the pack bond as you should, but it's not something that can be completely severed unless she's dead. If she is alive, no matter how they're blocking it, if you are strong enough you can find her."

"How the hell do you know all of this?"

Angel rolled his eyes. "I'm extremely intelligent and well-educated. And I've known more werewolves than you, Miss Recently-Bitten."

"What is he saying?" Derek asked impatiently.

Amber turned back to them. "That if I focus hard enough, and I'm strong enough, that I'll be able to find her." She paused, swallowing down the lump in her throat. "If she's alive."

"Then do it." Derek balled his hands into fists as though he were expecting the worst news. She couldn't even consider that as a possibility.

Footsteps from the end of the alley startled her and she looked up only to see Shane walking toward them.

"What the hell are you doing here?"

"Genevieve texted me," he said.

Genevieve immediately lifted her hands. "We need help, and we need someone else from the council there if we do find the sorcerer. They may not take our word for it. Shane was the only option I could think of."

Amber ground her teeth together but nodded. Genevieve was right and was thinking of all the things she hadn't.

"I'm here to help," Shane said firmly. "If Ceri has been taken by a sorcerer, I don't want to see her dead either."

"Does Jameson know you're here?" Amber asked.

He scratched the back of his head and pursed his lips. "Not yet."

"Will you get in trouble if he finds out you helped us?"

Shane shook his head. "That's for me to worry about, not you." He held his hand up before she could object. "I may be his beta, but I'm not his slave. That's not how this works."

She pulled back all her questions and worries and nodded, accepting that he could decide for himself. "What do you know about pack bonds?"

～

*A*mber sat sideways in the driver's side seat with her feet resting on the running board. Her hand was wrapped tightly in Genevieve's and she was trying to breathe deeply while she focused on the pack bond.

"This will be as natural as breathing one day, but for now, let the wolf guide you," Shane said slowly.

She tried to picture the wolf as she'd seen her that day during the Trials. Perhaps it was her imagination, but she thought she could see red eyes looking back at her. She focused on the pack bond strumming between herself and Genevieve.

Her pack's fear and worry rushed over her like a tidal wave. It was hard not to pull back just to protect herself from their emotions, but she couldn't do that. The wolf pushed her deeper, not caring what she felt. The sounds of traffic and Derek pacing impatiently began to fade away as other senses came into focus.

Each of her pack members felt like another heartbeat in her chest. She could sense where each of them was. The wolf looked around, touching each bond in turn. Genevieve. Close. Tommy. Far. She held her breath and she sank farther into her mind.

Ceri had to be there, she couldn't be dead. As she drifted deeper, she felt something dark slither across her mind. The wolf growled in her mind and crouched down. There was something pushing back. Trying to hide.

With a glimmer of hope that Ceri may actually be alive, she pushed back against the shifting shadows in her mind. The wolf howled and the sound grew louder and louder, making her head ache. She gritted her teeth and kept pushing. Angel said she just had to be stronger than whoever was trying to hide the bond from her. There was no power in heaven or hell that could keep her from Ceri.

She pulled strength from the pack and tore through the darkness. The bond that tied her to Ceri throbbed weakly in the back of her mind. She dug her fingers into Genevieve's hand so hard she had to be bruising it as she desperately reached for the bond. Ceri was alive.

"I can feel her," Amber gasped. "She's pretty far, not within the city limits."

"Where?" Derek growled.

"I don't know, but I can get there."

"I'll text Tommy," Genevieve said as she hurried around to the passenger side of the truck.

"I'll follow you," Shane said, before running back to his suburban.

They piled into the truck and Amber cranked it up with shaking hands. They had a chance if they could just get there in time. Ceri was alive, but she was in pain. And she was afraid.

CHAPTER 63

TOMMY

Witch's Castle in Forest Park. Call the police if I don't text back in one hour.

ommy dropped his phone in his lap and buried his face in his hands. The wolf was raging inside of him. He couldn't just sit here and wait.

"Is she alive?" Evangeline asked quietly, stopping her pacing abruptly.

"Yeah. For now."

She started pacing again. He wanted to tie her to a chair and make her stop. It was driving him nuts.

"What if…" she hesitated, picking at the hem of her

385

jacket. "These people hurt my mom, and they're not going to stop until we're dead. What if we go help?"

"And leave Eloise here alone?" He couldn't believe she was even suggesting it. He wanted to go get Ceri back more than anything, but he understood why Amber had asked him to stay.

Evangeline groaned in frustration. "I don't want her to die, but I couldn't live with myself if Ceri died either."

Tommy looked down at his hands. He couldn't even think about that. Ceri was the one that had convinced him to stay. She'd given him hope. He didn't want a life without her in it.

The floor near the balcony upstairs creaked and Tommy's head snapped up. Eloise was leaning against the banister looking down at them.

"Evangeline, you should go help them," the old woman said, her face set in determination.

Evangeline stared at her in shock. "You can't be serious."

"And why can't I be? Haven't I taught you to help people when they need it?" Eloise asked, her hands gripping the banister tightly to stay upright.

"But you know what this means. What it requires," Evangeline said quietly.

"I do. In fact, I think I know better than you," Eloise replied, giving her a serious look. "I won't tell you what to do, but I will give you permission, since it seems like you need it." With a final nod, Eloise pushed off the banister and began hobbling back toward the bedroom.

Tommy heard Deward's car turned into the driveway.

"What is she talking about?" he asked as he rose from the couch.

"She's talking about my demon side. The way that I saved her that night we were attacked." Evangeline dragged her hands down her face.

"Didn't you fly away with your mom or something that night? Can you do that now?" he asked, a plan forming in his mind.

"There's only one way I can do that right now," Evangeline said, her expression pained.

"How?"

"As a favor."

"I don't understand." They didn't have time for this. Tommy could feel the panic coursing through the pack bond. "A favor?"

"As part of a demon mark." Evangeline blurted out. Her hands trembled as she pushed her hoodie back. Her hair was blonde, like it had been the day in the forest. She'd grown paler though and had dark circles under her eyes. "The demon magic is limited during the day, but if you accept my demon mark in return for my help in getting you there and defeating the sorcerer and Zachariah, then I can use it."

"Then let's do it," he said without hesitation.

"You'd be indebted to me. How can you be so casual about it?"

"Are you going to demand I do something terrible?" he asked.

"No, I would never--"

"Then what is there to think about? I trust you, and I need your help. Please stop hesitating. We have to do something."

Evangeline looked stunned, but nodded. She lifted her hand. "Come here."

He walked up, standing within reach. She placed her hand over his heart. Heat rushed between them and her eyes lit up with power. "A debt for a debt."

The magic burned. He ground his teeth together to keep from reacting as the magic forced its way under his skin. She yanked her hand away like she'd been burned and took a step back but it felt like she was still touching him. Like she was part of him now.

"That wasn't so bad," he said despite the sudden dizziness at the loss of contact.

She held her hand to her chest and looked out the window. "I'm a parasite."

"Barely."

Eva glared at him, but the corner of her lip turned up in a half smile. "You're an idiot."

As she stood there, color bloomed in her cheeks. Her blonde hair darkened from root to tip as the horns grew from her head. Blue eyes became black. The effervescent glow of her skin became warmer. Healthier.

"Was that why you were sick? Because you wouldn't give someone your mark?" he asked, understanding dawning on him.

"Yes. It's a curse. A demon will die without at least one mark, and the more we have the more powerful we become." She glanced around the room furtively. "Don't tell anyone I told you that. Please."

He nodded, though he would have to tell Amber. Right

now, he needed Evangeline focused and an argument would distract her.

There was a knock at the door and he rushed over, yanking it open.

Deward looked startled. "What's wrong?"

"Deward, I need to ask you to do something both dangerous and possibly stupid." He stepped back and waved him inside, shutting the door behind them.

The troll raised an eyebrow, but didn't immediately object. "What is your request?"

"Ceri has been kidnapped by a sorcerer. My pack is about to try to rescue her, but they need all the help they can get. There is..." he hesitated, then decided Deward would appreciate the truth more than anything else. He pointed at Evangeline. "She is the girl on the news. The demon they are stupidly blaming for the no magic spots. It's a really long story, but her mother was hurt when the sorcerer and this half angel tried to kill her. She's upstairs, and we can't leave her defenseless in case someone comes here trying to hurt her, but I can't let my alpha fight alone."

Deward crossed his arms and looked at the floor, thinking. He tapped his long green fingers against his arm. Tommy knew better than to interrupt, but it was hard.

Finally, he looked up. "I see your dilemma, and I am willing to protect the woman. Perhaps this is reckless, but I find myself inspired by your fervor. I will do it."

Tommy sighed in relief. "Thank you."

"Also, just so you know, the house is kind of...sentient." Evangeline said hesitantly. "If someone tries to hurt you it may help. Trust it. And talking to it may not be a bad idea. It likes compliments. Isn't that right, Mr. Cottage?"

The cabinets flapped happily, and Deward jerked in alarm. "That should *not* be possible."

"Well it is, good luck," Tommy said, grabbing Evangeline by the arm and dragging her outside. The front door shut on its own and he heard all the locks click into place. The window shades dropped one by one and a wave of magic passed over the house as it turned itself into some kind of fortress.

He turned back to Evangeline. "Okay, how do we do this?"

"Um, just step back." She pulled off her hood and shook out her arms. Her horns, normally black as her hair, began to glow red. With a rush of magic that almost knocked him back, fiery wings exploded out of her back. Her eyes were completely black and her hands changed, claws extending from her fingertips.

He looked at her in awe. "That is badass."

"Shut up and get over here, teen wolf," she hissed, her voice changed by the sharp teeth in her mouth. He walked over and she awkwardly wrapped her arms around him. "Arms around my neck, and hold on tight."

Standing this close, for a split second, all he could think about was kissing her, but thoughts of what Ceri might be going through killed that as soon as it began. He wrapped his arms tightly around her neck and she kicked off the ground. They shot straight up and he squeezed his eyes shut, focusing on the bond and not the fact that he was flying through the air with a demon that had no clue what she was doing.

CHAPTER 64

AMBER

*A*mber stared at the old ruin. The roof of the house had rotted away long ago leaving only the skeletal stone structure behind. Moss grew on the exposed edges, dripping down the sides like mold. Deep in the forest, The Witch's Castle was rumored to be haunted but still attracted tourists daily.

Strangely, no one was here today. Perhaps they'd felt the ominous chill in the air. She shuddered as the wind picked up slightly.

"I can try to convince Jameson to come help if you wait," Shane said quietly.

"No. Ceri doesn't have much time." She scanned the ruins for any signs of life but the whole area was still. "It doesn't look like there's an entrance but I know she's here somewhere."

She walked into the ruins with Genevieve and Shane close behind her. Derek pushed ahead of her, jogging into the main room of the old house. They spread out slightly as they searched for whatever room or basement they had Ceri in. The pack bond throbbed painfully in her chest almost robbing her of her breath.

All her senses focused on the area around her. She thought she caught a whiff of Ceri but it faded quickly. It had rained sometime last night -- the forest floor had still been soft and damp -- and washed away the trail.

A loud crack startled her and she whipped around ready to fight, but it was just Derek. He'd kicked in an old cellar door that had been hidden under a pile of wet leaves and was peering inside. He nudged the now broken lock away with the butt of his gun.

"I saw a footprint near it," he said, waving Amber over.

She sprinted to him and helped him pull open the splintered door. The pack bond twisted inside of her, abruptly growing even stronger. The underside of the cellar doors had symbols drawn in what looked and smelled like blood. It had been blocking the bond.

Genevieve jogged up behind her, almost bumping into her. "Is this it?"

"Yes." Desperation filled Amber's heart as she felt the full extent of Ceri's suffering. She stepped down into the darkness without hesitation. The pain Ceri was in was almost overwhelming even through the bond. Her friend's fear screamed at her to move faster.

"Amber, we should make a plan," Shane said, trying to grab her arm.

She jerked it away and glared at him over her shoulder. "The plan is to rescue her and all get out alive. Don't you dare try to stop me. You don't have to come if you don't want to."

Shane's lips thinned in frustration, but he nodded. "I'm calling Jameson then I'll catch up."

Done waiting on him, Amber walked carefully into the cellar. The wooden steps creaked under her feet. She had to blink for her eyes to adjust to the impenetrable darkness. It smelled like earth, moss, and rat droppings down here. Ceri's scent mingled with all of it. She'd been brought this way.

"I can smell her," Genevieve said quietly from somewhere behind her.

"Me too."

"Is she close?" Derek asked. He had one hand on the wall guiding himself. She'd almost forgotten he wouldn't be able to see in the dark down here.

"Sort of. We're headed in the right direction, but she's still a good distance away." She picked up her pace, wanting to get to the bottom before the others, just in case.

The stairs led down into a what looked like an old wine cellar. Old, wooden racks rotted with age stood empty on either side of the room like sentries. Cobwebs draped over the aged wood. Even those seemed to be covered in dust. The floor was carpeted in a layer of grime that had been recently disturbed. A trail led through the center of the room to a door. It was propped open with a chunk of wood.

A strange smell drifted from the doorway. There was a hint of decay, but also of magic, and something else. Blood.

"Do you smell that?" Genevieve asked nervously.

Amber lifted her hand and motioned for the others to stop. "Yes, be careful. Derek, did you bring a flashlight? You need to be able to see now."

There was a click and light flooded the room as he pulled his headlight onto his head. He swung the shotgun up to his shoulder and aimed it at the door. Leave it to her brother to be prepared even in a crisis.

The smell grew stronger and there was a strange clicking noise, like claws on stone. Pale fingers wrapped around the door. They weren't human, exactly. The claws of a wolf extended from bony, human fingers. Fur grew in mangy patches on the knuckles, extending up to the wrist.

With a groan, the door was pushed open, and a horrible sight met Amber's eyes. She recognized this creature, or at least who he used to be. It was her maker. Peter.

His eyes were all white and his sallow flesh was spotted with rotten, black holes. He was hunched over like he had been caught mid-shift. Teeth too big for his mouth dug into his gray lips. He wasn't breathing. His heart wasn't beating.

The door swung all the way open, rattling as it hit the wall. Peter stepped into the room, stretching up to his full height, and howled.

CHAPTER 65

GENEVIEVE

Genevieve's heart skipped a beat as the howl echoed around them, signaling their presence here. This thing wasn't alive but it was walking and howling. Using magic for something like this was sick.

"Peter," Amber said, her voice shifting into a growl.

"Who is Peter?" Derek demanded.

"The wolf that bit us and changed us against our will. He used to work for Lockhart." Amber was shaking with anger. She could feel it pulsing through the pack bond, filling her with strength.

"I bought silver bullets after the issue with those golem monsters," Derek said, keeping his shotgun pointed at Peter. "Will they help?"

"I hope so." Amber took a step back and glanced at her. "Don't let him get near Derek."

"No shit." She hoped Shane would get down here soon. He had to have heard the howl.

"I don't have time for this. I need to get to Ceri," Amber said in frustration.

"I'll try to distract him so you can get past," Genevieve said, pulling her shirt off over her head. She was faster as a wolf, and she had a feeling she'd need all the speed she could get.

Peter cocked his head at them and curled his lips up into a twisted version of a smile. His muscles twitched slightly, then he exploded into motion. Amber ducked under the first swipe of his claws without shifting.

Genevieve launched herself toward him, shifting mid-air and ripping her pants to pieces. She caught his arm in her jaws and yanked him away from her alpha. A gunshot blasted through the room and the bullet hit Peter with a dull thunk, punching a hole straight through his chest. Viscous blood seeped from the wound but he didn't even flinch.

Peter slashed at her with his other arm and she ducked under it, scampering back a few steps. The gunshot hadn't slowed him down at all. If anything, he was getting faster.

Amber raced for the door. Peter tried to follow but Genevieve grabbed his ankle and bit down hard enough to crack the bone.

There was a loud smack and a grunt. Amber flew back from the door just as she tried to cross the threshold. She hit the floor and slid toward the stairs, stunned. A woman with red hair that looked like it had been hacked off with an axe stepped out. Her lips were sewn shut and her eyes had been cut out, leaving bloody holes in her face. Like Peter, her body wasn't right. Magical symbols had been carved into her bare arms and magic drifted up from them like black smoke.

The woman shambled toward Amber, who shifted, her clothes tearing away. Shane finally appeared at the bottom of the stairs, already in wolf form. He was snowy white and his eyes glowed bright yellow. With a growl, he launched himself over Amber and collided with the zombie. She grabbed him by the ruff of his neck and threw him to the side.

Genevieve danced in and out of reach as Peter slashed at her with his clawed hands. Her ears rang painfully as another shot echoed through the small room. It hit Peter in the leg this time, almost severing the limb. She watched in horror as the wound began mending immediately. The hole in his chest was almost filled in as well. The silver wasn't having any effect on him at all.

A scream split the air, coming from the direction of the door. Genevieve's heart clenched in her chest. Ceri.

"CERI!" Derek yelled, desperation clear in his voice. He tried to run for the door, but the zombie woman caught him with a kick, crumpling him. He rolled onto his back on the floor and swung his gun toward her, pulling the trigger. The blast hit her straight in the face, blowing out the back of her head and reducing her features to bloody gore. She faltered, legs wobbling underneath her.

Peter turned toward the sound of gunfire, distracted for a split second. Genevieve jumped and bit down on the back of his neck. His spine cracked between her jaws. She dug her claws into his back and ripped her head from side to side viciously, trying to tear his head off.

His hands grasped at her fur and ears. Sharp claws cut into her skin, but she didn't let go. They were hurting Ceri. They had to get to her now.

CHAPTER 66

CERI

The blast of gunfire shocked Ceri awake. A wave of pain hit her as her muscles protested the sudden movement. The light overhead made her head ache.

"They shouldn't be here yet," an unfamiliar male voice said, sounding very annoyed.

"I told you they might arrive early. It doesn't matter," another responded. This voice was familiar and unmistakable. It was the sorcerer. "They won't make it back here before we are ready considering the welcoming committee I left for them."

The sounds of fighting drifting down the hallway were faint. She craned her head trying to see the two men but they remained just out of sight. The other man was likely Zachariah Hudson, the half angel they'd seen on the news.

She still didn't understand why he would be working with a sorcerer, even to kill a demon. Half angels tended to be somewhat rigid about black magic use.

"Ah, our sacrifice is awake." The sorcerer drew closer. His aura was oppressive, as though a black cloud of magic followed him wherever he went.

He came into view and grinned at her, revealing yellow teeth and a scarred face. The freshest of the scars was on his cheek and looked like he'd stitched the wound closed himself. As she stared into the face of evil, despair grew in her chest. Her pack had walked into his trap with her as bait.

"Ceridwen, you don't look pleased to see me," he cooed, stroking her cheek.

"Is anyone ever pleased to see you?" Her voice cracked as she forced the words out of her bone-dry throat. She'd almost lost her voice from screaming before she'd passed out.

He cackled, then backhanded her so hard she lost consciousness again for a moment. "This might be even more satisfying than my other kills. I was supposed to get Donovan after he failed to deliver me the alpha I paid him for, but Selena got to him first." He grabbed her cheeks. "Now that is an interesting woman. She's everything you could have been. It's almost sad to see your potential wasted, but your magic will only make my spells that much more powerful. Already your pain has provided enough to--"

"Will you shut up," Zachariah hissed. "You talk too much."

The sorcerer sneered at the other man, anger contorting his features. "Talk to me like that again and you'll regret it."

"I'm paying you to do a job, not fuck around with this

bitch." He sighed, beginning to pace the room. Even in the midst of all this filth, the half angel was still beautiful. The darkness didn't seem to touch him. "Can't you just kill her already so we can get on with this?"

Panic curled in Ceri's gut. She didn't want to die here like this, her magic warped and used for evil.

"I'll kill her when *I* am *ready*."

Zachariah huffed in annoyance. "I'm going back upstairs. This better be done when I get back."

They kept sniping back and forth at each other, arguing about the timing of their plans.

Ceri looked around for Selena as she tested how tightly her arms were bound. Her earlier magic use had weakened them, but it would take another two or three attempts to break free considering how weak she was now. An offensive attack against the sorcerer was out of the question too. All she'd manage would be to piss him off. Selena's absence gave her a little hope though. Maybe she had a chance if it was just him.

A gentle breeze brushed up against her hair and she jerked her head around but no one was there. Frowning, she looked around carefully. It happened again, tickling her foot and she felt a gentle touch against her mind.

The room drifted away and the pain lifted from her mind like a fog clearing. It remained dark, but it felt different. This was just the absence of light rather than the stifling feeling that came with black magic.

Ceridwen, the voice whispered.

Can you help me?

There was a sense of uncertainty followed by determination. *I will try.*

Pain jerked her back into the room and she couldn't hold back the scream that wrenched itself out of her throat. A knife was buried up to the hilt in her leg and the sorcerer looked furious.

"That's not going to work again," he sneered.

Selena walked into the room just then. "I see you're getting started without me."

CHAPTER 67

TOMMY

*T*hey landed silently a few feet away from the ruins of the old stone house. Tommy was grateful to have his feet on solid ground again. Despite the awesome views of the city, he never wanted to do that again.

Evangeline took a deep breath and her hair faded back to blonde as the horns simply disappeared. The fiery wings drifted into ash that she brushed off her shoulders. "Do you know where they are?"

He shook his head. "I can tell they're close, but I don't know exactly where they are. I think they must be underground though. If they weren't we'd be able to see them."

They walked quietly toward the stone house. He kept his ears peeled for any hint of movement as he sniffed the air, hoping to pick up their scents. As the wind shifted, he thought he could smell Amber but he couldn't tell exactly which direction it was coming from. She must have walked all around this area.

A few broken beer bottles were strewn around on this side of the house. This was probably the favorite spot for the local kids to come drink, smoke, and get laid. He stepped over the glass and walked around to the other side of the house. A doorway stood empty, the door having rotted away long ago.

The ground looked slightly disturbed here and there was the slightest hint of someone unfamiliar lingering on the stone wall, as though they had brushed against it as they walked through the opening. He stepped over the threshold and looked around. The roof was missing so the room was lit by the afternoon sunlight that made it through the thick clouds overhead.

"Do you see anything?" Evangeline asked in a whisper.

He shook his head. "I smelled something though. Maybe the entrance is hidden."

Slowly, they paced the inner perimeter of the room, pressing on random stones and scuffing up the dirt on the stone floor to check for seams. Just as he was about to give up and look elsewhere, he heard a scraping noise and jerked around, motioning for Evangeline to be quiet.

The wall swung open, revealing a hidden door, and Zachariah stopped in his tracks, looking as surprised to see them as they were to see him.

"You bastard!" Evangeline shouted, flames bursting to life around her as she drew on the demonic power that coursed through her. Her hair turned black and the horns returned as her fiery wings flared behind her. The mark on his chest twitched and he felt the magic moving under his skin as if she were drawing strength from him.

Flames streaked from her hands. They crashed into Zachariah like waves breaking against the shore, rolling over and around him without harming him.

He sneered at her. "Your disgusting magic cannot touch me, demon."

"I bet my teeth can." Tommy shifted and charged the pretentious asshole that had tried to ruin all their lives out of blind hatred. Zachariah's eyes widened in fear as he frantically scrambled backward, hands grasping at thin air.

Just as he was about to collide with Zachariah, a flash of light blinded him. He hit something solid and searingly cold that threw him back with a wave of magic.

Shaking off the blow, Tommy looked up to see the half angel now held a shield that seemed to be made of pure magic and a strange sword that crackled with energy.

Zachariah shifted his feet into a fighting stance and turned his cold eyes to Evangeline. "I'll probably get a commendation for killing you myself."

"I'm going to rip you apart for hurting my mother."

A malicious grin spread across his face. "Your adoptive mother is nothing more than collateral damage. Killing your actual mother was a pleasure though."

Evangeline shrieked with rage as she launched herself at him, her wings propelling her up above the walls into the space the roof should be before angling down. Tommy forced himself back to his feet and raced toward the half angel as well. Zachariah moved his left foot back and held his shield up at an angle, his sword concealed behind it. He was going to skewer her.

Howling in warning, Tommy leapt as she sped down at him. His teeth closed around Zachariah's arm, wrenching the sword to the side just in time. Evangeline collided with him and they went down in a tangle of limbs.

Zachariah threw her back with a well-placed kick, then struck him with the shield. The magic flared painfully against his skin and knocked him off Zachariah's arm. He skittered back just far enough to avoid a swipe of the sword, but his skin went numb from the close proximity to the insanely cold magic.

He couldn't let it hit him or he wouldn't be able to walk. Flattening his ears against his head, he growled at Zachariah. The wolf was furious but also exhilarated by this opponent.

Flames rushed toward Zachariah again, but just like before, they washed over him ineffectively. If they were going to stop this guy, Tommy was going to have to do it himself. The half angel looked away for a split second and Tommy darted in, running behind Zachariah out of range of that sword. He nipped at his heels, his teeth tearing at the back of his ankle and drawing blood.

Zachariah shouted in pain and jerked around, swinging wildly in an attempt to hit him. The first two strikes missed, but the third came worryingly close as Tommy found himself backed into a corner. Tommy could smell the blood seeping into the fabric of his pants. He'd wounded him more than he'd realized.

Bunching his legs underneath him, he prepared to charge straight in, sword be damned. But then the air around them twitched and his legs faltered underneath him as gravity suddenly doubled. All three of them were knocked to the ground.

Zachariah looked up, straining against the overwhelming pressure, with a satisfied grin. "You're too late."

As abruptly as it had started, the pressure vanished. Zachariah jumped to his feet and ran. Evangeline turned to follow and he ran after her, but only made it two steps.

The ground split wide open right underneath Tommy's feet. Evangeline screamed but she was too far away to stop him from falling. A terrible feeling washed over him, stealing his strength. The wolf went silent in his head and he felt suddenly very empty. A shout tore from his throat as he fell into the gaping chasm.

CHAPTER 68

EVANGELINE

*E*vangeline watched Tommy fall in horror. A massive shockwave of magic lifted her from her feet and threw her back. She caught herself with her wings and shot up above the destruction. A chasm three feet wide and twenty feet long had rent the earth open.

As she drew closer to it, she felt the wrongness of it. It was the exact same feeling she'd noticed when she'd secretly visited the no magic zone near her school. She couldn't enter it even if she wanted to. She'd tried that day, but it had repelled her like a physical barrier.

Gritting her teeth together, she pounded her fists against the invisible wall. Tommy wasn't dead, but he was probably hurt, and there was no telling what effect it was having on him. Furious, she turned around, searching the forest for the angel. Tommy had taken the mark so that they could stop Zachariah and the sorcerer. She couldn't let him escape.

He still had his shield and sword which lit him up like a beacon even in the daylight. She dropped to the ground just outside of the house and grabbed a stone about the size of a softball. Her magic may not be able to touch him, but as Tommy had proved, he wasn't invincible. It was time to see if she still remembered how to throw that fastball that had been her signature when she'd played softball in junior high school.

She launched herself back up into the air and flew toward him as fast as she could. Her speed surprised her, she barely remembered fleeing with her mother, just racing against the sunrise. She didn't have to worry about the sun now.

Zachariah came into view once again and she flattened her wings against her back, racing toward him as she wove between the treetops. He was almost back to his car. She adjusted her grip on the first stone and threw it at him as hard as she could. It hit the back of his skull with a loud crack and sent him sprawling onto the ground.

She was on him in the blink of an eye. Every point of contact with him burned like she was touching an open flame. She faltered for a moment and he twisted, throwing her off. His shield blinked out of existence, but he kept the sword.

He swung it, slashing through her wing as she raised it to protect herself. Cold, burning pain rushed through her and it felt as though he'd severed a limb. She shrieked in rage and kicked out, catching his wrist, flinging his arm and the sword backward. It fell from his hand, rolling away on the forest floor.

He turned and scrambled after it. She jumped on his back and grabbed two handfuls of his hair. It hurt and her hands began to go numb, but she refused to let go this time. She slammed his face into the ground as he struggled underneath her, still trying to get to his sword. Her arms grew weaker the longer she held on. With a furious shout, Zachariah yanked one of her hands away and pulled her off balance.

Right next to the sword lay the rock she'd thrown at him. Dropping the other handful of hair, she launched herself at it, her fingers closing around it right as he grabbed his sword. She grabbed his wrist to stop him from stabbing her again and slammed the rock down on the back of his head. The blow dazed him and his body went limp for a moment.

She brought stone down on his head again and again, screaming in rage. Power flowed through her as his skull cracked under her attack. Rage, glee, and hate fueled her, replacing the strength his cold magic had stolen from her.

Memories of the pain in her mother's eyes as the fire had crawled over her legs, the exhaustion as she struggled to heal from the injuries, and the constant fear they'd both had to live with blinded her with rage. He was already dead, but she didn't stop until there was nothing left of his head but a mess of gore.

She paused panting, and that's when she heard it. A twig snapped and she looked up in alarm. A group of werewolves stood all around her, and they did not look friendly.

One of them stepped forward, an older man with a gray beard and a scar across his face. He looked at her, and the lifeless body in front of her. "Why have you killed Zachariah Hudson?"

She raised her bloody hands but otherwise stayed perfectly still so as not to startle them. "He was working with the sorcerer. He tried to kill me, and Amber's pack."

The old alpha looked her over critically, giving nothing away with his expression. "Show us where the sorcerer is. If you try to hurt one of my pack members or flee, I will kill you."

Swallowing down the fear curling in her throat, she nodded and pointed behind her. "They're at the Witch's Castle, the old stone house. I think they're somewhere underground in the new no magic zone."

Jameson's face hardened at the mention of a no magic zone. "Let's go."

CHAPTER 69

AMBER

*A*mber tore another chunk of flesh from the zombie's arm but she knew it would just grow back. They were fighting a losing battle and she was beginning to tire. No matter how they hurt them, the zombies simply healed. They couldn't tear them apart fast enough to disable them.

A blast shook the walls of the cellar, threatening the cave the whole thing in. Amber dropped to her stomach, ready to run for the stairs if needed, but the walls and ceiling held.

The zombies went strangely still, the unholy light behind their eyes dying. Siobhan stuttered, the symbols on her body flickering before snuffing out completely. She collapsed into a heap on the floor, lifeless once again. Peter fell as well, the half-shift vanishing and leaving him fully human, and fully dead, on the ground.

Amber took a step back, looking around in disbelief. They couldn't have just given up. These twisted creatures must have only been meant to delay them.

"What the hell was that?" Derek asked, leaning against the wall and panting as he tried to regain his breath.

She walked hesitantly toward the door, peering down the short hallway it led to. Light flickered in the distance casting strange shadows, beckoning her. Glancing back over her shoulder to ensure the others were following, she crept carefully down the hall.

There were three heartbeats in the room. She could hear Ceri's labored breathing, but the other two people in there were waiting for them silently. She paused, looking into the pack bond, then realized why she felt so strange. Tommy was gone. She couldn't feel him at all.

Fury rushed through her. She refused to consider that he might be dead. They must have taken him too, somehow. A growl escaped her throat as she wrapped what was left of the pack bond around herself and rose up to her full height, letting it burn in her eyes before rounding the corner and facing them.

The sorcerer stood in the center of the room, blocking her view of Ceri. In the corner, half hidden in the shadows, stood the last person she expected to see. Selena. The witch grinned at her, tapping a wooden wand against her thigh. She barely looked like herself. Her hair had been buzzed off and she looked ill.

Behind them, it looked as if the earth itself had split apart. A chasm filled with rubble stretched farther than she could see away from them.

Caligo grinned, spreading his arms wide as though he was welcoming them. "When Selena said she knew how to deliver you to me, I must say, I was skeptical. It looks like I was wrong to doubt her."

"Werewolves are utterly predictable," Selena said, her manic grin matching his own.

They were both insane. Amber lowered her head and growled. Ceri was so close, but she wasn't moving and her eyes were shut. She could smell her blood from here.

"Ah, I see you don't want to talk," Caligo said, throwing his head back with a cackle. His eyes were solid black when he looked back at her. "I guess it's time to finish this."

The rumble of falling rocks startled them both and Caligo took a step back so he could see behind himself while keeping Amber in his view.

Tommy stumbled out of the chasm in human form, but completely naked. He kept one hand on the wall to keep himself upright as he looked around the room. Amber wanted to howl in relief. When he took a step out of the opening, she felt the pack bond snap back into place. Tommy shuddered and seemed to instantly regain his strength. His eyes flashed yellow.

"The whole pack is here. How sweet." Caligo lifted his hand toward Tommy, magic pooling in his palm. Amber wasn't about to let him hurt Tommy. She raced toward him with Genevieve close behind.

CHAPTER 70

AMBER

*A*t the last moment, Caligo turned the spell on her. A black blur shot in front of her, blocking the attack right before it could hit her. Genevieve crashed to the floor, yelping in pain and black flames burned away her fur. She rolled, smothering it against the floor.

Amber howled in rage and ducked down, charging at him low. Her claws scraped against the stone as she launched herself at him. He yelled something in Latin and swiped his hand across her path. Her vision went completely dark for a split second and she was thrown to the side.

She hit the ground as gunfire cracked through the air. Her vision returned, though it remained slightly foggy. Derek shot at Selena again, driving her back as Tommy circled behind her, now in his wolf form. There was blood on his muzzle and dripping from Selena's arm.

Amber tried to stand but her muscles only jerked erratically. The floor under her was slick with what smelled like blood. As she twitched, the red stains grew darker, glowing with an unholy light. The spell seeped into her body, twisting dark claws into her mind. Her front paw moved, claws sliding against the stone. She hadn't moved it. She couldn't.

A growl came unbidden from her throat as she stood. Foreign rage filled her. The wolf howled, eager to kill. She screamed inside her mind, trying to wrestle back control of her body, but it did no good.

Caligo's voice whispered through her mind. *Kill them all.*

Amber's head swiveled around to face Genevieve, who was back on her feet and watching her carefully. Her lips curled back over her teeth and she growled at the small black wolf.

Kill.

She charged at Genevieve, her powerful muscles propelling her across the distance in the blink of an eye. Her jaws snapped close on air as Genevieve ducked underneath the initial attack, darting away to her left.

Kill.

Her next strike caught Genevieve's leg and blood filled her mouth. Genevieve yelped and tried to jerk away, snapping at her shoulder when she couldn't pull her leg free.

Amber used her weight to shove Genevieve off balance then lunged for her throat. The smaller wolf twisted out of the way, putting space between them. They circled each other, heads low and ears flat against their head.

There was a loud crash as Selena threw Derek back with a wave of her hand. His head struck the wall and the shotgun clattered to the floor as he lost consciousness. She turned her wand on Tommy who yelped in pain. Green flames engulfed him as he writhed on the floor, twisting in a frantic attempt to get them off of him.

Kill.

Amber charged Genevieve again. They collided in a tangle of limbs and teeth. Her teeth sunk into Genevieve's shoulder, ripping away a chunk of flesh. She yelped in pain and struck back with two vicious bites that grazed Amber's side, cutting almost down to the bone of her ribs.

Shane was circling Caligo, attempting to get close. The sorcerer held his hands out wide as if welcoming an attack. "Perhaps you should help Amber. It looks like she's having a little trouble controlling herself."

Shane growled and took another step forward, all his muscles tensed for an attack.

"The longer you wait, the less likely it is she'll--" Caligo's words were cut off by Shane's attack. The sorcerer brought his hands together with a loud crack. A shockwave caught Shane and tossed him back. He slid across the floor and hit the wall. As he scrambled back to his feet, a brilliant, shimmering cloud engulfed him. His legs collapsed beneath him and he clawed against the ground, trying to get away from the powdered silver.

Genevieve clawed at her gut and pushed her snapping jaws away with her other paw. She bit down on the leg, and the bone cracked. Genevieve yelped in pain but didn't stop fighting back. Amber had to jerk away as the other wolf snapped at her throat.

Something heavy hit her in the side, knocking her off Genevieve completely. She struggled against the arms that wrapped around her, trying to cut off her air supply.

Kill.

She snapped at the hand that held her, grazing it and drawing blood. Derek refused to let go but she was stronger than a human. Getting leverage with her back legs, she jerked free and turned on him, forcing him to the ground.

"Amber, look at me!" Derek shouted, pinned beneath her weight. "Don't do this! Fight back!"

"Am...ber..." Dylan choked out, blood bubbling out of his lips. "Hel...p...hurts..."

The memory crashed over her mind like an ice bath, shocking her into stillness as her jaws closed around her brother's neck. She trembled as the urge to bite and tear coursed through her. Something wasn't right.

Hands sunk into her fur, the touch gentle. "It's okay," Derek whispered. "If you remember this later, I forgive you."

Kill. The command came again. She hesitated, trembling under the weight of the magic.

No. It couldn't happen again. Amber whined and tried to let go, but her body was fighting her. She squeezed her eyes shut and sunk into her mind, searching for the wolf. The angry, hateful thing howling in her mind was all wrong. It wasn't the creature whose soul had joined with hers.

Wind ruffled her fur, bringing with it the sweet scent of Ceri's magic. Amber growled and fought back against the black magic that clung to her mind. Slowly, the wolf's power joined hers. The pack bond reignited inside her and she wrapped herself in its protection. Turning toward the darkness in her mind, she shredded the spell.

Her jaws released and she jerked away from Derek, chest heaving. He looked at her wide-eyed, staying perfectly still as if he was afraid to set her off.

The breeze blowing through the room turned into a sudden gale, almost knocking her off her feet. The sorcerer shouted in rage and turned toward Ceri with a furious expression. Her eyes popped open and she ripped her arm free of one of the restraints.

Shane was the first to move this time, though he was slow from the silver he'd inhaled, attempting to draw Caligo's attention away from Ceri. He darted in, barely dodging the first swipe of the sorcerer's blade, then latched onto the arm that held the dagger. Caligo didn't even hesitate. He flipped the dagger to the other hand and stabbed it into Shane's back, then kicked him away. Shane fell to the ground and didn't move.

Caligo ran toward Ceri, who had one hand stretched out toward Selena. The witch clawed at her own throat, choking as though she couldn't breathe. Ceri curled her hand into a fist, her face set in determination. Selena's lips began to turn blue as she was deprived of oxygen.

The sorcerer cast a spell that hit Ceri with a flash of light. Her spell faltered and she slumped back to the table, her body shaking erratically. Selena, freed from the spell, took off at a run. She disappeared through some door that hadn't been visible before.

Enraged, Amber howled as she charged the sorcerer. Her legs were shaky but they were responding to her once again. This bastard was hurting everyone she cared about, and for what? Power? Money? Nothing could be worth this amount of suffering.

Amber ran as fast as she could toward him, her heart pounding in her ears. Caligo slid to a stop next to Ceri and lifted the knife high overhead, his eyes locking with Amber's.

She launched herself at him, but it was too late. The knife plunged into Ceri's chest and she convulsed, her one free hand clawing uselessly at Caligo's arm. He ripped the knife free in a spray of blood in the same moment that Amber clamped her jaw around his throat.

She ripped out his throat with her teeth. Caligo crumpled to the floor as blood poured from the wound. Pain shot through Amber's chest as the demon mark dissolved, but she didn't care. All she cared about was Ceri.

Amber shifted back and pressed her hands against the wound in Ceri's chest. Her blood ran freely under Amber's hands. She'd seen wounds like these before in the emergency room. The victim was normally dead by the time they got to the hospital. She just had to stop the bleeding. She had to. Somehow.

Ceri gasped, blood bubbling up between her lips as it filled her lungs. Her eyes were wide with fear, but she still lifted a trembling hand to Amber's face, her mouth opening and shutting around words she couldn't quite form.

"Please don't die," Amber begged. She couldn't watch someone she loved die again. She wasn't strong enough for that. "Just hang on. I'll stop the bleeding."

Desperately, she pushed all the strength she had left through the pack bond, trying to give Ceri a little more time, but she was bleeding out so fast. The pack bond was a mess of pain and fear. Every single member of her pack was hurt. They had no strength to give. Ceri gasped for air she could no longer take in. Her lung had probably collapsed.

"Ceri!" Derek shouted, running over. Horror spread across his face as he took in the extent of her injuries. Looking up at Amber, he asked. "Can you save her?"

She stared back at her brother, tears slipping from her eyes. She couldn't say it out loud. She refused to.

Angel appeared in front of her, near Ceri's head. He was barely visible, just an apparition. "I can heal her."

"How?" she asked, pressing down so hard she feared she'd break one of Ceri's ribs. The witch didn't even flinch, she was too far gone to feel pain and barely conscious.

"Take another mark from me. I can't act without it."

Amber hesitated, hands trembling. She couldn't think, not with Ceri laying here like this.

"Amber!" he shouted as his body began to fade even further. "Take the mark or I cannot help you!"

His face flickered, shifting from the demonic to something almost...human. Amber reached her hand up, trailing her fingers across his cheek, then grabbed his hand and placed it against her chest. "A debt for a debt."

As painful as the first time, the magic seared the skin under his hand, burying itself in her chest where the other mark had been. She could feel him once again. His eyes met hers and she saw the satisfaction there.

She knew he hadn't planned this but he had found a way to take advantage. Dropping his hand, she put pressure on the wound once again. "Help her."

CHAPTER 71

CERI

*M*agic burned through her body like a lightning bolt. Ceri gasped as she was finally able to take a full breath. Every wound and ache was gone. For a brief moment, she wondered if she'd died and gone on to the afterlife, but then Amber was above her, tears dripping from her cheeks.

"Ceri? Can you hear me? Please say something, please," Amber gasped, shaking her lightly.

"What..." she blinked, still disoriented. What had happened? She remembered the knife. The pain. And darkness overtaking her.

Derek shoved his way in close and wrapped her in a hug. He was shaking and she felt still-wet blood in his hair when she put her arms around him.

Her eyes met Amber who was standing a few steps away. She was pale and looked like she was trembling as well. Amber's eyes strayed to the left and she nodded.

Ceri frowned. Caligo was dead at her feet. The demon's mark should be dissolved now.

Derek released her slowly, gently pushing her sweat-soaked hair back from her face. "Are you okay?"

"Yes, but I shouldn't be. What happened?" she asked, eyes flicking between Derek and Amber.

"I took another demon mark," Amber said, her lips pressed together into a thin line. "I couldn't watch you die, I'm sorry."

Ceri's face softened and she rubbed her hand over the place the knife had sunk in. She could be angry or blame Amber for making a foolish choice, but the truth was she was thankful she was alive. Amber hadn't had many choices. She met her alpha's eyes and said, "Thank you."

Amber's shoulders slumped in relief. "Get her off that stupid slab, I'm going to go check on the others."

Shane, who must have been the white wolf she'd seen, was slumped in a corner panting. As Derek helped her sit up, she saw that Genevieve was helping Tommy sit up with one arm. The other was cradled against her chest. Tommy's skin was red and angry from Selena's attack with the wand. Seeing his injuries only reminded her of the torture she'd endured.

Her fingers dug into Derek's arm as she struggled to keep from panicking. He pulled her into a tight hug and she buried her face in his shoulder, letting the scent of his sweat and cologne fill her nose, blocking out the rest of it. His touch grounded her and she slowed her breathing. Even though the physical wounds had healed, she couldn't escape the mental scars this day had left behind.

As Derek helped her off the slab she saw Amber and the others tense up. Amber walked toward the door, her hands clenched into tight fists.

Shane limped after her, catching her arm. "He's not going to hurt you," he croaked, still struggling for a breath.

"I'll believe that when I see it," Amber said shortly.

Jameson walked into the room, followed by a blood-soaked Evangeline and his pack. Evangeline looked basically unharmed, but the way her eyes were darting around betrayed her nervousness.

"You wanted proof, here it is," Amber said, sweeping her arm toward the sorcerer's dead body and the destruction behind them.

Shane locked eyes with his alpha. He was practically swaying on his feet but seemed determined to stand with Amber. "I saw the sorcerer attempting to kill them."

"And the creation of the no magic zone?" Jameson asked, nodding toward the rubble-filled chasm.

"We were fighting in a different room."

Amber gave him a withering look. "The sorcerer did it."

"It opened up underneath me when Evangeline and I were fighting Zachariah," Tommy said, walking up to stand beside Amber.

Jameson sighed and dragged his hand down his face. "Alright. I think it's obvious that neither you nor this girl is responsible for the no magic zones. You'll still need to keep her hidden or get her out of town. Hudson made too big an impact for her to go walking around without causing a riot."

"That won't be a problem. We'll be finding a safe place for her soon," Amber agreed with a nod.

Ceri slumped with relief. It was over, for now at least. With the new demon mark, they wouldn't be truly safe, but they had a chance now. Her eyes felt heavy. More than anything, she just wanted to sleep.

CHAPTER 72

AMBER

It was still daylight outside and that felt wrong considering the darkness they'd just endured. Amber looked at the sun where it hung low in the sky, partially blocked by clouds and tried to still the trembling in her hands.

She'd come so close to losing someone else, someone she'd come to think of as a sister, all because of a demon's mark. She'd hurt Genevieve and almost killed her brother. All she'd wanted was to protect them but she'd put them all in even more danger instead by dragging them into a fight with an evil sorcerer.

Angel was still floating around, observing Jameson and his pack as they milled around discussing what had happened. Maybe Thallan was right and she should kill him to protect everyone else.

Shane walked up beside her, startling her. "Sorry," he said, touching her arm gently. "Didn't mean to scare you."

"It's okay. I'm just jumpy right now."

He gave her a wan smile. "Understandable."

"What now? Is the council still going to try to punish me or something?" she asked, wrapping her arms around herself. She felt cold down to the bone.

"No. Jameson asked for proof, and you managed to give it to him." He hesitated. "Some of them may trust you a little less, or be assholes, but they can't do anything to you without risking punishment themselves."

She snorted. "That's comforting. I see how well that went last time."

"Jameson is on your side." Shane squeezed her shoulder gently. "I have to go. I inhaled a lot of silver earlier, and while the pack bond is keeping me upright, I really need to get treated."

She nodded. "Of course. I'm sorry you got drug into all this."

"No one dragged me into anything. I wanted to help because I care about you and this sorcerer needed to be stopped. Don't fret about it, okay?"

That was easier said than done. "Sure."

"I'll see you soon." He headed back toward Jameson. Ceri, Derek, and Evangeline were still talking to the old alpha, trying to work out how exactly the sorcerer had created the no magic zone.

She tuned them out and looked around for Tommy and

Genevieve. They were sitting out of the way. Both looked exhausted. Genevieve met her eyes and she had a strong urge to turn and just run but she swallowed down her fear and guilt and walked over.

She nervously crossed her arms and stared at her bare feet that were now completely filthy. It finally occurred to her that she was still naked, but it seemed they were all past being concerned about modesty. "Is your arm okay?"

Genevieve sighed and pushed up to her feet. Amber watched her warily, expecting a punch or accusations. Instead, Genevieve dragged her into a one-armed hug.

"It's healing, and if I hear one word of you blaming yourself for what happened, I'll break my other arm."

Amber laughed, though the sound was a bit hysterical. "I tried to kill you."

"The sorcerer tried to kill me." Genevieve stepped away and met her gaze, eyes narrowed. "Unless you've secretly wanted me dead all along?"

"Of course not!"

"Then why are you acting like you did it on purpose?" Genevieve demanded, jabbing her in the arm with her finger.

"I fell into his trap, I should have seen--"

"Blah blah blah." Genevieve rolled her eyes. "We're all alive, and the sorcerer is dead. We can analyze our strategy some other time."

Tommy snorted in amusement. "Gen, you may not be the best at comforting people."

"I'm excellent at it. You hush."

Amber shook her head. No matter what happened, they

didn't lose their sense of humor. Frowning, she looked down at Tommy.

"How the hell did you and Evangeline end up here? You were supposed to stay home." She crossed her arms and glared at him.

"About that..."

A hand on her shoulder startled her, but she looked back to see it was Ceri, her brother, and Evangeline. She avoided eye contact with Derek. That was a conversation she was not ready to have, not if she wanted to keep her shit together until she had a chance to be alone.

"Is everyone doing okay?" Ceri asked, leaning in to take a closer look at Genevieve's arm.

"As well as can be expected," Genevieve said, waving Ceri away. "You can look at it later. Let's go home."

Amber agreed with a nod. Nothing sounded better.

CHAPTER 73

EVANGELINE

*E*vangeline couldn't believe her good luck. When those werewolves had shown up, she was sure she'd be killed. The fact that they'd given her the benefit of the doubt after they'd watched her literally beat a man's head in with a rock was insane. Maybe there was a chance she could have a normal life after all...or at least be safe for a while.

They climbed out of the truck and she was tempted to run inside and tell Eloise they were safe now, but she held back and walked next to Tommy. It was strange how aware of him she was now. Kadrithan had dozens of demon marks at least but he'd never talked about how close you felt to the person that wore it. She felt Tommy's fear and pain as he'd fought, and she felt his exhaustion now. His strongest emotions were like a heartbeat at the back of her mind.

Ceri paused in front of the door. "There's something wrong. I should have noticed sooner, but I thought it was just because of the fight."

"What?" Evangeline asked, shoving in front of Tommy. "What's wrong?"

"There is a threat inside the house. The wards are activating."

Evangeline yanked the door open, but Amber's grip on her arm kept her from entering. "Get off of me!"

"Slow down. You can't help Eloise if you walk into a trap."

"Deward is supposed to be there with her. Can you see him?" Tommy asked nervously from behind them.

There was a strange thunk from upstairs and Amber rushed inside with Evangeline close behind her. She ran in front of the alpha and looked up toward her mother's room. An elf was facing off with Deward, the troll that always tutored Tommy, and his features were contorted with rage.

Deward's shirt was singed and he was standing in front of her mother who was slumped against the wall with a baseball bat in her hand. She could barely stand but her mother wasn't the type to go down without a fight.

"Get out of my way or I'll kill you too!" the elf shouted.

"Move, Deward," Eloise growled.

"I refuse."

"Get the hell away from my mother!" Evangeline yelled, wishing she could draw on the demon's power again. Now that she'd fulfilled Tommy's request, she wouldn't be able to access it until the sun set.

The elf's eyes turned to her and hate filled his face.

"Thallan, what the hell are you doing?" Amber asked, her

tone even and calm like she was trying to talk down a hostage situation.

"I waited but as expected, the demon has you wrapped around his little finger." He drew a gleaming blade from his belt. "SHOW YOURSELF KADRITHAN OR I'LL KILL THEM BOTH."

Thallan walked toward the stairs, the knife held in his hand like a shield. There was a strange, glowing sphere in his other hand. He lifted it and his eyes darted around the room. "I can kill them all. I know you've seen one of these before."

Amber stepped in front of Evangeline, shielding her with her body. A useless gesture if that was a firebomb. Evangeline eyed the door to her mother's room, trying to find a way to get to her and run before it was too late.

Her uncle appeared, looking at the elf with a bored expression. "This is beneath you, Thallan."

The elf sneered at him. "You murdered my wife."

Kadrithan raised his brow. "Your wife was killed in a car accident. I know you've always irrationally blamed me, but this is taking things a bit far."

Evangeline knew that tone. Her uncle was pissed. If he'd been able, he would have killed the elf right then and there, but of course, he couldn't.

Thallan's fingers tightened on the firebomb and Amber tensed like she was going to try to make a leap for it. If she missed, the whole house would blow.

Evangeline stepped around Amber and walked straight toward him, her hands held out to her side to show she had no weapons. "Stop it. If you want revenge, just kill me."

Thallan's eyes flicked over to her.

"Kadrithan wants me alive. He'd be devastated if I was killed. So, if you think you need some kind of revenge, then just kill me. Leave everyone else out of it." She took another step forward. "I'm sick of everyone around me getting hurt trying to protect me, so just hurt me instead."

"Evangeline, get away from him and stop being stupid," Kadrithan demanded.

Amber was trying to edge toward her and she could feel Tommy panicking. She didn't care anymore. She thought she'd done enough when she had killed Zachariah but they'd come home to another threat. It would never end, not as long as she was alive.

"Evangeline, no!" her mother screamed from upstairs. Her shout made Evangeline look up and she saw horror on her mother's face, but she couldn't turn back now. This was the only way to keep her safe.

Thallan adjusted the grip on his knife, then moved toward her like a flash. She lunged at him at the same time to stop Amber from getting in the way, but they never collided. Blinking she looked around and found herself...upstairs. Deward looked just as surprised as she did to see her standing next to him.

Her mother limped toward her and yanked her into a hug. "What the hell were you thinking?"

"I had to..." her thought trailed off as a woman appeared in the midst of the living room. Pale green hair fell over her shoulders in loose curls, framing a delicate face. She was beautiful...and transparent.

Thallan, whose legs had sunk into the floor like it was quicksand froze, his eyes going wide.

"Illya?" he whispered reverently as if he were looking at an angel.

She drifted forward, her ethereal feet not touching the floor. "I waited for you," she whispered. "Day after day, but everything around me grew dark. What have you done?"

Tears slipped out of Thallan's eyes and slid down his cheeks. "I was trying to find a way to avenge you. The demon, he took you from me. I didn't know you were here."

She shook her head, a frown marring her perfect mouth. Gently, she tried to stroke Thallan's cheek, but her hand passed through him. "It was an accident. Simple bad luck."

Her mother's hug tightened around her as if the mention of death scared her. It scared Evangeline too. Her mother was old. If she was attacked again she probably wouldn't survive. They might have gotten through this but all hope of feeling safe seemed laughable now.

"No," Thallan insisted, cringing away from her. "No, I can't..."

Illya leaned in close. "Stop looking for someone to blame. The man who killed me is already dead."

Thallan's body shook with grief but he couldn't look away from the woman.

Evangeline glanced at the others to see if they had any clue what was going on, but they all looked just as confused as she was, except for Ceri, who looked about as awed as Thallan.

"What is she?" Amber asked nervously.

"An echo," Ceri said in awe. "She poured so much magic into this place that a little piece of her stayed behind. The house isn't sentient, she is."

Illya moved away from Thallan, shaking her head in disappointment.

"You will not come here again until you hold no more hate in your heart," she said, lifting both hands. The house groaned and everything shifted, rolling in a dizzying blur, and then Thallan was gone.

The woman, Illya, glanced back at Evangeline and smiled brilliantly at her. She felt herself relax slightly.

"Don't be so hard on yourself. I can see the good in you." As quickly as she had appeared, Illya vanished, disappearing back into the house.

Evangeline looked down at the pack, stunned. "That was weird, right?"

"Extremely," Deward said, crossing his arms and shaking his head. "This pack is very strange."

CHAPTER 74

TOMMY

They'd all searched the yard after the incident with Thallan, but hadn't been able to find him. Amber had decided that they were safe enough in the house for now and she'd deal with him later.

Tommy pressed the palms of his hands into his eyes until he saw stars, then took a deep breath and headed over to talk to Deward. Amber had spent the last ten minutes apologizing and thanking him while also chastising him for going along with their plan even though it had worked.

He stopped awkwardly in front of the troll and scratched his head. "Sorry about that."

"I've never been called irresponsible or idiotic before," Deward said with a frown.

"I can't believe she said that." Tommy covered his face with a groan. "I really am sorry, I shouldn't have--"

"Do not apologize," Deward said, lifting his hand. "I think, perhaps, I did act rashly. Something I've never done before, but the result was satisfying. Despite your alpha's doubts, you joining the fight did seem to make a difference."

He wasn't sure how to respond to that. "Well, yeah, it did."

Deward nodded. "Then I shall take that conversation simply as a sign of concern from your alpha."

"Probably a good idea."

Captain Jack walked through the living room and pawed at Amber's leg, meowing loudly. Deward eyed the cat warily.

"I did notice something while you were gone. There is something wrong with your cat."

"Did he throw up or something?" Tommy asked, concerned.

Deward shook his head. "No, but before your ghost appeared, its eye was glowing. It looked as if it were about to attack. No one seemed to notice since they were focused on the demon and the elf."

Tommy looked at Captain Jack, brows pinched together. "Glowing?"

"Glowing green. It's possible the adrenaline caused me to mistake what I saw, but I'm almost positive that I remember correctly."

"Weird. I'll keep an eye on him."

Deward nodded. "I should return home now to give your pack privacy and discuss all this with my father."

"He won't tell anyone about Evangeline, will he?"

"No. My father never believed demons were responsible

for the no magic zones. He will not betray your pack's confidence."

"Great," Tommy said with a huge sigh of relief. "So, I'll see you in a few days for more tutoring?"

Deward shook his hand firmly, and pulled him in, pressing their foreheads together briefly before stepping back. "Yes. See you then, brother."

Tommy blinked, not sure what had just happened. It kind of felt like Deward had just declared him an ally or best friend or something. "Yeah, uh, see you then...brother."

Deward grinned and headed toward the door, waving his goodbye to the rest of the pack.

"Are you two dating now?" Evangeline asked drily, appearing next to him.

Tommy shrugged. "Maybe." He had managed to find pants shortly after they'd dealt with the Thallan crap, but no one had had a chance to clean off yet. He felt grimy but Evangeline was covered in blood. "Are you okay?"

She looked down at her hands. "I guess."

"I take it you killed that half angel?" He probably shouldn't be asking but he thought avoiding it might not be healthy either.

"I beat his head in with a rock."

"That's intense." He took a deep breath. "And kind of awesome."

She looked up at him and raised a brow. "Awesome?"

He nodded, trying to convince himself as much as her. "He tried to kill you and hurt your mother, and you protected her. That's brave."

She laughed. "Is it awesome that I liked it? That I reveled in crushing in his skull?"

Tommy shrugged. He'd been asking himself the same thing. When Amber had ripped the sorcerer's throat out, he'd been happy. He'd wanted to kill Selena and he'd wanted her to suffer when he did it. "Maybe it's normal for us. Demons and werewolves aren't...human, exactly. We're both predators. As long as you don't go full serial killer, I think you're good."

"That's real comforting."

"Just being honest," he said with a grin.

"Hey, Tommy, can you order pizza?" Amber asked from across the room.

"Absolutely." Today sucked, and nothing could change that. Food could make it better for a little while though.

CHAPTER 75

AMBER

A text from Shane popped up on her phone, confirming he was back to full health. Amber dropped her phone on her bed and sat down, unwinding the towel from her head.

Angel formed right across from her sitting in a black chair. He looked more solid than normal. There was no silly form this time either. She suspected this was his real face. It looked close to the glimpse she'd seen other day; the sharp jaw, aquiline nose, and tousled black hair.

"You better not intend on demanding I fulfill my mark right now," she said as she squeezed water from the ends of her hair with the towel.

He smirked at her. "Did you know Tommy bears Evangeline's demon mark now?"

She sighed, annoyed that he'd reminded her about that little complication. "Yes, did you come to gloat?"

"No, I came to tell you that I've found a safe place for Evangeline to stay. Someone will come to pick her and Eloise up in a couple of days."

"Did you ever find out how they located her?" Amber asked, surprised. She'd expected to have to keep Evangeline forever.

"Yes. It's been taken care of."

That sounded ominous and Amber decided she didn't want to know any details. "Great. Will handing her over to them fulfill my new demon mark?"

Angel threw his head back and laughed. "No, it's not nearly enough. Besides, I know you'd do it anyhow, so there's not much incentive for me to waste a favor on it, is there?"

Amber wished, once again, that she could punch him. "You're an ass."

"And you're a soft, squishy, easily-manipulated marshmallow." The smile on his face made him look easy-going but she couldn't forget the satisfaction she'd seen when he'd trapped her with another mark. She'd never forget that. Thallan was crazy, but he was right about the demon.

She got up and pulled her warmest pajamas out of her drawer. "Great talk. I'm going to bed now. Make yourself scarce."

"It was impressive what you did," Angel said, standing from his chair and prowling toward her. "Killing a sorcerer isn't easy."

"No, it wasn't."

He stopped right in front of her. Close enough to touch and leaned in. "You should be proud of yourself."

He lifted his hand like he meant to touch her face but she caught it and was surprised to find his fingers were solid.

"What are you doing?" She tightened her grip on his hand. His eyes strayed to her lips for a moment and she could practically feel his intent. She shoved him away. "Don't even think about it."

His grin widened. "Sleep well, Amber."

He vanished and her demon mark returned to its dormant state. She pressed her hand against it, wishing for the hundredth time she could cut it out of her chest.

Angry, she yanked on her pajamas and crawled into bed. Of course, that asshole had to come piss her off right before bed. The cherry on top of a terrible day.

She tugged the covers up to her chin, then grabbed a pillow and held it. That was still uncomfortable so she flipped to her other side and tried to squish her pillow into a better shape.

After five minutes of tossing and turning, a gentle knock at her door startled her. She sat up and heard Ceri just outside. Crawling out of bed, she hurried to the door.

Ceri stood in the doorway with a pillow tucked under her arm and tears streaming down her face.

"What's wrong?" she asked, pulling her into a hug.

"Can I sleep with you tonight? I know it's dumb, I'm not a two-year-old but––"

"It's not dumb. What's wrong?"

Ceri took a shaky breath. "I can't stand being alone right now. Every time I close my eyes I'm right back in that room."

Amber kept an arm around Ceri and walked her over to the queen-sized bed. "Come on. Just don't hog the covers."

They curled into bed together and Amber stroked her friend's hair gently. She would never admit it aloud but she was glad to not have to be alone tonight either. Small feet walked over her leg and a warm weight settled in the crevice between her and Ceri. Captain Jack's rumbling purr mingled with Ceri's heartbeat and slow breaths. It was comforting. She pressed her head against Ceri's back and counted the steady rhythm until she drifted off to sleep.

CHAPTER 76

GENEVIEVE

*G*enevieve hurried toward the rest of the old Lockhart pack. The challenge had already begun. Greer hadn't given her much warning. Part of her didn't want to watch this but part of her needed to. She wanted to see Greer win.

"Gen, wait up!" Steven huffed as he tried to catch up. He wasn't much of a runner. He'd stayed over because of the whole near-death experience thing, which he was still upset about.

"Walk faster, I want to watch," she said, not slowing down to wait.

She slipped through a hole in the crowd and stood at the edge of the circle they'd formed. Kevin, the temporary alpha she'd met at the last challenge, was already limping. The other wolf, a tall black wolf with a white patch near his nose who she assumed was Paul, stayed still as Kevin circled around him.

"There are so many werewolves here. Are they all part of this pack?" Steven whispered in her ear.

"Yes, but hush and watch," she said, pushing her fingers against Steven's lips. He sighed in annoyance but she didn't care. The only thing that mattered right now was this fight.

When Kevin charged, he moved so fast he was a blur. He went straight for the neck but Paul was ready. Ducking down and catching him under the jaw, Paul rose up on his hind legs and forced Kevin onto his back. Furious snarls filled the air and Kevin scrambled to get back up as Paul tested his defenses.

The sound made the hair on the back of her neck stand on end. When Amber had turned to her, eyes bright red, and attacked she'd thought it had to be a dream. A nightmare. But the pain had been all too real.

It felt like the pack bond had been ripped away the moment Amber's teeth had sunk into the flesh of her leg. She hadn't wanted to fight back at all but she'd known from the first instant that she *had* to. That Amber would never forgive her if she let her kill her. Amber would rather die herself. So, she had fought back...and lost.

Paul's jaws closed around Kevin's throat. The other werewolf thrashed underneath him but Paul had every advantage and the struggle was futile. Slowly, the thrashing stopped and Kevin shifted back to human form, staying submissive with his face against the ground.

After releasing his grip on Kevin's neck, Paul shifted and stood over him. "Do you submit?"

Kevin's eyes flicked up toward Paul, then he twisted sharply, throwing dirt into Paul's eyes. He stumbled backward and Kevin jumped to his feet, landing a single punch. Genevieve's heart stuttered fearfully and she curled her hands into a fist.

Paul rolled with the punch, then whipped around stomping down on the side of Kevin's knee. A scream of pain tore from Kevin's throat as his leg crumpled. With two quick steps, Paul got behind him, back to back, and wrapped his hands around Kevin's head. With his shoulder, he lifted Kevin off the ground, then brought him down sharply. A loud crack echoed through the silent crowd as Kevin's neck broke. He went limp and Paul tossed his body to the ground.

"I will not tolerate cowardly, dishonorable actions in this pack," he shouted at the shocked onlookers. Everyone shuffled nervously in place looking at the people standing next to them in disbelief. Then, Paul tilted his head back and howled.

The sound resonated in Genevieve's chest. This was power. This was pack. Maybe Greer was right and werewolves had become too tame recently. She might hate that people had to be hurt, but she couldn't deny how this made her feel. The pack would follow Paul now.

"That was intense," Steven said, already scribbling down notes.

It annoyed her to see him doing that, as if the werewolves were zoo animals he was studying. He might think what he'd just witnessed was "intense" but he hadn't felt it. He had no idea how powerful it really was.

"I'll be back, I need to go talk to him about my case."

"What?" Steven's head snapped up, his eyes focusing on her finally. "I'll go with you. I'd like to see--"

"No. This is pack business, it's not appropriate for you to tag along. Just stay here and don't bother anyone," she said, barely keeping from snapping at him. It wasn't really Steven's fault she was upset with him. She'd just been having a bad week and didn't have the patience for his quirks today.

"Okayyy, fine," he said, looking put out.

She hurried toward where Paul was standing, talking to a few of his pack members. They looked completely awed by their new alpha. Paul had always exuded a cool, give-no-shits vibe but he was standing straighter now.

As she approached, he turned and caught her gaze, then said something to the others before heading toward her. He was still completely nude but that didn't faze her anymore. She kept her eyes firmly on his face though.

They stopped in front of each other and Paul grinned at her. "I didn't expect you to come."

"I wanted to watch you win. Congrats by the way," she said, returning his smile.

He nodded his head in thanks. "Now I simply have to maintain the position for a month."

"Something tells me you won't have a problem after how...decisive your victory was." Her eyes strayed to Kevin's corpse. They hadn't moved him yet. If her research was correct, they'd wait for a council member to come and record the death, then turn his body over to the authorities.

She thought she should feel bad for the guy but he had been an awful alpha and person.

Paul snorted. "It wasn't what I intended but I will gladly use it as a teaching experience for the rest of the pack. But I know that's not why you're here. What do you need?"

She turned back, slipping into her business mindset. "Davie Johnson is sitting in jail, unable to be released on bail until his alpha vouches for him."

He sighed and scratched the back of his head. "I thought it might be about him."

"He never should have been arrested. The fight was started by someone else, he just happened to finish it."

"Davie is an idiot and a troublemaker, and he has been since the day he was turned. He was one of Lockhart's poorer choices."

"He may be an idiot, but he needs help. Maybe a respectable alpha to show him the error of his ways?" she prodded, trying not to be too blunt about bringing up his past mistakes.

Paul smiled and shook his head. "You certainly know how to guilt a man into doing what you want."

She shrugged and did her best to keep the smile off her face. "Just doing my job."

"I'll be there. You can text me the address." He nodded goodbye, then headed back to his pack.

Genevieve watched him go and felt...satisfied. She had done it. It hadn't gone how she'd hoped, exactly, but that didn't matter. In the end, she'd succeeded.

"Hey Gen, you ready to go?" Steven shouted from across the yard.

"Yeah, I am." She headed back to her pack and felt a little lighter on her feet. It was time to celebrate.

Today was Tommy's birthday -- the butthead had tried to hide the date but she'd found it out just in time -- and then tonight was the full moon. They hadn't run together as a pack in forever. She was looking forward to it.

CHAPTER 77

TOMMY

A chest plate crafted from one hundred percent tuna can. A helmet made from a measuring cup. A slingshot of rubber bands and chopsticks. And a saddle that was carefully sewn together from only the finest tire scraps.

"There's no way he can do it," Evangeline said, eyeing Woggy's get up.

"Quit being so pessimistic. We've been training for this. He can do it." Tommy adjusted the little helmet, strapping it securely under the pixie's wide chin. Woggy smacked his hands against it and almost knocked himself over but it stayed in place.

"I agree, the chances of success are low despite extensive preparation," Deward chimed in unhelpfully.

Tommy glared at him. "That's enough from both of you. You should be encouraging him, not assuming he'll fail."

Ceri knocked on the door to his room, slightly breathless from jogging upstairs. "Is he ready? The pixies are swarming out front."

Tommy looked down at Woggy who stared up at him with a determined expression. Outside? he signed.

The pixie nodded resolutely and signed, *outside* and *mine*. Standing there in his armor, he looked like a little warrior. It still pained Tommy to think of the pixies fighting since someone was bound to get hurt, but Woggy needed his yard. He couldn't live in fear.

Tommy handed Woggy the slingshot and the little bag of pebbles they'd chosen for this battle. With weapons in hand, Woggy marched over to Captain Jack. The cat paused, looking up from his belly licking, and seemed to sense that it was time. The two of them had a strange connection, and sometimes Tommy wondered how smart the cat was, exactly. Especially after the whole glowing eyes thing Deward had mentioned.

Once Captain Jack had rolled to his feet, Woggy climbed up the makeshift saddle, settling in place. The bag hooked over the front of the saddle, keeping his ammo within reach. Rubber band stirrups hung down from each side to brace Woggy's feet and help him hang on. Watching them race around the house for the past week had been hilarious. Even Captain Jack seemed to enjoy his role as the pixie's noble steed.

Riding with his head held high, Woggy pointed toward

the door and squeaked twice, signaling Captain Jack to head in that direction. The procession that led downstairs was somber, marred only by Amber giggling hysterically.

Derek clamped a hand over her mouth but that quickly devolved into a wrestling match.

Tommy walked ahead and grabbed the door handle, ready to open it, but he hesitated. "Maybe I should go out there with him. Just in case--"

"You can't," Ceri said firmly. "We talked about this and Deward is right. Woggy has to win their respect to reclaim the yard if we don't want to murder them all."

He sighed and nodded his head. They'd talked this over a dozen times. It was the only way. "Okay."

Stepping back, he pulled the door open. Woggy put a pebble in the slingshot and adjusted his position in the saddle. Captain Jack meowed loudly. And then they were off.

The cat could move fast when he wanted to. The crazed duo shot out of the door, both of them letting out a ferocious battle cry.

Their fearless charge startled the swarm of pixies currently hovering in the bushes near the porch. They scattered like a flock of startled birds, shooting into the air with a frantic flapping of their wings.

Tommy shut the door and hurried over to the living room window. Each window had the eager faces of the pack pressed up against it. Watching and waiting.

"Yes! That was the perfect shot!"

Tommy shoved his way in next to Evangeline and watched as Woggy unleashed his fury over the rival swarm.

Pebbles sped out of the slingshot, each one hitting its mark. A pixie crashed into the bushes, another onto the walkway that led to the porch.

As a few of the pixies began to fight back, Captain Jack darted here and there, dodging the rocks they threw. He caught one with a swipe of his paw and knocked it into the porch banister.

"Oooh, Jack is helping him," Amber said excitedly.

Tommy curled his hands into a fist and watched with bated breath. The scattered pixies were starting to regroup. They were flying at him now in groups of two or three trying to snatch him out of his saddle. They knew he couldn't fly. If they knocked him off...he'd be vulnerable.

"He's running low on ammo already," Deward said, watching intently. The troll tried to pretend he didn't care about this whole thing, but Tommy knew he wanted to see Woggy win. The pixie had a way of winning even the most cold-hearted over.

Woggy launched a pebble at a group of three pixies speeding toward him. He caught one in the head, but the other two grabbed his helmet and yanked. With an angry squeak he was dragged backward off the saddle, then tossed onto the porch. He hit the ground and rolled a ways before coming to a stop. For a moment, Tommy was afraid he wouldn't get up, but he did, shaking his head as though the blow had knocked him senseless.

The remaining pebbles had been scattered across the porch when he'd fallen. Woggy stuck his hand in the little bag and pulled out the last one. He loaded it into the slingshot and pulled the rubber band taut as he turned in a slow circle, searching for the next attack.

Captain Jack yowled and charged at some of the pixies, forcing the majority of the swarm back. One of them got through. This pixie was different from the others. He wore a paperclip necklace with a leaf dangling from it and had a distinctly fierce look about him. He swooped toward Woggy, zig-zagging in the air to make himself a harder target.

"He's only got one shot left," Ceri said, her face practically pressed against the window.

"The odds of him making the shot are--"

Tommy elbowed Deward. "Good. They're *good odds.*"

The pack went silent after that, watching the pixie close in with bated breath. Woggy pulled the rubber band back as far as was possible without snapping it. His big, bulging eyes narrowed as he focused in on his target. The old pixie darted left then right, then shot up into the air.

Woggy followed the quick movement, moving his left leg back to brace himself. With a rage-filled squeak, the pixie flattened his wings to his back and dove. Woggy released the pebble.

Tommy's fingertips dug into the window-sill as he watched the pebble fly up, up, and smack dab into the center of the attacking pixie's forehead.

The old pixie dropped like a stone as Woggy leapt out of the way, hitting the ground with a thud and lying still in a small, gray heap. Woggy froze, watching him with his sling-shot clutched to his chest. After one breathless moment, the pixie's leg twitched and he jerked back to consciousness. He pushed himself upright slowly, keeping an eye on Woggy.

The old pixie was a darker gray than the others. A scar slashed through his wide lips and his wings were notched and torn from old battles. He rose and limped toward Woggy, who brandished his empty slingshot like a sword. Then, he did the last thing Tommy expected. He yanked the leaf off his necklace and dropped it at Woggy's feet with a firm squeak. Woggy stared at the leaf, then looked at the other pixie, big eyes widening in surprise.

Woggy lowered his slingshot, then signed *friend*. The other pixie cocked his head in confusion, but awkwardly repeated the motion. The leader then turned to leave but Woggy squeaked, stopping him in his tracks. He turned back in confusion and Woggy signed *friend* again, then grabbed the leaf and ripped it in half.

All the gathered pixies squeaked in shock and horror, their wings flapping excitedly. The leader's lips curled back in a growl until Woggy held out half the leaf to him. He looked at the leaf, then looked at Woggy, who signed *friend* for a third time.

Something like understanding dawned on the old pixie's face and he took half the leaf, clutching it to his chest. He limped forward and Woggy held still, holding onto his own leaf. The old pixie squeaked, then very carefully licked the top of Woggy's head.

"Ew," Genevieve muttered.

Ceri smacked her on the arm. "Shhh, this is a beautiful moment."

Woggy returned the gesture, his long, slimy tongue wiping away the blood on the pixie's head. The leader repeated the sign for *friend*, seeming to finally get the connection.

Behind them, the other pixies began squeaking and swooping through the air in celebration. The ones that could still fly at least. Many of them were a bit worse for the wear.

Tommy let out a breath he hadn't realized he'd been holding. This was the best birthday present ever.

CHAPTER 78

DEREK

*D*erek had never really looked at the moon before, not like they did. Whatever their connection to it was, it seemed worshipful. All day they'd been full of energy and talking about their run that night.

He watched them shift while trying real hard not to think about the fact that his sister was naked. It was easy to watch Ceri instead. She was currently twirling in the middle of the yard, her face turned up toward the sky, and her skirt billowing around her. It was the first time he'd seen her *really* smile since she had been taken.

"Come on," Ceri said, holding her hand out to him with a brilliant smile.

"What?"

"Come run with us!" She started walking backwards toward the pack and they all looked at him expectantly.

"We can't keep up with them." He felt out of place. He wasn't part of the pack. They had welcomed him but it wasn't the same.

"You can keep up with me," Ceri insisted.

The wind danced through her curls and the moonlight highlighted the soft curve of her cheeks. She was looking right at him, into him. There was no way he could say no to her right now. Probably not ever.

He set his drink down and jogged after her. Amber took off at a run toward the tree line, a howl rising up that each pack member echoed. Ceri grabbed his hand and dragged him after her. She lifted her head and howled too, completely carefree.

He laughed and tried to howl too, but it came out more like a strangled yell. She laughed anyhow and tightened her grip on his hand. Their feet flew over the forest floor as the pack darted around them. Tommy was like a puppy, yipping and tripping over things. The black wolf, Genevieve, was so fast he could barely see her sometimes. She raced ahead with Amber, winding through the trees.

Something stirred in him as he ran with them. It was faint, but it felt like family. Ceri looked back at him, her blue eyes sparkling with pure happiness, and he knew he wanted to stay with them forever.

CHAPTER 79

CERI

*C*eri stared at the ceiling and wondered what the hell she'd been thinking. Well, she knew what she'd been thinking. She'd nearly died, been tortured, and had almost given in to the dark side. That and the full moon had made all sorts of things seem like a good idea.

Derek's snore turned into a snort and he shifted in his sleep, throwing his arm over her chest and burying his face in her neck. She sighed. Last night had been nothing short of perfect but now she had to deal with the consequences. Maybe they could try this…whatever it was. The damage was already done so she might as well enjoy it while she could. Or maybe that would make it worse.

She wished she could just go back to sleep and be blissfully unaware of all of this but sleep was no longer an option, not with her mind running through worst case scenarios like a hyperactive hamster on a wheel. Maybe if she got up and hid in the bathroom he'd just go back to his room and they wouldn't even have to talk about it.

"I can feel you overthinking this," Derek said. His voice was rough from sleep. He smoothed his fingers through her hair and the tension in her muscles relaxed slightly.

"I just--"

He quickly put his fingers over her lips, then pushed up on his elbow so he could look at her. "You don't owe me anything because of last night. I'm not going to pressure you. You said you didn't want to date me, so unless you decide you've changed your mind, let's not rehash all that."

She pulled his hand down so she could reply. "You're being way too accommodating."

He grinned and tugged on a lock of her hair, winding the curl around his finger. "I learned the hard way that there's nothing worse than chasing after a girl that doesn't want to be with you. I'm not doing that again. However, if you just need a distraction every now and then, I can certainly *accommodate* that."

She smacked him but couldn't help but grin. "This is a slippery slope. It's going to end in disaster."

He flopped back down on the bed beside her and dragged her over on top of him. "Then we should have fun along the way."

Winding his hands through her hair, he tugged her down for a kiss. She quickly pushed her hand in between them, covering his mouth, and wiggled her fingers, casting a quick spell. He flinched and grimaced at her.

"What the hell was that?"

"Breath freshening spell." She grabbed his head and closed the distance between them, letting his lips distract her from the worries in her mind. As his hands slid down her back, she melted into his embrace, letting her fingers trace the muscles in his arms. He was already in her bed after all, she might as well enjoy him while she had him close by.

CHAPTER 80

EVANGELINE

*H*er life fit into a backpack. The one she'd tried to steal that Tommy had instead given to her when he'd heard she was leaving.

"Are you okay?" her mother asked, putting an arm around her shoulders.

"Is it weird that I'll miss them?"

Her mother smiled and tucked a loose strand of hair behind her ear. "Not at all. I think it's the closest I've seen you come to having friends."

"Oh gods, don't make me sound so pathetic," she said, zipping up her backpack and swinging it over her shoulder.

"Then don't look so pathetic," her mother said, clapping a hand on her back. "We're getting a fresh start and you know they'll stay in touch however they can. Especially that *boy*."

She glared at her mother and held her finger up to her lips emphatically, shushing her. "They can *hear you*."

Her mother laughed as she hurried out of the room, cheeks flushed with embarrassment. As she headed down the stairs the front door opened. Kadrithan was hovering behind Amber in his ridiculous little, red devil form.

A man and a woman walked in. The man was tall and lanky with a slight stoop to his shoulders. He had on a baseball cap that was pushed back with black curls spilling out beneath the brim.

"Ms. Hale, Asshole Demon," he greeted the two of them in turn with a nod. His wife or whoever she was, smacked him on the arm.

Evangeline had to hide her laugh behind her hand. She already liked them. Anyone who literally called her uncle Asshole Demon was her hero.

"I'm Katarina, and this is my idiot lover, Charlie," she said, shaking Amber's hand. Her accent was Russian but she looked like she was half elf. Her ears were lightly pointed and her hair had a hint of pastel blue to it.

"Nice to meet y'all," Amber said, shaking her hand with a smile.

Eloise walked past her and hurried over to meet their new hosts. They were apparently being driven over the border, then flown to somewhere in South America, the location to be disclosed once they were there. Her uncle had promised her beaches and no strangers, so she hadn't complained. Honestly, it sounded like a paradise right now.

A mass of blonde curls suddenly blocked her view as Ceri

wrapped her up in an unexpected hug. "I know we weren't all that close, but I wish you well."

"Thanks," Evangeline said, pulling away. The rest of the pack gave her a brief hug as well, wishing her luck.

Charlie grabbed her mother's suitcase and headed out toward the car.

"We'll see you at the car," Katarina said with a gentle smile. She had a calming air about her that Evangeline had come to associate with elves. Except for Thallan. That asshole was insane.

Kadrithan followed Katarina outside, discussing some detail about their journey with her. Evangeline sighed and followed. As she stepped outside, Tommy stopped her, shutting the door behind him. He looked a little awkward. She could actually feel his nervousness through the mark, which was an odd sensation.

"Do you know how long you'll be gone?"

She shrugged. "No clue."

"Alright, well, keep in touch."

Acting on impulse, she put her hand over the mark on his chest and looked up. "I'll see you again, don't worry." She felt like an idiot right away but it was too late to take it back.

He smiled and placed his hand over hers. "Maybe you can come visit every now and then like your uncle."

Shuddering in horror, she shook her head. "That's way too creepy. I'll just text."

He laughed and dragged her into an unexpected hug. "Ok, that works."

They parted and she hurried to the waiting car, looking

back over her shoulder one last time. The pack had not been what she'd expected. They'd been good, even to someone like her who didn't fit in anywhere.

CHAPTER 81

AMBER

*I*t was almost Thanksgiving. The leaves had all fallen from the trees and it was getting genuinely cold at night. Amber curled her arms around her legs and stared up at the moon. It was waning now, but she could still feel the pull of it in her blood. The wolf shifted in her mind, watching alongside her.

The door opened and she jumped, still easily startled after the week they'd had. Derek walked out and shut the door behind him.

"I've finally caught you alone," he said, raising a judgmental brow.

"Has it been that obvious I've been avoiding you?" she asked ruefully.

"Yes." He walked over and sat down on the porch swing

next to her, making the chains clank. "I talked to Bernard and he's not going to evict us. Insurance will also cover the damage to the warehouse. We should be able to open the mechanic shop only two weeks later than planned."

Amber's shoulder slumped in relief. "Glad to hear it. I'm sorry it's been nothing but trouble since you got here. I really thought we could just get to work and not have all this drama."

He raised his brow at her. "I don't think your life will ever be drama free again. But that's okay. We've got this, sis."

"I really hope so but sometimes I wonder." She rubbed her forehead and sighed. "The no magic zone is different from the others. It's still expanding, which is freaking everyone out. Selena is still out there, probably murdering people as we speak."

"I know. We'll find her and stop her. The police are blaming her and the sorcerer for the no magic spots, so you'll even have help for once."

"They still don't understand how the no magic spots are created or why. Detective Sloan also said the sorcerer we killed couldn't have been responsible for them all." She shook her head, frustrated. They may have saved Ceri but the sorcerer had still succeeded.

He'd left his mark on the pack too. Ceri still woke up with nightmares. If Amber moved too quickly, sometimes Genevieve would flinch. She always tried to laugh it off, but Amber knew she had hurt her. Tommy spent every free moment training with Deward like he expected them to go to war at any moment. This wasn't what she wanted for them.

"What are we becoming?" she asked quietly, regretting the words a little as soon as they left her mouth.

"You're still who you were before you were bitten. You're just stronger, faster, and hairier now," Derek said with a smile, trying to lighten the mood.

"Am I though?" she asked, turning to look at her brother. "I've killed people, and enjoyed it. I almost killed *you*. Whatever this is, it's changing me. Maybe it's impossible to keep from becoming...evil."

Derek sighed and the smile fell away. He looked out over the yard and pursed his lips thoughtfully. "You're not a bad person, no matter how much you think you've changed. We both saw *real* evil that night. The wolf inside you is a predator, but you control those urges, and most importantly, you still control your own actions."

"If there ever comes a moment where I'm not in control anymore you have to promise me that you'll stop me," she said, holding his gaze.

"You have me and the whole pack watching your back, Amber. We won't let anything happen to you."

She rubbed her hand against the demon mark absently and forced herself to smile at her brother. "I know."

CHAPTER 82

KADRITHAN

"**I**s the girl safe?" Zerestria demanded.

"She is, and she has embraced her potential, finally. She gave one of the wolves her demon mark," he said, careful to keep his tone even and respectful.

Zerestria slumped back in her chair in relief. She was old, one of the few still left that remembered what it had been like before the Fall. Before the curse. "The girl's stubbornness was infuriating, but in some ways, I respect her resisting as long as she did."

"It was foolish. She is the key to breaking this curse, and she put that all at risk just because she didn't *like* what she had to do." He paced the length of the room, only looking up when he noted that Zerestria hadn't responded yet.

She looked at him with amusement, raising her brow.

"Oh, shut up, she's nothing like me," he said, rolling his eyes.

"She has your stubbornness and her mother's temper. It's a miracle she's still alive," the old woman said, shaking her head with a laugh.

"She might be my niece, but sometimes she's an asshole," he said grumpily.

"That's the angel half of her," Zerestria said with a smirk as she rose from her chair. Her back was slightly stooped with age, but the magic that kept them alive strengthened her frail body. Her long, silver hair fell over her shoulders like a shawl.

As she rummaged through her desk, he wandered toward the window. It used to be beautiful. It had been a paradise.

Now bare trees covered the barren hills, their arms stretching toward an orange sky. The air was dry and still now. There was no breeze. The seasons never changed. When their magic had been stripped from them, it had destroyed this realm.

He closed his eyes, and for a moment, let himself remember their glorious past. His mouth watered at the thought of the sweet fruits he used to pick from the trees. The gardens had been bursting with flowers. He and his sister had spent every afternoon swimming in the cool, clear lakes.

"Kadrithan, we need to get in touch with the others. I need to know if your cousin managed to get a mark on someone actually useful," Zerestria said, interrupting his pity party. She sealed the envelope and set it aside.

"I'll go ask in person, I've been meaning to check with my cousin as well," he said, extending his hand for the letter.

Once the dust had settled, a resistance had grown within their ranks. It had been scattered and ineffectual for centuries, but slowly, the elders had begun to work together instead of against one another. A plan had been formed. They hadn't realized someone like Evangeline would have to play a role until she was about five years old. They'd initially kept her alive just because of how badly the angels wanted her kind dead. His gut had told him she would be important.

Amber was both a complication, and possibly, an unexpected help. She didn't trust him at all now, but he could fix that eventually. She was driven by a sense of justice, and she had a thing for helping the underdog. If all else failed, he could make her help. She wore his mark.

That had been a bit of quick thinking. He smiled as he strode out of the tower. He wasn't really a demon any more than the angels were really angels, but he could play the part. He was good at it. Amber's mark was one of a hundred he wore. All different pawns in this centuries long war. He had more marked souls than any of his brethren.

One day, he would be rid of them all. His hand tightened on the envelope, crinkling it. One day, he would be free.

MAKE A DIFFERENCE

Reviews are very important, and sometimes hard for an independently published author to get. A big publisher has a massive advertising budget and can send out hundreds of review copies.

I, however, am lucky to have loyal and enthusiastic readers. And I think that's much more valuable.

Leaving an honest review helps me tremendously. It shows other readers why they should give me a try.

If you've enjoyed reading this book, I would appreciate, very much, if you took the time to leave a review. Whether you write one sentence, or three paragraphs, it's equally helpful.

Thank you :)

P.S. Who's your favorite character? Let me know in the Facebook group.

https://www.facebook.com/groups/TheFoxehole/

Follow Me

Thank you so much for buying my book. I really hope you have enjoyed the story as much as I did writing it. Being an author is not an easy task, so your support means a lot to me. I do my best to make sure books come out error free. However, if you found any errors, please feel free to reach out to me so I can correct them!

If you loved this book, the best way to find out about new releases and updates is to join my Facebook group, The Foxehole. Amazon does a very poor job about notifying readers of new book releases. Joining the group can be an alternative to newsletters if you feel your inbox is getting a little crowded. Both options, and Goodreads, are linked below :)

Facebook Group:
https://www.facebook.com/groups/TheFoxehole/
Goodreads:
http://goodreads.com/Stephanie_Foxe

The Witch's Bite Series is a complete series that follows Olivia Carter –

We all have our secrets. Mine involves a felony record, illegal potions, and magi–well...the last one could get me killed.

I've been living in a small town working for the vampires for the last six months. All I want is to save up enough to open an apothecary, so I don't have to heal the neckers anymore.

Of course, nothing in my life can be *that* simple.

Two detectives show up at my door asking questions about a dead girl and trying to pin the murder on my employer. Next thing I know, I'm dodging fireballs in parking lots.

The police and the witches want me to roll over on the vampires. The only problem is, I'm almost certain they didn't kill the girl. Although, my best friend and favorite vampire has been missing and won't answer my calls.

Time is running out for me to save my paycheck... and do the right thing or whatever.

Stephanie Foxe also writes with her husband as Alex Steele. In The Chaos Mages Series you will meet Logan Blackwell and Lexi Swift as they solve crimes in a world full of magic and myths, much like in Misfit Pack.

Vampires don't rob banks. Werewolves don't bust into jewelry stores. And Detective Logan Blackwell doesn't work with a partner.

Too bad all three of those things happened in one day. Supernaturals are getting possessed, wreaking havoc, then turning up dead. Blackwell has been tasked with finding out who is responsible and stopping them before they kill again.

After a series of unfortunate incidents that include blowing up part of the Met, Blackwell's boss is fed up. He sticks Blackwell with a partner who has issues that only complicate his life.

Assassination attempts threaten both their lives, but no one will tell him who is trying to kill Detective Lexi Swift, or why. He's already lost one partner, and he's not willing to see another die. It's a good thing she's tough and wields magic almost as chaotic as his.

Old enemies, new threats, and more destruction than his boss can handle are bad enough, but sometimes our inner demons are the most dangerous. When they find the person responsible, Blackwell will face a fight he never expected, and one he may not win.

But most importantly, will the pink ever get out of his hair? He should never have taken that bet...

www.StephanieFoxe.com
www.AlexSteele.net

facebook.com/StephanieFoxeAuthor
goodreads.com/Stephanie_Foxe